THE FEDERATION

BY JACK BROWN

THE FEDERATION

Bennett books may be ordered through booksellers or by contacting:

Bennett Media and Marketing
1603 Capitol Ave., Suite 310 A233
Cheyenne, WY 82001
www.thebennettmediaandmarketing.com
Phone: 1-307-202-9292

ISBN: 978-1-957114-16-3 (Paperback)
ISBN: 978-1-957114-17-0 (eBook)

Printed in the United States of America

CONTENTS

CHAPTER 1

ARRIVAL

1

"Come here, Jamarcus," Thor called as he lowered himself to his knees. Rhiannon placed Scar on the sand and he ran as fast as he could to Thor, who swept him up in his large strong arms. Scar squeezed Thor's neck while he and Athena hugged and kissed him.

"Did you just get home?" Thor asked, and Scar nodded, staying silent to keep from crying.

"Did you miss us, Jamarcus?" Athena asked, with Scar answering with another nod.

"Oh, we missed you too," Thor said, pressing his prickly black beard against Scar's face, tickling Scar as he tried to push him back.

"Thor?" Ra spoke up.

"Yes Papa," Thor said as he swung Scar around.

"You need to move your ship. It's in restricted space."

"Don't worry about it. It's just above the house," Thor pointed out, and when Scar looked up, she saw a silver disk shaped ship hovering above them that looked to be made of a single piece of metallic material.

"The air space above our house is still restricted for commercial flight," Ra explained.

"Really? When did that start?" Thor asked.

"When you left," Ra stated.

"Oh," Thor said as he got the gist of what Ra was saying.

"It shouldn't be a problem," Athena said. "No one is saying to move it now."

"You are the oldest, Athena," Ixchel chastised. "You know better. Stop trying to defend Thor."

"Come on, Momma," Thor said as he walked over to Rhiannon and Bernini. "It's been forever since we've been together like this. I just want to hang out."

"Hi, Thor," Bernini said in a muffled voice as Thor pressed him and Rhiannon against his chest.

"How have you guys been?" Thor asked.

"Good," they answered in unison.

"How many more years of University do you have left," Thor asked Rhiannon.

"This is my last year," Rhiannon said. "I give my dissertation in the spring."

"That's when you start your position of Light Bringer for Mangala?" Athena asked.

"Yes," Rhiannon answered a bit hesitant.

"Congratulation," Athena said as she knelt over to hug her sister.

"She still has to graduate," Ixchel reminded them as she and Ra walked towards them from the trail to the Chateau.

"She will," Athena said as she smiled into Rhiannon face. "Don't worry, it's scary at first, especially with all the attention. But you'll get used to it."

"Do you want to play in the water," Thor asked Scar when he noticed him looking at the ocean, with Scar nodding in response.

"Let me take your clothes off," Thor said, and Scar almost panic, but remembered that he was a child now. He had swam on the north shore of Oahu with Tasi and Nathans' little nephews while they were naked. It was no different now. Thor placed Scar on the sand and turned his white onesies into white light before it disappeared. Once Thor was finished, Scar walked into the water, still surprised that he couldn't feel the cold of the water even though he knew it was winter in that area. Thor followed Scar, occasionally picking water up with his hands and dripping it over his head while clothed as his own military style, blue fitted uniform got wet.

"How are you doing on Firmament?" Ra asked Athena.

"The planet is doing good now," Athena said with pride. "They just finished the latest legislative changes to move off of fiat currency. They're also beginning a colonization program in neighboring systems. It's been less than ten cycles, and they've done so much. I just watch amazed at what they're accomplishing." Scar watched Athena as she talked, and although there was happiness shining from her, Scar could still feel a bit of loneliness underneath.

"Did you have to make any political changes yourself," Rhiannon asked.

"I try my absolute best not too," Athena said.

"That falls on the planet's government and the Federation Parliament," Ixchel added. "We do not interfere with the political decisions of the planets we supply Light to, unless there are policies that go against our own ethics."

"I hope I don't have to do anything drastic when I get to Mangala," Rhiannon bemoaned as she walked to the water edge to splash water at Scar.

"You should just focus on school for now," Ixchel said.

"Don't worry so much," Thor suggested as he picked Scar up and swung him around, water trailing behind Scar from his hair.

"Hey Jamarcus, you want me to toss you in the air?" Thor asked, and when Scar agreed Thor put Scar's feet in his palm and waited until his balance was set.

"Ready?" Thor asked, and Scar nodded. Thor threw Scar straight into the mourning sky, the velocity of the throw blowing the air back to ruffle everyone's clothes.

"Aten Ka," Ixchel muttered as she watched Scar ascend above them.

"Hey, throw me," Bernini asked as he ran and grabbed Thor's arm.

"Wait till Jamarcus comes back down," Thor said, and after a few more seconds Thor reached up and grabbed Scar as he fell, his hair tangled and his eyes wide open with excitement.

"Come on, Bernini," Thor said as he picked him up. It didn't take long for Bernini to balanced himself in Thor's hand as he was thrusted upward, Thor chuckling as Bernini screamed as he left. When Scar bounced up and down with anticipation of being thrown, Rhiannon decided to pick him up and took her down the beach so she could throw him.

"How's your trading company?" Ra asked.

"I hit a bit of a slump recently," Thor said as he caught Bernini, who giggled as Thor swung him around. "After I bought a new cargo ship, I was hoping that I could exchange the resources I have in a few different systems and up trade."

"What happen?" Ixchel asked as she watch Rhiannon throw Scar into the air.

"You guys know about the trade dispute that some of the independent planets are having? How they want to base all resource trade around iridium because a small group of planets are in regions that are low in semi-conductive metals? That's causing a lot of planets to stamp the resources coming out of their regions. A third of my supply is marked now, which can't be traded until a fair trade solution is chosen."

"Did you lose any value in your resources?" Ixchel asked as Rhiannon caught Scar.

"You can't lose value of whatever resources you hold on too," Thor said as he threw Bernini up.

"In theory," Ra said. "We all know that flies in the wind once you ask for goods in exchange for resources.

"I thought I was going to up trade for a good bit, but in essence I have a third of my assets that is worthless because of an imprint on them," Thor complained as he caught Bernini out of the air, who fell on his back breathing hard when Thor placed him on the ground. Scar rushed over and climbed on his chest so he can fell his joy.

"Did you want to try trading with nations in the other Houses?" Athena asked.

"No," Thor said, his pride taking a bit of a hit as he heard the question. "I'll just have to go back to logistics shipping for a while."

"You were able to do it before, you shouldn't have a hard…" Ra began, then paused when a mental broadcast sounded out, letting all in their area know that a undeclared craft must vacate the air space and register at the local space port.

"You need to move your ship," Ixchel instructed Thor.

"Let me take Scar in the house and put some clothes on him," Thor said as he picked Scar up off of Bernini.

"Thor, just go move your ship," Ra said. "We changed the laws towards us so we no longer have executive privileges when you and Athena left."

"It will only take a moment," Thor said as he walked toward the Chateau.

"Thor," Scar spoke as he looked up at Thor, who paused in step for a moment before looking down at Scar.

"Go register your ship," Scar said, and Thor breathe in a sharp breath, biting his pride before letting it out.

"Yes your Highness," Thor said softly down to Scar.

"Take me with you?" Scar asked.

"I want to go too," Bernini said as he got up and ran behind Thor.

"Alright," Thor said, who then held Scar up and with a thought made light glow around Scar before it turned into a blue Federation military uniform. Thor then shifted the three of them on to his craft and directed it to the space port in the City.

"You know he's never going to change," Athena said to her parents as she held Rhiannon close to her. "You're too hard on him."

"We have to be," Ixchel said. "To all of you."

"He just wants to make you guys proud," Athena explained.

"We are proud of all of you," Ixchel responded. "He is just trying to build what we have. That takes time, millennia. He does not have too. He already has so much now."

"Maybe you should tell him that your proud," Rhiannon said, and Ixchel pondered those words as she leaned against Ra's hips.

"Are you guys hungry," Ra asked. "I can fix us something before Thor comes back." When the others agreed, Ra lead them all inside the Chateau to prepare breakfast before the rest of the family return.

2

Scar woke up when Athena tussled his hair as he laid next to her in the bed of her childhood room in the Chateau. Scar remained there a bit more, curling up in a ball and enjoying lying in Athena's Light. It felt good mingling your Light with someone who cherishes yours, and Scar just wanted to stay there in its love and warmth.

"The future scion of the family needs to learn how to get up early in the morning," Athena whispered, and as she rose out of bed, pulled the bed sheets away that left Scar uncover in only the blue suit Thor made. Military discipline kicked back in, and Scar crawled out of bed and intuitively tip toed to the bathroom before Athena picked him up.

Scar felt that Athena wanted to dot on him for a while, so he didn't complained as she carried him to the bathtub and drew warm water for them. She took her night gown and Jamarcus onesies off before she stepped in the tub with him. Scar couldn't help but laugh while he felt how happy Athena was as she washed him and played with his hair before she rinsing all the soap off of him.

Once done she climbed out of the tub and dried Jamarcus off before she walked back into her room and put on some simple cloths, a white button blouse and tan cotton like pants. She carried Scar naked through the Chateau, his Light illuminating the corridors they walked through, until they got into the nursery where she found a white shirt and dark green overall pants to put on Scar. She then looked through Scars toys to find something that he would like.

She found a green leather skinned like animal that looked like a reptilian unicorn, made from a solid piece of polished metal. She animated it and had it run around Scar, who laughed as he reached out to grab it, only for Athena to leap it out from his reached. Scar then looked around the room and pick another toy that was a large blue feline beast with blue wing like tuffs from its shoulders.

Scar made the predator chase after the unicorn all around the room, under the Crib and behind bookshelves, until the cat clipped the unicorn on the ground, with Athena laughing as Scar made the beast crawl atop his prey. They were about to pick some other toys to play with when Ra walked into the room, his Light buzzing with a dozen tasks he needed to do that day.

"Come on Scar," Ra said as he picked up the boy from the floor. "Some of your cousins are here to see you."

"Uncle Iolan and Iorad are here?" Athena asked as she followed Ra out of the nursery.

"They arrived about an hour ago. We didn't want to get you two because you were still asleep."

"I wonder whose fault is that," Athena said snidely as she flicked Scar's nose.

"You slept as long I did," Scar said with a huff, surprised on how mad he got at her accusation.

"No I didn't," Athena denied.

"Yes you did!" Scar said, energy raising inside of him as he was ready to argue with Athena. Athena only teased him with a stuck out tongue which made Scar shout back in retaliation.

"Will you two stop bickering," Ra said as he winced from Scar's cry. Scar face became solemn after annoying his father, then angry as Athena laughed at him. A smile then came across his face as he enjoyed these emotions he felt. He wasn't really mad at Athena, it was just his youth intensifying every emotion he had. When he was a young Jamarcus on Earth he didn't realize it, but now with an adult's mind he knew what was happening. He was literally living that proverb of knowing what one knows as an adult, but was now a child.

Ra arrived in a large dining area where the light of the rising sun flooded the room from the east, shining a yellow glow on the polished wooden floor and lower walls. The top half of the walls were painted white, except for the glass walls to the east and west, which allowed the sun to shine in at dusk and dawn. There was a large oval shape table where dozens of Pleiadean children, all dressed like Scar, sat and ate breakfast, all talking or screaming at each other.

Only Ra's brothers noticed when he, Scar and Athena walk into the room. They were as tall as Ra, but weren't as muscular, with long black hair and gray eyes that Scar noticed matched their gray shirts and black pants. Their wives were next to them, talking up a storm about all the gossip in the families. Iolan's wife was brown hair and brown eyed, with a yellow blouse and brown dress, with Iorad's wife being black haired and with full length green and grey dress.

"So here's my nephew," Iorad said in Pleiadean as he walked over to Ra and snatch Scar into his arm.

"Hello," Scar said in the same language.

"Oh, you know Pleiadean," Iolan said as he walked over to Scar to play with his hair.

"Only a little."

"When did you arrived from Earth?" Iolan asked.

"Last week," Scar answered.

"Was it tough?" Iorad ask before Scar nodded in response.

"It was tough for your father too when he descended. That was over four hundred cycles ago. Iorad and I would look down on Earth a lot back then, angry by how he was treated. Our father said it was for Ra's development, but we didn't understand then. In a way, I still don't."

"I do," Scar said simply, which made Iorad and Iolan laugh.

"I bet you do," Iolan said as he rubbed Scar's face.

"Is that Scar!" one of the kids shouted, and as the group faced the children, the whole lot of them screamed in excitement as they rushed from their seats and ran circles around the adults. A playful dread filled Scar, pondering what will happen once his cousins got theirs hands on him.

"You children settle down," Iorad's wife said as she hustle over and took Scar from him. Without missing a beat she manipulated the Light inside Scar and made it into a solid plasma field.

"Your cousin just arrived here so treat him nicely," she said, but the children hardly listen as they all snatched Scar into their hands and took off into the Chateau to play with him.

"Where are all the rest of the kids?" Ra asked after the children trampled off.

"These are the ones either not in Seminary or in University," Iolan said. "The older ones not in school were either busy at work or out exploring our universe."

"You would think that they would want to be here to see their cousin," Ra lamented. "Especially after all he went through on Earth."

"They're teenagers," Iolan said as he walked over to the table and grabbed some Nimian beacon off of one of the kids' plate. "Most teenagers are absorbed in what's going on in their lives at the moment. It's natural. They want to play with their friends, meet beings from other worlds. We did the same thing."

"Except that Mom was on our butts all the time to shape up," Iorad said. "Look at Ra, he went through the Ascension. Why can't you act like him."

"Sorry," Ra said with a shameful smile.

"Don't be," Iorad said as he walked over to Athena and gave her a big hug. "Look at what you have now in four hundred cycles. It takes some Lights millennia to accomplish what you have. If they don't quit along the way or decide to pass on to another life. You shouldn't be sorry. You even have a daughter here who is a Light Bringer to a system. How are you, sweety."

"I'm good, Uncle Iorad," Athena said.

"You're still feeling lonely?" Iorad asked.

"A little," Athena answered ruefully.

"You should have some of your cousins come to visit you," Iolan suggested. "I'm pretty sure they'll keep you busy. They're always doing something to…" and Iolan was cut off by a large thud heard from a neighboring room, followed by an eruption of laughter.

"You children settle down!" Iorad's wife screamed at them before she and Iolan's wife chased after the kids.

"Where is Ixchel anyway?" Iolan asked. "And Thor and Bernini? They're busy too?"

"Thor had some business he's trying to deal with now," Athena explained. "Bernini's at school. Momma went to get Aunt Chac'chel from her home in New Scarborough."

"They don't want to slide here?" Iorad asked.

"You know how discipline those two are," Ra said. "You have to admire them for that."

"I would have thought that Ixchel would want to be here to keep Scar from being murdered by the kids," Iolan laughed.

"She doesn't feel comfortable with all of your kids around," Athena said.

"Aren't you guys trying to have more children?" Iolan asked.

"We're always trying," Ra said.

"I see," Iolan said.

"Wait, their back," Athena said, her eyes widening as she felt their mother's car drive to the Chateaus entrance. The four of them walked that way, arriving just in time to see Ixchel in a simple Andean outfit walked through the door, dressed in a matching blue blouse and pants. After came Kukulkan, wearing a rustic brown and green suit and pants, with Chac'chel following behind. She was a bit shorter than Ixchel, and fuller, with a rounder face and belly. Her black hair went down to her waist, and she was cloth in an elegant navy and white vertically stripped dress. Her face was the same as her Light, strict and focus.

"Hello, Aunt Chac'chel," Athena said as she approach them.

"You're not going to say hello to Kukulkan first," Chac'chel said disapprovingly in Andean.

"Hello," Athena said as she bent over to hug Kukulkan.

"Hello, my dear," the old man said patting her on the back.

"Cousin Chab didn't want to come?" Athena asked.

"We sent messages to him, but he never received them," Chac'chel answered. "You know him, he stays in his own pocket universe pampering his sons."

"Where are the kids?" Ixchel asked as she closed the front door.

"There somewhere in the house falling into the Empty," Iorad said with a chuckle.

"Well, lets go see him," Chac'chel said before anyone else tried to strike up a meaningless conversation. The group walked the halls of the Chateau following the noise of play until they found the group running amuck in a large den, the children jumping around on the furniture or chasing each other with Scar's bubble in their hands. When they saw Chac'chel the group became deathly silent before she and Ixchel greeted their mothers.

"Hello Valka, hello Haleigh," Chac'chel said as each woman bent over to hug her.

"Hello, Lady Chac'chel," Valka said as she pushed back her brown hair back.

"Scar, say hello to your aunt," Ixchel order, and he was lowered to the floor before walking over to his aunt.

"Say hello to Kukulkan first," Chac'chel said before Scar could speak a word.

"Hello sir," Scar said as he stepped towards Kukulkan.

"Welcome back, your Highness," Kukulkan said as he rubbed Scar's head. "I'm glad your back. If you need anything, I will always be there for you. I live to serve your family. Remember that, Scar."

"Yes sir," Scar said before he turned back to Chac'chel.

"So, you can speak Pleiadean, but you can't speak Andean," Chac'chel noted.

"Sorry," Scar said with his Light.

"It's not that big of a deal," Iorad said as he went to pat Scar's shoulder. "He's only a baby now. He has cycles to learn everything he needs."

"If Scar is effectively becoming the Speaker for an entire Andean ethnic group, one should think that he should speak Andean," Chac'chel said not taking her eyes from Scar.

"She is right," Ixchel said with a small smile.

"I can learn now," Scar said eagerly, wanting to learn from Chac'chel. He felt everyone drawn away from Chac'chel's demeaner. But after years in the military, Scar felt what was underneath it.

"Your mother should have taught you this while you were on Earth," Chac'chel suggested.

"He was barely getting over the trauma he dealt with there," Ixchel explained. "I have only been able to teach him how to use the Light."

"How so?" Chac'chel asked as she picked up Scar. "Do you even know what a tenth density being can do?" she asked with Scar only shaking his head.

"Well we need to fix that right now," Chac'chel said as she walked away from the group.

"Keep everyone busy Honey, we will be back," Ixchel said to Ra as she and Kukulkan followed behind Chac'chel until they reached the Library.

"Make a blanket for us so we can sit down," Chac'chel ordered Scar, who after a bit of concentration, created a red blanket in the air before them and placed it on the floor.

"Go get your father's book on Density Theory," Chac'chel said as she sat on the blanket. Scar rushed away, climbing up the stairs and around the Library until he got to the bookshelf with the text he needed. After climbing up to get it, he rushed back to the three as they sat waiting for him.

"Come read it to me," Chac'chel said as she patted her lap for Scar to sit down on. "Can you read in Andean?" Chac'chel asked.

"Yes," Scar answered before he started. "There are many things that are not agreed upon about the capabilities of a certain density, but the common consensus is that a density is able to fully manipulate another density that is three loops below it. Per example, a seventh density can manipulate the fourth density, etc.

"A fourth density being can penetrate into the Waters of reality, effectively wrapping it around themselves. Because of this such a being can create, decrease, or manipulate gravity, and create windows to locations far from the subject. With this feat, such a being is capable of close to sound speed. They can make themselves invisible to a third density being also.

"A density can see or feel another being of the same density, so a being must be higher in Density than the subject it is hiding from. A fourth density being also has extra sensory perception, giving the subject telepathy and empathy with any sentient light, and limited telekinesis. A fourth density can also see inverted into any matter, allowing the object to become see through. Because gravity can be manipulated by the being, that person will have enhanced strength and stamina based on how much gravity is displaced. The density can also manipulate gas elements and molecules freely.

"As a light increases it's density, the established abilities are also enhanced, along with new abilities added. A fifth density light is now capable of remote-viewing, being able to see and hear across vast distances of reality. A being of the same density or higher is able to notice when they're being remoted-viewed. A fifth density is able to probe and control a light that is lower in density.

"They are also able to gain access to the White, the plasma field surrounding a universe that contains all the quantum fields of every energy and force that is found in that universe, but is not able to control most of these fields fully. While in the White, a light can travel far reaches of reality much faster than previously before, effectively granting that light faster than sound speed. Liquid molecules are fully able to be manipulated. Lastly, a fifth density is able to see into the future or the past in a limited manner, yet has little control of what they see. Also, they can only see into one's own personal timeline."

"Do you know who is like this?" Chac'chel asked as she rubbed Scar's head.

"Bernini?" Scar answered after a thought.

"Who else?" When Chac'chel asked again. Scar looked at her, then at Ixchel. When he looked at Kukulkan and saw his five loops of light, Scar pointed at him.

"See how you can tell?" Chac'chel asked, with Scar nodding in response.

"Keep reading," Ixchel ordered, and Scar quickly found the place he left off.

"A sixth density can travel outside an universe and travel to the Space Between. Many are not sure if the Space Between is a density or not, because as of yet no one has been able to control it, only traveling through it between universes. A sixth density can now travel instantaneously anywhere throughout a universe, and can also access the Matrix. In the Matrix, one can think of a location that they want to travel to and be sent there, as long as they were entangle with the target first.

"The Matrix is also nigh omniscient, limited to only what everyone's light in the Matrix knows. A being can also project their Light anywhere in the universe. They're able to control certain quantum fields in the White, gaining access to more fields as they increase their densities. Solid matter can now be animated and reconstructed fully. Finally, a sixth density is able to manipulate time, speeding and slowing time in an object, able to view the background radiation of an object to look into its past, and can passively look into different universes on timelines they may be connect with.

"Isn't Rhiannon like this?" Scar asked.

"Yes," Chac'chel answered. "You missed the part where it says they can supply light across a planet."

"Sorry."

"Don't skip any places, read all of this chapter. It's important for you to know."

"Okay," Scar said before he started again. "A seventh density is capable of traveling to another universe, most likely one that they are connected with passively with their personal timeline. Once a subject from any universe is observed, access to that universe is capable. A seventh density is now able to convert matter to any other molecular or elemental type, as well as create matter from pure matter they create from gaining access to the light. Seventh densities can now control more exotic energy and force quantum fields, and supply such energies across a star system or star cluster."

"You skipped the part where it says a seventh can now fully control a light or bestow powers upon anyone three densities below it," Ixchel point out in the book.

"Sorry," Scar said. "Thor and Athena are Seventh right? Athena has seven loops."

"Yes she does, now keep reading," Chac'chel urged.

"Here's where it talks about you, Aunt Chac'chel," Scar stated. "An eight density's range of influence and control now extends across a standard galaxy. That light can travel to more universes, and has complete control of all energies and forces in the White. Here's you, Momma. A ninth density light can influence an entire universe, and travel anywhere in a multiverse. A light is now able to create a pocket universe the size of a star system. A tenth density dight can access the plasma field surrounding a multiverse, control multiple universes, create a pocket universe the size of a galaxy, and see into other lights timelines."

"Can you see other multiverses?" Chac'chel asked.

"Barely. They're like groups of Aten Ka formed in more loops around the main one," Scar said as he rubbed his eyes.

"Are you getting bored with this book?" Ixchel asked.

"He has to keep reading about his density," Chac'chel said curtly.

"But you don't want to burn him out," Kukulkan said as he stood and picked Scar up into his arms. Chac'chel was going to respond, but remained silent.

"Lets find one of my favorite story books I used to read to your mother and aunt," Kukulkan said as he carried Scar across the library to find another book.

CHAPTER 2

26 CYCLES AFTER ARRIVAL

1

"Go sit in your chair," Sneeze said as she rummage through her toy chest.

"Okay," Scar said as he sat down in the seat next to the table in Sneeze's bedroom. Scar watched Sneeze for a bit as she searched for the right toys to play with, then glanced around her room to keep his mind busy.

Her bed was unmade, and Scar knew that always made Psssh mad, but Sneeze was too happy and focused with playing with him today to bother remaking it. The room was small and quite modest to Scar's surprise when he first came to visit. There was a single small bookshelf with children's books in them on one wall, books that Scar now had a renewed love for. Fairytales never change, no matter the culture or world, but that sense of wonder that they told felt good to read about again.

Next to her bed was Sneeze's dresser with a small mirror on it. On the bottom corner of it was a picture of them on Nima, with Scar hugging Sneeze tightly as they smiled at the camera in front of the Chateau. Other than that, there wasn't anything else, not even a window to let light in. A stand up lamp with vertical lights lined on its pole illuminated the room for them.

Sneeze finished digging through her chest and came to the table with a plastic tea pot, four plates and cups, and two toys. One was a mantis like robot that transformed into a vehicle, just like the ones Scar used to play with as a child when he was on Earth. The other was a female doll that wore Andean clothing with white shoulder length hair. After placing cups and plates in four sections on the table, Sneeze put the toys by two of the plates before sitting down across from Scar.

"What type of tea do you want," Sneeze asked, and Scar thought for a bit.

"Honey green tea," Scar suggested, and Sneeze picked up the tea pot and tilted it over Scar's cup, with green liquid light pouring out of it. Sneeze filled all the cups before placing it back down and turning to the doll.

"What do you want to eat, Hathor?" Sneeze asked before she took hold of the doll with her light.

"I want eggs please," she made the doll say. Scar reached out to the robot to make him speak.

"I want soft cakes," Horus demanded.

"They're called pancakes, kid," Scar giggled.

"We're not on Earth dad, sheesh," Horus said as he rocked back and forth on the table.

"Don't sass at your father, Horus," Sneeze clicked, scolding Horus as she whirled her hands in the air as if she was cooking food on a stove. Scar hid his thoughts in his mind as he watched Sneeze, not wanting her to know he felt slightly ashamed of how Sneeze wants to be a housewife. It was still lingering aspects of culture Scar brought with him from Earth, living in the United States at a time gender and sex rights were beginning to get figured out. There was no conflict in Sneeze's light about what she was doing. It made here happy believing she was cooking for her family.

Once Sneeze believed she was done she reached over to Hathor's plate and motion with her hand that she was using a spatula to place golden lit scrambled eggs on it before turning over to Horus and placing a steaming single pancake on his. Sneeze then placed some fruits that looked like kiwis with anthers sticking out the top of it on Scar's plate before she made Hathor eat her food. Horus walked over to Hathor's plate to try to take some eggs.

"Leave my food alone," Hathor complained as she tried to push Horus away.

"Let me have some," Horus demanded, reaching past Hathor's arms to steal her food.

"Horus, stop bothering your sister," Sneeze bemoaned. "Sonlig?"

"Listen to your mother," Scar said sharply at Horus, who pouted as he went back to his plate, which made Sneeze laugh madly. Horus and Hathor gobbled up their food before giving their plates to Sneeze, who put them all back in the chest.

"I bet I can run faster than you," Horus said as he transformed into an oval shaped vehicle and drove off the table, landing on the carpeted floor with a thud.

"No you can't," Hathor said as she leapt of the table and began chasing Horus through the room. Horus drove around the room, barely keeping ahead of Hathor as she tried to grab him. He steered under the bed and around the dresser's legs, then bolted out of Sneeze's room, with Hathor running closely behind. Scar and Sneeze chuckled and ran behind the two toys as they made their way through Sneeze's living quarters, which had a large living room with high end music players that glowed soft green light as they played Roi Son jazz music and couches in front of a holographic television where two mantis like Kaggen maids for Sneeze watched their soap operas.

Scar and Sneeze chased Horus and Hathor into the kitchen area where in the center of it was a table with no legged chairs surrounding it. Sneeze ran to the silver colored refrigerator where she grabbed two large green to dark purple colored berries, handing one to Scar so they could both eat them with ferocity. A knock was heard at the entrance to Sneeze's quarters, with Sneeze's light growing brighter as she felt who was there.

"I'll get it!" Sneeze shouted at her maids as she picked up Horus and Hathor up with one hand and pulled Scar along with the other to the entrance. Three of Sneeze's friends, two green and one red mantis females stood there, their lights glowing with anticipation of their friend joining them.

"Hey, Sneeze," one of the green ones said as soon as the door was open. "Do you want to go to the market? Those new necklaces are in."

"Okay," Sneeze said excitingly as she handed the toys to Scar. "Can you put these in my room?" she asked before Scar turned around and created a window to Sneeze's room and placed them in Sneeze's chest.

"Hi Sonlig," the mantis said.

"Hi Proclaim, how are you?"

"I'm good," Proclaim chirped happily.

"Hi Nibble, hi Whisper," Scar said.

"Hey," Nibble said while Whisper waved her red hand at Scar.

"Spy, Tilting, I'm going to the market with my friends," Sneeze said as she pulled Scar out the door.

"Be home before it's dark," Spy buzzed just before Sneeze closed the door behind them and the group rushed through the hallway that lead from Sneeze's quarters to one of the open level areas of Psssh's pyramid castle. The girls and Scar ran past all the people and buildings until they reached the great stairs that ran along the western side of the black pyramid, where the red setting sun blazed the jungle where Groen Stad laid, a city intwined in the jungle.

Scar felt nervous as he watch the large bulbous abdomens of Sneeze's friends bobbing up and down in front of him, something he knew made them giddy. That was Jamarcus still in him, and his desire for big butts. It made him embarrassed as all the adults looked at the group and him. It was bad enough that they were all naked, which made Scar's pale white and pink freckled skin and blonde hair stand out amongst the Kaggen. He could fell some of the passersby's thinking 'who is this white boy with our princesses'.

Once they got to the foot of the pyramid they ran through the many stone walkways in the city jungle. There were stone pillars with hieroglyphics and figures with vines circling them along paths that went in every direction. Some paths had stairs that went up and down hills. At each intersection were large stone floored clearings, squared with pillars at each of the corners where the red sun reflected of the grey surface. Everywhere were buildings in the forest, in which the structures were constructed around and with the jungle.

It didn't take long before the children reached a shop where wooden and multi-color stone necklaces and headdresses were arranged on stands. The adult women in the store towered above them as they walked through the store, eyeing all the wares. Most of the women had black patterns tattooed on their abdomens, describing what ethnic group or city they were from. The women who were single had a large black bar that ran vertical down the abdomen, while the married ones added lines along the side signifying how many cycles they were married.

Sneeze and her friends picked out a few necklaces and headdress that would be worn for a wedding and put them on Sneeze, all the while laughing as they felt Scar looking at them. Once they felt that they had the right assortment of jewelry on her they pushed Sneeze in front of Scar.

"Do you think she's pretty?" Proclaim asked, boring into Scar's Light.

"Sure," Scar said as he handled one of the necklaces.

"You better say yes," Proclaim said before they walked of and looked at more jewelry.

"Ooh, I like her tattoo," Nibble said as she peered at a blue green mantis down the aisle from them.

"That tattoo is from one of the central plain tribes," Proclaim said.

"Do you girls want to go to the tattoo shop?" Sneeze asked, and when they chirped in agreement, placed the goods back and rushed out of the store, Sneeze pulling Scar behind her and running to a nearby tattoo pallor. It was one of the few shops that was completely enclosed, with lights floating in the top corners of the shop to properly illuminate the space. The group watched through a window as mostly women and a couple men were receiving tattoos on their abdomen. The men had a harder time, because their abdomens were much thinner and more sensitive than the females. Scar watched the girls fantasizing about what tattoos they would like to get, and how their boyfriends would react upon seeing them.

"I'm bored," Whisper said, being not particularly interested in the tattoos.

"Do you want to go over to my castle," Proclaim asked.

"No, that's on the other side of the planet," Sneeze said. "My father wants me to stay close to home when Scar's here."

"Lets go to the beach," Nibble suggested, and Scar watched as their Lights brighten as they imagined Scar in the water. Without a word Sneeze grabbed Scar's hand and they were off to the beach east of the pyramid. When they arrived there were still children playing in the surf as the sun was close to setting behind Psssh's castle. Parents laid in the sand and watched as the kids flew, ran, and tossed water at each other with reckless abandonment.

When Scar and the girls first ran into the ocean, Sneeze wasted no time and grabbed some water around her and shot it at Scar, who blocked most of it with a plasma field.

"That's not fair!" Proclaim shouted as she and the two other Kaggen girls grabbed onto Scar, holding on to his arms and one of them trying to keep a hand over his eyes to keep him from making another field. Sneeze hit all of them with another blast of water, making all of the girls giggled with delight. Scar managed to wrestle his way out of their grasps, and ran in desperation down the beach where he was mentally making a circular sand fort with an opening facing the waters to withstand the girls assaults.

"Don't let him get in there!" Proclaim yelled, but Scar managed to get in the structure just in time to dodge a few more water attacks. A few boys joined Scar in his fort, and they mustered all their will to repel all the attacks the girls on the beach made to take the fort. Wave after wave of girls kept coming, propelled by endless youthful energy. When some got tired, they rushed off to get a drink or a snack from a parent.

"That's bogus," one of the boys said as he watched the girls eat. "They got us cut off from the food."

"What are we going to do?" another asked, and then everyone stopped as their attention was directed at a large ship that flashed in above them. It was Thor's cruise yacht that looked like an ocean vessel. While the boys looked up in amazement, the girls took the opportunity and rushed the fort, driving all the boys inside and drenching them. As the boys laid in the water and sand defeated, Scar felt Bernini and Thor shift near the entrance of the fort.

"Hey Sneeze," Bernini said as he rushed over and picked her up, swinging her around. Sneeze's friends watched on with a bit of jealousy, but were more focused on Thor, intimidated with his size yet still intrigued.

"Why are his feet weird?" Proclaim quietly asked.

"He has feet like my father," Scar answered, almost laughing at how they were staring at Thor.

"Ready to go kid," Thor said as he picked up Scar and spanked his naked rear.

"Yeah," Scar said when he was back on the ground, running over to Sneeze.

"I'll see you later," Scar said as he hugged Sneeze.

"Bye," Sneeze said as they held each other, their friendship and nervousness binding in each other's light. The longer they held on to each other, there more they didn't want to let go, and soon they were both crying.

"Come on Jamarcus, you'll be back," Thor said as he summoned Scar over with his hand.

"I talk to you soon," Scar said as he rushed over to Thor.

"I love you," Sneeze said as her friends held her in their arms to comfort her.

"I love you too," Scar replied as Bernini played with his wet hair.

"You know you guys are always connected, right," Bernini informed Scar.

"It's not the same," Scar said as he wiped away his tears. Thor shifted the three of them on his ship, and as Scar watched with his Light as Sneeze waved goodbye to the ship, Thor lifted the vessel up into the air, taking it into the Space Between and back to their home universe.

2

"So what I was thinking is that I wanted to set up a way station here in this clearing of water," Thor said as he pointed to an open area of space amongst stars in the holographic image he had in front of him.

"How far is that from our system?" Prime Minister Taz-in asked from his hologram. He was a tall gray, cloth in a white head wrapping and a black cloak with white outlining and red trim.

"It should be about twelve sound cycles from your system, Prime Minister," Thor answered as he scrolled through his image to Taz-in's home world to double check.

"You mean light cycles?" Taz-in asked a bit puzzled.

"I'm sorry Prime Minister," Thor laughed. "Yes, light cycles. It's the closest area of water that provides clearing for the station that is also closest to the other star systems of your nation."

"That will take most of our commercial cargo ships at least one cycle to get to the station."

"Do you have any other area in mind?"

"Yes, there is a clearing four light cycles away from our home system," Prime Minister Taz-in said as he manipulated the star map to another clearing.

"Yes, I know what clearing you are talking about," Thor said as he recalled notes on it from a holographic tablet. "When I talked to the other systems they said that it was too far for them. They believe that it would create too much of a trade advantage for your home world."

"Bla'nik is the center of our civilization, Lord Thor," Taz-in explained. "It should be the center for our commerce also. The outer worlds will have to adjust."

"I understand that you feel that way, Prime Minster," Thor said diplomatically. "But I am just a logistic provider. I don't want to get my business tangled in any political disputes. My only true goal is to provide a service."

"Just in it for the resources," Taz-in chuckled.

"To be blunt, Prime Minister."

"What did the other worlds suggest?" Taz-in asked.

"Actually, two of the worlds mentioned a clearing of space that was about twenty light cycles away from your world and at the most eight from them," Thor said as he began scrolling through the star map.

"Why?"

"I'm giving this information to you in good faith," Thor said. "A few nation states want to begin colonization in this region. Mostly business that want to get the upper hand on mineral deposits found in the region."

"We have a free market in our civilization," Taz-in said with a huff as two more individuals walked into his image, females in similar clothing, one in blue and the other in gray. "If they want to colonize, by all means. We on Bla'nik don't need to suffer the resource fallout for it."

"Secretary Aiesh-shan, Deputy Mai-shan," Thor said in greeting to the two women.

"Lord Thor," Deputy Mai-shan said as she handed an information device to Taz-in.

"That's why I've suggested the clearing that I've shown you," Thor spoke up. "I did the same for the other worlds. It is a neutral location where no particular world would have any advantage over the other."

"Yes, I see that," Taz-in said grimly as he looked at his device, then smiled as he peered over Thor's shoulder. "It looks like your brothers are in pain listening to our conversation." Thor turned around in the circular white room to look at Bernini and Scar, leaning on each other as they sat on a curved leather couch that was beneath a glass window. The window revealed the stellar bodies surrounding Thor's ship. Both were dressed in plain Andean clothing, with matching white shirts and green cotton pants.

"Scar wanted to listen in on our trade deal," Thor explained. "He's going to be the Speaker for House Xkit and he wanted to see how I worked for future reference."

"They're so behaved," Taz-in said, which immediately prompted Bernini to do something mischievous. When Thor continued his conversation with the prime minister, he yanked on Scar's blond hair which made Scar wince. Scar retaliated by tucking on Bernini's ear. Bernini wiggled his head until he was free from Scar's grasp, then popped Scar in his belly, making Scar belch out in surprise.

"Cut it out you two," Thor said to them. "If you're going to act up then go somewhere else." With that, Scar shot Bernini's face with a plasma blast, then shifted out of the ship. Filling himself up with light, Scar sped around the yacht with Bernini close at his heels. Bernini sent blast after blast at Scar, but Scar managed to barely dodge them.

"Why aren't you going faster!" Bernini yelled at Scar, knowing how powerful Scar was. Scar didn't answer, wanting to enjoy his older brother hot on his tail with a fierce anger. Scar was more powerful and stronger than Bernini and Thor. He had lost all the baby fat and was becoming more tone like Thor and Ra. Bernini wanted Scar to fly loops around, showing off how fast he was. Scar felt how proud Bernini was of him, but Scar limited his light when he was with his family. Right now Scar wanted to be the little brother being bullied by his bigger one.

Bernini managed to land a shot on Scar, who went spiraling out of control before he compose himself. With a grunt, Scar chased after Bernini, slinging plasma shot after shot at him as they flew around Thor's yacht, then towards Thor's other utility vessels. As they traveled through the waters, Scar looked at the surrounding stars, nebulas, and far away galaxies, marveling at the sight of them, beginning to feel like he was home.

Bernini evaded Scar enough to head towards one of Thor's larger cargo vessels, a massive gray tube shaped ship that stretched for miles with dozens of other smaller vessels docked to it. Bernini dashed between the ships over the surface of the cargo vessel, Scar close behind still trying to blast him. At one point Bernini dodge a shot by shifting inside the cargo hull, then flew around the large circular microwave engines with Scar barely keeping up with him. All along its inner corridors blue skinned floating androids, with legs cut mid-thigh, performed all the functions for the ship.

"Don't break anything, tadpoles!" Thor bellowed at them in their lights, and Bernini shifted out of the vessel, flying a fast as he could away from all the ships. Scar shifted right behind, trying the best that he could to keep up.

"Go faster!" Bernini yelled at Scar, wanting Scar to increase his light. Frustrated, Scar did as such, dashing forward with new found speed, grabbing on to Bernini's foot before he turned and grappled Scar in his arms. They wrestled out in the vastness of the waters, Scar screaming silently in anger and joy as Bernini overpowered him, gripping Scar's neck under his armpit.

"Lets go guys, or I'll leave you stranded out here," Thor ordered, and instantly Scar and Bernini shifted onto Thor's yacht, right behind him as Thor just finished saying goodbye to the prime minister and turning the hologram off.

"Are you finished," Scar asked as he stood at Thor's feet, barely tall enough for his head to be above his knees.

"Yeah, their nation is giving me five cycles to build the satellite city," Thor said, his light brimming with anticipation and concern.

"You've been working on this for a long time, haven't you?" Scar asked as he stepped on Thor's toes. "You're close to having your own city state. Your own personal Timbuktu."

"Yeah," Thor said as he bopped Scar around on his leg, his joy flickering in his light.

"What are you going to call it?"

"New Nippur," Thor said dreamingly, looking into his own future.

"What's the problem?" Bernini asked as he felt the bit of concern in Thor.

"Nothing, it's just that one of my cargo ship's hull doors has a broken system that's keeping it from opening. The system is part of a model from the

Federation that has security systems that is owned by Papa. If I can't get the right parts, I'll have to replace the whole door system."

"I can get it for you," Scar suggested as he jumped of Thor's leg.

"That's okay," Thor said, with a waver in his pride.

"No, I'll do it," Scar said wanting to make Thor happy. "I'll take it out of the resource account that's set up for me. I don't even use it anyway. Got to be millions of tons in it. You'll just have to pay me back. With interest, so Papa doesn't get mad at us."

"Yeah, that does sound like a plan," Thor had to admit. "If not I'll have to wait months until I get the right parts."

"Come on, lets go," Scar said, eager to go to a new location he hasn't seen. Thor pushed light into the yacht's field until they were into the White. Thor scrolled over the universe screen below the ship until he dove the yacht back into the waters and by a large metropolitan trade satellite in a red nebula surrounding a newly born star. It was mostly a giant sphere construct, with large tubes sticking out of it as new sections were added on. Thor navigated his ship to one of the tube sections at the top of the city that was open to space, so they didn't have to go through decontamination procedures. After docking Thor shifted the three of them onto the docking bay, and as they flew to a check-in counter, they could feel all the gazes from the workers on them.

"Hello Lord Thor, Lord Bernini, your Highness," the clerk said as they approached a counter.

"Hello, I'm trying to find the section of the station where you have door systems for Sirian class cargo ships."

"For standard size entrances or large industrial entrances?"

"Industrial."

"That's going to be in the central hub of the station," the clerk said as he handed them three passes into the station. "You'll have to go through the decontamination portal over there."

"Aten Ka," Thor muttered as he floated towards the portal. "Come on tadpoles." Scar and Bernini followed behind him, with Scar looking out into space to see more ships docking and leaving the port. It was a bit unnerving seeing the plane of the port at a perpendicular angle from the main sphere of the station. The more he looked at it, the more it made him feel like he should fall towards the doorway.

They soon entered the portal, a room that served as a pressurization chamber for beings to enter the atmosphere control hull. As the door closed behind them the room was filled with a mixture of gases and antiseptic sprays to kill any bacteria on them. Scar mistakenly breath in and winced as his lungs filled up.

"Don't breath, dummy," Bernini warned Scar.

"I'm trying not to," Scar said as he hit Bernini's arm. They fought while the room was blasted with strong UV rays, and Thor lead them through the open portal in front of them. The three oriented themselves to the entrance of the door, and as they passed through the field at the entrance, they fell to the floor as the station's maintained gravity well effected them. They walked through the corridors of the station, occasionally taking lifts to the central section of the ship, all the while feeling the gaze of the people they walked by.

All small number of them wore pressurized suits. Most were Andean, with other species littered throughout. All stared at the boys, especially the women staring at Thor. Scar was reminded of how it felt when he walked with Rhiannon at her university, with the students staring at them like celebrities. The three of them walking together made Scar feel like male actors walking down Rodeo Drive. There was a point of time when Scar would have mocked such people with contempt, but now he couldn't help feeling proud walking next to his brother.

He could also see why the women couldn't keep their eyes off of Thor. His mixed Pleiadean and Andean heritage gave him a hapa appearance, a termed Scar learned on Hawaii that described a person that was mixed Caucasian and Asian. He was also tall for a Pleiadean, about eight feet tall, with his physique showing through his form fitting blue suit. He cut his beard after Ixchel complained about, but a black stubble grew back that match his black crew cut hair.

Bernini looked Andean like Ixchel, but he lost a lot of the baby blue skin tone as he became more pale white like their mother and Scar. He also kept his hair wild, preferring it that way. He's grown taller also, although Scar was catching up with him in height, his Pleiadean ancestry revealing itself. Bernini started noticing girls more often now, his eyes darting around to see if any were looking their way. When two white and black Lyrans stared at him he turned shyly away, prompting Scar to giggle and receiving a punch in the arm for it.

They arrived at the industrial section of the station, a large multi-storied warehouse with meters high metal shelves storing everything that a ship needed, from engine parts, hull pieces, and weapon systems. When the three received security clearance to go in from the security guards, they walked up to another counter where an Andean man was busy going over holographic files.

"Excuse me sir," Thor said after waiting a bit.

"Wait a dot," the man said as he pressed a few icons on the screen he was looking at before he flicked it away in disgust.

"Oh, what do you need, my Lord?" the man asked plainly as he recognized Thor.

"I was hoping that you had an industrial door system for a Sirian class cargo ship."

"What model?" the clerk asked as he made another holographic screen appeared.

"Her-wepes model."

"Yeah, we got it," the clerk said as he scrolled through the files on the screen. "Do you need it with or without the weapon system?"

"Without, please," Thor answered.

"Yep, follow me," the clerk said as he waved his hand at a gray and yellow industrial robot that was floating nearby. The robot grabbed the handle of a large flat palette carrier and pulled it along as the clerk guided the three brothers between the many aisles of the warehouse. Soon they arrived at the location where the motor and pully parts of the system were found on the top shelf high above them. The robot levitated up to the system and created a field surrounding the machinery, lifting it up and carefully placing it down on the carrier that audibly strained under the weight.

"I'll have my robot take it to the counter," the clerk said as the robot floated back to the floor.

"I'll do it," Scar said excitedly as he ran to the handle and pulled it behind him as he walked over to hold Thor's hand. The clerk looked on astonished as Scar easily pulled the tons of parts behind them as the three made their way back.

"So how are we going to pay for this?" the clerk asked as he created the hologram appear again.

"Can you take the funds out of my account, please?" Scar asked.

"Alright your Highness," the man said as he pressed a few icons.

"And what are we doing?" Ra asked behind them. Thor, Bernini, and Scar turned around to find Ra standing behind them, dressed in a rural red dress suit and brown pants.

"I was getting a door system for Thor," Scar said hesitantly. Ra walked up to Thor, looking up into his eyes.

"You know this is wrong," Ra said. "You shouldn't have used your brother's status for this purchase."

"I was going to pay him back with interest," Thor explained silently.

"It's my fault," Scar said, frighten by Ra's emotion. "It's all my idea. I'll pay it off to you."

"You're too young Scar," Ra said, his eyes never leaving Thor's. "You may still believe that you're an adult, but you're in a child's body now, and will think that way. You, Thor, know how unethical this is. It undermines your Mother's and my authority. And Scar's."

"Yes sir," Thor said.

"I can take the system back, Lord Ra," the clerk offered.

"That's alright, Baba," Ra said as he finally turned his gazed at Scar. "Don't do this again."

"Yes, my Lord," Scar said.

"Yes, Father," Ra corrected.

"Yes, Papa," Scar responded. With one last look at Thor, Ra turned and shifted away. And amongst Ra's light of love for them, Scar felt it. Like a gray dot floating on the surface of a sun. Disappointment. Thor walked over to Scar and rubbed his hand through Scar's hair, trying to cheer him up.

"Don't worry, he's always like that," Thor said, but it did little to make Scar feel better.

"Man this sucks," Scar mumbled to himself.

"Lets head back," Bernini said. "We should watch a movie from Earth and eat some ice cream to make Scar happy."

"That's a good idea," Thor said, and the three quickly made their way back to Thor's yacht with the door system and back to his fleet of ships. They went back to the circular room and searched through movie files until they found an awful horror movie Scar remembered. After a robot arrived to give them bowls of ice cream, they dimmed the lights and watched the flick. During the whole movie Thor kept pestering Scar, playing with his face or tickling him. When Thor tried to push Scar's nose in his armpits, Scar leaned back on top of Bernini's lap, trying to push his toes into Thor's nose.

"Smell it…smell it, now eat it," Scar said as he tried to get them in Thor's mouth, who grabbed his feet and tickled them. Scar giggled as he ripped his feet from Thor and came to a rest, lying between his brothers, feeling the light of their male pride and goofiness. It made Scar feel a little better, and tired from the day he soon fell asleep.

CHAPTER 3

35 AA

1

A group of guards stood along a road with Scar as they watched over the visitors approaching in their personal vehicles. They stood before a large high class coliseum that is surrounded by large manicured grass fields and a controlled forest. Scar and the guards wore black and white suits and ties, and were link mentally in Scar's light from orders of Twin Pillars, the head security director for Athena.

The section of the road that Scar stood by was the gated entrance to the coliseum that had tall bushes hiding the metal barrier. Dozens of Firmian paparazzi stood by the entrance, trying to take pictures or get interviews of the celebrities arriving. Most of the arrivals drove in with expensive luxury cars, the majority of which were oval and elongated in shape. The visitors are all brown to dark gray in skin tone, with the males in slick dress suits, and the women with exotic and chic dresses designed by up and coming fashion designer. One man in an extravagant brown and white pictograph dress that matched his skin tone burst out of his car with arms stretched to the sky, saying hello to the press who ate up his entrance.

"That Pythagoras is a Source damn trip," one of the guards chuckled under his breath. Scar laughed as he watch more guest arrived down the road. There were a few political figures who arrive that was a pain in the neck to accommodate. They had their own state security units that coordinated with Twin's team, and each nation state wanted to make their own special entrance.

There were also huge commotions when any aristocrats showed up, especially when some arrived in carriages drawn by horse like beasts that were slightly scaled and thick haired.

"Hey Jamarcus, head over to my location. Your sister is almost here," Twin Pillars ordered in Scar's light. Scar shifted to Twin's positioned, the tall double door main public entrance to the coliseum. Twin Pillar stood on the steps in front of it, his six foot tall slender frame poised as the upper class gossiped around him waiting for Athena's arrival. Scar quickly stood next to Twin Pillar, looking at his stern gray face. If it wasn't for his skin tone, bald head and slightly larger eyes, he would look human.

"Once your sister arrives, you're going to escort her as quickly as possible to her seat," Twin Pillars said, not moving his eyes from the crowd. "If you don't then everyone here will want to talk to her until the sun comes up. The opera won't start until she's seated."

"What if she wants to talk to everyone?" Scar asked honestly.

"Then encourage her to go to her seat," Twin Pillar responded. "You're the head of the House, right? Use that."

"Dude, it doesn't work that way," Scar laughed as he watched the crowd turn to face a long brass tinted limousine heading their way from a secure pathway away from the public.

"Go grab your sister," Twin Pillar ordered, and Scar walked to the road in front of the entrance where the vehicle stopped. As a guard open the door, the crowd of celebrities and dignitaries rushed in much like the paparazzi did to them, each trying to take a picture or talk to their Light Bringer. Tall Athena stepped out of the rear door of the vehicle, followed by four fancy dressed teenage girls. Athena wore a stunning black and red evening gown with a long trail and longer white silk scarf, the dress trail carried by the four girls. Her shoulders were bare which showed of her long neck that was covered by her shoulder length black hair. Her dress gave her the appearance of arriving at her wedding.

"Hi, Jamarcus," Athena said as she walked over to Scar, bending over and hugging him. Scar felt a bit embarrassed when Athena kissed him twice on the check,

"Don't you look handsome in your suit," Athena said before she rubbed her hand over Scar's shaved scalp.

"You cut your hair. When did you do that?"

"Last week," Scar answered.

"Why did you cut your hair?" Athena asked in a disapproving manner.

"I'm still not use to having blond hair," Scar admitted. "I'd probably wouldn't feel as bad if it was black."

"Trust me on this, Jamarcus," Athena said as she rose and faced the crowd. "If you don't get used to it, you'll never be able to find joy in yourself. I know."

"Okay," Scar said as he followed Athena who walked into the crowed and hugged some of her friends who all repeated how beautiful she was. When Athena spotted Pythagoras, she rushed over to him as fast as her dress would let her, screaming all the while.

"Girl, you look so beautiful," Athena said as she embraced Pythagoras in her arms.

"I know I do," Pythagoras said boldly and stepped back as Athena bent down to look at the figures on his dress.

"Jamarcus, get your sister inside the coliseum," Twin Pillar instructed Scar, who poked at Athena's arm.

"Athena, Twin is about to kick my ass if I don't get you inside the building," Scar pleaded.

"My own brother can't give me any freedom," Athena said as she hugged Pythagoras. "I'll see you later."

"Bye sister," Pythagoras said as Athena held on to Scar's hand and had him guide her to the door.

"Do you like my dress, Twin?" Athena asked as she walked by him on the steps to the door.

"It's beautiful, Lady Athena," Twin Pillar said while keeping his eyes on the guests.

"You haven't even looked at it," Athena said, piercing her light into Twin Pillars who turned away.

"I saw what I needed," Twin Pillar admitted, which satisfied Athena enough for her to enter the coliseum with Scar.

"He is such a man sometimes," Athena groaned.

"How else do you want a man to act?" Scar asked before being yanked by his sister.

"Don't you take that tone with me," Athena reprimanded Scar as she slipped her arms around him. Scar lead Athena through the inner corridors of the building before they arrived at the open air grass field that was separated by a blue tiled moat from the other seats above and around them. On the upper levels of the coliseum the other guests took their time finding their seats as they mingled with each other. Scar took Athena to a few row of seats lined with blue flower bushes that were placed before a circular stage at the far end of the coliseum.

As Scar sat down with Athena, he looked at the stage and marvel at the workmanship of the building. He haven't been in an amphitheater before, let alone a coliseum. The actors were going to use their lights to create illusions for the audience, but it still amazed Scar how the building itself was going to amplify the actors voices.

"Do you want to go behind stage?" Athena asked when she felt Scar's curiosity.

"How do I get back there?"

"Just climb up on stage and head back there. You're security."

"You're sure?"

"Go," Athena urged Scar, who stood up and walked over to the stage. After climbing up he walked behind the curtain where a stage hand was looking at a clip board and a radio in his ear, checking off items as dozens of actors and production workers rushed around them.

"Oh, hello your Highness," the stage worker muttered as he looked up from his board.

"Hi," Scar answered, amazed at all the work going on behind the scene.

"Did you want to have a look around?" the stage hand asked as he looked at Scar.

"Can I? My sister wanted me to."

"Go for it," the stage hand said waving Scar off as he spoke into the radio while checking of another item. Scar walked about, looking at the props that will be used as aesthetics for the opera's illusion. There were hundreds of costumes hanging on racks everywhere. There wasn't much of changing rooms for the actors, just open door rooms with white sheets dangling at the entrance. When Scar saw the changing room for the female actors, he immediately turned and went in another direction. In a sudden whirl the production crew back stage and above got into positions, making final preparations for the opera, and dozens of actors flood the side areas, ready to go on stage as the event began.

The opera was about the forming of the Firmament, a set of philosophies founded thousands of cycles ago that created the modern culture of the world, even having the planet named after it. The main characters of the story was

Farrar-in, a general of one of the powerful armies of an ancient empire that was led by the other protagonist, Man-in, the emperor at the time.

The two friends will clash once world dominance was secure about how to rule. Farrar-in wanted the ethnic group of the empire to rule, with their already established values and norms. Man-in wanted to create a government that was ruled democratically, based on the trifecta of the Firmament, the Path, the Knowledge, and the Source. Terms that are similar to the Federation's Discipline, Education, and the Light.

A civil war broke out in the empire, which happens when they're spread out and the cultures of the conquered nations meld into the central one. Farrar-in led a coup for rule of the empire, and in the process fatally wounded Man-in. While Man-in laid dying in his arms, Farrar-in listened as Man-in warned him that all of this has happened before, and will keep happening until they do something different. Moved by his friends death, Farrar-in abolished the empire and created the first global government that would become the basis of their modern civilization.

While standing on the side back stage, Scar looked out at the audience, and realized why the coliseum was built the way it was. The building was built not so long ago, a gift to Athena for being their Light. As Scar observed the seats above Athena where everyone else was separated from her, it became clear. All the celebrities, kings and queens, diplomats and government officials sat in the seats above. Separated by the moats that looked like the blue sky was where Athena was, where the gods sat. Scar noticed Athena waving for him to join her, and almost walked out on the side of the stage floor, completely forgetting about the opera.

"What are you doing?" a stage hand whispered at Scar in a harsh voice. "You're ruining the immersion." Humbled, Scar shifted next to Athena, who held on to him tightly, laughing at how she got him in troubled. Scar sat uncomfortable in her arms, wanting to say how beautiful she was. He knew that all she would do was scoff at him, so he stayed silent. Scar felt Athena's memories, ones of her when she lived on this world over four hundred cycles ago. Athena's light even looks like a dark gray Firmian. Scar just sat in her arms, feeling her love and happiness for the people around her, mixed with that small bit of loneliness.

2

Scar stood by a doorway into the Chancellor's office in the executive building for Firmament's government. Scar's back was against one wall while Twin Pillars stood across from him, looking out one of the windows onto the buildings grounds. Along the walls in the hall they were in are simple furniture, a small table made from red tinted wood or a chair with a yellow cushion. Along the walls are also paintings, depicting important events in the global government's past.

Across from Scar was the picture of a meeting that happen ten cycles ago, one of different heads of state signing the resource trade pact, officially ending fiat currency. A shadow loomed on the leg of the current Chancellor at the time, cast from a general in the room. Scar guessed the artist put that in there to represent the conflicts that erupted around the planet at the treaty signing, conflicts that are still occurring.

Twin Pillars scratched his nose before looking at Scar, who looked back with a 'what' look. Twin Pillar smiled before adjusting his business suit and using his eyes to bore holes into the Chancellor's door. Scar smiled back, studying Twin Pillars' light. Scar didn't know how old he was. Athena was able to lift certain individuals up into the fourth density that were pre-approve by the government. Athena's security attachment is such a group, and since one ages much slower once in the fourth density, Scar guessed he was in his late thirties or early forties. He served in the planet's central army for twenty cycles before he retired and joined a security firm, something Scar did when he was on Earth. There were other similarities that they shared, their love for music similar to metal on Earth, sunrises from the ocean and sunsets making the water turn red. That was probably why Twin Pillars always had Scar attached to Athena's personal guards when he visited.

But there is a deeper reason in Twin Pillars light that he didn't want to say or was willing to admit. Scar could feel how much he was head over heels for Athena, something Athena could see also. But it's hard for a man in a traditional patriarchal society to say how he feels to a woman who is in no simpler terms better that you in every way. How do you ask a goddess out for a date? At least with Scar he feels that there is a high density being he could compare himself too. He knew that Scar was immensely powerful, but their education level and military experience are the same. Those facts subconsciously gave Twin Pillars confidence to stand next to Athena. Scar turned his face to the door, feeling Athena's emotions in the room before releasing a sigh of relief.

"She's ready to leave," Scar said looking over to Twin Pillars. "She wants us to go in there and rescue her."

"Tell the other men to bring the cars around," Twin Pillar said as he open the door into the room. While Scar gave out the call, they walked into the chamber where Athena, dressed in a light red business suit was seated on a couch watching while the heads of states in the room shook hands with each other. Athena herself smiled and grabbed Scar's hand as he and Twin Pillars approached her.

"Leaving so soon?" Chancellor Manifest asked as he walked over to them. He was a tall dark brown man, over six feet tall, and large belly in is blue business suit. But Athena still towered over all of them as she stood up, being as tall as Ra.

"Since the meeting is over, I wanted to head out to get my guards something to eat before heading home," Athena said, prompting Scar and Twin Pillars to give each other a glance.

"And this is your little brother," Chancellor Manifest said as he reached over to place his hand on Scar's shoulder. "How are you, your Highness."

"I'm good, Mister Chancellor," Scar answered as he placed his hand on the President's arm.

"I won't keep you then," Manifest said as he walk back to the group.

"Lets get out of here," Athena whispered to Scar and Twin Pillars before they made their way to the door.

"Lady Athena," a woman's voice spoke out, and the three turned around as a light gray women in a dark gray dress suit walked up to Athena and hugged her.

"It was so wonderful seeing you," the woman said, her light ecstatic to be in Athena's presence.

"It was wonderful meeting you too, Chancellor Marble," Athena said as she bent over to hug her. "I hope to meet you again."

"I do too," Chancellor Marble said as she waved goodbye as the three left the room.

"Where do you guys want to eat?" Athena asked, her light wanting to let loose for a bit.

"Anywhere is fine," Twin Pillars said, ready to accept anywhere that Athena wanting to go.

"I asked where you wanted to eat," Athena said, annoyed by Twin's answer.

"Hey, there is this barbeque place that the guys love to go to that's an hour from here," Scar suggested, almost laughing from feeling how Twin Pillars wanted to strangle him.

"That's great," Athena said, looking excited. "Road trip. This will be fun." As they exited the main entrance to the executive building, a small number of guards, all dress in business attire, escorted them to three vehicles waiting by, with Athena's brass tinted limousine in the middle. Scar followed Athena into her vehicle even though Scar was almost tempted to suggest he ride with the rest of the men and Twin should ride with Athena. Once seated in the back, Athena wrapped her arms around Scar as she turned on the flat screen television in the car. As the driver began his way to the lunch spot, Scar and Athena watched the news coverage of the talks that they just left.

"Did everything go alright?" Scar asked.

"Not everything goes as you want in those meeting," Athena said as she flipped through the channels until she reached one where the analysts on a news show blasted the results of the meeting. "But we at least came up with a solution that we can build upon in the future."

"So the peace treaty is in effect?"

"The two nations agreed upon a cease fire a while ago really," Athena said as she listen to one of the analyst complained on how much she was interfering too much on sovereign nation's affairs. "The meeting was just a formality. But it also served as a means to bring both nations into the global fold and hopefully into the Federation."

"Are you nervous that it won't hold?" Scar asked.

"Very," Athena said. "You have to remember. We only bring light to the people that request it. Nothing more. It's fine if other nations don't want to join in, but if their personal military conflicts affect the nations I provide for, I will act. I have to. Selfishly, it's to protect my bottom line…"

"But we must defend the people in the House of Xkit we swore to protect," Scar said as he watched to news cast.

"Exactly," Athena said as she hugged Scar. Scar looked up at Athena, feeling proud of what she's doing. He wanted to say so, but stayed silent. Saying so would only agitate her. They rode in silence the rest of the way until they reached a small suburb in a lower middle class neighborhood filled with modest low oval shaped houses. The vehicles stop by a small restaurant that was at a corner of a block. The place was called 'Granite Bar and Grill,' with a neon sign where some of the letters aren't lit.

"Oh, this place should be great," Athena said, anticipating eating the food inside.

"It isn't the greatest shop," Twin Pillars said as he walked over to them. "It's just a hole in the wall."

"Those are the best restaurants," Athena said as she followed the men inside. "Jamarcus, remember that one mom and pop place on one of the islands at home?"

"Yeah, I loved their roasted Nimian hens," Scar said as the men stopped in front of the cash register. The store owner came out from the back kitchen, and when he saw the group his light brown face spread into a huge smile.

"Afternoon, fellas," the man said, and then his face went pale as he saw Athena standing above the group, with Scar next to her. The group chuckled as the owner took a moment to composed himself, walking over and placing his hands on their shoulders.

"Lady Athena, your Highness," the owner stuttered, trying to come up with something fancy to say to the two.

"Don't freak out, Tur-in," one of the guards laugh. "She doesn't act as high and mighty as she looks."

"Hey!" Athena said, reaching out to hit the guard.

"What do you guys want then?" Tur-in asked, feeling a bit at ease.

"Hey, lets have Lady Athena try out a whole grilled prairie stalker," another guard suggested.

"Yeah, that's awesome," Scar said, wanting to see Athena's face when she saw it.

"Alright, I'll have it grilled up for you in a quarter section," Tur-in said before heading back to the kitchen. As the group sat around the few tables in the restaurant, Scar noticed that a couple of the cooks stuck their heads out from the back to get a glimpse at him and Athena.

"You guys want to show Athena one of the dances we do around these parts?" one of them suggested.

"We don't have to do that," Twin Pillars said, wincing at the thought of having Athena seeing the dance.

"Come on man," another guard said, wanting to show off the local customs. All of the guys and Scar got up and formed a circle, their hands clinched together and their backs facing inwards. The group began to dance as twice they moved forward and back, then twice dancing to the right. One of the men began to sing about Athena, about how smart, beautiful, and strong she was. Athena watched with a smile on her face as they twirled around and around. At certain points of the song, the men would shout out how they felt they were with their relationship with Athena.

"Friend," one called out.

"Uncle," another said.

"Father," yet another stated.

"Brother," Scar said.

"Brother," Twin Pillars said, but Scar felt that he wanted to say something more intimate. It wasn't long before cooks appeared from the kitchen carrying a large steel platter with what looked like a large iguana grilled with a brown sweet and tangy sauce, surrounded with baked taters, looped shaped pasta covered in white cheese, and shredded lettuce like green leaves.

"That looks delicious," Athena said as the plate was placed before her.

"I was sure she would freak out," one of the guards laughed as they all stop around the meal, each taking portions.

"Do you guys think that I'm just some princess that stays in her tower all the time?" Athena asked as she bit into her food.

"Well, yeah," one answered.

"I see what type of friends you are," Athena laughed as she nudged Scar on his shoulder.

"Thanks for this," she said.

"No problem," Scar said, feeling Athena's loneliness fade away a bit.

CHAPTER 4

59 AA

1

Scar stood in front of a mirror of the guest room Rhiannon built for him, trying on dozens of outfits that she bought for him to wear. Many of the clothing were high end designs made from the most expensive brands in the Federation. Scar tried on an ensemble that combined a purple long sleeve silk shirt, black pants and black leather belt with a gold buckle. After feeling squeamish looking at himself in the mirror, he changed his cloths.

Next he tried on a set that consisted of a black and white shirt that ran down to his mid thighs with silver buttons, matched with loose fit black pants lined with silver colored seams. Scar looked at the clothing, then at his face for a while, then took off that outfit. He finally settled on the set of clothes he had his eyes on from the beginning. Clothes from Earth, a brown motorcycle shirt, fit blue jeans and a bomber leather jacket.

Feeling good about himself after looking in the mirror, Scar left his room to roam Rhiannon mansion while he waited for her to get dress. The house was large, but contained very little. The few possessions that Rhiannon purchased for her home though were of the best quality, balancing out a kind of minimalist styling. Scar walked out into the outdoor viewing room that overlook the large lake at the bottom of the cliff Rhiannon's home stood above.

The afternoon sun reflected of the crystal blue water surface as it gently rolled in on the arid shoreline. There are houses littered along the shore, high in property price since Rhiannon moved in above them. Most of the homes were constructed from clay brick, with open windows that allowed the dry air to freely flow in and out. The houses are scattered about the sparse trees and brushes, where the rest of the land is arid steppes, created from mechanical weathering millions of cycles ago when there was more water on the surface of Mangala.

Mangala was mostly a desert world, red sand with large ocean lakes separated by the collective land mass of the planet. The world now ships most of its usable water from the outer ice cloud at the edge of the system since Rhiannon freed them from most of the planet's energy consumption. That allowed the people on the world to leave much of its environment as is, pristine and beautiful.

"I figured you would wear that," Rhiannon said as she step out onto the deck with Scar. He turned to face her as she walked towards him in a flowery dress with a V neck that went down to her waist with a puffy mid-drift that fluttered halfway down her thighs. She wore black stiletto style shoes that were mostly straps on her feet.

"Sorry," Scar said as Rhiannon walked up to him, hugging him and placing her chin on his shoulder. His recent growth spurt got him to about five foot seven in Earth's measuring, making him just as tall as Rhiannon. Scar guessed that when he becomes a teenager, he'll be just as tall as Ra and Athena. As Rhiannon held on to him closely, Scar could feel her boredom, her light brimming to have some fun in her new free adult lifestyle.

"It's a good thing I bought these clothes for you," Rhiannon as she played with his jacket. "You'll probably just wear a Federation suit if I didn't."

"I'll go put on something else if you want," Scar said to appeased her, brushing her black hair from his eyes.

"Don't worry about it," Rhiannon said as she walked towards the edged of the deck, her arms stretched up to the sky. "Aten Ka, lighten up. I want you to have some fun. I have a whole day planned out for you."

"What do you want to do first?"

"We're going to the market to meet up with my boyfriends and for a bit of shopping," Rhiannon said as she led Scar to the garage. Inside were three vehicles, a large cargo one for shopping, an turbo charge all terrain vehicle, and a super sports car that looked like a Pagani. After the two lowered themselves into the sports car, Rhiannon linked her light to it, then reached out to open the garage door. She sped out of the garage and down a curved road to the opening gate of her property, turning onto the public road and accelerating off.

"This place is more gated off than our home on Suburbia," Scar said as he looked at all the mansions they drove past.

"Ha, this place is modest compared to where the government wanted me hole up," Rhiannon huffed. "They were going to build this castle for me, secluded away from any major city. They were planning to have security escort me around and everything."

"It's just a security measure," Scar said. "Any prudent lower density civilization would do the same to give themselves some peace of mind."

"Or they can just trust me," Rhiannon scoffed. "There's no way they're going to treat me like Athena. You feel how lonely she is."

"Yeah."

"Beside, I think that the last thing you want to do with a walking weapon of mass destruction is have it coup up all by itself," Rhiannon noted. "It may blow up on you. Anyway, I know how to defend myself, I served in the Marines for three and a half cycles. Thor taught me how to fight too. You should have him teach you."

"That would be cool," Scar said, smiling at the idea. After half a section they arrived at the market, a large multi-complex building with all types of clothing, accessories, jewelry, and electronic stores. It took them forever to find parking, and once they did, walked over to the sidewalk on the edge of the market, where Rhiannon looked all over with a confused look on her face.

"Deva, Sura, where are you guys?" Rhiannon called out with her light.

"Where on the upper levels," Sura answered.

"Why are you up there?"

"We found parking near the clothing stores."

"Argh," Rhiannon groaned. "Stay there, we'll meet you." Rhiannon lead Scar through the market where hundreds of shoppers walked by. There were sparse numbers of off world species, but the majority of them were the navy blue skinned Mangalans, all dressed in the similar style clothes Rhiannon tried to get Scar to wear. After climbing a few stories, they managed to find Sura and Deva standing along the glass window of a store. Deva had his hair tied in a ponytail, while Sura had a crewcut like Scar. They stood a bit taller than most of the shoppers, both just over six feet tall.

"Hi boys," Rhiannon said as she kissed both of them.

"Hey, Lady Rhi," Deva said.

"How's it going, your Highness," Sura said as he grabbed Scar into a headlock.

"Augh… good," Scar grunted as he tried to get free.

"Have you done anything fun since you've come planet side?" Deva asked as he pinched Scar's nose.

"No," Scar buzzed.

"You boys done making out with each other?" Rhiannon asked as she watched them annoyed.

"What? We have to mess with our little brother here," Sura said as he tried to pull Scar's jacket over his head.

"Come on, lets go," Rhiannon said as she yanked both Deva and Sura's hands into hers. "I want to get done here so we can go dune jumping." Rhiannon tugged the two close to her as she lead them further into the market, aware of the side glances the people around her gave them and loving it. They soon arrived at a women's clothing store, with showcased clothing with multi-colored material. The tops were all midriff or tubed top, with matching scarfs that wraps around the head and shoulder. The bottoms were either slim fitted or loose pants that all fasten around the ankles and waist. While the boys stood by as Rhiannon examined her options, one of the store clerks shyly walked up to Scar, tapping him on the shoulder.

"Excuse me sir, I know you're an alien, but you can't enter the store without any shoes on," the clerk said as she looked at Scar's light shining from his body.

"Oh crap," Scar said as he looked down at his feet. "I didn't even think about that."

"I forgot about them too," Rhiannon said as she stepped up beside Scar. "I'm sorry ma'am, that's my fault. Do you have any toesies for off-worlders?"

"Yes ma'am, I'll be right back," the clerk said as she left, barely able to take her gaze off of Scar, which Scar felt made Sneeze a bit mad.

"You don't wear any shoes?" Sura asked.

"Andeans don't wear shoes," Scar said as he flexed his toes. "Besides, most planets that I go to, everyone knows who I am, so they never bother saying anything about them."

"We're going to a shoe store next," Rhiannon said as she went back to picking out clothes she wanted to try on. "Didn't you feel her coming to you, Scar?"

"I don't probe everyone's mind. That's rude," Scar snapped at her. "I felt her coming. I thought she wanted to talk to you."

"Whatever," Rhiannon said as she rolled her eyes. The clerk arrived again to give Scar a pair of disposable socks, still eyeing his light. Scar didn't pay any attention to the stare, not wanting to get Sneeze any more pissed off at him. After thanking the clerk he followed Rhiannon as she walked to the dressing room to try on the outfits she liked. She went back and forth from the dressing area, asking Deva and Sura how they liked each one, settling on the one that she liked and she felt from her boyfriends that they liked how she looked in it.

Satisfied, she kept it on while placing the other outfits on one of the racks nearby. As she walked over to the cash registered to pay for her outfit, Scar had to smile about how she felt. To be young and successful, to be beautiful, to have two hot boyfriends that you know think that you're beautiful. It must be the life.

"I'm going to wear this out," Rhiannon said as she handed a small gray periphery port to the clerk, who took it as she looked at Rhiannon's shining skin.

"Are you Lady Rhiannon?" the clerk asked as the transaction went through.

"That's me," she answered with a weak smile and a shrug.

"Hi, my name is Ulu. I never thought I would ever meet you."

"Oh, I'll probably pop in and out of her a few times. Just between us."

"Sure," Ulu said before turning to Scar. "Is he your brother, Scar?"

"Yes he is," Rhiannon said plainly as she turned to him. "Say hi Scar."

"Hi," Scar said shyly as he waved at the clerk.

"That was weak," Rhiannon said snidely.

"I don't want to keep you up," Ulu said as she handed the port back to Rhiannon.

"That's no problem," Rhiannon said shaking her hand. "I'll see you later, Ulu."

"Bye," Ulu said as the four left the shop, Deva draping his arms around Scar's shoulders.

"I wonder what she would say if she found out you're not even a pre-teen," Deva remarked.

"Dude, shut up. My fiancé hears everything I do," Scar lamented.

"She looked like she was going to mount you Scar," Sura laughed. The two teased Scar all the way to the shoe store, where Rhiannon bought Scar a slick pair of toe sandals. They then separated, with Rhiannon taking Sura to her car and Deva taking Scar to his SUV like vehicle. They rendezvous out of the market and travel back to Rhiannon's home where the quickly left their vehicles and climbed into the all-terrain one, an open air vehicle made from spacecraft grade material to take the hardest impacts. After Rhiannon changed into shorts and a small t-shirt, she grabbed a cooler she had set aside and drove them out to an area of desert near their city that some of the locals visited for some outdoor madness.

"I'll show you how to drive this thing Scar," Deva said as he and Sura took off in the vehicle while Rhiannon set up a blanket on the sand. She screamed at them as the ATV ramped up the dunes and into the air, landing in big puffs of sand. Once in a while Deva would miss a landing, tumbling the vehicle over. When it would land on its bar roof, Rhiannon would fly over to flip them back on the wheels, telling them to keep driving. She enjoyed watching them, feeling their male hormones in their rushing blood.

"You're bored already?" Rhiannon asked as Deva and Sura drove back to the blanket.

"We want to get something to drink," Sura said as they watched Scar and Rhiannon eating and drinking.

"Switch then, I want to drive Scar around," Rhiannon said as she yanked her brother off the blanket, her Light growing bold. After strapping into their seats, Rhiannon drove the vehicle slowly away from her boyfriends, not wanting to throw sand at them. When they were far enough away, she poured a bit more light into the ATV, and pressed hard on the accelerator, picking up sand behind them as they sped towards a nearby dune. When the vehicle flew into the air after reaching the top, Rhiannon giggled from the weightlessness as they landed hard on the bottom.

Scar only let out a chuckled himself, which pissed off Rhiannon. She drove around finding more dunes to leap, filling the vehicle and their clothes with more sand that Scar ever had to deal with in Iraq. All the while Scar just smiled feeling how happy Rhiannon, which wasn't what Rhiannon wanted. Rhiannon pick out a particular high dune which side had almost a vertical angle. Rhiannon dash up the side of it with enough speed that the vehicle hovered a bit in the air after reaching the top, making Scar give out a yelp.

"Yeah!" Rhiannon shouted, satisfied with Scar's reaction before the ATV landed with a huge bounce, filling the vehicle with even more sand. They spent a few more sections of the day playing around on the dunes until they ran out of food and decided to go back to the mansion. They all took showers once they got back, Scar in his room and Rhiannon, Sura and Deva in hers. When he was done, Scar took a nap, not wanting to bother the three while they were busy.

Scar woke up in the middle of the night, searching out the see what Rhiannon and her boyfriends were up to, then regretting it when he saw. Laughing, Scar got up and went out to the deck, looking at the surface of the lake that reflect the spectacular night sky above him. It was ironic that Scar reached out to Rhiannon at that time, and how Sura and Deva teased him earlier. He didn't want to say it earlier, but he knew why Ulu originally came over to him. When he was Jamarcus on Earth, how was he supposed to know how hormones affects you when you become an adolescent. Now he does, and they hit him like a freight truck.

He tried to ignore the clerk, because he knew that if he even began a conversation, he didn't know what his hormones would make him do. That made him miss Sneeze even more. They weren't allow to play together as much now because of that reason. And Sneeze was definitely changing in her light and her body, her human physiology taking over. Especially her butt. She was starting to get a perky butt that seemed to defy gravity. When Scar began thinking about her, he felt a rush in Sneeze's light, which made the situation worse. Scar leaned against the balcony, never realizing that he would be in a time where he would love and hate being a kid again.

2

"So you just bought this salt mine, right?" Scar asked as he and Thor stood on the bow of his yacht as it flew over a large dry lake desert.

"Yeah," Thor said, scratching his beard while looking up at the blazing sun. "It's on one of the planets that Firmament found for mining. They let me buy it in exchange for setting up a neutral trading site for their nation."

"Way to work both ends," Scar chuckled.

"Hey, if you want it, go get it. That's capitalism," Thor stated. "And it's a good spot for us to spar."

"You're not going to kick my ass, are you?" Scar asked.

"Damn right I am. You're more powerful than me, so you shouldn't be holding back."

"Then how would I learn?"

"Yeah, keep thinking that way," Thor laughed. "Sooner or later you're going to have to get use to your power. I know Momma hasn't fully trained you yet. I don't know why."

"I kind of do," Scar said. "What type of fighting style are you going to teach me?"

"There's this instructor at Coba Private Seminary Academy in New Scarborough that coaches an elite fencing squad. They've had a lot of fighters that have won global and Federation championships. You should think about enrolling there when you start Seminary."

"Okay," Scar agreed as the ship came to a stop in a valley at the bottom of a dead caldera.

"Anyway, he taught me how to fight with a spear," Thor said as he lead Scar off his ship, flying down onto the salt bed below them. "I'm pretty sure you know basic combat skills from Earth, but you need to experience fighting someone from higher densities."

"Roger that," Scar said eagerly.

"I'm thinking we can bust up the side of these mountains," Thor said as he looked about him while he flexed his muscular body in his naval uniform. "It'll make it easier for me when I start mining for ores here."

"Always about getting that resources, aren't you?" Scar said.

"Yes, your Highness," Thor answered before he frowned at Scar. "Are you going to dress like that?"

"You think I should change?" Scar asked as he looked down at his simple Andean clothing.

"Into a Federation military uniform."

"Alright," Scar said as he turned his clothes into white light and then into a black fit form outfit.

"So you're thinking Marines?" Thor asked.

"You don't have an Army," Scar noted

"Aten Ka, Jamarcus. You're always hating on the Navy."

"I have to," Scar explained.

"Never mind. So first I'm going to teach you how to make a weapon," Thor said as he stretched out his arm in front of him. Light bloomed in his hand, then stretched out in a horizontal line. When the light dissipated it left a tri-tipped spear that looked to be made of a light metallic material that was pale in color.

"Reached out and feel how the spear is formed," Thor instructed, so Scar observed Thor's spear, noticing that it was made of a mix of titanium, carbon fiber, mercury, and gold, among other compounds. Scar made his spear, matching Thor's length so he didn't have a reach disadvantage.

"The material in these weapons allow you to pour your light into it," Thor said as his began to illuminate. "That allows the welder to attack at faster than sound speed and the weapon to take a lot of damage."

"Cool," Scar said as he made his spear glow.

"Basically, the most important thing you need to learn is probing your opponent's mind," Thor began explaining. "That will fundamentally tell you what you need to do in the fight. Attack, block, high, low…"

"Okay."

"Also remember to block you mind too," Thor said as he slowly walked towards Scar. "It may seem hard at first, but you'll get used to it. I'm going to attack you now."

"Wait, how do I block?" Scar asked as his heart rate jumped.

"Probe my mind," Thor said before he launched at Scar, creating a large cloud of salt and shatter ground. Scar instinctively slowed down time, just able to stay ahead of Thor's high speed. Scar dove into Thor's light, knowing that he was going to attack on his right, and somehow knew to spread his legs and to step into Thor's attack with the shaft of his spear. When their spears collided, the ground and air around rippled behind Scar like air being blasted into water.

Scar whole being shook from the impact, and he was almost about to allow himself to be happy about it when Thor spun around, bringing the butt end of his spear colliding with Scar's open left side, sending him cartwheeling head over feet, salt popping into the air as he landed in a heap. Scar got up as quickly as possible, his numbness on his left side fading while readying himself as Thor came barreling down on him. He stayed focused this time, blocking every strike he felt coming from Thor.

"Block out your mind!" Thor demanded as he fainted with a sweeping strike at Scar's head. When Scar went for the block, Thor intentionally missed, and with the carried momentum swiped kick Scar's legs. As Scar dangled in mid-air momentarily, Thor struck out at Scar like a person hitting a tossed up ball with a baseball bat. Scar filled his body up with light to match Thor's, bracing his hands and feet against spacetime to stop himself in mid-air, leaving a mist trail behind. He lounged at Thor, and while not entirely sure how to block his mind out from Thor, made a small wall of light in front of his head.

A small smile spread on Thor's lips as he easily dodge Scar's thrust at him as he also made a wall in front of his face. When Scar saw this, he slowed time down even further, forcing his light into Thor's before Thor stabbed his spear between Scar's legs, trying to strike at one of them. Scar flew up into the air, then came flying down at Thor, spear ahead of him. Again and again Scar thrust his spear at Thor, who easily swatted them all away.

"Don't always strike at the core!" Thor advice as he once again stabbed between Scar's legs. This time Scar simple leapt into the air, and as Thor did before, varied his attacks from high, low, left, right, with and without a weapon. Their sparing went on for a few minutes like this, each able to counter each other, with Thor occasionally getting the upper hand.

When Thor felt that Scar was able to fight him on mental reflex, he increased his light tremendously and intensified his attacks. When Scar felt this, it was like a sun bloomed from within Thor, pushing the waters of reality away as his lethal intent jumped forward in his light. Scar was caught off guard by his assault, and when he blocked a swipe at him, the force of the blow created a bubble shockwave that threw the ground and the air away from them in all directions. Scar didn't have time to recover before Thor stuck out at Scar again, sending him flying uncontrollable into the air. Scar skid himself to a stop against the waters again, but this time thought strategically, waiting for Thor to attack him.

When Thor took Scar's bait, lunging into the air to continue his attack, Scar shifted behind Thor as he got near. When Scar struck out at Thor, he easily parried Scar's attack, then shifted above Scar for his own attack, which his brother barely dodge. Again and again they shifted around the valley trying to evade each other's attacks, and when their weapons collided they created more shockwaves that seemed to suddenly explode out of nowhere.

Scar began to understand that skill wise he wasn't going to beat Thor. He had nearly two hundred cycles of experience on him. Scar decided to allow Thor to strike him, faking a missed block which allowed Thor to kick him hurtling towards the side of the caldera, debris exploding away from the impact. Thor rushed at Scar ready to stab him in the chest. Scar feigned that he was going to block, and just as Thor was to strike Scar drained all the light from his body. Thor's spear easily plunged through Scar's abdomen, and as Thor looked at the wound in shock, Scar raised his light back up again, and while blocking out the pain gripped Thor's spear in one hand and struck out with his spear in the other, slicing Thor's cheek.

A bigger smile spread across Thor's face, like the one that was on Scar's. Thor yanked the spear out of Scar and was about to strike again when his whole body relaxed as he felt Ixchel shift in behind them. Scar quickly healed his wound while he and Thor stood at attention as Ixchel floated towards them, dressed in her favorite gardening clothes, black soil still clinging on her knees.

"Scar, do you not think that you are fighting a bit too recklessly?" she asked as she wiped her hands clean with a cloth.

"No ma'am, I was," Scar answered obediently.

"I think you have been playing with your siblings for too long now. Go back to your room and start studying again for Seminary."

"Yes Momma," Scar said as he changed his clothes back to their Andean style and shifted to his Suburbia bedroom.

"How have you been, Thor?" Ixchel asked when they were alone, wiping the sweat from her shaved scalp.

"Fine, Momma, how are you," Thor responded silently.

"Good. Except my garden has been giving me problems lately. So is this the mine that you bought?"

"Yes ma'am."

"I am proud of you. You and Athena are doing very well in this region."

"Thanks Momma," Thor said with a small smile.

"Thor, you should not encourage him," Ixchel said. "He still believes he is an adult, but he is not."

"Yes ma'am," Thor sighed.

"I do not mean to be angry at you," Ixchel said, feeling Thor's anxiety. "It is for Scar's own good. He needs to spend time being a child, learning how to be happy again, to not fear or have any self-doubt. He needs to learn how to love again."

"I get it," Thor admitted, trying to come up with the right words to say. "It just that… it feels like… the only time you and Papa ever speak to me lately is when you're mad at me." Stung by those words, Ixchel drew in a deep breath, closing her eyes before letting it out. She floated over to Thor and hugged his neck tightly.

"I love you, Thor," Ixchel said as she tried to pour her light into him. "You know that right?"

"Everything you do is out of love for us," Thor said as he patted Ixchel's back. "It can be a little harsh sometimes." Ixchel reached up to Thor's hair when she heard that, running her hands threw it as her feelings began to leak out.

"You are my baby boy," Ixchel whispered into Thor's ear. "You are my handsome baby boy."

"I love you too, Momma," Thor said as he held up Ixchel in his arms.

"You grew your beard back," Ixchel said a bit annoyed.

"Yes," Thor chuckled.

CHAPTER 5

65 AA

1

Marshal lied awake in bed late in the afternoon trying to go to sleep, but his anger wouldn't let him. He stared holes into the ceiling while his mind kept going over what happened earlier at work that day. It wasn't his fucking fault. No matter how many times he tried to tell his shift manager, nobody listened to him. 'You know company policy,' his manager said to him, 'You been with the firm for over ten years'. Marshal tried to get in contact with his client, but he never answered his calls, never responded to his emails.

Marshal slowly got up and sat at the edge of his bed, reaching out to his whiskey bottle to take a swig. Fucking asshole. He tried to tell his client about the changes to state law that could affect his investment accounts. 'You need to move your funds to a different state' he told Andy. It's not his fault he procrastinated. Marshal sent email after to email at Andy telling him he needs to change locations for his savings. In one email he told Andy that he was being a fucking moron for not acting. So Marshal moved the accounts for him. You're welcome.

Marshal swallowed some more whiskey before putting the bottle down to get dress. 'You can't do that without the client's permission,' his manager told him. Bullshit, they know he was right. Marshal saved his client a few thousand dollars just by moving the locations of his accounts. Fuck anger issues. There wouldn't be any anger issues if people would listen to him. It was a bullshit move to take his client away from him. Marshal didn't buy that Andy wanted him gone. He and Andy knew each other. Andy understands him, he can be as frank with Andy as he wants and he didn't mind.

After getting dressed in some slacks and a polo shirt, Marshal walked through his small apartment to the refrigerator looking for some leftovers from yesterday. Why didn't people understand him? If people didn't listen to you, anyone would get angry. Especially if what you're trying to tell someone will help them. Even Marshal's wife turned on him. 'I can't be with you if you're angry all the time'. The bitch needed to listen to what he was trying to tell her. Marshal busted his ass off for her, made all the money they could need. She didn't need a job. Just stay home and watch the kids. The fuck is this nonsense with 'I don't need a provider, I need a good husband'. A good husband is a good provider. See how good you do providing for our daughters now. Thank Jesus for pre-nuptials.

Marshal took a few bites out of the baked chicken he brought home yesterday before throwing it in the trash. He looked down at his almost full trash container, his anger simmering over. He suddenly went to his couch to grab his green Celtic jacket, then slipped on his shoes before stepping out of his apartment. The building he is in was disgusting. He had a nice house in Bristol, Rhode Island, in a great neighborhood. It was everything that his wife should have wanted. Now he had to live in Harvard Square with all the lowlife college dropouts trying to make a living in Boston. And it isn't the safest place to live either. But since his firm moved him from Andy's account, he had to go back to working on the bottom dwelling earners. Most of them were minorities with no idea how to use the money they got. They deserve to be poor.

Marshal got in his blue sedan, leaned over to his glove compartment and checked his twenty two revolver to see if it was loaded. He closed it back up, reached into the back seat and grabbed his beanie cap, pulling it over his brown hair. He looked at himself in the mirror, his mid-day scruff and shoveled bangs giving him a delirious look.

It was that Frank, Marshal thought as he turned his car over and began driving back to Rhode Island. He's the one that put the idea in his wife's mind to leave. 'He's a better Christian than you,' his wife said. Marshal did everything a good Christian man is supposed to do. He tithe, worked at volunteer programs at church and work. He took his family to church every Sunday. What else should a Christian do. 'There's no love in you'. Bullshit. Everything he did for his family was out of love. He got them a nice house, gave his daughters the best clothes and toys they could afford. Got them into a good school, got a luxury sedan for his wife. An exercise machine so she can stay in shape. He got everything that they could need. How else are you supposed to love your family?

After an half an hour driving Marshal slowed his car into a parking space across the street from another rundown apartment building. What the fuck could Frank do for Marshal's wife and kids if he lived in a dump like this? Working at a restaurant, living off of tips. No man should be in a situation where they need the woman to help get by. Why can't Marshal's wife see that this loser is using her. She's barely making ends meet putting a roof over their daughters heads. How much can Frank actually help with things? None, that's how much.

Marshal's heart skipped a beat when he saw Frank step out of his apartment with a bag of garbage to take to the dumpster behind the building. With a panic Marshal reached into his glove compartment to grab the revolver, shoving it into his jacket's pocket before stepping out of his car. As he hurried across the street to catch up with Frank, Marshal's anger was ready to explode. Piece of shit. He's not even good enough to be with his wife. She was a model for a while, using that career as a means to pay for med school before Marshal met her. He was better than this loser.

Marshal managed to close the gap between he and Frank in the alley to the dumpster, and when he pulled out his gun and pointed it at Frank, Scar flinched, mentally causing Frank to flinch too, turning around in shock to find Marshal pointing a weapon at him. Marshal stood there stunned for a moment, not sure what to do next, which gave Frank enough time to lunge at Marshal and try to wrestle the gun from him.

"Stop it right there," Chac'chel instructed, so Scar froze the universe they were watching.

"You were doing an excellent job up to the point when your reflexes got the better of you," Chac'chel said as she floated next to Scar in the Space Between. "But you're young. The body naturally reacts to situations like this at your age."

"Yes ma'am," Scar said.

"You have to stay focus while observing an universe," Ixchel said as she ran her fingers through Scar's hair. "You may be able to automatically probe into a lesser densities' light, but your light is separate. Their emotions are not yours. Do not be influence by the lights of others around you. Be your own."

"Yes, Momma."

"Always ask yourself this question," Chac'chel said. "What am I? So many lights believe that what they are defines who they are. Makes them righteous beings. Their I am. Is that true?"

"No," Scar answered.

"What are you?" Chac'chel asked.

"I am not."

"And how do you define your I am not?" Chac'chel asked.

"By my actions," Scar answered.

"How would you define Marshal's I am not?" Chac'chel asked.

"Should I?" Scar asked.

"We're not asking you to judge his character. Marshal's actions does that. We're asking you to make a judgement of his actions."

"He is an individual who needs to identify himself with his genitalia. So he props up everything in the material, his family, his work and religion, as a mental reinforcement for his righteous genitalia. And I thought I never had to make such a statement."

"Rewind time back," Chac'chel instructed. "Make sure you erase everyone's light while you do it."

"Yes ma'am," Scar said before reaching out to the universe and rewinding it back for about ten seconds. After he manage to pull the light memories from the universe and having them fall up to Aten Ka above them, Scar released time so that Marshal returned behind Frank, pulled out his pistol and shot Frank twice in his back. Frank let out a painful cry before falling to the ground, grasping at his back believing he can somehow grab at the pain and yank it from his body. Marshal stood over Frank for a moment, his mind not grasping what he had done yet, then bolted for his car, getting it started and driving away erratically from the apartment.

"You were able to stay calm during that," Ixchel commended. "You have improved over these last few cycles. You seem to be able to handle universes that are in the Empty fairly well."

"That's because there is hardly any light in such universes that one has to deal with," Scar said.

"We should then move you up to dealing with those in Aten Ka then," Chac'chel said, and scrolled the universes below them until they came to some whose light tangles were stronger than those universes in the Empty.

"That one, observe that universe," Chac'chel said as she pointed at one window below them. Scar looked down onto a dense forest where a group of reptilians, armed in rusted chained or clothed armor, rested at the foot of a moss covered stone hill. Some of them sat on large roots that grew out of the stone as the group got ready for their trip to a new land.

This group was part of a larger army that assaulted a Sirian fortress a day's march away to the west. Their platoon were disenfranchised the whole time they marched towards the battle because their clan was one that didn't have much battle experience. Most of them were young and very poor, and couldn't earn the right in battle to move up in social ranking to mate or hold land. Groups of older reptilians came down upon them months ago with whips and slurs, slashing at them, forcing them into military wear as they forced the young men into a larger regiment of soldiers.

The whole time they marched the other reptilians forced them to do all the labor for the older, more battle harden platoons. All day and night they clean the shit holes, served the food, tended the shadow hounds pins where a couple of them lost their lives. Everyday was a nightmare for them until the night they came upon the Sirian city that they were going to attack.

The group huddled together, cold and scared in there poorly constructed armor, as the war flames from the other platoons of reptilians around them lit up the overcast sky. The soldiers screamed war chants at the walls before them as plasma bolts showered down from the sky, randomly piercing one of the young reptilians bodies. If that reptilian was lucky, the bolt would kill him instantly instead of that reptilian having to fight through the pain.

A horn blared over their heads and drums shook their bodies and ground, and their enforcer whipped at them, forcing the young reptilians forward to their doom. Somehow by chance an plasma shot plunged right through the enforcer's heart, who fell forward with a confused look on his face. Another horn blast sounded, and all the reptilians bellowed in rage as they rushed past the young platoon and into the ensuing battle. Someone in that platoon grabbed a fellow soldier to flee, and soon the young reptilians fled the battlefield heading east.

They ran all night and during the day, trying to stay in the cover of the forest to help shield their eyes from of the sun. The whips of the enforcers was still hot in their lights, forcing them to keep running from the nightmare they had escaped. They ran until they all but collapse at the hill they were at now, discussing amongst themselves on where to go. They couldn't go back north, which would be suicide. To the south were cites of Pleiadeans, who hated them just as much as the Sirians. Their only option was the east, where there was secluded areas of wildlands by settlements of their people. Hopefully they could stay there and avoid being detected until they came up with another plan.

A horn trumpeted above them, and the reptilians stood in horror as they saw an Sirian in gleaming bronze armor, his brown hair that grew from his elongated head fluttering in the wind standing at the top of the stone hill. In terror the reptilians dashed as fast as they could from the Sirian, only to be ran down as dozens of Sirian calvary flew or leapt down upon them. The reptilians tried to surrender to the gray skinned Sirians, but they didn't know the common tongue of the land, and as they pleaded only saw the eyes of the Sirians grow even more filled with hate.

What happen next was one of the most horrifying things that Scar has ever seen. The massacre was over in less than a few minutes, but when one is being torn apart, it feels like an eternity. All the young reptilians was chased and cut down by either sword or spear. Those who managed to get a good distance away were still shot by well-placed plasma bolts. Scar began to cry when he felt the existential terror of an reptilian who laid on the ground as the Sirian who pinned him down continue to plunge his sword into the reptilian until he died.

All the emotions began to overwhelm Scar, from the blind hate of the Sirian soldiers, of the fear of one Sirian as he stood by and watched the scene happen. The helpless pleas of one of the reptilians as he called out for help to some unknown cosmic savior to help him, to give him a life of peace that he desperately wanted. The apathy of the Sirian captain who understood the language of the reptilians but ignored their surrender.

Scar witness all of it, his anger brewing in his light. Just feeling the lights of all the beings below them reflected upon his own, making his light want to act. But he watched with discipline as Ixchel and Chac'chel taught him. He floated and looked in grief and a stiff upper lip until the last reptilian was slain.

"That was very good," Chac'chel told Scar trying to calm his light, but the compliment didn't help.

"You wanted to help them, did you not?" Ixchel asked calmly.

"Yes," Scar answered as he wiped his tears from his cheeks.

"Would that be ethical?" Chac'chel asked.

"No," Scar answered from repeated instruction. "The scene I just witness is happening continuously, in an infinite number of universes and in an infinite number of combinations throughout the omniverse. Why should I help these and ignore the others when it is impossible to help all of them."

"What is the most important thing though?" Ixchel asked, which Scar pondered until he could come up with an answer.

"If we were to help the reptilians, then we would stunt there Ascension into Aten Ka," Scar guessed. "One can never know what the outcome of any event can be, but the choses by the individuals must be made by them and not us so that they can learn from their actions. If we were to help the one reptilian who called out, then how would he learn to help himself."

"Correct," Ixchel said.

"You must always remember to be an individual," Chac'chel said. "You may be caught up in the mentality of the masses, but you know that the opinion of the many is not the same as the ethical one. We are teaching you the right thing to do in many situations, and you have been bless with the power to stand alone in that ethical decision. You must stand strong in your light, and not be swayed by what the masses may do before you. You will often be judged unfairly, but always be the righteous individual. Don't make excuses for yourself."

"Yes ma'am," Scar said as his aunt scrolled over more universes to observe.

2

"Wake up, Scar," Ra said as he turned on the light in his bedroom. Scar pulled himself out of his sleep and lied in bed for a few moments. He looked at Bernini's old clock that was on a dresser next to the bed and saw that it was four in the mourning. With military discipline Scar made himself get up and sit on the edge of Bernini's bed. He looked around in the room, which was plain like Jamarcus' apartment in Fort Walton. Scar took a look at the snow cover ledge outside his window before he finally shoved himself out of bed and walked over to Ra who stood at the foot.

"Good morning, Papa," Scar said as he hugged Ra's waist.

"Good morning," Ra said as he rubbed Scar's face before he went to the bathroom to shower. Afterwards he clothed himself and silently walked out of his brother's room, not wanting to wake Ixchel who was still sleeping. When he went downstairs and into to the kitchen he saw that Ra had fixed a breakfast of fruits, baked taters and a cup of fruit juice ready for him on a small eating table. After gobbling down his meal and downing his drink he went into the living room, grabbing a few of the books he was studying while Ra went back upstairs to join Ixchel in bed.

Scar looked out at the backyard through the invisible wall of the living room, watching the snow fall around the tree from a black sky. It was peaceful to look at, almost soothing for his light. It made him think that any child would be blessed to have the life he has and to see this sight. Scar shook his head, waking himself up as much as he could before he sat in the middle of the living room floor. He increased the light inside of his so he could read the books he pulled and open the one that taught languages.

"Good morning," the book broadcast in Scar's light in the Andean language.

"Good morning," Scar whispered a replied in kind as he read the response.

"How are you this mourning?" the booked asked in Sirian.

"I'm am fine, thank you," Scar answered.

"How is your day going?" the book asked in Lyran.

"It is going well, thank you," Scar said.

"How is your day going?" the book asked again.

"It is going well, thank you," Scar said again, trying to pronounce his words correctly. The book broadcast its language lesson in Scar's mind in more languages, increasing in vocabulary. After a section Scar picked up another book, this one broadcasting languages at an advance level. It took Scar longer to finish this book, with it wanting to hold a simulated conversation with Scar. He kept his voice low, not wanting to wake his parents, which made it hard for the book to hear his response.

After he was done with his language lessons, he switch to a book on time manipulation ethics. He was at the part where it discussed the use of time viewing for investigative and court purposes. There is actually few legal scenarios in Federation law that one can use time viewing when investigating a scene of a crime, such as when a patrolmen needs to find a victim that is missing and time viewing is needed to track down the person. If a body is found, time viewing must stop because a strong light could manipulate reality to fit any new crime scene that would fit into said light's narrative.

Certified viewers will arrive at the site to make sure that the crime scene was not tampered during the analysis process. More legal language existed to prevent any evidence that might have been obtain due to time viewing. Outside of verifying non-tampering, prosecutors must use physical evidence to convict a suspect, even if one were able to clearly see into the past and witness a crime committed by a suspect.

Scar stopped reading, his light getting tired from all the inputted information. He looked out into the back yard again, seeing that the sun has risen. Snow continue to fall out of the white sky onto the deep snow. Scar stared at it with a smile on his face when he heard Ixchel climbing down the stairs.

"How far did you get this morning?" Ixchel asked as she walked over to Scar, wearing a red shirt and a pair of puffy multi-color pants that looked extremely comfortable.

"I finished the language books," Scar said as he got up and hugged his mother, resting his chin against her head "I'm working on time ethics right now."

"Did you eat?"

"Papa fixed me something this morning after he woke me up."

"What time did you wake up?" Ixchel asked as she walked to the kitchen.

"Four in the mourning."

"Why so early?"

"I wanted to meet Aunt Chac'chel this afternoon for lunch."

"What for?" Ixchel asked as she rummaged in the refrigerator for something to cook.

"There is something I want to ask her," Scar said as he sat down next to the text books, reluctant to open any more.

"You do not want to tell me what you want to ask?" Ixchel questioned, feeling Scar's blockage.

"Not till after she answers," Scar said.

"Why not stop for a while," Ixchel suggested, feeling Scar's mental exhaustion. "Go out to the back yard a play for a bit."

"Okay," Scar said, surprised by how much his light increased with enthusiasm. He got up and rush to the stairs, then slowed himself realizing how his youth was getting the better of him. Scar went to his room to put on a warm jacket and a thick knit cap before heading into the backyard. His bare feet crunched the snow, the cold spreading over his warm skin as he walked to the tree. He stood there for a moment, his Light reflecting off the ground as he planned what he wanted to do.

He wanted to build a snow fort that he and Bernini would make during the winter months. Just thinking about it made him wish Bernini could come home from University. With a bit of melancholy, he went to work rolling large balls of snow, going around in circles to make the floor of his buildings. He scooped up large amounts of snows in his hands, slowly making walls along the paths he made. He then gathered more snow, bunching it up into balls and creating a pile in one of the rooms he made. He stopped suddenly, realizing that he was making all of this for only himself. Maybe Ixchel and Ra wanted to play, Scar thought, but felt a bit weird wanting to play with his parents when he still felt like an adult.

"Scar, come in and get something warm to drink," Ixchel spoke into him, and Scar quickly walked into the house, seeing Ra sitting on the couch as he watched the news on the television hologram, wrapped in a blanket and drinking from a steaming cup. Ixchel handed him one when he went into the kitchen, filled with a popular strain of Andean hot cocoa.

"What time is it?" Scar asked, wanting to know how much time he had to play with his parents before his lunch meeting.

"It is a quarter section after twelve," Ixchel said.

"Crap," Scar said looking at the clock. "I was out there that long?"

"You did build an elaborate fort," Ra said as he looked out back. "You and Bernini love to build those things. You don't even use them, just build them."

"I got to go," Scar said as he drank his cocoa, standing still for a moment to enjoy the warm sensation in his belly.

"Do you want us to take you?" Ixchel asked as she watched Scar head for the front door.

"No, I was going to take the bus. Thanks anyways," Scar said as he left the house and walked out of the driveway. He marched through the snow out of the neighborhood they lived in Suburbia, realizing now that the area needed a bus stop nearby. It took him half a section to get to one that was at the end of the road at the bottom of the hill the local houses sat upon. Thankfully, it didn't take long for a bus to arrive. After he got on and argued with the bus driver to let him pay he sat in a seat by a window, looking out and thinking how beautiful the houses were.

It would have been better if Bernini was there to ride with him, to share his emotions with so he didn't feel weird feeling like a child being in awe with everything he saw. But the rest of his family were older and out of the house because of the significant difference in their ages. Athena was one hundred and fifty cycles old when Thor was born, and she practically babied him when she got a chance to visit while he was growing up. Rhiannon and Bernini were closer in age, which explained why they acted like how a normal brother and sister would.

Scar accepted how lucky he was that he was able to spend close to sixty cycles with Bernini before he left for school. Sixty cycles of being a kid. It was a bliss that he didn't know how to handle, and Bernini being there and making everything seem normal or teasing him when he acted like a goof helped. Nobody wanted to talk about Ixchel having so few children and their separation of age. And it wasn't from lack of trying that they didn't have more kids. Scar heard that almost every night when Bernini left and Ixchel was feeling empty nest syndrome. Scar understood now why Athena could feel happy and lonely at the same time.

The bus made its way off of Suburbia island and on to the main bridge to the Metropolis. When he arrived at the bus hub into the city, Scar got off and transferred onto another bus that slipped through the snow until he arrived at the downtown district. Scar looked at the passengers on the bus as he got off, feeling a bit funny how hardly anyone dressed like it was freezing outside.

He walked through the busy streets until he came to a business building where the restaurant he was going to meet Chac'chel was at the top floor. Scar took an elevator up, ignoring the looks from the adults in business attire looking at his plain Andean clothing. After exiting the elevator, Scar walk up to the entrance of the high end restaurant where a concierge stood and informed him of his reservation, and almost giggled as the concierge expression went from mild disgust to exasperated bewilderment when he found out who he was. The man quickly guided him to where Chac'chel was seated, who was wearing another off-world gray dress.

"I was wondering when you would arrive," Chac'chel said disapprovingly as Scar was seated.

"Sorry," Scar apologized. "I was building snow forts in the back yard and… wow, that's a bad excuse."

"You're still a child now," Chac'chel said as she gave her order to the waiter who promptly arrived.

"Should I change clothes?" Scar asked after he ordered, looking at the other patrons in the restaurant. "I feel a bit underdress."

"No no, you're just like your father. Ra dresses the same way no matter what the occasion is. He even got Ixchel dressing like him sometimes."

"You don't dress like most Andeans," Scar teased.

"But I do dress for the occasion," Chac'chel pointed out with a stern eye.

"Yes ma'am," Scar said.

"What did you want to talk to me about?" Chac'chel asked as she took a sip from her water cup.

"I wanted to ask you something, but I'm not sure how," Scar explained. "Actually, I'm not sure if I'm even allowed to."

"Why?"

"It's hard to explain. It's not an issue of my youth. It's an adult request. I want it to be an adult request. I feel like an adult, but I'm still a kid. Barely an adolescent. I know what I want to say, but it feels weird when I think it out."

"I understand," Chac'chel said as she study Scar's light. "Your parents and I experienced the same thing after we went through the Ascension process. Athena did also, even though she wasn't sent down through densities. She was a random light that Ascended on her own and happen to be your mother's first born. It's probably why she didn't want to go through the process again."

"She's part of the reason why I wanted to talk to you," Scar said. "Well… her, Thor and you."

"Is that why you're blocking your thoughts from me?" Chac'chel asked.

"I'm just nervous about asking you want I want to ask you," Scar explained. "Thor and Athena are mad at me. They don't want to admit it, but they are."

"You know that's not true, Scar."

"You're mad at me too," Scar said, which prompted Chac'chel to be silent. "I know all of you wanted to be the Speaker of the House. I feel how you spite me for that."

"You know we love you," Chac'chel noted.

"And I love you," Scar said, confusion setting in. "I love you guys so much. I wake up everyday and know that I have the best family that anyone in the omniverse could ever want. You can't believe how happy all of you make me feel. But it feels wrong sometimes, like I don't deserve this happiness."

"Or you won't let yourself be happy," Chac'chel said.

"Yeah, you're right," Scar chuckled. "But I know what makes you guys happy, and when I do that, it makes me happy. That's why I want to ask if you want to share the title of Speaker with me." Chac'chel sat up straight, looking into Scar as centuries of experience kicked in as she tried to guess what Scar really wanted.

"What do you mean?" Chac'chel asked cautiously.

"I still want to be Speaker," Scar said. "I mean, I believe that I do. I want final say on things, but I want your voice heard too. So that every decision that you make will be considered the same as mine."

"That sounds like keeping your friends close and your enemies closer," Chac'chel said.

"Look, I know you see me as Scar," he began. "All of you. But I'm still Jamarcus. The memories are still there. All the pain and grief. I had love in my life for a brief moment and it was gone before I knew what it was. And now I have love in my life again. I don't want any other emotions diluting that light. I just want to be surrounded by love. Does that make sense?"

"I suppose," Chac'chel said as she look out the window, surprise by what her nephew offered.

"That's why I kept it a secret," Scar said. "I just didn't know how to phrase it. It is an adult decision. I want it to be an adult decision. But it's based on childish emotions. It's hard to explain." Scar looked at Chac'chel, whose large brown eyes looked down at the table, not moving even when the waiters brought their food and placed it before them. All the while she blocked an emotion that was building up inside her, not wanting it to break her demeanor.

"So," Chac'chel said as she composed herself and looked Scar in his eyes. "How do you want to do this?" Scar smiled as he explained his offer while they began their lunch.

CHAPTER 6

66 AA

1

Scar shifted to the neighborhood where he need to catch the morning bus to Coba Private Seminary. For what Scar was able to research, Seminaries in the Federation are the equivalent to colleges on Earth, while Universities are doctorate schools. Because most beings in the Federation live such long lives, on average a few hundred cycles, it's normal for children at the age of one hundred cycles to start Seminary, since they've had plenty of time to learn from information imputing books or shows on television networks.

What's more, the Federation allows children after graduation from Seminary to get jobs. A number of children get jobs as explorers, traveling to distant galaxies and worlds. It explains why in most UFO cases on Earth, many people describe the beings they see as always like children in appearance. Who would of thought that was because they are.

Scar walked alone along a street, feeling the late summer breeze flow over his black and grey school uniform for Coba, looking at the houses surrounding the bus stop. They weren't the same as the houses on Suburbia, because most on the people on that island were very well off. But Scar could tell that it was a upper middle class community. That and the clothes. Almost everyone that Scar saw walking to the bus stop wore designer clothes with their uniforms. Some even wore name brand toe sandals.

"Look at tall he is," Scar heard a one girl whisper to another, feeling their gaze on him. He was taller than all the children there, his height the same as he was back on Earth and growing, and the other children were at the most chest high to him. That was the only reason they didn't talk to him. And there was his light. Some just stared at the seven loops he allowed himself to show, compared to the five that most of the children here had. There was contempt in some of the eyes.

"He's got to be an old light," Scar heard another kid say. "They're always a bunch of try hards. Parents probably forced him to Ascend so he can make resources for them."

"Hey man," Scar heard someone say to him, which caught him off guard that he didn't feel his thoughts. Scar turned to an Andean boy, whose backpack hung low of his skinny frame.

"Hi," Scar said, ignoring the fact that he was blocking his thoughts.

"I didn't mean to stare into you, but you're an old light from Earth, right?"

"Yeah, man. You too?"

"Yeah," the boy said laughing. "I didn't probe your mind. It's just that your light still looks like a black male on Earth."

"You're the first one to say that to me," Scar laughed in English. "Does it look that weird?"

"Few here knows what we're talking about," the boy said in the same tongue. "They see stuff like this all the time. They wouldn't know how weird that is to us."

"Fuck, right? I tried telling my parents and aunt about it the other day, but they said that I'm still seeing only in the material, not the light."

"They're right," the boy said. "I guess it's hard for old ways of thinking to go away. My name is Popol."

"Sonlig," Scar said shaking Popol's hand. "Did you grow up in the U.S.?"

"No, Britain. So I guess you died in two thousand twelve. I was ninety five when I passed. How old were you."

"Thirty four."

"That young," Popol gasped with wide eyes. "Were you sick?"

"Yeah, kind of," Scar said with a shrug. "I don't talk about it that much. My parents want me to talk about it, but I don't want that to be my theme in school."

"I understand," Popol said as he turned to the yellow bus that was slowing to a stop in front of them. "It's hard to think that we have to go through the same damn nightmare of school again. Tell you the truth, I'm looking forward to it."

"I can't say the same," Scar said as they climbed onto the bus. "Aten Ka, they have yellow buses."

"Ha," Popol snorted as he sat down by a window. "I never gone to college, so this is new to me."

"I literally got my bachelor's just a few weeks before I passed." Scar said as he sat down next to Popol. "It's still going to be like high school. I'm not looking forward to that."

"I can say one thing," Popol mentioned as he looked at the kids on the bus. "You won't have a problem getting a girlfriend."

"Yeah, I don't think so," Scar said with a roll of his eyes. "I wasn't able to hold on to a girl on Earth. Besides, I'm spoken for."

"Sonlig, look mate," Popol urged, and Scar looked out at the bus and noticed that most of the girls had their eyes on him. A short hair one on the seat next to them didn't even blink as she stared down Scar when he turned to her.

"These girls are into your light," Popol observed in almost disdained awe.

"Aten Ka, I couldn't get a girl to even notice me in school on Earth," Scar whispered, then nudged Popol in the chest as he let out a laugh. "It doesn't matter anyways. Like I said, I'm spoken for. Sucks to be them." Popol eyes widen a bit when Scar said that, then let out a nervous laugh as they continued to talk the shit about Earth until they arrived at the school.

Coba Private was a large red brick campus that was located in a high end suburb at the edge of New Scarborough. As the school bus rolled in front of the school to let the students off, Scar saw other students being dropped off by their parents in luxury cars. Scar could feel that it was just as important to the parents to let their kids off in style as it was to their kids.

"What's funny," Popol asked when he heard Scar laughed.

"Nothing, I'm just laughing at the kids driving the cars."

"What?"

"Nothing man," Scar said as they walked towards the main entrance to the building. Looking around, Scar saw that Popol's observation was spot on. Almost every girl and a couple guys, pale skinned to dark tanned looked in his direction. One of them even reached out and swiped her hand through his light, which pissed off Sneeze to no end. Scar then noticed the other stares looking his way. The ones from the boys. Not all of them, just the very few ones that had six loops. That look of contempt bore into his light.

Scar and Popol walked their way through the halls until they came to the school's auditorium, where all the new students began to sit in their little cliques. The two took their seats and sat quietly until all the students were seated and the school faculty walked on stage. The teachers gave their roll call, and when the attendance finished, the students were told which class group they would be in.

"Mate, you're in 1A?" Popol asked in astonishment as they called Scar's assignment.

"Like I said, I already had my bachelor's on Earth. But this is like the first grade. There shouldn't be any difference so far now."

"I don't think so," Popol said. "I was actually looking forward to hanging out with at least one old light here."

"Don't sweat it," Scar said. "I'll make time to meet up. Plus I got my own place, so we can hang out after school."

"Your parents let you move out?" Popol asked.

"They didn't want me to, but we don't live in New Scarborough. I wanted to go to school at Coba because my brother was coached by the fencing instructor here. So I got a job and moved here."

"So you're basically free?"

"My parents are always watching me. But they're pretty chill about the stuff I do. As long as it's not stupid."

"That's awesome," Popol marveled. "What do you do?"

"I was in the Army for eleven years and security for four, so I got a job at a security firm here on Nima. It helps that I'm biracially Pleiadean, because my height made it easier to get accepted."

"Sonlig!" a faculty staff called, and Scar twitched a bit as he looked at the stage, then frowned when he say four other students walking towards the stage, all six looped except for a Andean boy, tall for his race and proud faced, who was seven.

"Crap, I got to go," Scar said as he got up. "Do you want to hang out at my place. I don't have work tomorrow and I got a game console we could play."

"Sure," Popol said as he watched Scar walk towards the called students.

"All right, I'll see you tomorrow," Scar promised as he followed the faculty through the school until they arrived in a room with a large oval table with five seats pulled up to it. Bookshelves lined the wall between windows on one side of the room, while on the other computers sat next to one another on desks.

"Hello students," an Andean woman said, dressed in a smart gray and black business suit that matched the school uniforms. "If you can please take a seat, I'll explained quickly why you're are here." Scar sat down in a chair closet to the door while the other students sat closer to the teachers, all with eager lights reflecting off the table.

"My name is Principal Ixtat," she said once everyone was seated. "And I'm pretty sure everyone here seated knows why you have been summoned. Every yearly class has a student council that facilitates any interaction for the students with the school staff, to allow the students to better become more independent as they fundamentally join Federation society as proper adults. You have been chosen because of your entry test scores and because of your densities. This is a prestigious private school, so I cannot understate the opportunity serving in the student council will provide for you.

"That said, I will like to let all of you know the seats that has been opened for you due to the group decisions of the teacher staff. Sonlig, because of your high score in all areas in literacy, athletics and light manipulation, along with your experience in your previous life, the seat of president of your class was chosen for you."

"Yeah, sorry Principal Ixtat, I'm going to have to turn that down," Scar said, with the other students swinging their gazes at him in shock.

"Sonlig, I know you feel this way, put you know your parents would like for you to take this seat. Think of the doors that can be opened for you."

"I understand," Scar said as he stood up from the table. "I just don't have the time. Truth be told, I just want to go to this school to get coached by Master Chuy. That's about the extent of extracurricular activities that I want to do."

"You can't possible want to give up the presidents seat," the proud face Andean said to Scar, his anger flashing at him.

"Don't get too work up Chaac," Principal Ixtat consoled. "It's still only an offer, and everyone here has a right to turn it down."

"But how can someone turn down being their class president," Chaac protested, a bit of jealousy shining through.

"I really can't man," Scar tried to explain. "I got a job after school, one where I have to go to tonight. So I really don't have the time to do anything outside of school and fencing."

"Your parents aren't willing to help you with school," Chaac scolded Scar in a condescending tone.

"They could, but I don't want them to. Maybe because I still think I'm an adult. Look, I know what this seat offers. The chance to interact not only with the staff here, but with other clients and entities that work for or facilitate all the needs of the school activities. But I got real stuff to worry, an apartment, the food in my fridge, the clothes on my back. That requires a job, which I have to go to tonight. There is a difference between acting like an adult and being one."

"The staff here respect your decision," Principal Ixtat spoke up. "If we're holding you up, you can leave Sonlig."

"Sorry guys," Scar said as he left the room, still feeling the burning gaze Chaac gave him. That gazed bugged him as he left the school and shifted to the inner city area that his apartment was located at. It was much like the apartment that he stayed in on Oahu, except a bit better and safer, like living in Brooklyn in New York City. The quality of life for citizens in the Federation is great, but there is still a stark difference between those that have high densities.

Scar hurried into the apartment building, saying hi to the neighbors he walked by. Almost everyone in this part of New Scarborough were fourth density lights, working services jobs for the city that primarily served as a business and political hub for the planet. You can't get much resources one could from mining off world, but you can still make a decent living due the mandatory standard of living the Federation requires employers.

"Sneeze, are you busy," Scar called out as he open the door to his apartment, but he could feel her ignoring him. Sighing, he tossed his school blazer on the couch and slouched down on it, turning on his game console, wanting to play for a bit before getting a short rest and going to work that night. He played a fantasy game that both he and Sneeze loved to play, but got annoyed by not having Sneezes' presence in him.

"Come on Sneeze!" Scar yelled into the room, but she still gave Scar the silent treatment. Scar looked around his room, not getting any joy from playing alone. It was a spacious apartment, with a living room and a separate kitchen. The bedroom also had a large bathroom. It was pretty nice for his budget, a place that he needed top dollar to afford back on Earth.

When he knew that Sneeze didn't want to play with him, Scar got up in a huff, took off his uniform, and laid down in his bed in nothing but this boxer briefs. He tried to go to sleep, but Sneeze just kept probing into him along with giving him the silent treatment. It got to the point that Scar sat up in his bed, growling at the ceiling, trying to be as quiet as possible to not disturb his neighbors.

"What did I do?" Scar asked, yet Sneeze still remained silent.

"You know what Sneeze, I got to go to work," Scar said hotly at her. "If you're going to be mad at me, just disconnect so I can get some rest. I can't sleep if you're going to be pissed."

"Why do you have to disconnect?" Sneezed ask, angered by Scar's suggestion.

"Why are you mad at me? I don't do the silent treatment thing. If we can't communicate, then there is no need for us to entangle. And disconnecting is not a hard decision for me."

"Why did that girl have to touch your light?" Sneeze asked.

"I can't control what people are going to do around me," Scar said.

"Yes you can."

"No I can't! Wow, that is so crazy. I can't force people to do what I want them to do."

"Why did all those girls have to stare at you like that?" Sneeze said, a hot flash popping into Scar's light.

"I'm pretty sure that if there was any other guy with the same light as me, the girls would look at him," Scar surmised.

"But they were looking at you like they were going to swallow you up. You can't tell me that you weren't a bit tempted to do something."

"Yeah, no, sorry babe," Scar said as he plopped back down on his bed. "I still feel like an adult, so going out with any girl here would feel Source damn awkward."

"What about me?" Sneezed queried.

"You're different. You're like a sister to me."

"Oh that's nice," Sneeze said getting more angry.

"Will you just feel what I'm trying to say in my light," Scar growled. "Don't you get it. I have a long relationship with you. You. It's like when Kathrine died and I didn't want to date anybody else. How can you be in that deep in a relationship with someone and then try to start over with another person. I don't have the patience for that. You're my best friend, my sister. I need you in my light. To have to start that all over again with another person is not something that I want to do."

"Don't you think that those girls in your school are pretty?" Sneeze asked, her hesitance piercing up.

"Sneeze, sweetheart, listen to me," Scar said in an even tone. "I don't look at the form anymore. I've been on too many worlds now with different looking specious to know that there is no standard reference for beauty. I only look at the female light. And let me tell you, if I wasn't with you, there wouldn't be a female in the multiverse safe from me. She could have four wings, three horns, and twenty tentacles. If she has trim, you need to hide her."

"Is that supposed to make me feel better?" Sneeze asked a bit annoyed.

"Aten Ka, woman, don't you get it," Scar said exasperated. "I love you. I've known you for seventy cycles. To have that stop and to start over again until I'm in that comfortable spot will probably take another seventy cycles. I'm not doing that. I don't think you understand how much I need you."

"If you say so," Sneeze said softly.

"ANYWAY, what did you do today?" Scar asked, ready to switch to another topic.

"Oh, my friends and I just got our tattoos today!" Sneeze said excitedly.

"Cool, I want to see," Scar said, creating a window into Sneeze's room where she was. Her heart jumped a beat with Scar looking at her. She had grown since the last time that Scar saw her. Her human DNA was expressing itself also, so that her bare breasts held up firmly on her, just like her perky butt. If it wasn't for her large almond shape eyes, she would look like any shaved head black woman on Earth with small lips and nose.

"Look," Sneeze said as she turned around, happy with how Scar looked at her. She had black makings of geometric glyphs across her derriere, with some of those symbols representing her royal status on her world. There was also a large black dot with wiggle lines protruding from it along the side of one cheek.

"Is that supposed to be me?" Scar asked as he reached out with his mind and touched the dotted symbol.

"Yes," Sneeze said as she stood still, allowing Scar to touch her.

"What else did you do today?"

"Not much. We got our tattoos just after school, but my friends' parents are mad that they spend so much time in Groen Stad, so they went home afterwards."

"You don't want to go over to their cities?"

"Daddy doesn't want me to leave the city so that everyone can keep an eye on what I do here."

"It must suck to be a princess," Scar mumbled.

"You have more freedom than I do," Sneeze pointed out.

"That's because I got my own place and a job," Scar said. "Otherwise I'd have to stay home with my parents. And it's weird there when I'm the only one in the house."

"Do they act funny?"

"No, they act normal, or what normal parents do with their kids. When Bernini was home he at least treated me how any normal older brother would. That feels normal no matter what age you are. But it feels weird when my parents…you know… act like parents."

"They love you," Sneeze said as she laid down on here bed facing Scar.

"Yeah, I know that," Scar said as he moved the window to face Sneeze. "But it doesn't feel right. I know that I'm a kid. But I don't feel like a kid. And when they act like parents, I feel bad for not feeling like I should."

"Maybe you should try being a kid and enjoying yourself," Sneeze said as she reached out to Scar with her hand.

"Everyone says that," Scar said as he held Sneeze's hand. "I just don't know how to." Scar started to run his fingers along Sneezes arm, which he felt made her heart beat speed up.

"I can't wait until fencing season starts so I can do something outside of work," Scar said as he moved his finger along Sneeze's hip. "Or maybe I should have joined the student council to keep busy. What do you think I should do?"

"I don't know," Sneeze whispered, not listening to what Scar was saying. When Scar looked at her light, Sneeze stared right back at him, waiting to see where he was going to touch her next. When Scar reached out to cup her breast, she held her breath, her heart pumping even harder as Scar ran a finger over her nipple.

"You know we can see you, right?" Ixchel said in their lights, and Scar snatched his hand back, releasing the window so it can snap back into place. He laid in bed with a guilty grin on his face while he felt Sneeze silently laughing with her hands over her eyes.

"Aten Ka," Sneeze giggled.

"Oh man," Scar laughed. "That was so not smooth. And you think I'm actually free to do whatever."

"I stand corrected," Sneeze said. "What time do you have to go to work?"

"Five sections from now."

"I'll let you go to bed then. I don't want your mom mad at me too. Love you Sonlig. Get some rest."

"Love you too," Scar said.

Chapter 7

68 AA

1

"I don't think you understand how tired I am," Scar said as he laid on the stage in the school auditorium, looking at the ceiling.

"I thought higher densities aren't supposed to get tired," Popol mentioned as he sat next to Scar looking down at him.

"Yeah, whoever said that is full of shit. Like, your body isn't tired, right? But your mind can go numb if you keep doing things that required a lot of mental attention."

"Maybe you should quit your job," Popol suggested.

"Yeah, that's not going to happen," Scar grumbled.

"But you're too tired from fencing practice and school."

"Well I'm just going have to suck it up, now don't I," Scar said. "Plus, it's only one night out of the week that I have to go straight to practice and then straight to work. It's just that yesterday Master Chuy kicked our asses."

"Holy shit mate, everyone heard that," Popol said. "That's the first time I heard a fight like that. Those shockwaves scared me for a bit there. I thought we were under attack."

"You never heard the fencing team practice before?"

"No. My parents moved to New Scarborough only a few weeks before the school started. As soon as they found out I got accepted they changed their whole life around so I can come here."

"It's a wise investment," Scar said. "The resource income between a fourth and fifth density is pretty significant in the interstellar market now a days. Are you thinking about getting a job in astral communications after school. Hey, a fifth density navigator is in high demand lately."

"Actually, my parents were miners in the system I used to live in. I want to start our own business in mining so my parents don't have to work for anybody else."

"You can give them access to more resources and travel to more worlds faster than the competitor," Scar guessed.

"That's the idea," Popol agreed. "I love my parents. They bust their ass to give my family the life style we have. I'm not trying to say that the Federation doesn't give everyone a better standard of living than anything a regular family could have back on Earth…"

"With unlimited resources, there's no excuse," Scar said.

"Right. But a person with the right attitude can bust their ass for a few decades and live like a rock star for a century. And we have a large family. My parents worked for centuries to give my family the comfort we have. My brothers and sisters would be happy just working alongside them, but I want to make life better for my parents. Or maybe that's just the human in me."

"No, it's because you're an old light," Scar said. "That's one criticism I can say about most people in the Federation. Because quality of life is so good, a lot of people get complacent. There's really no drive for someone to ascend in density. So those who are born with higher densities are the ones who get the best jobs and pay, instead of the ones who work the hardest. It's no different than Earth, where the rich stays rich and the poor stays poor. Except on Earth we placed social barriers that make it almost impossible for most to succeed without immense hard work."

"And we just happen to know what hard work can accomplish in life," Popol surmised.

"Exactly."

"All right students!" a teacher called out as she entered the auditorium. "The bus is here. Make sure you bring everything you need for the field trip. Don't forget your lunches, because there are no restaurants in the middle of the ocean."

"Like that's going to make a dumbass remember to bring their lunch," Scar said as he continue to lie on the stage.

"That means you too, Sonlig," Popol said as he stood up.

"Dude, help me up," Scar said as he reached up to Popol, who visibly winced when he saw Scar's uniform shirt become untuck.

"Tuck your shirt in there," Popol said as he pulled Scar up.

"What, you don't like to see my pale skin?" Scar asked as he pulled up his shirt, showing his tone abs that shined white from within. "I've got to be the whitest person in here, and I never believed I would say that. Be blinded by the light!" With that threat Scar ran around the stage, laughing menacingly while chasing down everyone with his light. They all chuckled or screamed as he came near, especially some of the girls.

"Be blinded!" Scar said as he approached Popol, wrestling his head against his belly. When Popol popped his head back up and gave Scar a menacing look while blocking his light, it made Scar laugh even harder as he guessed how mad he made him.

"Don't forget your food," Popol said as he scooped up Scar's bag.

"Thanks man," Scar said as he grabbed it from Popol before they jumped off the stage and followed the rest of the class out the school and into the late spring mourning. All of the students were corralled unto the school busses and began their section long trip to the pier that was near the eastern part of the indented sea that lies at the western part of the island continent.

After all the kids got off the busses, they hurried onto a small white and black cruise ship that waited for their arrival. When the students and teachers all came aboard and the ship was untethered from the pier the captain silently navigated the vessel out into the open sea. Most of the students stood at the edge of the top deck, taking pictures of the shoreline, where there were scattered towns at the foot of tall snow topped mountains. The mountains ice levels were raising back up the mountains because of the warmer weather, leaving green trees on the sides.

Scar and Popol stood at the bow of the ship, watching all the students and teachers walk about and talk within their own groups. Scar noticed that a small clique of sixth density kids sat alone with their fan club sitting by on a higher deck. Scar almost started laughing as he felt their condescending auras about them.

"I'm too sexy for this boat, too sexy for this boat, and my fancy coat," Scar sang as he looked up at them.

"What are you singing?" Popol asked as he gave Scar a weird expression.

"Nothing man, I'm just making fun of the cool kids upstairs."

"Aten Ka, you see those other kids just hanging around them like puppies?"

"You know, that is a medical condition," Scar began. "It's called aura hypnosis, when a person can become almost non-cognitive when in proximity to a high density light. Especially if that person's light is two densities below or more."

"And where do you keep all this useless information at?" Popol laughed.

"Pop, I've got to know this stuff. That's why I don't just go talking to random people like normal kids do. I've seen chicks just stare at me and not know that they're doing it."

"Like almost every chick on the boat," Popol observed.

"What?" Scar asked and looked around and only then noticed how a number of the female students that were looking their way.

"They could be looking at you," Scar said.

"No mate, they're looking at you," Popol corrected Scar. "I wonder why they don't just come over and say hi if they're interested in you."

"Probably because they think we're together," Scar joked. "Quit cock blocking me dude."

"Shut up, man."

"I kid man, I kid. Besides, like I said, I'm already spoken for. And that person is always watching what I'm doing. Which I don't mind."

"Whose that?" Popol asked while blocking his mind.

"Somebody, Jesus," Scar laughed. "Why did you have to freak out like that. What, you thought it was somebody you might like?"

"No," Popol groaned.

"What, dude, is she on this boat?

"Yes," Popol said after a pause.

"Oh man, you got to tell me."

"All right kids, we're here at Arrow's Head reef," one of the teachers yelled into the students. "Let's all go below deck and observe how the sea life is here in comparison to our other destination."

"This ought to be cool," Scar said as he began to follow the rest of the students below deck. Popol silently followed Scar as they descended down into the lower decks of the ship where there was a corridor along the outer hull. The hull had a clear glass wall that showed them all the hundreds of fish swimming along and under the vessel.

"I want you guys to take notice of how the animals, plants, and reef looks here," the teacher began here. "This reef is the prime source of bio-diversity along the river oceans surrounding our island continent of Axtal. The reef here receives much of the natural nutrients that comes from the ocean currents flowing from the west. That's why there is such an abundance of sea life at this location. But as we know, life evolves differently due to environmental changes, so that some species of fish may have certain characteristics here, but off shoots species may diverge as we go north and south of Axtal.

"As an example, I believe that the students on the north side of the ship are able to see a school of Axtal brims. See how this large fish is red with dark purple dots along its side in a nice line at the center. That is why it's call a brim. When we go north, you'll find a species of brim that are red with blue to violet spots, while at the southern end of the continent, you'll see brim that is entirely red.

"Another nice creature down below us is called a sea ferret, a hyper active sea slug that is more mobile than its other cousins of the genus. It has long feathery antennas that it uses to detect nutrients in the ocean stream. This species here has a red base with black bands that run from the antennas to its foot. To the north you'll find a species that has block spots running down it's back, while to the south there will be a species that looks similar to this one but the antennas will be smaller and non-feathery.

"Aww, it's so cute," one of the girls whimpered next to Scar and Popol as a ferret swam under the ship.

"Pop, go get that fish and show it to the chicks," Scar joked at Popol.

"No, why?" Popol asked confused.

"It'll impress the girl you'll like."

"I don't think that'll work, Sonlig."

"Sonlig, do you want to volunteer to grab the ferret for us?" the teacher asked as he overheard Scar.

"Sure," Scar said as he gave a sly grin to Popol.

"Aten Ka, who are you trying to impress?" one of the sixth density students asked in a patronizing tone.

"I'm too sexy for this trip, too sexy for this trip, I'm too fucking hip," Scar sang as he swirled his hips, making some off the students laugh.

"Sonlig," the teacher sneered.

"My bad," Scar said before he raised his light, prompting some of the girls to ooh at him. Scar shifted out into the water, using his light to keep himself dry. He quickly caught up with the sea ferret and encircled it in a curvature bubble before shifting back into the vessel. He splashed Popol with the water in the bubble before handed it over to him.

"Right bastard," Popol groaned at Scar as he blocked his mind, which made Scar chuckle, guessing how pissed off Popol was. Soon Popol was surrounded by a gaggle of female students, all of which were awing at the ferret Popol was holding. The uncomfortable look on Popol's face made Scar laugh even harder before the teacher told Scar to place the fish back and continued her lesson.

<2>

"Have any of you guys been following the news back on Earth?" Oki asked as he scratch his brown and white feline fur under his chin.

"Why, what's up?" Scar asked as he looked down at the sidewalk he, Popol and Oki were walking on.

"Fucking Peru declared war on the U.S.N.A," Oki said.

"The hell," Popol gasped. "It wasn't going to take long for them to do that. America had it coming."

"Do you think the Federation's going to help Peru?' Oki asked as he looked up at the apartment buildings they walked by.

"We can't," Scar said. "We only integrate with worlds when at least fifty percent of the population has accepted the terms with joining the Federation. Earth only has about twenty percent, and most of those countries were developing nations. Plus, if Peru declared first, the Federation will most likely stay out of the conflict."

"But it's what the forces in Peru did that's got the whole planet freaking out," Oki explained. "They took the Panama Canal."

"Wait, what?" Scar asked. "How? Why?"

"I know. Crazy right!" Oki exclaimed. "They took northern Chile and Argentina, western Bolivia, Ecuador, a good part of western Brazil…"

"They took all that?" Popol asked.

"Wait, I'm not done," Oki said. "They took Columbia and the eastern part of Panama. The Federation League took practically the western part of South America."

"Holy Christ," Popol hissed.

"It makes since," Scar said. "The U.S.N.A has been setting up guerrilla camps in some of those nation so they can mine resources in Peru. I guessed the League got pissed about having mercenaries invading Peru all this time."

"How did they take so much territory?" Popol asked.

"It was mostly ground forces," Oki said. "Their versions of Marines. It only took them two weeks."

"Holy shit," Scar said. "Two weeks? Damn, Earth just isn't ready to deal with fourth density warfare."

"Earth forces got some defenses against them, but the Leagues forces was led by this guy whose name was Anub Akina."

"No wonder," Scar said. "I know that guy. He's one of the few people on Earth that has ascended to the fifth density ever since they enter that dark matter cloud back in the twenty twenties. He served in the Navy for the Federation, in a galactic patrol unit. My parents met him. They say he's almost sixth density."

"Your parents work for the Federation?" Popol asked.

"Yeah," Scar said quietly.

"That explains why you're seventh density," Oki said. "Are they high up in the government?"

"Something like that."

"Where do you live anyway?" Popol asked as he looked around at the apartments.

"Umm," Scar said as he looked down the sidewalk. "It's down the block."

"It's about time," Popol mumbled.

"It's about time," Scar mumbled back at Popol. "Dude, quit bitching."

"If Anub is sixth density, he's got to be the most powerful person on Earth," Oki suggested. "Why would the U.S.N.A try any bullshit in Peru if it would provoke that kind of response."

"Well, one, the United States has a long history of starting bullshit in countries. We all know that."

"True," Oki agreed.

"Two, Earth isn't as knowledgeable as we are about the light," Scar said. "They only just entered that dark matter cloud. It's going to take time before scientists there are able to separate the metaphysics from the hard science about what they are capable of doing."

"Or they could have just listened to the Federation delegates when they visited," Popol suggested.

"It isn't that easy," Scar countered. "Essentially, all the beliefs and religions on Earth was first confirmed, then blown away in a matter of years. It'll take time for Earth's cultures to catch up."

"We did," Popol said.

"And we were pretty much outcasts on Earth for that, if you recall," Scar said. "Anyway, here's my apartment."

"What floor do you live on," Oki asked as he looked up at the light blue building.

"The fourth."

"We have to walk up there?" Popol moaned.

"Aten Ka, there is an elevator," Scar snarled at Popol. "Dude, are you still mad at me about the trip."

"No," Popol said as he block his mind.

"Yeah you are," Scar laughed as they walked into the building and summoned an elevator. Soon they were up to the fourth floor and into Scar's apartment, with Scar taking of his school blazer and flinging it onto his couch.

"What games do you have?" Oki asked as he sat down in front of Scar's hologram set.

"Mostly MMORPG's. I'm playing Xbal's World right now. I got two level eighty characters on it."

"What classes?" Popol asked as he sat down next to Oki.

"One tank and one heals that can double as DPS," Scar said as he laid down on the couch behind them.

"Don't you have work tonight?" Popol asked as he looked back at Scar.

"Nope, not tonight," Scar said. "And I didn't have practice either. And since we're gearing up for end of the year exams, we don't have any homework, so I got all night for us to goof off."

"Okay," Popol muttered as he turned back to see Oki start playing a game.

"I've never played as a tank before," Oki said as he moved Scar's character around. "Is it hard?"

"Yes and no," Scar stated. "If you build your character right and have pretty decent skills in this game, then no. If not, then it's real hard and nobody will want to play with you. Trust me on this."

"So what, we're going to watch Oki play all night long?" Popol asked a bit agitated.

"No, the game has four way local play," Scar said as he got up and sat down next to Popol. "I wanted us to make new characters and start a fresh game together."

"I never played a MMO before," Popol said. "I don't think I'm going to be all that good with a hand controller either."

"No problem, we can link up with the game with our lights," Scar said as he grabbed the controller from Oki. Scar went through the option menu in the game, and selected light link. After picking what numbered player was going to be picked, Scar handed the controller to Oki, then Popol until each had a character that they could mentally control.

"Now were going to select character races," Scar said as he quickly scrolled through the options and made a dark tan Andean with a bald head.

"Trying to look like how you did back on Earth?" Oki asked as he made his character.

"I just feel weird playing any other type," Scar said.

"I feel you," Oki said as he made a female Lyran with scant clothing and huge attributes.

"Why do guys always play female characters on games?" Scar lamented as he watched Oki admire his creation.

"If I'm going to play a game for hours on end, I at least want to enjoy what I'm looking at," Oki explained. Scar sighed as he watch Popol make a female Andean character himself, just as scantily clad but with brown hair.

"I guess I'm going to be surrounded by waifus here," Scar mumbled. "Okay, now we're going to pick classes."

"What type of classes are there?" Popol asked.

"Well, there are many types but there are three major archetypes. Tank, support, and DPS. So do you want to feel important or do you want to be a team player?"

"What's the difference?"

"If you want to feel like your skills and decisions make an impact on the team's success, then play as a tank or support. If you don't care about the rest of the team and think that the only thing that matters is how much damage you knock off a boss, then play as DPS."

"Well, since this is my first time playing this game, I think that I should play as a healer," Popol said. "Healers fight on the front lines, right?"

"No, you just stand back and heal everyone," Scar said.

"Okay," Popol said as he went through the class selections.

"What class are you going to be Oki?" Scar asked.

"I'm thinking berserker, because it can be a tank and DPS. I want to try being a tank."

"Cool, I'll be an assassin," Scar said with a sly smile. "I never played this class. They're mostly glass canons." The three finished with the selection process and were sent to the world of the game were they ended in the midst of hundreds of players, all running or riding mounts in a large village.

"All right," Scar said as he maneuver his character in front of Oki and Popol. "We can go through the tutorials of your classes, but that takes a bit of time, and the game is pretty simple to learn. It's one of those games where it's easy to get into but requires much skills to master. I love games like this."

"Yeah, I know," Oki said. "I hate those games that are only stat stackers and make people feel good about standing still and pushing an already determined sequence of buttons."

"Right?" Scar laughed. "The last game I played was like that and I hated it…" Scar paused as he noticed an heavily armored player walk up behind Popol and began to seductively dance behind him.

"What in the Empty is this guy doing," Scar said, stunned as the player began to perform a twerk like dance.

"Does he know that I'm a guy?" Popol asked, not sure what to do.

"Does it matter," Scar said as he move his character to confront the new player.

"That's my waifu, beat it dick," Scar said as he made his assassin slap at the player, who in turn gave Scar an emphatic middle finger before walking away.

"All right, what should we do?" Popol asked.

"I know a good place for us to level up before we take on some missions," Scar suggested as he lead Oki and Popol out of the village.

The Federation

CHAPTER 8

71 AA

1

"Today we are going to practice going over how to access the White," Mr. Hulneb stated in the front of the class. "Now that everyone moved their desks to the edge of the classroom we can begin without fear of someone getting their homework disintegrated. First, what is the White? The universe that we see is the result of the positronic and lepton interactions that we can detect from our senses. The reason that the sky is blue is because the molecules' electromagnetic fields reflect light at certain frequencies so that it hits our eyes at the color of light blue. The reason why metal has it reflective and sturdy appearance is the same, light reflected back to us at certain frequencies.

"Now if we were to take a single atom of oxygen, or a single atom of iron or carbon, we would be able to see the electrons, protons and neutrons in said atoms. But we won't be able to see the electromagnetic field surrounding the atoms. The reason why is because the particles inside the atoms all come from the waters of reality around us, and not separate fields mixed together. The neutrinos, muons, leptons, and such all come from the same pool. The electromagnetic fields attached to these particles come from the White.

"The White is the collective quantum fields of every known energy, force, or particle that exist in the omniverse that are connected to particles. So far as we know. The best way to think of it is that it's a large book, and each page is specific to a certain quanta. One page is sound waves, another is a page on gamma energy, there is a page on celestial energy from a single god, so on and so forth."

"Now, the best way to access the White is by increasing our densities, so that we may raise into it a density, but not too much that we are completely in its loop. Everyone try it now." Scar and the rest of the class raised the light inside themselves until they saw the classroom spread away from them like being inside of a bubble, and then the bubble flowed down towards their feet as they raised into the White, a universal plane of white light as far as one can see.

"Don't go too far into it," Mr. Hulneb warned. "We just want to access it so we can have a window readily available to us. Now, slip back inside the classroom but keep the window open to the White." Scar moved the window to the classroom up and over him so that he stood with the rest of the class, who all had shining widows of white light above their heads or to their sides.

"This technic is essential for certain jobs after you graduated," Mr. Hulneb continued. "We all know that travel in the White is in high demand in the job market since there're always new civilizations joining the Federation. You can get a job as a light bringer for a company, city or nation state, supplying whichever energy source that they may desire, rather it is electricity, thermal, or infer-red. Light densities like Sonlig here can provide energies like fusion, temporal, or even his own light energy field to give other individuals access to higher densities."

"Way to point me out right there," Scar grumbled.

"What I taught you to do is the way that you can easily access the White," Mr. Hulneb said, ignoring Scar. "Remember how to do this, and practice it so that it becomes more reflex than a task. Now that we know how to access the White, how do we acquire certain fields in the White. It may seem hard at first because all the pages in the White are all packed up against each other; that's what gives that density its color.

"First we are going to create our own little pocket dimensions, so that we can access theses fields without blowing up the school. First, we are going to make our own bubbles of water so that there is no reality inside of it. Everyone gather up some water, not too much that you're going to strain yourselves. Sonlig, I want you to pull more, because you're going to be grabbing more exotic fields today." Scar waved his hand in front of him, making reality ripple back and forth. Scar gripped a rippled and pull on it, until a large ball that looked like oil flowing through water appeared in front of him, and Scar strengthen the walls of the bubble, making sure that there is no outside reality inside of it.

"Your bubble is huge," a student gasped next to him, and when Scar looked around he saw that all the other students bubbles were the size of bowling balls in their hands, while his was as large as he was.

"Now that we made our bubbles…" Mr. Hulneb said, grabbing the class attention, "…we can create a gravity well inside of them to make sure no excess energy leaves. Each bubbles has its own reality in it, so it shouldn't be a problem for all of you to grab the waters at the top of your bubbles and make a gravity well." Scar waved his hand at the bubble, making the water inside the bubble ripple, and grabbed a ripple at the top, pulling it down and holding it so that a stable gravity well is sustained.

"So the best way to access a page of the White is to observe any phenomenon and vibrate that into the White. Once this is done, a person can just recall that sensation from memory and will be able to access that field at will. Lets start off with something easy like radio. You should have made a vacuum in your bubble, so there is no air to vibrate. Extend the window of the White to touch the inside wall of your bubbles, and then find a radio station and play it."

All the students moved their White windows inside their bubbles, widening it so that it touched the inner surfaces. After the students reached out to their favorite music station, each bubble began broadcasting different genres of music, from pop to folk, rock to jazz. Scar reached out to Earth and started to play a Rush song. One off the students accessed a Nimian dubstep channel, blasting it as loud as she could, making all the students dance and cheer like maniacs.

"The next energy field that we are going to access is the electric filed," Mr. Hulneb said, bringing the dancing to a stop. "Make your windows smaller first so that we don't fry everything. Alright? So it should be easy to find an electricity source and to vibrate that into the White." Each student reached out to find a local electricity source, then played that vibration in the White. Arcs began to shoot out inside the bubbles, all spiraling out in the same pattern.

"Notice that spiral that the electricity spits out in," Mr. Hulneb instructed. "Some of you may already know, but that pattern is the same as Aten Ka. That's because Aten Ka is connected to everything in the omniverse, in the White and the waters of reality. That's is the main reason it's theorized that Aten Ka is the source of all reality.

"We will learn how to access the other basic fields of energy on another day, but right now, since we have a Seventh Density student here, I want Sonlig to show us the more exotic quantum fields. In particular, Sonlig is able to access the many fields of quarks to create matter right out of the waters. Now to access these fields by themselves is a very dangerous process, because they're capable of tremendous destructive force. I hope that your field is strong, Sonlig."

"It is now," Scar said as he harden the wall of his bubble.

"So if you remember form our previous classes, quarks are always fluctuating, because the energy from a muon emits a gluon, which hits another muon, which changes that muon and makes it emit another gluon, and on and on. Each state of a quark is assigned a color, to make it easier to identify them. Sonlig, first shrink the size of your window to make it very small, and then I want you to access a blue quark."

Scar reached out into reality until he found an anomaly that produce the desired effect he wanted and vibrated it into the light. A huge flame of blinding light blasted out from his inside of his window, giving all the students a shock as they covered their eyes from the energy emission.

"I want the class to notice that when I ask Sonlig to change what particle to access, the brightness and stream of energy will change also. Sonlig, may you please access a lepton." When Scar did, the brightness of the plume soften but it became more solid, almost like a solid thin blade of white light.

"The reason that the energy expression has changed is because the amount of energy that is produce and the frequency of that energy is based upon the quantum field, even though Sonlig is vibrating the field the same way. Now we're going to try something different. Sonlig, try to access anti-red."

"Huh," Scar mumbled, trying to figure out how to access the field. He first tried to dig his light as deep as he could into the environment around him, but couldn't find what he wanted. He then sent his mind out into the Space Between, but didn't know where to look. Every universe he observed was made of the same matter.

"I don't know how to do that," Scar admitted, rubbing his head in frustration.

"That's right," Mr. Hulneb sighed. "Your past life was on Earth. Earth thinks more particle than wavelength. You probably just searched out trying to find something in the waters of reality that could help you but didn't."

"Yeah," Scar said right before the class bell rang.

"Everybody put your desks back!" Mr. Hulneb yelled out to the class before the students headed for the door. "Tomorrow we're going to delve into alpha and beta particles, so make sure your read up on them first."

"Mr. Hulneb, could you teach me how to access antimatter?" Scar asked once the class left the room.

"Sure," Mr. Hulneb said. "So your first mistake was thinking that you can find what you need by searching in the universe. That is not always that case. The White contains every wavelength that can exist in a universe, even if that universe doesn't have all the particles for the White. If an universe did, that universe would explode into complete information and flow back into Aten Ka. Just remember that everything is wavelengths, not particles."

"Okay," Scar responded.

"What you should have done was search out in the White, have the White vibrate in your light, and once you found the vibration you wanted, place energy into that field. Try it now."

Scar closed his eyes, delving his light into the White, letting it's energy vibrate his core. He started out in the lower frequencies, like sound and radio, then moved up to electricity and inferred, then up to x-rays, ultra violet and gamma. His light went higher into more exotic wavelengths, like fields that in some universes would be considered sources of magic because they can only be access by the light and not machine. There were other fields that seemed attuned to certain powerful beings throughout the multiverse. Scar laughed when he found the energy fields connected to his parents.

Scar's whole body shudder when he felt the fields that were associated with antimatter. They all seemed to flow in reverse and upside down, a sensation that felt a bit creepy to him at first.

"You just found it, didn't you?" Mr. Hulneb asked.

"Yeah," Scar responded, then opened his eyes when he noticed that they were closed. He saw that the next class was entering the class room, with most of the students staring at him while he was searching.

"Crap, I got to go," Scar said as he grabbed his backpack, felling a bit ashamed by all the eyes on him.

"You can practice more in tomorrow's class," Mr. Hulneb suggested as Scar left for the door.

"Ok Mr. Hulneb!" Scar shouted over his shoulder as he left the room. His next class was on the other side of the campus in the engineering wing, and students weren't allow to shift or fly on school grounds. The next bell rang as Scar was half way there, pissing him off more that he was late for class. He knew it shouldn't be such a big deal, but after being taught by Aunt Chac'chel for almost seventy cycles made him realize how entrenched it was for him to always be on time and to always do the ethical thing.

Scar eventually made his way into the engineering wing and into his aerodynamic class, with the classroom laughing as he neared his seat.

"I'm glad you can join us," the teacher said as Scar sat down next to Popol.

"Sorry Mr. Metnal," Scar said.

"I have your model plane up here, but since your late you don't have to finish today. You can try tomorrow."

"It's almost done," Scar said, actively suppressing a small panic attack. "There should be enough time for me to finish before the end of class.

"You don't have to worry about it, Sonlig," Mr. Metnal said dismissively to Scar, and Scar felt the teacher giving an impression that he believes Scar's status made him not take anything seriously, which silently enraged Scar.

"Look, Mr. Metnal," Scar said as he reached out and manipulated the plane on the teachers desk. The propeller spun fast enough so it hovered over Metnal desk for a moment, and after moving the wings and tail of the craft, Scar flew the plane around the classroom a few times before having it hover and then softly landing on the teachers desk.

"The plane is almost done," Scar said in a serious tone. "I just need to attach the motor and I'm finish. May I please do that?"

"Okay Sonlig," Mr. Metnal trepidly agreed before Scar walked up to his desk and retrieve his plane before sitting back down at his seat.

"You alright mate," Popol asked as he watch Scar begin to assemble the parts of his aircraft together.

"Yeah man, I'm chill," Scar said as he drew in and out a deep breath.

"How come your late?"

"I had Mr. Hulneb teach me how to access antimatter quantum fields."

"The White manipulation class sounds fun," Popol laughed. "I hear stories about how every once in a while that class spontaneously combust."

"Shit, it may have almost did today," Scar laughed with Popol, feeling a bit better.

"You have to work today after school?"

"Right after school ends," Scar said as he continue to work on his plane. "The firm wants me to escort some really rare minerals owned by a planetary nation state's subsidiary into their facility in New Scarborough. My boss is all hype about how my presence may bring in some new business for the job."

"Sounds important," Popol said as he work on the wing of his plane.

"I have tomorrow off, if that's what you're wondering. I get out of practice at four, so you can come over then. Oki won't be there if you don't mind hanging with just me."

"I don't mind," Popol said while blocking his mind.

"Yeah you do," Scar laughed. "Wow, do you hate my presence that much."

"No," Popol mumbled. "I don't mind coming over."

"Alright man," Scar said before they began concentrating on their projects.

2

Scar stood at the entrance of an industrial plant, staring out of the glass double door entrance with four other fifth density security guards. They were all dressed in squared away khaki uniforms and topped off with black berets, to give them that extra professional aesthetic. The berets were a bit too much for Scar, and also a nuisance. He had just gotten used to having his hair grown out, and then had to shave his head for this contract. When he was told about the uniform dress for that day, he wasn't sure rather he was relived or pissed.

The firm had a few more guards assigned to the large building that were on patrol that night, but those employees were dress in regular black and white office clothing. Ever since Scar began working with the company, the area managers always had him come to every new business pitch meeting or contract renegotiating to give their office an elite status of having a seventh density individual in their employ. Scar was first worried that he would be utilized as a combat contractor, but he ended up being more of a model.

"Hey Scar," one of the officers called out to him. "Did your parents ever talk to you about the planet that owns this building?"

"No, but I overheard some stuff," Scar said as he walk over to the four. "Paneta just joined the Federation about five cycles back, when one of their exploration ships found planet Lahmu."

"Are they a fourth density civilization? The ones that work here are."

"No, they're still Third Density. My family raises the densities of the workers here on request of their government."

"I never heard of a nation with the government running everything," the guard said.

"That's because most planets that join the Federation are led by divine rulers that act more like gods," Scar said. "Or call themselves gods. We had certain nations like Paneta on Earth where I spent my past life. The type of government was called a communism."

"Did you live in a government like that?"

"Me? No, a federalist republic," Scar answered.

"Kind of like the Federation," the guard guessed.

"Almost. Most of the governments of Earth were democratic also."

"So why is Earth having a hard time joining the Federation?

"It's the economy. It's not resource base, but currency."

"Oh," the guard whispered.

"Yeah man," Scar laughed. "I've noticed that too. It's harder for nations that have currency based economies to join the Federation. It's like it's impossible for them to understand that you don't need money to ensure the quality of life of your citizens. You just need to be good moral beings."

"The Federation schools teaches that civilizations that uses currency do it to convince their population that the ones with the most currency are gods," the guard noted.

"Yeah," Scar agreed. "That's how it is on Earth. Paneta was already a communist state based on resource trade, and had figured out interstellar travel when they discovered us. It was no problem for them to join. I think the only hiccup they had was when citizens of the world wanted to gather resources for their own. Like this company."

"Nothing wrong with being rich," the guard said.

"Am I supposed to say no to that?" Scar laughed as they watched their manager appear out of a nearby room and lead the other security guards towards the glass doors.

"Scar, Ahau, come on, the caravan is here," the manager said before he went outside. Scar and Ahau followed the rest of the group as they walked out to the dark road lit by floating light disks. Scar looked behind them at the plant, a fifty story tall office building of black walls and glass. The building stood above a large hill that looked out at Arrow Head Sea, where the road by the building ran down to a highway which a caravan of trucks and black bulky vans turned off from.

It only took the vehicles less than a minute to pass through the security gate at the entrance to the plant and up the hill where the manager walked up to the first large van. A large muscular red man with ridges that ran parallel in his black hair step out of the vehicle in a fancy gray and white pinstripe business suit, shaking the managers hands.

"Hello, Mr. Teuila," their manager said. "My men here are going to escort you to the bay doors at the back of the building. Let me introduce you to Lord Scar, who works for us."

"How are you, your Highness?" Mr. Teuila asked as he gripped Scar's hands.

"I'm good sir, thanks."

"Lets be on our way sir," the manager said before all of the men climbed in the van and traveled to the back of the building where workers in white overalls waited to open industrial size bay doors. The trucks backed into the bays where remote cargo lifters hovered into the truck containers and picked up pallets with blue colored barrels on them. Scar and his guards followed the lifters as they floated over to large elevators that swiftly took them to one of the top storage floors, where more workers guided the lifters to their designated locations.

"This floor will always be patrolled by multiple guards at all times," the manger said to Mr. Teuila as the group watch the lifters hover away. "And at least one planetary patrolmen will be on site on all shifts. As you can see, we have some of the finest security personnel that anyone can find in this universe."

"Excellent," Mr. Teuila commended. "Thanks for guiding me up here. Do you mind showing me the rest of the plant."

"No problem, Mr. Teuila," the manager responded. "Scar, Ahau, standby here until the other caravan arrives from the port."

"No problem, captain," Scar said as the group walked back to the elevators.

"Do you remember much from your previous life?" Ahau asked when they were alone.

"Everything," Scar answered as he looked out of the floor's window.

"Did you like your time on Earth."

"No. Don't forget that I went through the Ascension process there."

"Oh yeah, I forgot," Ahau sighed. "So it must have been rough."

"I was miserable, but I don't regret it," Scar replied. "I have so much now. Well, I've always had what I have, but I appreciate it so much more. No, that's not right. I guess that I don't want the status I have, but I understand how to use it. I think that's what I trying to say."

"I think I understand," Ahau said. "Do you think that Earth will ever join the Federation?"

"I don't know man. It's hard to convince people who has only lived one way of life that there are in fact better ways to live than the one you know. And for everyone on the world."

"I would have thought that after Earth's delegates came to visit Nima, they would have been convince then," Ahau said.

"It's never going to be that easy. There's so many culture barriers to keep the people on Earth thinking the way they do, it's insane. Here's a perfect example. The whole currency versus resource thing. Earth has this misnomer that a person who works hard deserve all the success that they receive in life. Philosophically, that is true, but the application of it is sometimes faulty, and no matter how many times an enlighten mind try to convince others that way of thinking is faulty, you'll get religion or communist thrown in your face.

"We know that the Federation has a better application of objectivism, or I think it does. A person in the Federation can get a ten year mining or farming permit, or twenty year ones if they want to receive light assistance from the Federation. Or they can strike out on their own if they choose, relying on their own light like my friend Popol wants to do. That person can go out in the universe, mine ores in an isolated asteroid field or raise livestock and crops on a farm world and become richer than anyone on Earth can do on their own. An individual.

"On Earth, yes, a person can achieve some success on their own, but if they want more, they have to get others to work for them. But many on Earth confuse the work of others as their own work, and the profit that the workers achieve as theirs to claim."

"That always did seem strange whenever I had to work on a third density planet," Ahau noted. "I would always be like, 'Why do you give your workers so little if they're doing so much work, shouldn't it be the other way'. And the person would be like, 'I'm the boss.'"

"Right," Scar agreed. "Granted, the technology on most third density worlds make it hard for individuals to gain as much resources that the Federation can offer. So over coming that obstacle is always going to be a hurdle for any rising civilization. But the one glaring problem with objectivism is the notion that the amount of resources or currency that one accumulates is directly tied to happiness."

"But their is no currency in the light," Ahau said with a confused look.

"Exactly," Scar said. "One can only find happiness in their own Aten Ka. But on Earth, currency is god. We create religions to support that notion. Empty, we even put 'In God we trust' on the currency of the nation I lived in."

"What in the Empty," Ahau muttered.

"Right, creepy isn't it."

"Scar, can you head to the front," their manager broadcast in Scar's light. "I think that the next caravan is coming our way."

"Roger that, captain," Scar said. "I'll be right back man."

"I'll be here," Ahau said as Scar summoned an elevator and traveled to the bottom floor. He went out to the street by the double glass doors and waited for a quarter section, wondering if the caravan was ever going to arrive.

"Captain, are you sure that the caravan is coming this way?" Scar asked.

"I think I made a mistake," the manager suggested. "Head up to the storage floor and stand by, please."

"Oscar Mike," Scar said as he went back inside and up to the storage floors.

"Have fun?" Ahau asked when Scar arrived.

"Tons," Scar grumbled. "What were we talking about?"

"I think we were talking about happiness," Ahau said.

"Okay," Scar said. "So, hmmm… yeah. Look, I'm not saying that the pursuit of gaining wealth can't make an individual happy. If that's what makes you happy, cool. But let's not pretend that happiness is tied to wealth. Wealth may be associated with happiness sometimes, but happiness is independent from wealth, and always will be. There are hunter gatherers on the world my fiancé lives on that have everything that a person can want while still living in balance with their neighbors and the environment. Isn't that wealthy?"

"Empty, a person can go into the Services, raise their light to the fifth or sixth density," Ahau said. "That person can travel the universe and have no worry at all. I'm still thinking about doing that."

"But we can't forget that we are higher density individuals," Scar pointed out. "Look, I'm not self-righteous. We have it made living in the Federation. Yet currency is a great social tool for large amounts of beings to interact with one another. But there are other ways of doing it. And there is only one way that a person can find real happiness."

"Hey Scar," the manager called out again. "I think the caravan is heading our way now. Head out front, sir."

"I'm moving," Scar said with a twirl of his eyes. "I'll be back."

"Don't get lost," Ahau joked as Scar left and made his way back to the street. This time he waited silently for half a section for vehicles to show up, but none came.

"Captain, are you sure that the vehicles are coming?" Scar asked.

"Scar, just to inform you, I'm watching the highway for the vehicles to arrive. I got a call from the port that they are on their way but there seems to be a hold up. Just stand by at the storage rooms for now. Thank you."

"Jesus Christ," Scar moaned before he returned back with Ahau.

"When are these vehicles going to show up?" Ahau asked as he watched Scar's annoyed face.

"I don't know," Scar mumbled. "Alright, here's my point I was trying to make. The people on Earth seem to think that capitalism and socialism are different, that Marxism and objectivism oppose one another."

"And those are?" Ahau asked.

"I'm sorry," Scar apologized. "Their just different ends of theories based on the use of currency. But the thing is, there both the same, not in the ends part but in the use of the means. There both systems that believe that happiness can be found with the proper use of fiat currency. We know that wealth doesn't means happiness, right?"

"Correct," Ahau agreed.

"And that happiness can only be found in Aten Ka. You can't find happiness in the material. The material form can be discriminated, disenfranchised, starved, sicken, torture, etcetera. And if currency can be used as a tool to do these things, how can currency also be a tool for happiness, and who's to say that the use of currency doesn't do both at the same time.

"We in the Federation know that the only place to find happiness is in our own lights. To do that is with our actions, specifically to always act with love. So it doesn't matter what form of currency theory you use. The most important thing do is to act with love to other sentient lights first."

"Scar, the vehicles are coming now," the manager broadcast. "Meet me out front."

"Are you sure?" Scar asked.

"I think so, I saw a group of trucks heading down the highway."

"You know what," Scar groaned, his last bit of patience wearing thin. Compulsively, Scar shifted out of the window and fell almost fifty stories, coming to a still just before he placed his feet gently on the concrete sidewalk.

"What was that all about?" the manager asked nervously as Scar walked up to him.

"Do you know if the caravan is coming?" Scar asked again.

"They should be coming soon," the captain said.

"You know what man, I don't know if you know this or not, but I'm not an object, I am a light," Scar stated to his manger in an even tone. "I get what you are doing. It makes sense to have a high density light for your clients to see. But I'm starting to get a little pissed having to go back up and down this building every five seconds."

"I'm sorry, Scar," the captain said. "If you want I can wait right here…"

"No, I'll wait here," Scar suggested as he looked downhill towards the highway. "I'll let you know if the vehicles are coming. Just hang out with Mr. Teuila."

"Thanks Scar," the manager said before he left Scar outside, alone in his memories.

CHAPTER 9

74 AA

1

"You know, I've never been to a party before," Scar said as he looked at the other children in the spacious living room, all dressed in designer clothing.

"You never went to any parties while you were in high school?" Oki asked as he took a sip of juice from his plastic cup.

"I mean, I just hang out with my friends and played D&D, if my mom let me."

"What, you were a nerd?" Popol asked moving to Oki's side to get out of the way of some classmates that were running through the room.

"Actually, yes I was," Scar side with a strong smile. "And I'm fucking proud of it."

"You didn't know any of the popular kids in school?" Popol asked.

"You cannot believe how lame that question sounded," Scar said. "These guys are kids. We actually have lights of adults."

"Or we are children that just happened to do adult things," Oki said.

"I can't argue that," Scar agreed.

"Why did you bring us along anyway?" Popol asked Oki.

"Yeah, the girl who lives here is in one of my classes," Oki said as he walked towards the living room couch once he saw the kids sitting there move. "She knew that I hang out with you guys, so she asked me if I wanted to come, and wanted me to bring you guys."

"So you're using us to get in good with the chick," Scar assessed as they sat down. "Nice, I like your strategy."

"My only problem is that I think she wanted to talk to you," Oki said.

"Why doesn't she come over and talk," Scar grumbled.

"Because you two are always together," Oki said. "People think that you're a couple."

"What, Popol is my waifu," Scar chuckled.

"Mate, that's not funny," Popol moaned as he blocked his light, which made Scar laugh even harder.

"That's got to be so weird," Scar heard a boy say behind him. "How do you live on Earth as a black guy and be reincarnated as a white dude."

"Who does he hang out with?" a blue and silver Doggan asked as he rubbed water on his gills. "Does he hang out with Pleiadeans, Andeans, reincarnated Andeans who were black?"

"So you never wanted to go to parties when you were a kid?" Popol asked Scar.

"No, just the concept of parties just seemed weird," Scar said. "Okay, so to be asked to go to a party, someone has to figure out what type of person you are."

"You can be a friend of the person," Oki said as he played with one of his furry ears.

"Other than the chick who lives here, do you know anyone else?" Scar asked.

"Shit, I don't even know the girl all that well," Oki admitted.

"There's nothing wrong with that," Scar said. "But most people ask random folks to their parties because they think they're nice, or God forbid, cool. And how is that figured out? Do you wear the right clothes, listen to the right music, does your parents make enough money?"

"We all wear school uniforms at Coba, man" Oki said.

"Almost everyone here are the sixth density kids at Coba," Scar pointed out, with Popol and Oki looking around the see if it was true. "If it's just a bunch of people wanting to hang out to have fun, I have no problems with parties. But this isn't it. I just feel weird here."

"Maybe you're carrying something back from Earth," Popol said.

"You may be right," Scar said as he leaned back on the couch. "But still, I ask you, in principle, what's the difference between hanging out with you guys at my place or being here?"

"Hanging with your friends," Popol answered.

"You could just go talk to someone," Oki suggested. "You know, try to be a friend. Don't wait for other people to do the work for you."

"You're right," Scar said. "But everyone here is a kid. An over one hundred year old kid, but a kid none the less. Which also means they're kids stuck in their ways. I can't relate to kids. Besides, everyone here are so focused on their lights."

"Yeah," Popol agreed. "It's like since they're sixth densities they think I'm supposed to automatically like them or think that their special. Bitch, you haven't done anything but be born."

"You guys are just haters," Oki said. "Just chill out and have fun."

"Easy for you to say, you're the cool one," Scar said.

"Wait, how am I'm the cool one?" Oki asked.

"You're the cool one of the trio," Scar explained. "Popol's the shy awkward guy, and I'm the tall brooding loner guy."

"Your assessment of us is freakishly accurate," Popol laughed.

"I do admit though, I do hate," Scar said. "I shouldn't, but I do. I just hate how everyone just looks at densities, and not the light itself. Maybe it's because we did grow up on Earth. You know people on Earth care about stuff that doesn't mean jack shit. And no, I'm not being the asshole 'nice guy'. It's the same thing here, everyone here is focused on the wrong thing. Who cares how many loops you have. We're all the same."

"No, we're not," Oki said. "We're not the same, and there's nothing wrong with that. There's nothing wrong with you being a seventh density. It's your actions that define you, that tells us if your light is good or bad."

"Where have I heard that before?" Scar chuckled.

"That's got to be the lamest thing to happen to you," one of the boys behind him spoke up again. "To have to be in the body of a white dude."

"I bet he has no problems picking up chicks though," the Doggan said. "Every girl in here is looking at him."

"Better chance than if he was black," the first on laughed.

"Let's go somewhere else," Scar said through clinched teeth as he stood up from the couch.

"Where to?" Oki asked as he stood.

"Let's go on top of the roof," Scar proposed as he began to head towards the stairs. "I want to see the sunset over the sea."

"Shouldn't we ask if we should go up there?" Popol asked as he followed Scar and Oki up there stairs.

"Dude, I don't care right now," Scar said as he went over to Popol and pulled his head under his arm. "Just have some fun, man."

"Get off me," Popol said while he blocked his mind, punching Scar in his chest, with Scar running up the stairs away from his onslaught.

"Wait, how do we get up there?" Oki asked as he looked at the upper floor hallway.

"Shit, come here guys," Scar said as he grabbed both Oki and Popol in his arms before shifting onto the roof. Scar felt Popol heart jump a bit when he did that, and ruffled his hair when he put them down on the roof.

"Dude, don't freak out man," Scar said as he laid down beside Popol.

"Warn somebody before you do that," Popol said as he and Oki sat down and looked out at the houses surrounded by autumn trees, their red to gold leaves falling to the ground. To the south they could see the lights of New Scarborough shining like diamonds in a metropolis. To the west was the sea, with the light of the red sun reflecting off of its surface as it slipped under the horizon. All the while ships traveled in and out of the sea, either by water or air.

"I almost forget how beautiful this place can be sometimes," Oki said quietly.

"Doesn't it make you feel kind of funny?" Scar asked. "Like your heart skips for a moment, and your skin tingles from the air blowing over it. Your body is just in ecstasy."

"That's call being happy," Popol informed Scar.

"Is that what that is?" Scar asked in genuine shock. "Wow, that actually feels good."

"What, you never been happy before?" Oki said.

"Maybe. On Earth, not really. When I'm with my family here, yes. I thought it was just being young again."

"You must have had a hard time on Earth," Popol said.

"You have no idea," Scar said. "No, that's wrong. I didn't have it bad. We all know that there were people who really suffered on Earth. Suffered horribly. I know, I've seen it."

"Don't get depress now, man" Oki said. "This is a new life. A better one, one that you earned. Look at you man, you're a seventh density. Your life must be set after you graduate."

"My parents are still going to school me after I graduate," Scar said. "They want me to go to University and the military, so I can be eligible for congressional service. Once I do all that, they have a position set up for me working for them."

"Brutal," Popol mumbled.

"What are you going to do after school?" Scar asked Oki.

"I don't know," Oki said. "I was thinking moving off world and working as a navigator. But I want to see the universe. Travel to some exotic galaxy and date some hot chick on a world I never heard of."

"That sounds like too much fun," Scar said.

"I can't wait till I graduate," Popol said. "I already got plans set up for my family. We're going to mine like crazy in a dark debris field in free space that we found recently. My parents already got the permits to mine there, but when I'm done, we can cancel it. Then I'm going to set up a storage company on my world, then a trade firm. I have plans, mates."

"That is awesome," Scar said. "To bad we can't hang out as much if you're going to be working so much."

"More like you annoying me," Popol said.

"That's why I love hanging out with guys," Scar laughed. "You treat me like the dumbass I really am. It's why I love you so much Popol. You don't take any shit from me."

"Do you have to say love," Popol moaned, blocking his light again.

"Ah, feel weird," Scar teased Popol, flicking Popol's ear. "Don't feel comfortable being in a bromance."

"Bromance," Oki laughed out. "God, I haven't heard that said in a century."

"Mate, you need to stop that," Popol said as Scar kept plucking at his ear.

"What are you going to do?" Scar baited, waiting for Popol to pop him one, then went silent when Popol bent over and kissed him on his lips. Scar laid for a moment, thinking first that it was Popol playing a joke on him, but became more confused when the kiss lingered. He laid there dumbfounded a bit longer before Sneeze's presence flared up in his light, her anger jolting Scar to move Popol off of him.

"Holy shit," Oki laughed.

"Dude, was that a joke?" Scar asked, but when Popol kept his eyes locked on Scar, his confusion turned to comedic joy.

"Dude, are you gay?" Scar asked, and when Popol pulled back and put his hands over his face, Scar and Oki howled in laughter.

"Why didn't you say you were gay?!" Oki asked Popol.

"Oh my god," Popol moaned in his hands.

"Jesus, I'm sorry dude!" Scar laughed.

"Don't say you're sorry," Popol snapped as he looked down at his lap.

"Man, you should have said something. I would have stopped bugging you."

"That's why I didn't say anything," Popol said.

"You should have told me you were gay," Scar offered. "I wouldn't have acted the way I did. Is that why you're always blocking your mind."

"I was blocking my mind because you were always blocking your mind. I thought you liked me."

"I do," Scar said. "I love both of you guys. A guy can have a love for another man. It doesn't mean I want to bang you both. Especially, you Oki. There'd be hair all over the place."

"Fuck you, you racist bastard!" Oki shouted as he punched Scar in the stomach.

"But you always block, Sonlig," Popol said as he looked at Scar.

"I have to," Scar retorted. "Besides, your still blocking now. If you stop blocking, I'll stop blocking."

"Yeah?" Popol asked.

"Dude, Popol, I swear, don't bug me man. I hate when people hide something from me, especially when they're mad at me." Popol looked at Scar a bit more, then let her guard down, revealing her feminine light.

"Dude, you look like your character on Xbal's World," Oki blurted.

"God dammit woman, you should have told me," Scar said. "Why didn't you try to go after any other guy that you know is gay?"

"Because you were always there."

"Wait, have I been the one cock blocking you this whole time?" Scar laughed. "Sweetheart, I'm sorry."

"Don't say sweetheart," Popol said.

"My bad, I won't do it again."

"No, it's just that when you say it, I know you mean it. You're just like my brothers."

"Well, yeah," Scar laughed. "You guys are like my brothers. Sister now, I mean."

"You haven't live up to your part of the bargain, Sonlig," Oki pointed out. "Everyone's letting out their deepest secrets, you got to now." Scar looked out to the ground below them, making sure no one was able to see what they were doing.

"You got to promise not to tell anyone," Scar demanded.

"What the Empty could you be possible hiding?" Popol said, her heart feeling a bit better.

"I mean it guys, I'll make you fucking pinky swear."

"Alright dude," Oki agreed. "Cross my heart, hope to die, stick a needle in my eye."

"Popol?" Scar beamed at her.

"I promise," Popol said, a bit worried. Feeling satisfied Scar released his light a bit, only letting enough out so that ten loops buzzed about his body. Popol and Oki watched stunned at them, struggling at what to say.

"I kissed the next Speaker of House Xkit," Popol whispered.

"Your Highness," Oki stuttered.

"Bro, say that again and I'll kick you in the knee," Scar threaten.

"I kissed the next Speaker of the House of Xkit," Popol repeated.

"Really, that's all you can think about?" Scar asked.

"Wait, aren't you engaged?" Popol asked.

"Oh, yeah," Scar said as Sneeze's light pushed forward, Making Oki and Popol jump back.

"I'm sorry, Princess Sneeze, I didn't know," Popol apologized. "Fuck, Sonlig, you should have said something."

"You're sorry," Scar smiled. "I'm going to hear it all night."

"Holy fuck," Oki said. "Man…Sonlig, I can't look at you the same way."

"And that's why I hate going to parties like these," Scar said. "Everyone looks at me like that. You were the only two who didn't."

"Dude, what do we do now?" Popol asked looking up at the sky. "This evening has been bat shit crazy."

"I'm just going to watch the sun set out in the sea," Scar said while decreasing his light, looking out at the horizon. "There's one thing we can say though, Popol. At least we got to make out with someone before Oki did."

"Man, that fucking doesn't count," Oki said, lashing out at Scar with punches to his shoulder as the sun disappeared into the sea and the stars began to multiply in the sky.

2

Scar stood in a line of students in the indoor gymnasium, each with a spear in their hand, practicing repetitive strikes over and over until Master Chuy commanded them to change attacks. Across from them were more students, each with arched Nimian curved swords, all performing similar strikes. All were dressed in gray slim fitted uniforms with the school's symbol of a crescent moon over their hearts.

As Master Chuy gave out commands, each student would count out their movements, attacks or blocks, all the way up to one hundred, then would move on to their next movement, for over a section. When the team lost their tournament last week, Master Chuy remained silent all the way back from the competition, which always meant that they were going to eat shit the next practice.

"Partner up!" Master Chuy shouted once the team finished their movements. "Spear to spear, sword to sword! Get it done so we go cross weapons!"

"SIR, YES SIR!" the team responded as the students spilt up into pairs facing each other for close quarters combat drills. First the partners stood a few feet from each other, one performing simple single strikes at the fighter across from them, who would block and counter attack in suit. Since their blades were made of steel, there was no need to hold back, and Master Chuy was making sure that no one was.

After the groups moved up to more complicated attacks and blocks for half a section, the group spread apart across the gymnasium so they could practice lunge attacks. Scar looked across from him at the other students, most with smiles on their faces, some more serious. The fighter with the most strict face was Chaac, staring down his opponent with a fierce glare.

"Are you paying attention?!" his partner yelled at him before she was about to strike.

"My bad," Scar laughed as he prepared himself, which earned him a condescending glance from Chaac. Scar began his lunges and blocks like the other students, an organized sequences of attacks like before for another half a section. Once they were done with all their like weapons drills, the students moved on to close quarters cross weapons. Each student paired up with a student on the same skill level, which left Scar pairing up with Chaac.

"Strengthen your stance" Chaac ordered Scar as he prepared to strike.

"I got you, man," Scar said with a smile.

"If you had done that the last tournament, you would have won more points," Chaac scolded Scar.

"I still won that match," Scar said with a confused expression, which infuriated Chaac, causing him the attack without warning, which Scar blocked and countered as taught. Humbled for just a bit, Chaac stayed quiet untiled they finished their attacks and block techniques and the teams moved to lunge attacks.

"Strengthen your stance, Sonlig," Chaac demanded again as he ready for his strike.

"All right," Scar said. "I'll do it. But you have to do something for me. Block your mind."

"Excuse me?" Chaac asked.

"Block your mind, man. You telegraph your attacks too much. You would have probably gotten a perfect score in you last fight if you had done that."

"I'm still faster that any fighter out there," Chaac retorted. "What does it matter?"

"Look, man, I'll show you," Scar offered as he prepared to attack. "Look, I strengthen my stance for you, so there is no excuse for me being too slow. So I'm going to block my mind, okay. Are you ready?"

"Yes," Chaac said as he prepared himself, placing his crescent curved sword in front of him.

"Are you sure?" Scar double checked.

"Yes, I'm sure I'm…" was all Chaac was able to say before Scar lunged at him, the floor splintering away from the force of his launch. Chaac barely had enough time to understand what was going on before Scar landed next to him, lightly tapping Chaac cheek with tip of his spear blade.

"See man," Scar said as he stood his spear up, resting on its shaft. "You got to block your mind."

"That's not fair," Chaac scoffed. "You caught me off guard when you keep asking me things."

"Yes, that's what's you're supposed to do," Scar laughed. "Catch people off guard."

"Sonlig, are you going to fix that floor!?" Master Chuy yelled at Scar as he appeared next him. Scar looked down at his instructor, an elder Andean man with white scruffy hair the same pale white as his glowing white skin. He was mostly skin and bones in his uniform, except for his pot belly. After Scar looked at him he glanced behind himself, only now noticing the damage he caused.

"Oh shit, sorry Master Chuy," Scar said before he reversed the damage to the floor while the other students laughed at him.

"If you showed that same enthusiasm in your last fight, you would have gotten a perfect score yourself," Master Chuy informed Scar.

"Yes, Master Chuy," Scar said.

"Sonlig's right, Chaac," Master Chuy told Scar's partner. "You broadcast your attacks too much with your light. Blocking your intentions is the first rule of higher density combat."

"Yes Master Chuy," Chaac answered with a sigh.

"It still wouldn't have helped you," Scar chuckled as he took an exaggerated swing at Chaac with his spear, which Chaac easily blocked. "I still would parry any swing you toss at me."

"Is that so, Sonlig," Chaac said in an almost disgusted voice. "You actually think you can beat me? Some off-world country bumpkin who thinks that since you gone through the Ascension process that you can beat someone from a family of seventh densities."

"You assumed too much about me," Scar said. "And yeah man, I think I can, straight up."

"Since we finished our drills, you two can be the first to spar then," Master Chuy said before turning to the class. "Alright, you bunch of tadpoles, everyone over the sea. Last one there has to do one hundred laps around the planet!" With that threat, the team all but disappeared as they shifted to their usual meeting place over the sea just west of New Scarborough, floating in the late afternoon autumn air.

"Chaac, Sonlig, you're up," Chaac instructed the two. "And tournament rules here. First to ten points in one minute."

"Alright coach," Scar said as he flew out over the water to his starting point.

"I'm going all out," Chaac said as he flew to his point, his confidence filling his light as he hovered in a ridged stance. "Just to warn you."

"Bring it then," Scar said nonchalant, floating with his spear leaning on his shoulder. Chaac eyes bored into Scar's light in anger as he watched Scar seemingly belittle his challenge.

"Start!" Master Chuy shouted, and Chaac dashed through the air at Scar, aiming at his head. Scar quickly moved his staff into position to block and counter Chaac, but Chaac anticipated his move, ready to strike at a different angle with his speed. He was caught off guard when Scar dropped a bit out of the sky, Chaac's sword swiping just above his hair and Scar seamlessly striking out at Chaac's exposed belly.

"Point, Sonlig!" Master Chuy shouted as Chaac stared at Scar, rubbing his belly from the spear poke.

"You hit me," Chaac said in shock.

"Yes I did," Scar agreed.

"Did anyone see that?" one of the students asked.

"No," the person next to him said.

"Ready up," Master Chuy ordered, and the two combatants went back to their positions. Chaac anger flared up inside of his light, using it as fuel for his next attack.

"Start!" Master Chuy shouted, and once again Chaac lunged forward, trusting in his speed. This time Scar simply blocked all of his attacks, then at one point struck out at Chaac, coming a bit short of his target. Chaac smiled as he tried to take advantage of an open attack, but once again was caught off guard when Scar swung his spear around again to hit Chaac as he came in for a strike.

"Point, Sonlig!" Master Chuy said.

"Source, dammit!" Chaac shouted in frustration.

"You got to block your mind, man," Scar offered. "And don't attack all the time. You leave yourself open when you do."

"Ready up!" Master Chuy instructed. Chaac's anger smoldered as he returned to his spot, but this time he decide to change his tactic.

"Start!" Master Chuy shouted, and Chaac stayed where he was, blocking his mind and waiting for Scar to attack.

"He can learn," Scar whispered as he flashed forward, striking in earnest at Chaac, who was shocked at how fast Scar's attacks were. Chaac blocked all of Scar's attacks that came his way, waiting for him to make a mistake for an opportunity. All of a sudden Scar flew down away form Chaac, who gave chased after him, confused at what Scar was doing. He stopped short above the sea, not wanting to get wet as Scar plunged in, a large spray of water erupting after his entrance.

"What are you doing, Sonlig?!" Chaac asked before he realized that Scar had appeared in the middle of the mist, striking out and hitting him in the chest.

"Point, Sonlig!" Master Chuy announced again, with Chaac screaming out at the sky from the third point Scar got in a row.

"Ready up!" Master Chuy instructed, and the two returned once again to their spot, Chaac looking across at Scar who floated soaking wet before him.

"Start!" Master Chuy announced, and once again Chaac stayed where he was, blocking his mind and waiting for Scar to attack. Scar obliged, dashing forward and swiping at Chaac with precision attacks, trying to keep the pressure on Chaac. Scar suddenly stopped his assault, swiping at the air and sending a gust at wind at Chaac, who hovered with discipline, guarding himself for Scar's next attack. He was not expecting Scar to send another wave at him, this time of spinning reality.

When the wave of reality hit Chaac, his heart skipped a beat as it seemed that Scar was rushing at him faster than normal. He calmed when he got in the middle of the wave, with time slowing down and Scar flying at him, his side exposed as he prepared to strike out with his spear. Chaac's light grew in anticipation for Scar's strike, then a panic came in as he touched the other side of the reality wave and time speed up, Scar flying at him faster than he thought. Chaac slash out at Scar, but as he came out of the wave, time slowed down, leaving him open for Scar to hit Chaac on his head.

"Point, Sonlig!" Master Chuy said.

"Source dammit!" Chaac screamed. "Only a coward with no honor use tactics like this! No on would truly respect you on a battle field if you did this!" Scar eyes widen after Chaac's rant, and then his expression went calm and his light even tone as he flew back to his starting position. Chaac flew back to his, deciding this time to rely on his speed to defeat Scar.

"Ready, up!" Master Chuy said, and Chaac clinched his body and light up, ready to strike out as fast as he could.

"Start!" Master Chuy announced, and Chaac attacked as fast as be believed he possibly could, and struck down at Scar's chest, the sword's blade contorting as Scar stood there, allowing the weapon to hit him.

"Point, Chaac!" Master Chuy said, and before Chaac could think about celebrating, Scar reached and clamped down hard on Chaac's wrist. Stunned, Chaac tried to yank free from Scar's grasp, but could only look in confusion as Scar brought his spear up and struck down hard at Chaac like hitting a block of wood with an axe, flinging Chaac down and crashing into the seat water.

"What in the Empty are you doing, Sonlig!" Chaac yelled as he emerged from the water, then watched as Scar shifted in front of him, his light intensifying so much that a ring of darkness surrounded it, his lethal intent shining from it as he prepared for another attack.

"Sonlig!" Master shouted, and Scar stopped, shifting before the instructor with a bow, his spear at attention next to him.

"SIR, YES SIR!" Scar answered.

"That's one hundred laps for you, around the solar system."

"Yes sir," Scar said as he stood up straight.

"What the Empty is your problem?" Chaac asked as he shifted behind Scar right before he was to depart.

"Have you ever killed anyone?" Scar asked Chaac.

"Excuse me?" Chaac asked.

"Have you ever been in a battle? Fought in a war?"

"No."

"Bro, you don't have to listen to what I have to say, but hopefully in the future you'll listen to the words," Scar stated. "Never begin a battle you know you'll win. Only if you're willing to die for what you're fighting for." Scar then turned and flew up and out of the atmosphere to begin his laps.

CHAPTER 10

77 AA

1

"**T**en fucking cycles," Scar said as he looked out at the large number of his student body walking into the city's civic center, dressed in ceremonial black and gray gowns. "Ten cycles of torture over. God damn, I forgot how good graduating school was."

"Jesus man, it wasn't that bad," Popol said as she fidgeted with her yellow stole. "You complain about everything. I had fun. I'm going to miss going to Coba."

"I'm going to miss Coba," Scar mimicked Popol in a squeaky voice before Popol whacked him on the back of his head.

"It's that we're institutionalized," Oki said. "Going to the same school for cycles, meeting the same friends in class, acting like kids…"

"We are kids," Scar said.

"You know what I mean," Oki grunted at Scar. "Yeah, fine. We are kids. It's fun being a kid again. Empty, we're not even teenagers yet and the universe is at our finger tips."

"It's kind of scary," Popol said as she evened out Oki's orange stole. "You believed that the universe is open to you. Then you graduate and realize, shit, the universe is open up to you. What do you do?"

"Wait, you can't be scared," Scar laughed at Popol. "You're going into a business where you're literally going to find unknown reaches of space to mine."

"What, I'm scared," Popol snapped. "I have a plan. Just executing it is going to be scary."

"I kid," Scar said. "I get it. I felt the same way when I got out of boot camp when I was on Earth. You get used to waking up at four in the morning, exercise, eating, training; the comfort of a ridged schedule. Then you graduate and you're free in a sense. Freewill is a nice notion to talk about, but when you're put into a position to understand what it is, it's fucking terrifying."

"Dude, we should head in," Oki said as he began his way towards the civic center's entrance. "What are you guys going to do after graduation?"

"My parent's already got working on that mine field," Popol said. "I'm going straight home to help out. Hopefully by the end of a cycle, we'll have enough to build a cargo ship and we can get our business going."

"No rest for you?" Scar asked.

"No, can't hang out and do dumb things for a couple of decades. What are you going to do, Oki?"

"There is this far off galactic nation that just got accepted into House Shou in my home universe. I convinced my parents to let me go out and explore it. Maybe I'll get a job navigating or translating. Meet some chick, hang out until she's old and move on to the next one."

"Holy shit, that's just fucking wrong," Scar laughed.

"Thus the many perks of being nigh immortal," Oki said.

"You don't find that at all a bit creepy?" Popol asked.

"Nope. I don't have a prearrange marriage like you do, Sonlig. Sucks to be you, nerd."

"Ha," Scar snorted.

"What are you going to do, Sonlig?" Popol wondered as she peered into Scar's light, seeing if Sneeze was listening.

"My parents got more studies for me. They want me ready when I go to University on Saltal."

"No rest for you also?" Popol consoled Scar.

"I'm going to be Speaker of my House," Scar said as he looked around to see if anyone was listening. "Would you want the Speaker of a House just meandering into their position, not even ready to take on the job."

"God, no," Oki muttered. "We saw that on Earth. I had enough of that."

"It's rough," Scar admitted. "I wouldn't wish what I've been through, what I got to do on anyone else. But I wouldn't want it any other way. At least I can say that when I become Speaker, I earned it."

"What type of training?" Oki asked as they passed through the centers door and came into the entrance hallway that will lead them to the building's main auditorium.

"Well, for now my father wants me to be an advisor on some staff meetings, especially dealing with the universe Earth's in. He wants me to make final decisions on some diplomatic and domestic issues. Basically throwing me to the wolves."

"Brutal," Popol whispered.

"I got to get used to it," Scar said. "My aunt's been drilling it in my head that I can't get emotional at everything that goes on out in the multiverse. Not every issue that we have to deal with is going to end with a happy ending. And I have to make some dark choices too."

"Christ," Oki hissed.

"Yeah," Scar agreed.

"Yeah man, you're right," Oki said. "I don't want any idiot just accepting the Speakership of a House. And I don't want your job either."

"Thanks," Scar laughed sarcastically as they finally arrived into the auditorium, where the family and friends of the graduating class sat above them in the upper levels, and the students sat in seats in front of the stage where the faculty staff sat.

"I hope this doesn't take long," Scar said. "I want to hang out with Sneeze as long as I can this week before she has to go home."

"You sure you don't mind us tagging along?" Popol asked as they took their seats. "I figured you'd want to be alone with her."

"Which is why my parents want me to bring you guys along," Scar said. "Besides, I want to show you guys my family's islands."

"Islands," Oki stated. "This dude said islands."

"Bro, shut up," Scar said as he looked around, absently playing with his golden cord that laid on top of his purple stole. "It's my home. Don't knock me for it. What, Popol's probably going to own an island herself in a few decades. Maybe her own nation state."

"Don't curse me," Popol warned Scar before the principal approach a pulpit to welcome everyone to the graduation ceremony. Different teachers got up to speak, handing out rewards to students for their scholastic accomplishments. It was an awkward moment for Scar when he and Chaac got on the stage together to receive rewards for their Federation's amateur fencing singles championships, and also being inducted into the school's athletic hall of fame. It then came down to the speech of the valedictorian, who made her way to the pulpit amongst the roaring applause of the student body.

"Principal Ixtat, faculty of the school, student council. My family and friends, you know you! And all the students in the graduating class of '07.

Thank you for giving me the opportunity to speak before you as this year valedictorian. I want to first thank my parents for raising me, and for dealing with me at times. As some of you know, my old life was on a war torn third density world, and some of those habits and culture that is imbedded in you is hard to let go. So I'm very grateful for my parents for being patient with me, and for my brothers and sisters for not being patient at all.

"I thought about what I wanted to base my speech on. Will I speak about my family and how they nurtured me?. Will I talk about my friends, who help me understand the worlds that I discovered? Will I talk about this school, about how much fun I had learning and getting into trouble? The reason why is because it is always the unpopular decision of most valedictorians to give a speech based on one common theme. The more and more I thought about it, the more I realize that it's actually a good topic to use. So for everyone's disapproval..."

"Oh Source, no," Scar mutter as other students began to groan in anticipation.

"I'm going to base my speech on the road not taken," the valedictorian announced, laughing as she was greeted by the cries of denial and comic anguish from the graduating class.

"It's weird," she began. "Almost every culture that I've studied has a poem or story that's based on the idea of this concept, this theme of a road that an individual either wished they traveled on or were happy that they did. But why? What would cause an individual to look around and ponder on their life. To reflect on where they are or what they've done. To see the material around them and get either satisfaction or anxiety. Ponder on if they had done things differently, would they be somewhere else physically?

"Would they look at their home, and the condition of it, or maybe they don't have a place to call home. Maybe they would think about the people or family around them, if they love or despise them, or maybe this individual is alone. What about the person's job, if they have one? Are they happy doing it, or does it give the person grief? But really, that's what it is. Happiness. A person looks at all the external objects in their life, and after reflecting on them, wonder if that person is happy. And then that person would think that if I would have done things differently, would I have ended down a different path? Would I have ended up in a place where I would be happy?

"Except there is a fundamental flaw in the idea of going down a different path. There is only one true road. And that road is paved by the decisions that we make. Also, the goal is not a physical location or object at the end of a particular path, but the person you want to be once you reach your destination. A destination you never want to reach. Do you want to be a rich and famous actress, or do you want be recognized as one of the best actors that has ever performed the craft. One of the choices may not give you the other, but the most important thing is if you are happy. And if so, it shouldn't matter if you're rich or recognized. Although it would be nice to get paid for what you love.

"The most important thing to understand is that the destination is not to be found in the material, but in one's own light. If you can look inside yourself, like the hypothetical traveler I describe at the beginning of my speech, and after reflecting everything around you upon your light, if you found that you are happy, then you did it right.

"If not, the path you need to seek is not in the material but inside yourself. You need to make the right choices for yourself in order to find happiness in you. Because no matter how much you try to go somewhere different, interact with people known or unknown, try a new activity or retry old ones. If you're not seeking happiness in yourself first, you'll never find it in the material. Aten Ka. The real destination, the one and only true road leads to the Light."

2

"How long is your leave?" Scar asked Bernini as he sat in the back of their parents car, holding Sneeze's hand.

"A month, for now," Bernini said as he drove their mother's car dressed like a chic hipster from Earth. One of his hands was on the steering wheel, the other arm resting on the open window of the door. "My ship deploys at the end of the month."

"I can't believe your family owns these islands," Oki said as they drove through Suburbia and towards the Citadel in Metropolis.

"It's a home," Scar said.

"I just don't understand how a family with all the resources in a multiverse drives around in a simple sedan like this," Popol joked as she looked out her window from her front passenger seat at the rolling grass hills around them.

"If you don't like, you can walk," Bernini said as poked at Popol ears.

"Where are you going to deploy?" Sneeze asked as she leaned towards Bernini, still holding Scar's hand.

"My ship's going to deploy to another universe where a few new nation planets just joined House Shou," Bernini said. "We're supposed to help facilitate logistic services for them until they can get going on their own."

"They don't have navigators yet," Oki told the group. "That's what I was talking about earlier, that's where I want to go to work soon."

"Yeah, they'll need it," Bernini said as he drove the car onto the bridge that connected Suburbia with Metropolis. "I'm loving my tour there. It's so much fun interacting with a civilization that is just entering the fourth to fifth density. Everything is new and an adventure to them. They appreciate things I took for granted growing up. I thought everybody could travel through the White, but when I worked on an explorer ship last cycle, the sense of duty and courage that emanated from those travelers was amazing."

"That sounds really cool," Oki said, almost transfix by how Bernini describe his job. "But wait a dot. How can you serve if you're not one hundred and eighty cycles old."

"Parents permission," Bernini explained.

"You can go into the Service when your one hundred cycles old," Scar said. "It's just that you can only serve in Congress once your one hundred and eighty cycles old. That's why so many people wait until they go into the Service and then go to University around that age, so they can get it all done at one time. Besides the fact you can spend decades being a free teenager"

"I'm paying my way through University with the Navy," Bernini said as he turned on the radio to an Earth rap station.

"You're going to University first though," Sneeze said to Scar.

"Momma and Poppa are paying for my tuition," Scar said. "That way they'll have more say on what courses I'll take."

"You're not going to be able to pick any of your courses?" Popol asked. "That sounds a bit harsh."

"I'm going to be the Speaker of our House," Scar said. "You don't think that my parents or the nations in our House are going to just let me go to University and get a doctorate in any random field, do you?"

"Did you want to be Speaker?" Sneeze asked Bernini.

"No," Bernini answer sharply. "I mean, yeah, I would love to be a Speaker of a House. Who wouldn't want to be a god king. But the process. I don't know how you did it Scar. And on the first try down, too."

"Yeah, I know," Scar agreed. "That'll probably never happen again for a thousand cycles. The was just a statistical anomaly."

"Why did you decide to go through the Ascension process?" Popol asked Scar.

"I was straight up naive," Scar said as he looked out over the water towards the Citadel, the large glowing white monolith in the center of Metropolis. "I wasn't even ten cycles old. Poppa was just talking about it one day and I was like 'I want to do it!' like an idiot."

"Dude, what?" Popol asked astonished.

"Yeah, girl," Scar laughed.

"No fucking way," Oki said.

"We tried to talk you out of it," Bernini said. "Rhiannon and I tried to explain it to him. You said you knew what was going to happen. I think you saw it more as a challenge than a life decision."

"I don't know what the fuck was wrong with me," Scar said as they drove onto the island of Metropolis. "But I did it, no matter what may be."

"To bad some of the students at Coba didn't know that," Popol mentioned. "Chaac probably wouldn't have looked down at you if he knew who you are or what you've done."

"Why did he need to know?" Oki countered. "He was an asshole. It's like you said Scar, some people only think about their light, not what the light does. Screw Chaac."

"Chaac is a product of his environment," Scar said. "He's just trying to live up to the standards of his family, his House. You have to respect that. I know I learned from that. Besides, I didn't mind being called a country bumpkin. What's wrong with your parents pouring everything into their child so you can have the best life anyone can have in any universe?"

"I still think you should have told people who you were," Popol said.

"Yeah, that was pretty shitty of me. Definitely with you Popol. I thought that I could hide who I was and be an ordinary person for a while. Make some real friends like you two…"

"And me," Sneeze added.

"You're my wife…ah…fiancé, that doesn't count."

"How does that not count?" Sneeze asked as she bored into Scar's light.

"I loved you for a while now," Scar said. "But to have friends… anyway, Popol, you taught me I shouldn't hide who I am anymore, because I may end up hurting people I care about."

"I think maybe it should be to love yourself a little bit more," Popol considered.

"You're right about that," Scar admitted as Bernini parked the car in a VIP parking at the foot of the Citadel, the building towering above them like a small mountain. Everyone climbed out of the car and walked towards the white monolith. Scar walked behind them all, watching as Sneeze and Bernini fooled around ahead of Oki and Popol, who were a foot shorter. They all wore simple Andean clothing compared to how almost everyone else dressed in Nimian business suits coming to and from the Citadel.

"Don't you get a bit jealous with the way Bernini and Sneeze act together," Oki asked as he slowed to walk with Scar.

"Nah man. Sneeze is just so into our light now as a family. She's just not my wife… no, fiancé dammit. She's my sister. Our sister."

"Your soul group," Oki agreed.

"Yep," Scar said as they enter the Citadel through a large white stone entrance, its arch towering above them. Inside the bottom floor was a large open dome of the same white stone, with thick, tall pillars scattered about that was the support for the structure. There were many buildings inside of the dome, almost like a small village, mostly for visitor services. Bernini lead them to one of the buildings where a number of staff stood waiting for them, all dress in sharp brown and black work outfits with white long sleeve shirts.

"Good mourning everyone," a women spoke as they arrived. "Lord Bernini, Princess Sneeze, Your Highness and guests. Welcome to the Citadel. My name is Ahluic, and I'm the Director of the Citadel's visiting services. I hear that your parents wanted us to take you on a tour here?"

"Yes, please," Scar answered.

"Alright. If you can follow me, I'll take you around the visitor district," Ahluic pronounced as she lead the group amongst the buildings.

"Is everything connected to your family's light," Oki asked as he observed how everything in the dome had some form of curvature about it.

"Yeah, my Mom and Dad's," Scar said. "That's why we have the four large cables that run from the Citadel through the city, to fuel everything."

"That's why you have to go through the Ascension process?" Popol asked. "So you can have enough light to fuel everything?"

"Yeah," Scar said. "We don't just fuel everything here in this city. This monolith is entangled with every nation that has asked us for our light. You need a lot of light the fuel all of them."

"I wonder why you need to go through the Ascension process to increase your light any way," Popol wondered.

"Do you study Gucumatz hypothesis?" Scar asked.

"I didn't take advanced Aten Ka theory," Popol said. "You did, most high densities do."

"My bad. Well, he said that the reason is because of Xiuh's barrier…"

"That's like Einstein's constant right?" Oki asked.

"Right," Scar said. "Because our densities is above the barrier, there is no resistance to it as we increase our light. So the most any person can channel is enough light to displace one universe on their own. You max out at the seventh density. It's like a swimmer trying to swim as fast as they can in an ocean.

"Light outside the ocean of reality can go as fast as the speed of sound because they don't have to worry about Xiuh's barrier. There is no water to work against. The only problem is that you max out at the speed of sound due to no resistance. Lower lights in the water can't go as fast as the speed of light because you'll end up splashing water out of the ocean of reality. But if a light below Xiuh's barrier learns how to swim at the speed of sound, that light theoretically can now raise their density exponentially. That's what allows high density lights that goes through the Ascension the reach higher densities, or that's the running hypothesis."

"What density were you when you Descended?" Popol asked.

"I was sixth going on seventh," Scar responded.

"You were that high without going vegan yet?" Oki asked.

"Scar was the highest density out of all of us," Bernini jumped in. "I was born fifth. The closest was Athena, but she was born fifth going on to sixth."

"But you're not vegan now," Popol noticed. "I wonder how high you'll get when you do. Did you want to go vegan?"

"Momma doesn't want me to until I'm one thousand cycles old. By then most people's forms are developed."

"Or contemplating reincarnation to relieve their boredom," Oki said as they followed Ahluic through the inner town. The group enter all the different shops or restaurants, buying souvenirs or snacks as they traveled along. After they visited all the buildings, Ahluic lead the group up through the many levels of the Citadel, using lifts that are built into the many pillars of the monolith. On the upper levels many nations had their own embassies and small little districts that had the same types of shops on the bottom floor, but unique to their home world.

"Why did we eat downstairs," Sneeze complained as they walked by a restaurant where roasted avian beasts hung glazed in the window, the smells from it causing all of their mouths to water. Ahluic then lead the group to the top of the Citadel, where they came out to a flat white surface that overlooked the Metropolis. Over the edge they could see clouds below them, curling around the building as it created its own weather patterns.

"Do you guys want to get your picture taken?" Ahluic asked as a camera drone floated their way.

"Okay," Sneeze answered as she hugged Scar tight around his waist. The group scooched close together, all with their arms around each other, waiting for the camera drone.

"You guys set?" Ahluic asked.

"No wait," Scar pleaded before he reach over to kiss Sneeze on her lips, her light blooming as he did. The camera flashed and processed their image before showing it as a hologram before them. The group laughed as it showed all of them giving a last dot glance to Scar as he kissed Sneeze. All but Scar, who kept looking at the blond haired alien kissing his wife.

CHAPTER 11

147 AA

1

Scar looked out the window of his parents spacecraft, an silver egg-shaped mass that traveled through the White on their way to Saltal. Sneeze sat next to him, sitting quietly yet her light shining with a bit of hesitant excitement as she sat in the same vehicle as her fiancé's parents. Scar looked into her obsidian never blinking eyes, looking over her face as he loved to do sometimes. Kathrine used to hate when he did that to her, saying that she wasn't pretty, and Scar had to tell her that it's not about being pretty, it's that he loved her, thus loved how she looked.

The three lumps Sneeze had on her forehead were gone now, and she looked almost like a black woman on Earth with a bald scalp that stood almost eight feet tall. She was just as tone as Scar is but not as muscularly thick as he became. And her female human anatomy filled out too, her breast and buttocks now adult size and just as perky as when she was younger.

"What are you looking at?" Ixchel asked as she peered back at Scar and Sneeze from her place next to Ra, who sat on the navigator seat at the front of the passenger room.

"Nothing," Scar said ruefully as he and Sneeze leaned against each other, trying to hold in their laughter.

"Hmmm," Ixchel mumbled, staring into their lights, then turning back when she was satisfied that they weren't up to any hanky panky. Scar grabbed Sneeze's hand and squeezed it, with Sneeze smiling at him as he did. Luckily Sneeze was dressed in some of Athena's old clothes from home, otherwise Scar defiantly would have had a hard time keeping his hands off of her. It was the main reason why he was very seldom allowed to visit her on Roi Son, and if he did they were never alone. When she comes to visit on Nima, Ixchel would have the both of them doing chores, or helping out in her garden, or doing anything other than what normal teenagers would do if they were dating.

"We're here," Ra announced as he plunge their craft out of the White and into the waters of reality above Saltal, a metropolitan planet covered in a white plasma field of curvature, the equator of the field bulging out like a ring. Through the field Scar could see that it was as populated as Earth was when he left, with the night part of the planet lit with artificial lights.

Ra navigated their craft into a lane of other crafts entering the planet's atmosphere, then allowed the planet's navigating service to take control and direct them towards an spaceport that was in the heart of a continent the shape of a upside down Y, the upper tail and double bottom both veering off to the east. At the center of the continent was the largest city that Scar had ever seen on a planet's surface, taking up most of the land mass of the continent's intersection.

"Teotihuacan is huge," Sneeze muttered as she looked out if the front window.

"I was just thinking that," Scar added. "I thought that the Andean council didn't want cities being this big."

"It is because of Teotihuacan that we made that policy," Ixchel answered. "It is still beautiful though."

"Yeah," Scar muttered.

"Now after we land we are going straight to Ya'ax Mont University," Ixchel told Scar. "The first thing we are going to do is register you for your classes.

Then I want to talk to the president to see what she has planned for you there. I do not want you doing anything other than focusing on your degree. You did register for Federation political science theory, correct?"

"Yes," Scar answered.

"What else are you going to do?" Ra asked.

"There's an Earth based sports league organized by old Earth lights. They made a scholastic American football league, so I'm going to try out for it."

"As long as it does not take away from your studies," Ixchel reminded Scar.

"Yes ma'am," Scar said.

"I also want to look at your dorm facilities," Ixchel said. "Just to be sure that you will have everything that you need."

"I still have resources saved up from my job," Scar said. "I saved up to pay for tuition for half of my courses. That should be enough to pay for anything else I might need."

"We are paying for everything, Scar," Ixchel said as their craft began its last descent onto a clear landing pad on a remote part of a busy spaceport. "You should not have to worry about anything. Just let us know what you need and we will help you out."

"Momma, you don't have to do that," Scar insisted. "I'll be fine."

"Listen to your mother," Ra demanded into Scar's light, and Scar sighed in defeat.

"Yes sir," Scar answered.

"You will tell us if you need anything," Ra ordered.

"Yes sir," Scar said as the craft came to a floating stop a few feet above the tar mat of the spaceport, where a few technicians waited for them to exit their vessel. The family left their seats and climbed down inside the ship to the exit hatch that opened from the hull like water parting. The open section of the hull formed steps for the group to walk down to one of the techs waiting at the foot of the stairs.

"Good day, your Majesties," the worker said looking up at the group. "What do you have to declare on your ship?"

"We didn't bring any food," Scar said as Ra and Ixchel walked to the back of the craft to get the family sedan. "Just this ship and a car."

"May we inspect the ship?"

"Go for it," Scar said as he and Sneeze stepped aside to allow the techs on to the craft. Ra drove the sedan next to the couple, and after the tar mat crew inspected the vehicle, Scar and Sneeze entered and were driving to the school.

"I don't think I like this place to much," Sneeze said as they drove along on a highway. "There isn't enough green around."

"There is some," Scar said as he looked about. "But the city design is definitely leaning towards the urban aesthetic."

"They do it to appeal to other civilizations that don't appreciate nature as much," Sneeze said with small disdain.

"You have to," Scar said. "Not every nation is the same, and there are countless cultures in those countless nations. We have to make the Federation's capital as appealing to as many as possible. You piss off everyone while doing it, but the small part that everyone agrees on is where you find progress."

"Well, I don't like it," Sneeze admitted. "I don't like a place where you can't feel the soil under your toes."

"Maybe there's a park on campus that we can chill out for a while," Scar suggested. "We got all day. Maybe we can have a picnic there."

"Sounds fun," Ra said as he drove the vehicle through the dense traffic of the mega city. Its scale dwarfed the Metropolis back on Nima. Above all the high rise buildings was a massive upper level driving freeway that was supported by its own gravity well that seemed to fill the horizon . Lanes of flying cars crisscrossed the cloudy sky in patchwork fashion. Everything was so dense, compacted together on all sides.

"This place is like Coruscant," Scar said.

"What's that Sonlig?" Sneeze asked confused.

"Nothing," Scar said as Ra finally drove onto Ya'ax Mont's campus, a huge group of buildings that stood on top of a large wooded hill. The road they drove on winded up the hill through different departments of school's learning curriculum. At the top of the hill was the area that held the major sports open and closed facilities, as well as the campus' main office and auditorium. Ra pulled his vehicle into a designated parking space and the group climbed out and walked towards the campus's office.

"This place is much better," Sneeze said as she held onto Scar's waist. "There were way too many buildings coming here. This feels like a place you can breathe."

"That's a huge football field," Scar said as he looked out towards the athletics fields. His eyes then looked about them to all the different species that walked about. Scar had never seen so many different species with so many type of gene expressions. There were beings that floated with no legs, some that slithered, some that walked on two legs, or four and more. There were beings that flew with or without wings. There were beings shorter than Ixchel, and beings that were as tall as the buildings around them. Scar was surprised when he saw a group that looked like globs of white light that flowed in a row, and then those beings looked with annoyance at Scar for staring at them.

"Sonlig, don't stare at people," Sneeze laughed as she squeezed Scar, who looked down in contrite fashion. They were all amazing to Scar, and he couldn't help a sense of joy swelling up in him. He knew that the planet Saltal was the center of the Federation's multiverse, but seeing what it meant was something different. Just the chance to interact with new species and to learn about their cultures was making Scar's heart race.

"I think we go this way," Ra said as he with Ixchel in hand lead the group to a building where a sign that imprinted in your light read 'student registration'. They walked into the glass door entrance where dozens of students stood in line to register for their classes. When they got to the end of one line, a blue skinned winged student smile back at them, then stared stunned at the group. He was trying to come up with something to say, and before Scar and his family thought about introducing themselves, they saw everyone else stare at them in the corridor. They were all seventh density beings, and were transfixed by the nine loops around Ixchel and the ten around Ra and Scar.

"Hello," the family heard someone call out to them, and they looked out to see a faculty member in a red and white dress walking towards them in a rush.

"Hello, your Majesties," the person said as she brushed her green hair behind her ears on the side of a large peach colored head. "My name is Haniel. Welcome to Ya'ax Mont."

"Thank you," Ixchel said as she grabbed and shook her wrist.

"And you must be Scar," Haniel said as she looked up at him. "You're here to register, I assume. If you may, please follow me and we'll help you out."

"No ma'am, we're fine," Ra said.

"Are you sure?" Haniel asked.

"This is the line for student registration?" Scar asked.

"Yes," Haniel answered, understanding their gist.

"We're good," Scar said with a smile.

"Well, just to let you know, the president wants to meet with all of you after you're done. You can find us in the offices over to your right."

"Thank you, Haniel," Ixchel said before she departed. It didn't take long for the line to be processed and soon they were standing in front of glass enclosed counters where processing clerks worked on hologram computers before one of them called the group over.

"Name?" the obsidian skinned woman with white short hair asked, clearly not caring who was in front of her.

"Scar Amun," Scar answered.

"What course are you taking?"

"Federation political science and theory," Scar said.

"What is your F.I.N.?" the woman asked, and after Scar answered, a hologram appeared in front of the four that listed all the classes and credits that Scar assigned for himself.

"Sweetie?" Ixchel spoke as she looked over the curriculum. "You have two Earth based classes here."

"I wanted to take Earth history, pre and post 2024," Scar explained.

"You are not planning to change courses are you?" Ixchel asked.

"No Momma," Scar said. "I just figured that I take courses that I know I'll get an easy five in."

"You know that history taught on and off a world can be completely different?" Ra asked.

"Yes sir, I know," Scar answered with a sigh.

"Do you want me to change the course?" the woman behind the glass asked in an absent monotone voice.

"No, no," Ixchel answered. "If you want to take these classes, you may. Just stay with your degree."

"I will," Scar said as he bent down to hug and kiss Ixchel. After they confirmed Scar classes and stepped from the counter, they saw a small number of the faculty staff waiting for them at the entrance of the side offices.

"They are really desperate to meet you," Sneeze said.

"They probably want to use Scar presence here to boost admissions to the school," Ra said.

"Besides the fact that it's already one of the most prestigious universities in the multiverse," Scar said.

"Why be one of and instead be thee?" Ixchel proposed. "Do not worry, Scar. We will talk to them. We want you to only focused on your studies. Go around with Sneeze and explore the campus. We will meet you later."

"Okay," Scar said as he and Sneeze walked out of the building hand in hand.

"Do you want to go look at your dorm room?" Sneeze asked as she looked up at the signs for directions.

"That sounds like a plan," Scar said as he followed where Sneeze pulled him through the campus buildings. Scar did feel a bit in his comfort zone as he walk amongst the students, then realize that it's going to feel weird again when he graduates and the universe is open for him again. The fact that he was going to join the Marines gave him at least some piece of mind.

There was something that Scar began to notice as he and Sneeze walked together. Everyone gave them a side glance as they walked, which is to expected since Scar was a tenth density. But their eyes lingered because of Sneeze. She was biracial Kaggen, and it was her Kaggen heritage that Scar saw give the students a sudden start.

The Kaggen were notorious for their exploration behavior back in their native universe, the same one where Scar spent his previous life on Earth. The Kaggen rule that universe, and although they maintain a peaceful existence with the Federation, the explorer sub-culture of their species were very empirical. Scar learned in history class that many of the interactions some species had with the Kaggen were just like the UFO encounter stories that Scar researched back on Earth. Cold and scientific in nature, with no regard for the individuals the explorers studied.

So when people gave Sneeze a nervous glance, it made him feel closer to her, or perhaps protective. He pulled Sneeze beside him at one point, grabbing one of her butt cheeks in his hand, which gave Sneeze a pleasant start. Those negative stares did make Scar feel normal, which deep down he knew was wrong. If she wasn't there and everyone was just staring at him, he would have felt miserable, not knowing rather they were staring at his light, at him, or even both. He still didn't feel normal inside his form, which he knew was very wrong. Yet he still couldn't shake it.

"Are you okay, Sonlig?" Sneeze asked, looking into Scar's light, which snapped Scar at out his train of thought.

"No, I'm fine," Scar said as they approached the dorms, upscale apartment buildings that had colored trimmings along the corners of the building based on what major the students was in. Scar and Sneeze made their way to the purple trimmed ones and into the student check-in station where a group of students sat behind a circular counter with hologram computers displayed before them.

"Good mourning, ma'am and sir," a formless student spoke from a pocket dimension with half a dozen green and black tendrils protruding from it. "I Am, and I can help you with your check in process. What is your name?"

"Scar Amun," Scar stated as he looked about the station, which was much like a recreation room, with dozens of television screens floating about, tuned to different channels. There were arcade games, some digital and some material based placed here or there, with some students gather in small groups as they competed with each other.

"I'm going to have to start a D&D club up in here," Scar muttered to himself.

"Is that game all you think about?" Sneeze asked.

"Yes it is," Scar answered proudly.

"There you are," I Am said, finally finding his name on the list. "I went through the catalog a couple of times, then I looked at your light and decided to look at the suites list."

"There are suites on a college campus?" Scar asked with a confused expression.

"There are here," I Am said as he rolled from his place behind the counter and next to Scar and Sneeze. As it rolled, reality seemed to slip around it also, giving I Am the appearance that it was in and out of reality at the same time.

"I can lead you to your room if you like?" I Am stated.

"I want to see it," Sneeze said excitedly, which made Scar feel a bit better that she was excited. That might be a blessing in their relationship, Scar thought, with Sneeze finding some pleasure in material things. Because Scar barely could. If he wasn't going to marry her, he would end up having all the resources that could buy an intergalactic empire and wanting nothing to spend it on.

I Am rolled before them, leading the two pass a couple of apartment buildings and to a gated area where smaller dual two story house complexes stood between manicured lawns and maintained trees. I Am finally presented them to one of the houses, where in the front yard was a swimming pool with lounge chairs and even a barbeque pit with a stone gazebo near it.

"This is great, Sonlig," Sneeze said as she looked about while they walk through the front door. Inside was all the commodities that a person needed in a house to live comfortably. There was a simple living room with a television hologram and couch seated before it with a table standing behind it for guests.

There was a full kitchen also, with Scar and Sneeze being surprised that it was stocked with food already.

"Wow, this place has everything you need," Sneeze said after they finished exploring the bottom floor, then paused for a bit in thought.

"Do you think that's the point?" Sneeze asked Scar.

"I think so too," Scar agreed as he turned to I Am. "Thanks man, I sure we can find our way around."

"Let me know if you need anything," I Am said before it rolled out of the house.

"Well, as prisons goes, this isn't bad," Scar said as he lead Sneeze upstairs, his hand still firmly gripped on her rear. The upper level of the house was one large room with wooden beams placed in even intervals to support the roof. There was a bed that was placed before a window that showed Teotihuacan shimmering from the large hill. There was also a study area with a desk and a leather and steel seat, with a hologram computer set up for Scar. The bathtub and shower was also open air, with the shower surrounded with green stained glass. In a corner floated a metallic box that had many appendages that cleaned the house for the occupant.

"This is so nice," Sneeze said as she left Scar side and walked over to the bed to feel the sheets. "You're going to have fun here… what's with that face?"

"There seems to be a problem,' Scar side as his face twitched a bit. "That ass isn't in my hand."

"Come over her and get it," Sneeze said in a stern tone, slightly peeved at Scar for demanding her at his side, then giggling as Scar approached her in an aggressive manner. Scar pushed her onto the bed and laid on top of her, Sneeze staring into his eyes as he looked down at her.

"I guess this place is nice," Scar said as he kissed Sneeze. "It has a great view. I don't know why the pool's out front. I'll probably never going to use that."

"Hmmm," Sneeze moaned between kisses.

"I should go back to the campus to see where my classes are for this semester. You don't mind, do you?"

"Hmmm," Sneeze answered again, and Scar noticed that she wasn't paying attention to much of what he was saying. Her eyes were always staring, but her light was blinded, waiting for him to kiss her again. Scar decided to oblige, shifting her legs up to fit his hips between hers. He really starting going at it when he was kissing Sneeze's neck and grabbing one of her breasts, which made Sneeze sigh in a way Scar enjoyed.

"Are we not supposed to have a picnic?" Ixchel asked into their light, and Scar and Sneeze stopped, hugging each other tightly and laughing into each other's bodies.

"Yes ma'am," Scar said.

"We're heading to the park," Ra said. "Do you want us to buy from anywhere in particular?"

"I'll buy," Sneeze said as she dragged Scar off the bed and down the stairs.

"Are you sure?" Ra questioned. "It's no bother for us."

"You guy's already took care of me so much so far," Sneeze pleaded. "I want to. Please?"

"Alright, Sweet Pea," Ixchel said. "We will be in the park then."

"Okay," Scar said as they rushed out of the house, smiling at how happy Sneeze was as she lead him through the campus grounds and to the food district.

"Do you want fast food or deli style?" Sneeze asked as they looked at all the food vans that were parked on the edge of the campus park, which was a large grass area where a statue of the school founder stood, surrounded by a ring of green trees with white, pink, blue and red flowers blossoming on them.

"Let's get something from the vegan stand," Scar suggested. "I'm going to have to get used to that diet anyway when I join the Service after school."

"Okay," Sneeze said. "Wait here Sonlig, I'll be right back." As Sneeze walked to the food truck, Scar walked over to a bench nearby and sat down, looking out at the park as the midday sun shined through the trees. Since Teotihuacan was located just north of Saltal's equator, the weather was always nice, and the breeze was prevalent on top of the hill where the school stood. Scar soaked in the scenery while a Zeta came and sat next to him with her meal.

"Hi," she said to Scar.

"Hey," Scar answered.

"New to the campus?" she asked.

"Is it that obvious?" Scar asked as he looked at his simple Andean clothing.

"No, it's your light," the Zeta said. "There aren't many tenth density beings here. Actually, I don't think there are any period."

"Yeah," Scar said shyly.

"What are you majoring in?"

"Federation political science."

"So, you want to serve in Congress in the future."

"Something like that," Scar said.

"If you need any help around campus, just let me know," the Zeta offered as a Pleiadean woman sat down across from Scar

"Hi," she said, completely ignoring the Zeta, who angrily stood up and walked away from them. "You're new here. Have a name?"

"Scar," he answered, watching the Zeta as she left, feeling a little upset about what happen himself.

"My name's Anu," she responded with a sly smile, brushing back her brown hair. "Are you here with anybody?"

"Yeah, my fiancé over there," Scar pointed out as Sneeze arrived with a bag full of food.

"Oh," Anu said as she looked up at Sneeze, not sure what to say.

"Are you ready?" Sneeze asked as she ignored Anu.

"Yeah, Sweet-pea," Scar said as he stood and grabbed the food from Sneeze.

"Who's that bitch?" Sneeze asked as they walked towards the park, loud enough so that she knew Anu heard her.

"Wow. Okay, first, I'm sorry that I pissed you off if you're mad at me. Second, don't you think you're being a bit harsh? She could be a friend you might like."

"The first woman you talked to wanted to be a friend. That bitch was a resource digging skank," Sneeze said. "I'm actually glad your parents boarded you into your house. And I don't want you using that pool too."

"Yes dear," Scar laughed.

"Unless I'm there," Sneeze added.

"Ha!" Scar snorted as they walked through the park, finally finding Ixchel and Ra waving at them from under the shade of a pink flowered tree. Ra made a blue blanket for them to sit on, and Scar pulled out the food for everyone so they could begin eating.

"Thank you, Sneeze," Ixchel said.

"You're welcome, your Majesty," Sneeze said, which made Ixchel's expression grimace.

"Do not call me that, Sweet-pea," Ixchel said.

"What do you want me to say?"

"You can call me Ixchel."

"I'm not saying that," Sneeze contested.

"You can say Mother," Ra suggested.

"I'm not ready to say that either," Sneeze said.

"Why not?" Ixchel asked in a serious tone, which made Sneeze laugh nervously.

"Are you liking the school?" Ra asked Scar, who looked about the park at all the students walking by, or sitting in the shade of the trees or playing some group sport. He saw them, but wasn't attached to them yet.

"I'm happy right here," Scar confessed.

"Give it time," Ixchel said. "You will get use to this place. It is okay for you to be happy. Remember that.'

"Yes ma'am," Scar said in between a bite of his meal.

"Let's go look at Scar's place before we leave," Ra said. "I want to see how much this place has changed since your mother left here."

"Sounds like a plan," Scar agreed as he watch his family eat in bliss in front of him, allowing himself to feel just the same for a little bit.

Chapter 12

150 AA

1

"Now I know that some of you in this class still have a view point that's still biased from your previous life," Professor Hipparchia said as she brushed some of her silver white hair about her elongated head. "Keep in mind that this course is being taught by individuals that are not native of Earth, so I don't have any view point from that world. It is strictly from a point of view of a historian from the outside looking in.

"This class in particular will focused on some on the major events that happened between 1850 and 2024. With that in mind, let's start off with the most important one, and that is the Great Resource War, or the Great Oil War, that lasted predominantly throughout that entire time period.

"The Great Oil War actually started when oil was beginning to be refined in the nation call the United States of America, not to be confused with the now United States of North America. At the time the world's largest distributor of oil was Standard Oil, a corporation from the U.S. This corporation was so large that it was forced to split into three companies that still exists now, Chevron, Exxon Renewable, and the third a major part of BP Interstellar.

"Standard Oil still had the world's monopoly on oil production and refinery, even making oil centers in the Pacific and Indian Ocean. However, oil was being found in a competing nation to the United States, the then Russian

Empire. Oil was found in Russia much earlier than this time period of the nineteenth century, and Russia began the drilling and refining of oil at the turn of the century, becoming a major global rival to the divided companies of Standard Oil. It is these companies' need to secure oil reserves, and the nation states backing them competing with one another, that eventually lead Earth into it first official military conflict, something the people of that planet called World War One."

"World War One was started because of the assassination of Arch Duke Ferdinand," a student stated. "There was already saber rattling going on at that time; nations just used that as an excuse to actually go to war."

"The group that assassinated the Arch Duke was associated with a revolution party, the Young Serbians," another student interjected.

"That's right," Professor Hipparchia said. "But the Young Serbians was one of many groups funded by western European financial institutions to disrupt the oil power in Russia and eastern Europe. Some of these institutions, located in France and the United Kingdom, were business partners with Standard Oil. Much of the war, and subsequently World War Two was fought over the location of oil reserves and refinery plants throughout Europe, the Near East and Africa. It can be stated that if one nation, the Ottoman Empire, had allied themselves with the United Kingdom instead of Germany in World War One, that much of Earth's conflicts after World War Two would most likely never have happened."

"Okay, now World War Two was fought to stop the fascist regimes of the Nazis in Germany and Italy," another student objected. "Plus the Japanese Imperial Navy spread across the Pacific. It was the Japanese that attacked Pearl Harbor and brought the United States into the war. And there was the Holocaust."

"How many students in this class had pass lives on Earth, especially in the United States of North America?" Professor Hipparchia asked, then laughed as she saw a small number of hands raised. "It still surprises me how many lights from that area of the world still object to an outside telling of world events. It isn't an attack against the United States. Or any other country for that matter. I'm only telling events of Earth's history."

"But oil had nothing to do with World War Two," the student insisted.

"Japan attacked Pearl Harbor in hopes of eliminating the U.S. Pacific fleet, so the United States couldn't stop Japan's acquisitions of Standard Oil's refineries in the Pacific and Indian Ocean. Germany lead its campaign into Russia to secure its oil reserves. The Nazi regime was performing acts of genocide while trading with U.S. oil companies. Not to take away from the travesties that happened during the wars, but the true reason for both World Wars was for the control of oil.

"Before World War Two, the United states lent its support to the then burgeoning Communist Party that was about to fail during reconstruction in Europe after World War One. Corporations in the United States, including Standard Oil, gave their financial support to the Bolsheviks, the main communist revolution party in Russia at that time, which would later on form the Soviet Union.

"Companies in the west did this in hopes of being partners with the new Soviet Union and its state owned oil fields. Standard Oil purchased fifty percent of the oil reserves in the region known as the Caucuses, and even built refineries in Russia for the Soviet Union."

"How is it that we didn't learn about this in any history class?" an old Earth light student asked.

"Well, for one, did you actually pay attention in history class?" Professor Hipparchia asked.

"Holy shit," the student laughed.

"Plus, and this is no offense to those who lived in the United States. That nation has a terrible track record of rewriting history that paints any of its most important figures in a bad light.

"This actually leads up to the next subject in today's lesson, and that is the First Cold War that started just at the end of the Second World War. Corporations in the United States went out of its way to help establish the Soviets, with banks helping to establish governments and loaning political parties money for stability."

"Do you think that this lead to some of the communist scare that happened in the U.S. at the same time?" a student asked.

"Largely," Professor Hipparchia answered. "The Soviets had not become the dreaded enemy to the U.S. at that time of history yet. Many of the ties that the U.S. created in Russia also made cells in the United States to try to spread communism in the naton. But it wasn't a conflict of ideologies that was the main problem, but the financial backing of such institutions, which were mostly oil companies.

"It has been theorized that the purpose of oil companies, especially the remnants of Standard Oil, of doing this was to create a large global nation state ruled by one particular type of political system, which at first was socialism and communism. Not for the purpose of spreading communism, but for the control of resources by these oils companies.

"However, there were still resistance to this spread of communist ideology, specifically in the part of Earth that you call the west, primarily western Europe and the United States. So these corporations in the west that still supported and profited from the Soviets helped to secure trade deals between the two factions, which secured the Soviet Union supplies to produce military assets."

"What a dot," a student interrupted. "You're saying that the United States gave the Soviet Union the supplies it needed to produce military arms to extend the Cold War?"

"Precisely," Professor Hipparchia answered, which was welcomed by the grumbles of the class. "The best example of this was the Vietnam War."

"Hold up," a student said. "I was following everything up to this point. But to say that the U.S. supplied the enemy in Vietnam is too much. This is tin foil hat territory right now."

"Like I explained before, I'm only stating the facts of an off-world observer. I would like to clarify that I did receive my Doctorate in the study of the First Cold War on Earth. So I would like to say that I'm one of the leading authorities in this matter.

"The reason why this sounds incomprehensible to believe is because it's fool hardy for the United States to actually give the Soviet Union weapons and strategic equipment such as radar and other military equipment. These items were considered 'strategic' to the U.S. The resources and goods needed to construct these devices however were not. So the remnants of Standard Oil traded to the Soviet Union with these goods and resources, who then created strategic assets and gave them to the communist party in Vietnam, which prolong the war.

"The only reason why the war in Vietnam ended, as much of you well know, is because the world's public was sick and tired of the violence, which is a natural progression that any civilization takes as they progress into the Light. Both the Soviet Union and the nations in the West decided to stop all hostilities and withdrew from Vietnam, which became a communist state and allied itself with the United States soon after, which made the war in that nation all but pointless.

"Without the Vietnam war, and the crushing lost in Afghanistan, the Soviet Union soon collapse without outside financial or resource support it received during the Cold War. So the oil companies in the world tried a new experiment to get the nations under one global government.

"This is beginning to sound like something from Info Wars," a student joked.

"What was needed was another war," Professor Hipparchia continued. "One which the world governments knew they could succeed in because of the Soviet Union's collapse. So they decided that the next best target was the Near East. In particular, Egypt, Libya, Iraq, Iran, Syria, Yemen, and Lebanon. So the oil companies started with Iraq."

"Didn't Iraq invade Kuwait unannounced?" someone asked. "Didn't Saddam try to rebuild ancient Babylon?"

"Dude, we told him to do it," Scar said.

"What?"

"Saddam Hussein was a U.S. asset," another student added. "We put him in place as a puppet once we took out Iraq's Shah, but he turned on us. And it was Kuwait that was allegedly stealing Iraq's oil. Saddam Hussein met with the U.S. ambassador to Iraq at the time and asked her if he could invade Iraq, and she told him the U.S. didn't care. That's practically a green light."

"Correct," Professor Hipparchia said. "It was then that the U.S. sent troops not only into Kuwait and southern Iraq, but also created a permanent presence in Saudi Arabia that still persist now, now due more to goods trade since oil production has drastically decreased on Earth. It was then that world governments focused on trying to access and control the oil reserves in the Near East.

"What finally stop this western expansion was the re-emergence of the Russian Empire, led by its own oil conglomerates. Thus started the Second Cold War, one that pitted all of the oil companies backed by western or eastern military might against each other. What truly started the Cold War again was events that followed the U.S. failed attempt to prevent terrorist attacks in its home soil.

"The United States responded to the attacks by invading Afghanistan, a country that had nothing to do with the attacks, which was actually perpetrated by Saudi Arabian agents," Hipparchia dictated, which caused all too knowing chuckles in the classroom. "It was then the United States seized it's chance to go back into Iraq and take out Saddam Hussein, while also trying to establish a pro-western government in his absence, a gamble that eventually failed.

"Tell me about it," Scar muttered.

"But resistance sprung in Iraq, which was face front backed by neighboring Muslim nations opposed to the western presence, but they themselves were back by eastern oil finances. The Russia government would themselves declare that they were also in the fight against terrorism, but it became unclear which groups were the terrorists, since there were groups funded by the west and groups funded by Russia. Since they all fought in Near Eastern nations with or against each other, and eventually into Ukraine, the world was confused by who was fighting who. But in earnest the conflict in that region was competing oil companies fighting for control of the oil reserves. And to reiterate, the Second Cold War may not have happened if the Ottomans had allied with Britain.

"All of this will eventually come to an end post 2024, after the Earth's solar system enters a pure matter cloud and thrust the Earth into the fourth density. That end's it for today's lesson, class. Next week we're going to go over the Rise of the American Empire, and how it changed its tactics to coerce or co-opt other nations and its own citizens to remain in power."

2

Scar hurried to finish the last few sentences of his report on his computer, going over the wording again and again to make sure he edited his assignment the best he could. When he was satisfied, he hit a few icons on the glowing keyboard and it faded out from above the desk he sat at. He quickly walked over to the drawer that was next to his bed, pulling out his Dungeon Master

Guide, a felt bag filled with many different types of dice, and his folder filled with loose pieces of charted paper.

After he grabbed everything he needed, he rushed downstairs and out of his apartment, saying hi to his neighbor who was hosting his girlfriend and buddies at the pool that afternoon. They tried to offer a chance for him to hang out, but he quickly declined, his light focused on getting to the rec room as soon as possible. He greeted all the students he knew as he entered the student registration area, walking to a table where four other students sat, two Andeans, an green scaled Anunnakian, and a brown feathered Pamolai.

"Hurry up," Katah squawked at Scar as he sat down next to him.

"Sup, Nerds!" Scar said as he laid his items down and poured his dice out on the table.

"You know it's going to take us forever to make characters, right?" Uncir complained as he grabbed some die in his sky blue hands and began rolling them with enthusiasm.

"Dude, I didn't want my mom bugging me all night because I didn't finish my assignment," Scar mumbled.

"That was so funny," Utu hissed in laughter. "Man, every five minutes your mom's light would pop up and ask 'Is your report done?'"

"That must suck having your mom be able to read your light from across a universe," Chamahez said as he grabbed a sheet of paper and began writing stats down.

"Which means she can hear everything you say," Scar said.

"I don't care. She aint my mom, loser."

"God I can feel the love," Scar laughed. "Alright, what characters are we going to make?"

"So you're still going to be paladin, right?" Katah asked.

"Yes," Scar answered as he rummaged through his folder until he found an old character sheet.

"If that's going to be the case, then I'm going to be bard. Our feats would have good symmetry together. That should give the party some nice bonuses."

"I thought that I was going to be the paladin," Utu protested.

"Shoots, alright," Scar said as he flipped through some more paper. "I can make a new character then. Maybe I'll try a mage this time."

"I got the mage class," Chamahez informed Scar.

"Wait, okay. And Uncir, you're the cleric, right?"

"Yep," Uncir said as he rolled for his attributes.

"Crap, I guess I can be a fighter. I haven't played a fighter in Dungeon and Dragons for over one hundred and fifty cycles."

"You should play a barbarian," Katah suggested.

"Oh man, that would be perfect!" Uncir shouted. "You're half Pleiadean anyways. You look like a Source damn Nordic brute with all that muscle. And your name is Scar! It's fucking perfect."

"Wow, thanks for calling me a Nordic brute," Scar muttered.

"Dude, that's a compliment," Utu laughed. "You won the lottery when you reincarnated."

"Yeah, you keep saying that," Scar said as he began to work on his barbarian.

"Hey, are you mad?" Utu asked.

"No," Scar answered.

"Yeah he is," Katah noticed.

"You alright man?" Uncir asked a bit concerned.

"Yeah," Scar said as he stopped writing, closing his eyes and taking a deep breath. "It's hard for me to talk about. No matter how I say it, I feel like shit thinking the way I do."

"It's because you were black back on Earth?" Uncir asked.

"Yeah," Scar said.

"You know that's still racist?" Utu stated with a laugh.

"That's why I feel like shit every time this comes up," Scar said. "Damn, I still shave my head because I can't get used to being a blond."

"Holy shit dude," Chamahez said, hitting Scar's shoulder. "It's weighing down on you that much?"

"Yeah," Scar sighed. "Aten Ka, I feel like absolute shit."

"Well, it's better than what happen to me," Utu said. "I went from being black to being Reptile from Mortal Kombat."

"Test your might," Uncir softly said as he moved his arms in horrible martial arts motions.

"Dude, I would have been so happy to be Anunnaki," Scar said. "At least there is some link to ancient African traditions with the Anunnaki."

"There are African cultures that worship Pleiadeans too," Utu reminded Scar. "I know some old Pleiadeans who are proud the have been African."

"I know," Scar said. "My dad's one of them. Maybe it's because I lived on Earth when everybody began bashing on white men."

"Privilege, conservative white men," Katah corrected.

"But what does that mean?" Scar argued. "By all accounts, I was a privilege black male growing. I lived in an middle class home. My dad was an officer in the Navy back in the States. My mom was a teacher. I grew up well off. Is there a good old boy mentality with upper echelon jobs where white men only know and interact with each other? Yeah. But man, EVERYBODY does it. Including black people. That's good ol' boy mentality when you have communities that don't intermingle with each other. There's no difference between the Crossbones and Alpha Phi Alpha."

"Now wait a minute," Uncir laughed. "I can't agree with that."

"I looking at them by their means, not their ends, "Scar explained. "I knew some southern good old boys when I served in the Army…hell, one of them saved my life in Iraq. This guy was born poor, and most likely stayed poor. Wealth is inherited, rather you have it or not. If you're born rich, you'll stay rich, and vice versa. If you compared our lives, then I was the one who was privilege. My sister was a multi-millionaire."

"Yet you feel like shit because of how you look?" Katah guessed.

"I know that it's only skin pigmentation," Scar said. "You are not defined by who or what you are, but what you do. But dammit, it doesn't help if you're reincarnated into the body of a seven foot six inch tall, blond hair, blue eye white freckled dude who just happens to be one of the richest beings in the multiverse."

"With, like, the coolest name ever," Chamahez added.

"You know what, I have to agree with that," Scar laughed. "Scar Amun is a cool name."

"So you don't want to be wealthy?" Katah asked.

"That's not the point. But I'd rather be a dirt poor nobody in the eyes of many, but as long as I'm happy and without need, I'm good."

"I guess I was lucky," Katah mentioned. "I was Indian living in Maine when I was on Earth. I was so happy when I came back to my higher density form. It felt like I came home."

"How old were you when you went through the Ascension?" Uncir asked.

"I was one hundred cycles old," Katah answered.

"Me too," Chamahez commented. "My parents explained the process to me, and for some strange reason, I wanted to do it."

"I was nine cycles old," Scar said.

"That young," Utu groaned. "Man, no wonder you're still having a hard time. You haven't really formed an identity yet. No wonder your light still looks black."

"You think that's the problem?" Scar asked.

"Maybe?" Chamahez offered. "Or you could just be racist?"

"Damn!" Scar chuckled. "You cut me deep Shriek, you cut me deep."

"Yet you don't carry any of the culture traits back on Earth," Utu noticed.

"That's because I never did hang out with anybody growing up," Scar explained. "My closest friends were from Hawaii, and I loved the culture there, but they didn't like Mainland people on the islands, so culturally I don't belong anywhere. I feel Andean more than anything else. I loved growing up on Nima. It was the first place where I knew that I was happy."

"That's probably why you dress Andean," Uncir said as he played with Scar's sleeve.

"Don't mock me," Scar snarked back. "At least I don't dress like a bunch of preppy rich douches."

"Aten Ka!" Utu howled.

"Man, what in the Empty," Uncir laughed.

"You're just a hater because I look so sexy," Katah said as he stood up and flexed his arms, all the while being rooted on by his friends.

"I'm sorry," Scar giggled. "I know there's nothing wrong with being what I am. I guess it's going to take time for me to get used to it."

"Well, you don't act like some self-centered young light who thinks that everyone must worship them," Chamahez said. "Like, ninety percent of the dummies here act like that."

"Right, I thought that was just me," Katah said. "That can grate my feathers sometimes."

"Anyway, lets make these characters!" Scar shouted as he banged the table. "You know what, I am going to play a barbarian. And I'm going as Scar." With that Scar made illuminated armor appear around him, and pulled out a massive longsword from his side and pointed it into the air. "Crom! Grant me one request. Grant me revenge!"

"Dude, you have to go shirtless," Uncir scolded Scar.

"I'm not going half naked in the rec room dude," Scar laughed.

"All right, so I'm going to be the mage," Chamahez said, as he made himself looked like a black cloaked, silver belted wizard, with a red pointy hat and a pseudo-dragon that perched on one of his shoulders.

"I'll get my muse on," Katah said as he was dressed up in elegant medieval noble garment, with a golden lute with speakers built into them.

"I'm your sword and your shield," Utu swore, encasing himself with silver chainmail that was covered with dark blue and silver garments with the image of silver dragon on them. He also pulled out his sword that was encased in radiant light.

"May Kelemvor protect us," Uncir prayed, as he clothed himself in in chainmail also. He held up high a holy symbol, a crest that had a skeletal hand holding a scale imprinted on it.

"Okay, gentlemen," Scar began. "We find ourselves on a remote road along the Sword Coast, because the last town we were in believed we were a bunch of murdering hobos…"

"We aren't?" Utu laughed.

"So someone suggested that we try our luck in Waterdeep," Scar continued. "On the road there it seems that we see what looks like refuges heading our way from a recent battle. What do you guys want to do?"

CHAPTER 13

151 AA

1

"I'm hoping that some of you have taken the course on Earth history pre 2024," Professor Three Squares told his class, staring them down with his large dark almond shape eyes. "You won't be able to appreciated the changes that happened on Earth unless you know how drastically global culture had changed in the previous century, and how events following 2024 changed everything just as abruptly.

"April 17, 2024 was the date when Earth's solar system entered the pure matter cloud, bosons that the people on Earth called dark matter. Nothing particular happened at first, because it took time for the density of the pure matter to effect those who had on their own began their Ascension.

"The dark matter entry was a sensation on the planet, with many fearing the gravity of the cloud would tear the solar system apart when it was first detected. Scientists around were quick to announce that yes, the gravity from the cloud did effect the Earth, but it happened through out millions of cycles, in events such as meteorite strikes that caused global extinctions.

"It became apparent around the summer of that year that the cloud was causing some type of effect on certain individuals. Those who had already opened their energies nexuses in their light would randomly go unconscious from spontaneous light travel. However, these events were quickly denied since there was no proof that these individuals experienced any light manipulation phenomena.

"Later that year an increasing number of people were demonstrating more abilities associated with light manipulation, such as telepathy and empathy, telekinesis, and flight. Much of the population who experienced these events had mental break downs, because they hadn't learn to keep their consciousness out from the surrounding population. The more peculiar trend that popped up was the significant increase of individuals who claimed to be a messiah and would save the planet from an end of the world event."

"My neighbor did that," a student claimed, with everyone laughing around her. "I'm serious. I lived in Frankfurt, Germany, and my neighbor across the street started claiming that he was Jesus Christ, and started shining his light on everyone. When I showed him that I could do the same, he called me a demon. All the neighbors laughed at him."

"I saw that it caused a stir in the global culture," Professor Three Squares continued. "It was at the beginning of the next year that physicists on Earth found out that the pure matter cloud increased the amount of light in the body, or what they called mass. This allowed humans to create their own biological plasma fields, entering Earth into the fourth density.

"The major event that happened following Earth's Ascension was the revelation that not only did certain ethnic groups of humans contained Anunnaki DNA, but there were also kingdoms of the Anunnaki engineered organisms called the Igigi on Earth side by side with humanity. This created quite a stir, with many developing countries descending into mob mentality to rid themselves of their Reptilian neighbors."

"That shit was scary," another student the class said. "I was in church when that happened to me. Everyone freaked out about it, and my friends who I knew at that time for decades started calling me Nephilim, or a fallen angel. People I knew my whole life. Thank Aten Ka my wife on Earth was smart and said that it was because almost everyone had the genes in them since we were genetically modified by them."

"It also helped that the Anunnaki kingdoms on Earth stayed calm throughout the whole ordeal," Professor Three Squares said. "And for a few years, there was relative peace and acceptance until the leaders of the Anunnaki kingdoms began to offer their light for resources, which many nations rejected. It all came to a head on March 30, 2029, when Pierre Boucher agree to supply the nation of France light for five hundred and fifty million Euros a year. That sent a shockwave through the global currency market, when it looked like a leading economy was ready to get off of oil or natural gases.

"Other nations began to follow suite, such as developing ones whose economies couldn't compete with the global super powers. Now these countries were energy independent, and would rather trade with the Anunnaki who practiced equal mass trade instead of with richer economies who kept them in debt with currency trade.

"A particular bad scenario happened in the country of Sudan, where the southern population were mostly Reptilian and wanted to secede and join nations to the south with predominantly Anunnaki ethnic groups, but northern Sudan wouldn't allow them because of the resources of gold and other minerals that were located in the south."

"That was all the United Sates doing that," someone claimed. "We paid off mercenaries to go into southern Sudan and set up illegal mining operations. So when there were natural military conflicts, the U.S. tried to use the excuse that Christians were being attack to go in. It was sick."

"It was then that the Federation decided to extend an invitation to Earth, to offer our support in helping humanity through the Ascension," Three Squares continued. "Scar, your parents met with some of the earth delegates that came to your home world. Do you want to describe what happen?"

"Nothing much," Scar said as he sat up. "Umm…my parents showed them around the planet for a week, just for them to see how our culture and economy was like. We even had them stay at our family castle in New Scarborough. But when my Mom and Dad offered them the conditions to join the Federation, they flat our refused.

"Which is to be expected," Three Squares said. "To inform everyone, the conditions all planets must comply with in order to join the Federation is to move off of oil, natural gas, fission and fusion fuel, and to provide light to all Earth citizens. Earth was to also eliminate currency and individuals had to intermingle with someone of a different haplogroup. If fifty percent of the planets population was able to do this within one hundred cycles, then they would be granted access into and considered persons in the Federation."

"Must be nice to have parents that have privy knowledge to all the answers in the class," a student snidely remarked behind Scar.

"You know what," Scar said as he leaned backwards to look at the student upside down. "If you want to go through the Ascension process like I did and live through all that misery, be my guess bruh."

"I'm sure he meant no offense Scar," Professor Three Squares said. "The summit was a failure but to note two important individuals were present at that meeting. Senator Jennifer Biggs from the United States and Anub Akina from the Independent Caribbean Alliance, both who were offered and accepted to join the Federation Service, both in the Marines, and both went to University during their military stint.

"While they were serving and going to school, there was a reconstructing of Earth's economies as most countries with large Anunnaki populations, such as in western South America and Central Africa began to form their own independent Federation League. This caused former political and military enemies to form a new fiscal alliance. The new G8 became the United States, Russia, China, Britain, Germany, Iran, and Saudi Arabia, economies that stayed oil and currency based to bolster their own currency based market.

"There was an attempt for this new fiscal alliance to begin clandestine operations in the new Federation League when Anub and Jennifer returned to Earth. At that time Jennifer was elected to serve as President of the first global nation-state of the Federation League. With her and Anub they provided security for over forty cycles for the new nation until Jennifer Biggs died on August 8 2082 in the capital of the Federation League, Nairobi, Kenya."

"Holy shit, the United States, China and Russia celebrated that death," one of the students lamented. "There were television and radio stations that were playing 'The Wicked Witch is Dead' from the Wizard of Oz."

"At this time a new G8 was formed," Professor Three Squares said. "It would be the U.S.N.A., India, Russia, China, Iran, Saudi Arabia, Italy, and Germany. Britain decided by this time to join the League, but Germany was convinced to stay by being given tariffs breaks, since they were beginning to think of joining the new European block of the Federation. Only thirty percent of the world's population had decide to go through with the Federation's demands, and it was feared that if Germany joined, it would be the domino that made other nations follow.

"Because of the death of Jennifer Biggs, it was believed that the League's best strategic asset was gone, since at that time she was the only full fifth density being to have ever used their light manipulation capabilities on Earth with military application. So once again nations around the world funded illegal miners to infiltrate League territories, this time in South America, in hopes to sway global opinion against the League for denying individuals access to resources to sale for currency.

"The Federation League tried their best to deal with the problem fiscally with Earth's market, but the Federation only deals in equal trade of mass; a pound of fruits for a pound of linen. Earth's economic profile couldn't accept such terms, so incursions into League land continued, until one faithful day. July 27, 2084 was the day when armed smugglers were confronted with Marines from the League in Western Peru, and when demanded to leave, the mercenaries attacked our Marines with a microwave pulse warhead. No Marines were lost that day, but the League realized that action must be taken.

"The next month came to be known as the Great Incan Road War. Lead by Anub Akina, who at that time was sixth density, led a coalition of Earth citizen forces to claim land in South America. As you know, they took control of all territory in Ecuador, Columbia, and Bolivia. They also took the northern parts of Chile and Argentina, Western Brazil, and most importantly Eastern Panama to control access of the Canal. Anub himself with the help of his daughters physically moved all war ships out of the waterway, just as a show of power.

"That ceased all future incursions into League land for over a decade, and peace actually prevailed for a bit, until Germany tried once again to join the European Federation Block. The G8 offered Germany deal after deal to keep them in the currency based market, but Germany decide to part ways and joined the League, which prompted Poland to consider talks with the Federation.

"Tensions rose on Earth when Western Ukraine decided to separate and join the League. Even though Western Ukraine would allow Russia access to their oil refinery plants in the region, having Western Ukraine secede would give Poland incentive to, which would cut the sub-continent in half, and also would eventually lead other European nations into joining the League and the collapse of the global market in its entirety.

"The G8 countries declared war on Ukraine at that time, in April of 2095. The League decide to stay on the defensive, much to the displeasure of Anub Akina, who wanted to use this opportunity to not only attack Earth's forces, but to claim other nations who quietly wanted to join the League, which would make the last currency based countries give up the fight and the vote to join the Federation would pass.

"For two months the Federation kept a shield up around Western Ukraine, preventing anyone or anything with military value from entering. Then on June 10th of that year the U.S.N.A. launched a supersonic missile using top-secret water sliding technology at Ukraine. It was carrying a neutron bomb, since by then Earth learned that pure matter produced by such a bomb is the closest thing to the light that can be artificially produce.

"The blast killed thousand of lights that had Ascended into the fourth density and weren't ready to block the neutrino shockwave. Anub Akina acted alone and destroyed the only facilities that could produce such weapons, one in Russia and the other in the U.S.N.A. within a matter of minutes. It took that long because he made sure to destroy the facilities and not harm the personnel there."

"The war was called off when the G8 then acknowledge that Anub could easily destroy all military assets on the planet and there was nothing they could do about it. A week would pass while the G8 waited for a response from the League, who stayed quiet. The League at that time approached the Federation and asked for protection, but we couldn't give it to them since we don't like using military solutions in planetary disputes in joining the Federation. The League then decided that on April 11th, 2095, the highest densities on Earth would link League territories into their light an Ascend up into the White, effectively leaving third density Earth and ending the war.

"That's all for today class. Later this week we will go over how based on fiscal stress that the United States faced on the decline of oil use on Earth, the U.S., Canada, and Mexico decided to rework the North American Free Trade Agreement and become one nation, and thereby embrace Mexican culture."

2

Scar sat among many of his football teammates in the campus' indoor gymnasium, which held the hard floor Jai Alai and Pitz court. The football team sat together in their orange and yellow number uniforms on bleachers as fellow students began to arrive and be seated next to the team. There was a cheerleader squad who hyped up everyone who entered the gymnasium, and the students welcomed in joined in the spirit of the sports rally, with the sense of nostalgia filling the arena.

When Scar became a teenager, he had believed that he was on the tall and large side of alien species. His father was just as tall as he, but thinner due to his required vegan diet. Thor was taller, but was as muscular as Scar. The men and women on the team were athletes compared to Scar. The Reptilian and Draconian linemen were a foot taller than he, being massive walls of flesh. He wanted to be receiver, but most of the receivers on the team stood a few inches taller than him. Because he was physically stronger than the receivers, he got the starting half back position, where he also double as the return man. The team didn't run much because of his Andean feet being a liability without light, so he performed mostly chip blocks and short field catches. But what they all did together was good enough for the team to get into Saltal collegiate championship game that school year.

Scar began to notice some of the female gaze that the team was getting from the students, and began to feel uncomfortable when most of the stares turned to him. Scar didn't want to return any of the looks because he knew Sneeze would get pissed, and it was hard to get to sleep at night when she was mad at him. When he saw his role playing crew enter into the arena, he gladly left the team and walked over to sit with them, far from most of the crowd.

"Sup nerds," Scar said as he sat down next to Katah on a bleacher.

"Hmmm, excuse me Principle Carter, the football players are bullying us again," Uncir stated in a nasal nerdy tone.

"Dude, shut the fuck up," Scar laughed as he punched Uncir's shoulder.

"Help, help, school bullying!" Chamahez yelled, dodging away from Scar's strikes.

"You guys are assholes," Scar said as he slouched back onto the bleachers behind the party.

"Come on man, you leave yourself open for it," Utu said as they looked at all the happy students in the gymnasium. "I can't believe everyone still gets hyped up about football."

"Yeah, me too," Katah agreed. "You can feel the testosterone overflowing over here…oh wait, that's you Scar."

"You know what guys…?" Scar grumbled at the party.

"I guess you're not a nerd anymore," Katah lamented. "We lost our barbarian, fellows. It was good while it lasted."

"I wish I could play on the team," Utu admitted.

"Yeah," Chamahez agreed. "Jokes aside, it would've been nice to see what it's like on the field in a legit game."

"Why didn't you guys try out for the team?" Scar asked.

"Dude, look at the size of all the players," Uncir noted. "They make you look normal, Scar, and you're huge."

"Well, I wouldn't mind one of you on the team if it meant I didn't have to deal with all of your harassment," Scar said.

"I tell you what, the way some of the women in the seats look at you is crazy," Katah said, observing a few women looking their way.

"If I was you, Scar…" Chamahez said.

"You'll still be a nerd who can't get a date," Scar laughed, this time dodging Chamahez blows.

"You got to admit that you enjoy all of this, right?" Utu asked Scar.

"I love playing the game," Scar said, brushing the bangs of his blond mohawk away from his eyes. "The attention, not so much."

"If you were single, would you mind?" Uncir asked.

"Do you want me to get murdered?" Scar asked, staring holes into his skull.

"I'm not the one with a ball and chain keeping me from the best bachelor's life ever, loser."

"I swear, you guys aren't content until you make me feel miserable, aren't you?" Scar asked.

"You have a princess fiancé and you're on the football team," Katah said. "I'm jealous, but damn dude, you don't think that's too much."

"Okay, there are like twenty divine princesses over there next to us," Scar said as he pointed to the cheering students following the chants of the cheerleaders. "Just go over and talk to one of them. You guys are practically gods yourself, if not in name but in status anyway."

"Dude, I'm not a god," Katah said as he gave a snide looked to the students. "A lot of these kids are so full of themselves."

"That's unfair," Scar said. "I used to think like you do when I was a kid, but wouldn't admit it. 'Would any of these chicks give me a chance if my density was lower'? You guys are still thinking like you're back on Earth."

"Says the person who's still not comfortable in his own skin," Chamahez laughed.

"You're right, but I admit it," Scar said. "Yes, people date within their social status. That will never change as long as any society has any form of stratification. And there is nothing wrong with that. But you guys are in that same status now. If the opportunity presents itself, go for it. Source knows I tore myself up when I was on Earth over that. I don't want to go through that trauma again."

"Yeah, but you were lucky enough to have Sneeze with you almost the entire time you were on Earth," Uncir stated. "I may bust your chops about it, but being that close to someone to share your light with them? I would love that."

"Then take a chance man," Scar said. "Look, that Lyran right there. She looked over here twice now, and not at me. Go make a move, dude."

"She wasn't looking at me," Uncir said in an almost dejected voice, pissing Scar off enough that he got up and attempted to walk over to the woman before Uncir pulled him back down.

"Fuck man, chill," Uncir grunted at Scar.

"Go, man!"

"Dude, no," Uncir said. "The last thing I want is to have some chick looking down at me."

"Alright, you know what guys?" Scar started into the group. "I'm going to tell you in the face. The whole 'I'm a nice guy' schtick is so full of shit. No chick is going to find you acceptable unless you present yourself as acceptable. And no one wants to date someone who looks down on them. Just for a second, did it ever occur to you guys that the chicks over there think that you're too good for them?" When the party looked at each other in silence, Scar smiled when he knew he was getting his message across.

"Look, we make straight fives in school. We nail all the light manipulation classes. Even if you guys aren't in any divine royal houses, you are all but set up to start your own. Most of the students here got by in life for centuries on just their innate born abilities, not even trying to get better. They look at you guys and see your success and get intimidated. When we were in Seminar, yes the rich kids and the high density jocks ruled the campus. But when they all grew up, these gods realized that it's not young lights that ruled the multiverse. It's us old ones."

"Nice speech," Utu moaned.

"Fuck you dude," Scar snapped back at him. "All I'm saying is that we intimidate them. We have so much more experience than they do. There is this guy I went to school with, Chaac, that I was on the fencing team with. There was this one time when I was goofing off with him because I thought the same way you did. He yells at me like 'Why do all of you 'old lights' look down at me.' These kids aren't used to being around people who aren't impressed with who or what they are. Those princesses are used to guys fawning over them, but they don't know how to talk to you if you don't give two shits about them. And you'll never get the girl if you keep waiting for one of them to recognize that you're nice. You should try being nice to them."

"Hey Scar, get up here!" one of the female cheerleaders yelled at him from in front of the students. When Scar looked over, he saw that the star quarterback, wide receiver, and linebacker all stood next to each other waiting for him to join them.

"Oh, fuck no," Scar muttered.

"Oh no, great Roshi," Chamahez pleaded to Scar. "Please show us the ways of acceptance. Show us how to be nice to the other students here." The party laughed as Scar made his way to the other players, giving them the middle finger as he walked away. Once Scar stood next the other football players, the cheerleaders began a cheer that got all the students pumped up, waving their school color pom-poms in the air and chanting along with the cheerleaders.

"Lugh, Lugh, he's our man, if he can't do it, no one can!" The cheerleaders yelled with the crowd, as the quarterback gave a quick wave to the students.

"Lugh, Lugh, he's our man, if he can't do it, Nimrod can!" the cheer continued with the Anunnaki receiver raising his hand.

"Nimrod, Nimrod, he's our man, if he can't do it, Fenrir can!" the crowd said as the black haired linebacker clapped his hand.

"Fenrir, Fenrir, he's our man, if he can't do it, Scar can!" and once chanted there was a loud ovation from the students, many from the women. Scar pointed to the students, and winced when he looked over at the party, who all gave him a slow soft applause. Scar could do nothing but give them a weak sarcastic smile back.

3

"Wake up Horus," Scar said as he leaned down on his bed in his military house to kiss Horus on his cheek. Horus wanted to sleep with him that night so he could spend as much time with his father before Sneeze came to pick him up later that day. Horus squirmed for a bit, and almost fell back to sleep before Scar poked his pale white cheeks, this time annoying Horus enough that he wiggled around to avoid Scar's touch.

"Come on, time to take a shower," Scar said as he picked up his sleepy son out of bed and into the bathroom. He took off both of their clothes and turned on the faucet water before Horus stepped into the shower and stood underneath the stream. He blinked his dark eyes to keep the water out as his white haired became drench. Scar took a bar of soap and lather both of them up, letting Horus do the same so he can copy him as he washed.

After the two rinsed off and left the shower, Horus quickly ran off like a little bouncing lamp to his room so he could put his clothes on without any assistance. After Scar put on a shirt and a pair slacks, he went to check on Horus progression. Horus stood before his little bed with his briefs on, but was struggling to put his shirt over his head. He always managed to get the sleeves in the wrong position.

"You want me to help?" Scar asked as he approached Horus.

"No!" Horus insisted as he pulled his shirt on the wrong way again, then look at what his father was wearing.

"You wearing that?" Horus asked.

"Yeah," Scar answered, and watched as Horus put the clothes he first picked out back and chose new ones that looked like what Scar was wearing. When he struggled with his new shirt, Scar shifted it around until Horus had it on properly. Horus didn't wait to says thanks before he went to put on a pair of pants, then pulled Scar out of his room and towards the kitchen.

"Eat breakfiss," Horus demanded as they stopped in front of the fridge.

"What do you want to eat?" Scar asked as he looked inside. "Do you want fruit salad? Eggs?"

"Eggs," Horus ordered, and he held on to Scar's pants as Scar picked out eggs to cook. After taking some Nimian butter and choosing a frying pan, Scar turned on the stove and lathered the pan with some butter before cracking all the eggs into it.

"I want to cook!" Horus yelped as he bounced up and down next to Scar.

"It's too hot," Scar explained before he picked up Horus and guided his hand near the stove.

"Hot," Horus said when he felt the heat from the stove.

"See," Scar giggled. "When you're older and aren't able to feel the heat, I'll teach you how to cook." Horus nodded in Scar's arm as he watched his father finish their breakfast. Scar placed Horus down and put their eggs on plates and took them over to the table so they both could eat. Scar tried to help Horus eat his food, but Horus just grew a temper tantrum when he tried.

"Eat!" Horus ordered Scar, so Scar went back to his food so he and Horus could eat like equals. When he was done, Horus rushed off to his room while Scar picked their plates to wash them. Horus quickly returned with his bubble container and headed to the front door.

"Bubbles!" Horus yelled at Scar, who quickly washed their dishes before he joined Horus outside. It was a beautiful spring mourning, with the trees surrounding the military housing blossoming white flowers. The neighborhood children too young for Seminary played outside in packs of gangs running or flying everywhere. Horus sat down on the grass in front of Scar's house and open his bubble container, taking the top off and trying to blow bubbles into the breeze. He had a hard time, and when Scar tried to help him, Horus would push him away until he was able to get a good stream, and only then would he give the top to Scar so he could blow some.

They did that for a couple of sections before Horus got tired of it and wanted to go to the store, desiring snacks for his trip back home to Roi Son. After placing the bubbles back in his room, they walked hand in hand to the corner market, but stopped midway when kids in a park saw them walking by.

"Horus!" they yelled, and Horus' light bloomed and became solid as he anticipated playing with his friends.

"I'm playing with my friends," Horus informed Scar. "Stay."

"Okay," Scar laughed as he sat down in the grass and Horus dashed to the park, roughhousing with all the kids there. When he got a little too excited or out of breath, he would run back into Scar's big arms to rest for a bit, but after a moment would burst off again to join the ruckus. When Horus began to desire a snack, he remembered that he and his father were walking to the store to buy some. He said bye to his friends without waiting for their answer and ran back to his father, yanking him up and continuing on to the store.

They were only there for a short time, enough to buy some treats and a drink before they began their march back home. Horus walked happily along side Scar, his hands covered in crumbs as he ate from one of the hard bread packages. When they got close to home they saw the large, black, block shaped vehicle that Sneeze was driven in in front of Scar's house, with Sneeze standing next to it, dressed in another of Athena's set of Andean clothing, waving at them.

"Hi Mommy!" Scar and Horus yelled as the rushed over to hug Sneeze.

"Hello my boys!" Sneeze said as she picked up Horus, making sure to wipe the crumbs off his fingers.

"Are you boys having a good time?" Sneeze asked as she kissed their cheeks.

"Yes," they answered simultaneously.

"Do you have everything packed up?" Sneezed asked Scar.

"Yes," Scar said before he went inside the house and grabbed Horus things from his room, placing them in the back of the vehicle when he returned.

"Give your father a hug before you leave," Sneeze instructed Horus, who ran to his father to get snatched up.

"Love you Daddy," Horus said into Scar's neck.

"Love you too, son," Scar said as he walked over to Sneeze to hug her.

"Are you going to visit Groen Stad soon?" Sneeze asked kissing Scar.

"Yeah," Scar said. "I'll have leave in four months hopefully. There some shit going down…"

"Sonlig, Horus is listening."

"Sorry," Scar said with a rueful smile. "There's a conflict going on in Dwarka space near Mangala. The Federation can't openly act, but Aunt Chac'chel wants special forces in the region in case anything needs to happen."

"Just be careful," Sneeze said as she continued to kiss Scar.

"I will," Scar said as he hugged Sneeze and Horus in his arms, holding them there when he didn't want to let go.

"We got to go, Sonlig," Sneeze spoke into Scar's cheek.

"Okay," Scar said reluctantly as he let his family go. After they climbed into their vehicle they were driven down the road, with Horus waving out the window until they disappeared from sight. Scar waved goodbye until they were gone, then turned back to his house, stopping in front of the door and waiting, not wanting the dream to end.

CHAPTER 14

1

Scar stood on the twenty yard line on the football field late in the evening, his Light drained from his body, slowly breathing in and out the warm evening air to keep himself calm before the kickoff. It was late in the fourth quarter with almost two minutes left in the game. The scored was tied, and Ya'ax Mont had this one chance to run the clock out and score, giving them the championship.

It was a brutal and low scoring game, with the defense doing most of the work and keeping both teams in the competition. Throughout the game one black maned lion linebacker from Ashanti University, Aboagye Sai, hounded Scar the whole time, over powering him and making his life blocking for the quarterback miserable. Scar was never able to get his rhythm going the whole game, leaving the other receivers to pick up his slack.

Ashanti University students screamed at the top of their lunges, trying to get into the players head before kickoff, but Scar completely blocked it out, just looking at the football, mentally going over his technique before the ball went into the air. He managed to take one quick look into Ya'ax Mont's section to find the party, waving at him before the start of play.

"CRUSH YOUR ENEMIES!!" they roared at him, making Scar laughed as he clapped his hands above his head.

"CROM!!" Scar screamed back at them, the group howling with laughter as Ashanti University prepared for kick off. Scar's body went limp, his feet dancing below him as the opposing team kicked the ball into the air. He followed the balls ascent into the air above, feeling a little happy that he had to move forward because of a short kick.

He gave one last glance to his side to see if anyone snuck on him in his periphery, and panicked when he saw two defensive players closer than he expected. He clinched up instinctively, momentarily pausing time, then quickly drained his light and waved his and to signal for a fair catch. He hoped that nobody caught his mistake, but the referees blew their whistles before Scar caught the ball in his cupped arms. He stood there with cinched teeth in anguish, the opposing team rushing by him as one swatted the ball out of his hand.

"Infraction on the receiving team," the head ref announced to the audience with his light. "Illegal use of light, number twenty one on the offense. Fifteen yard penalty, first down."

"Fuck!" Scar screamed at himself as he ran to his team huddle on the field, knowing he just put his team on the five yard line.

"That's our bad Scar!" one of the guys on the special team yelled at him, but Scar didn't listen to him, his frustration boiling over as he stood next to his teammates.

"Shake it off, Scar. Just focus on the next play," Lugh said, slapping Scar on his helmet. "Lets drive this fucking ball down the field and win this game. Lets be heroes, alright. Panther, Tango hook, Yancy slant, Jimmy long, X-ray hitch, break!"

"Break!" the team yelled as they clapped, everyone getting into position for the play.

"I got you, your Highness!" Scar heard a yell from across the scrimmage line, and Scar looked over to Aboagye staring him down, his black mane flowing out of his black and silver helmet.

"I'm going to make you wish you never crawled out of your castle!" Aboagye roared at him, his teeth glaring from the stadium lights.

"I'm right here, punk!" Scar yelled back as he hunched down, ready for the ball to be hiked.

"Fifty three mike!" Lugh informed the line, pointing at Aboagye. The lineman shifted their stance to prepare for him, but Aboagye didn't care, confident that he could burst through the line and get to the quarterback.

"Ready, set, HIKE, HIKE, go!" Lugh yelled, attempting to draw the defense across the line. When the ball was snapped, the tight end and the right receiver dashed down the field, the tight end swirling around back to the line of scrimmage, the receiver turning more inward towards the center of the field, hoping to draw in of one the safeties.

Lugh wanted to wait to see what the safeties were going to do, but Aboagye burst through the line past the linemen. Scar blocked him the best he could, but Aboagye over powered him too, practically running over him and forcing Lugh to throw the ball early, the tight end barely able to touch it before it fell to the ground. Aboagye roared into Scar's face before he went back to the rest of his teammates, who all slapped or headbutted his helmet.

"Shake it off," Lugh said once everyone was in the huddle. "Alright, Panther, Tango slant, Yancy long, Jimmy slant in, X-ray chip. Break!"

"Break!" the team shouted with a clap. Scar heart pumped a little harder as he got to his position to the left of the quarterback. Right on cue, Aboagye was back at it again, harassing Scar.

"You're done with your support group, because you're going to need it!" the linebacker snapped at Scar. 'Because I'm been bullying you all night long!"

"Come bully me, I'm right here!" Scar shouted back before getting ready for the next play.

"Ready!... set!... HIKE!... go!" Lugh yelp before the ball snapped. The receivers all ran down the field, and just as before, Aboagye burst through the line. Scar block him, but immediately released, just at the same time when the receiver on his side turned right and ran to the center of the field, leaving the left side with an empty hole. As hoped, Lugh threw the ball over Aboagye's head and Scar caught it, running for only six yards before the defense sniffed out the play and tackled him, forcing their team to call a time out. Looking at the clock they only had one minute and thirty five dots left.

"Lets keep moving," Lugh said in the huddle. "Panther, Tango slant, Yancy long hook, Jimmy long post, X-ray chip and hook, on Hike, break!" The teamed broke the huddle, lining up in their positions. Both teams jarred at each other before the ball was snapped.

"Ready...set...Hike!" Lugh said, catching the defense off guard when he quickly snapped the ball, with the tight end and the receiver on the right running down the field, with the tight end slanting towards the center. Scar chipped block Aboagye and released like before, and Aboagye hesitated, wanting to chase Scar but deciding to go after the open quarterback.

When the right receiver and Scar hooked back towards the line of scrimmage, the defensive players all followed suit, leaving another hole open for a small window of time down the left side of the field. Lugh braced himself for a hit as he released the ball, being tackled while the ball found his target with the left receiver for a thirty yard gain, but he was tackled before he could get out of bounds. With their team calling timeout, that left them with just a minute left and one timeout.

"Going back to you Scar," Lugh said in the huddle. "Panther, Tango slant, Yancy long, Jimmy slant in, X-ray chip. Break!"

"Break!" Scar yelled, and searched across the line but didn't see Aboagye in front of him. Aboagye fell back near the safeties, while another linebacker lined up on Scar's side, ready to blitz.

"Fifty five, mike!" Lugh informed, pointing out the new blitzer. "Ready… set…HIKE…HIKE…go!" When the ball snapped, the linebacker before Scar didn't blitz, only following Scar as he ran up the field, while at the same time Aboagye faked going up field, but blitz through a free lane in the center of the line, chasing down Lugh who was forced to throw the ball out of bounds.

"Shit!" Scar grunted at himself as he ran back to the huddle, thinking he should have stayed and blocked. Aboagye went right up into Scar's face to let him know about this mistake.

"What's wrong, little prince," the linebacker said into Scar's helmet. "You scared now? You don't want to block me?" That only got Scar hot as he pushed Aboagye away from him, creating a small scuffle before the refs pulled everyone apart and on their line of the scrimmage.

"Hey, Fifty Three is after Scar," Nimrod said once the team was back into the huddle. "Lets use that."

"Alright," Lugh agreed. "Ignore the sideline guys, this is our plan. Ranch, right gash, on Hike, break!" The team clapped their hand and when they made their running formation, their sideline erupted in anger trying to make them stop and almost calling a timeout. Lugh waved them off that idea, and prepared the blocking assignments for the run.

"Hey, I'm coming right at you!" Scar yelled at Aboagye. "I hope you're ready, cause I'm going right over you!"

"I'm ready little prince!" Aboagye roared back. "I got my kitchen open! I'm serving L's tonight!"

"Ready…set…HIKE!" Lugh sounded, handing the ball to Scar who patiently waited for a seam to open, and when he punched through, Aboagye slammed right into to him, taking Scar off his toe cleats and into the turf.

"You don't want any of this, little prince!" Aboagye screamed at Scar as he got up, but Scar ignored him as they rushed back into his huddle, the quarterback waving off the coach who wanted to call a timeout.

"Play action, Ranch sprint left, Yancy chip, break!"

"You know his a king, right?" Nimrod told Scar before they went back into their running positions.

"Hey, King Sai!" Scar yelled at Aboagye when he got to his spot. "I'm about to dethrone you! I'm going to rent out your throne!"

"Keep talking, little man!" Aboagye snapped, clearly mad yet cheerful, seeing Scar trying to get under his skin. "My shop's open! Come get another serving!"

"Ready…set…HIKE…HIKE…go!" Lugh commanded, lunging to Scar's left, slapping Scar in the chest. Scar held his chest tightly, and when he cleared the line tried to break for open field before Aboagye wrapped his legs underneath him. The linebacker was about to cheer but noticed that Lugh threw the ball to Nimrod, who was wide open after a chip blocked. The Ya'ax Mont students erupted in jubilation as Nimrod ran towards the goal line, but was chased and tackled just five yards shy of it on the left side of the field. Everyone rushed down to the goal line as quickly as possible, and when Lugh snapped and threw the ball to the ground, there was nine seconds left and they had only one time out left.

"Lets run the ball down their throats!" Lugh shouted at the team once they were in the huddle, getting everyone as pumped as he was. "Okay, Tango sprint left, play right, on second Hike, break!"

"Break!" the team shouted and clapped as the got in the running positions. This time both teams stayed quiet, with Ashanti University's students yelling at the top of there lungs to keep the offense from hearing the snap. Scar was surprisingly calm through this, even a little sad when Aboagye didn't dig into him. Win or lose, this sensation that everyone was feeling at that exact moment was to Scar the best part of the game. The only thing that made it better was Sneeze's light in his, enjoying all the adrenaline rushing through him and the sensation of his physical form, clearly being excited by it.

"READY…SET…HIKE…HIKE!!" Lugh screamed, and all at once all the players on the line lunged to the right towards the open field, drawing the defense with them. Except for the tight end and Scar, with Scar leading the head block while Lugh moved towards the spot where Scar was supposed to be, then stepped back to put the ball in the tight ends hand.

Scar stayed low behind the linemen, hoping the he was blocked from sight, and when he reached the end of the left side of the line, saw Aboagye trying to sneak in and behind the line to catch the runner who was supposed to run right. Caught off guard, Scar blocked upwards at Aboagye, knocking him off his feet, which made the entire audience 'woah'! in amazement. That block allowed the tight end to plow over another linebacker before barely reaching the endzone, who then spiked the football down as hard as she could when she scored, screaming at the top of her lungs as the rest of team ambushed her.

When the offense rushed back to the sideline and the special team unit ran out and performed a routine field goal, that gave Ashanti University only two seconds left to try and tie the game and send it into overtime. While Ya'ax Mont students shouted at the top of their voices, waving their yellow and orange ribbons and flags in the air, the football team all held hands or knelt, praying to Aten Ka to somehow change the fate of the game, which would be an illegal play. Once the ball was kicked off to the opposing team, the yelling went from a constant state of panic when Ashanti received the ball, to joy for Ya'ax Mont when the Ashanti player was tackled moments after he caught the ball.

Scar ripped the helmet off his head and ran onto the field, running in any random direction as the Ya'ax Mont players screamed in joy at their victory. It took forever for the coaches to wrangle all the players together so both teams could congratulate each side for a good game.

"Nice block!" Aboagye said as he grabbed Scar in his arms. "I didn't even see you from behind the O-linemen!"

"Man, you were the best player on the field!" Scar yelled into Aboagye ear to make sure he heard him. "To bad you can't go pro. You could probably make it onto a Federation pro team!"

"Man, no aristocratic school athlete can make it onto a team!" Aboagye laughed. "Beside, we both know I can't. It sucks being a divine god, right."

"Right!" Scar laughed. "See you next year!"

"We'll beat you next year!" Aboagye shouted as he dashed off to join his team in the locker room. Scar searched the stands for the party, who waved him down to one end of the stands.

"The lamentation of the women!" they shouted as they slapped Scar's shoulder pads.

"Yes, that is best!" Scar yelled back at them.

"Hey man, they're presenting the trophy!" Katah pointed out as he looked onto the field. "You better get out there!"

"I'll see you guys later!" Scar said as he slowly jogged his way to the team, a bit melancholy now that the season was over.

2

The party arrived at the campus park at night where students of Ya'ax Mont gathered to celebrate the football team's championship win. As they walked along the campus paths, Scar looked into the sky where large holographic screens floated in the air, modulating as they also blasted music into the night sky. The screens would switch views from students to students, who would either dance, make out, or look like fools for all to see.

Inside the park large groups of students congregated together, shouting and dancing as deejays that played on a stand next to the school's founder statue work their magic, trying to create as many beats out of their light's as they could. As the music dove into the participants light's, the combine sense of euphoria and naivety made all the students almost forget all sense of decency. To Scar, it looked like any normal rave on an Ivy league campus. The more Scar thought about it, the more he concluded that perhaps that's why he went through the Ascension, to noticed this detail. Knowing this made Scar aware of the things he knew he should and shouldn't do, but maybe that was also what was taking a small amount of joy out of him.

"This party is lit," Utu said as they walked through the dense crowd. "Man, these girls have lost their minds."

"No, they know what they are doing," Katah said. "You still thinking like a man from Earth. Those rules don't apply here."

"Yeah I see that," Uncir said as they watched a hot pale gray Sirian chick put the moves on a Doggan fellow seating next to her. At one point she slid her hands between his legs, and the Doggan flicked his blue to green fish scales in nervousness, which pleased the Sirian woman who took another swig from her plastic cup.

"To bad girls back on Earth didn't do this," Chamahez said as the party arrived at a food stand. "It would have made dating so much easier."

"That's because they would have been labeled a slut," Utu informed the group.

"Remember when that one NASCAR chick dated, like, two guys at the same time?" Katah asked.

"Shit, everyone tried to make a big deal out of it," Uncir grumbled. "Let the woman get some dick. Damn, she earned it. That's the whole point of moving up in status in a culture. You attract more possible partners to you. What's wrong with dating as many of them as possible until you find the right one?"

"Or three," Scar added.

"Word," Utu agreed.

"I'm just saying," Chamahez continued after munching down on a morsel from the stand. "We kind of had the shit end of the deal growing up in on Earth when it came to dating. Guys were still stuck with asking the girl out, even though women wanted to be treated the same as men."

"That was only in the U.S.," Scar said. "I've been other places where women put the moves on me and no one blinks an eye."

"The U.S. was always fifty years behind everyone else when it came to social issues," Katah said. "Like women who bust their ass to get a good job, but wonder why there aren't any men on her level that she can date when she took the job of one of them."

"The whole dating down thing?" Uncir asked as he took a drink of alcohol from a plastic cup.

"Fuck yeah," Katah continued. 'Like, if you want to create a world where the sexes are equal, then the social responsibilities got to be shared too. You can't take a good job, and still expect to marry someone who pays the bills. You moved in status, you took that role, now go get your partner."

"Like I said, men get the shit end of the deal back on Earth," Chamahez said. "We're stuck having to be the man, which was equivalent to being the bread winner on Earth. If we were to marry a chick on Earth who made the money in the house…"

"Which there is nothing wrong with that," Scar chimed in.

"…Then that guy's a loser. His less than a man. But if a woman marries a man in that equal society, she won the jackpot. There is no penalty for her."

"No, Katah's right," Scar said. "That's only in the U.S. man."

"Yeah, well, women back then needed to change their perspective. They asked men to change, but didn't account that they needed to change too. Like, if you're still in the concept of not dating down, then you eliminate so many guys that could make you happy."

"Dude, were you spurned by some chick back on Earth?" Utu laughed.

"I'm being serious here," Chamahez insisted.

"I think you hit the booze to hard," Uncir said snidely.

"No, I get what you're saying," Scar sympathized with Chamahez. "Look at Frig over there." They all turned to see the tight end who scored the winning touchdown as she danced in the midst a women who either danced by her or had their hands on or in her clothes.

"She's living the life right now. As she should. You can't expect to have someone that athletic, that gorgeous, and that high in the social status to not have trim dangling all over her. If she had men all over her now, nobody here would have a problem with it; this just happens to be a culture that sees the light more than the form the light is in. But if she was on Earth and had guys all over here, she be stigmatized."

"But that's not what I'm trying to say," Chamahez countered.

"I know," Scar concurred. "What you're saying is that if she had the mentality like most women in the U.S. did back then, and wanted to be seen as equals, but only wanted to date up, there wouldn't be a single male in that section of the universe that would meet Frig's criteria. And she would probably wonder where all the all the 'good men' are at.

"For the longest time on Earth the only way a women was able to move up in status was to marry up. That's why Prince Charming didn't really matter in all those Disney movies, or if the princess actually loved him. It was his social status that's more important. But only women are allowed to date up, not men. I get it, it's bullshit."

"So what does a guy have to do to get a date?" Utu pondered.

"On Earth, we'd have to wait for a woman to ask us out since we understand it all," Scar assed. "But we know that would never happen. Here, there's no excuse. We are theses gods equals. And there is nothing wrong with dating on the same social status."

"We could date down," Uncir suggested.

"Yeah, would you be satisfied by a person who wasn't an old light that was lower in density than you?" Scar asked. "It's like having to go through the Ascension process again after going through it once. Fuck that shit."

"Okay, that's hypocritical of you, you know," Chamahez pointed out. "You were engaged as a child, and your fiancé is like your best friend who stayed with you during the whole process. And she's lower density than you."

"Touché," Scar agreed with a laugh.

"It's still intimidating though," Chamahez said. "Okay, I get it. I still got that Earth mentality in me. But man, look at these woman. They're goddesses, man. There so beautiful, and smart."

"And powerful," Utu added.

"And so much better than us," Katah chimed in.

"Dude, you're equals," Scar said. "So it would be easier if these chicks were lower density. If that's the case, you all should have been married by now with a girl completely enamored by your auras. But what do you have to lose with asking out a divine supermodel? If they are enlighten, they would give you a chance. If not, there's another one right there."

"Hey Scar!" a female voce called out, and the group turned to see a short Zeta in a little red dress walk up next to Scar to get something to eat.

"What up, Three Spheres," Scar said. "What are you trying to do up in this party? Get some dick?"

"Hopefully," Three Spheres said. "How's Sneeze. Is she with you right now?"

"No, she's taking a nap. She didn't want to be bugged by all this music all night."

"It's got to be rough on you guys being on different sleeping patterns," Three Spheres said. "You really can't share your light all the time like you want."

"No, we do," Scar said. "We share it all the time. And I mean all the time."

"I stand corrected," Three Spheres said as she looked at the rest of the party. "Who's your friends?"

"Party, this is Three Spheres," Scar said to his friends.

"Hi," the party said in unison.

"Hi," Three Sphere said as she gave a drink to Katah. "What's your name?"

"Katah," he answered as he took the drink.

"I see you're an old light like Scar. Are you from Earth too?"

"Yeah."

"I love your feathers," Three Sphere's said as she ran her fingers through his brown foliage. "It's like you're some bird of prey. I bet you can snatch any girl out there."

"I don't think so," Katah said.

"But wait, you don't have a phallus like most male sexes do. You have a cloaca right?"

"Holy shit," Uncir whispered.

"Yeah," Katah answered nervously.

"So, you have the have sex like women have sex together, right?" Three Spheres asked as she pulled Katah towards the central area of the park so they can dance.

"Damn," Scar said as the party watched them leave. "I didn't know Katah was a one drink ho."

"She didn't buy dinner or anything," Utu joked.

"You know, like, take me out to a movie or something," Chamahez complained as they watched Katah dance with Three Spheres. Three Spheres continued to question Katah, placing her hips firmly against his. When Katah glanced back at the party, they all gave him an emphatic thumbs ups.

"Okasan, Otosan, I'm going to be a man tonight," Scar muttered as the rest of the party laughed in agreement.

CHAPTER 15

155 AA

1

Scar stood in front of his refrigerator, looking inside for something to eat that would take him half a section of his time before he meets with his professors to give his dissertation. He was somewhat proud of himself that he managed to stay in school that long. The road to your doctorate was hard in Federation curriculum, due to the fact that you have to come up with an original idea out of an infinite number of ones in a multiverse. One would think that with that amount of individuals to study throughout the history of the multiverse, it'll be easy to come up with an original. That's when most students learn that no matter what form or what culture a Light is in, that Light is the same no matter where you find it. So it's actually very hard to find an original idea.

Out of the first group of students Scar was in class with, the majority quit school once they reached their Master's equivalent. Even Uncir, Utu, and Chamahez quit after they got their degrees and found girls they can settle with. It does help if you have two women in your head that loves you but won't take any excuses from you either to get your doctorate. Still, no matter what the professors say at this point, after cycles of internships in different planets congressional halls, writing laws for the lawmakers who are supposed to write them themselves, Scar can safely say that he feels he accomplished something. Which will mean jack shit in a couple of hours when the professors reject his thesis.

After Scar picked out some items so he could make a sandwich, he walked back upstairs to his bedroom and turned the computer back on. He skimmed through his dissertation a few more times, trying to make sure everything was edited properly, that the phrasings and meaning was easily conveyable. To make sure that there was no misunderstanding on what he thought was an excellent idea.

He knew that he was going to have a hard time presenting his thesis. His teachers and parents told him that all old lights usually present a thesis on how to better integrate third density beings into the Federation, like the one he was trying to present. And all of them failed. That's why he did what most of them did and made a second thesis, knowing that he won't get as good a grade as the first one, but still a passing one. But you never can tell; perhaps Scar would be the first.

"Hey Scar, you busy?" Fatah broadcast in his light.

"No…no…what's up?"

"When's your dissertation? Three Spheres and I want to go to the plaza and buy a new outfit."

"It's in a few minutes," Scar said as he turned his computer off and went over to his closest to change his clothes.

"Oh shit, my bad," Katah apologized. "Do you want us to wait?"

"No dude, you guys go. I'll meet up with you later. There's a drama festival that has a new play that's going to open tonight. Lets go there after I get out."

"No way man. That's why Three Sphere's wanted to go shopping. She wanted to hit the club tonight to celebrate her thesis getting accepted."

"Oh dude, she got her doctorate?!" Scar shouted. "Tell her congrats. Shit, I don't want to bog you guys down. She's probably wants to get you liquored up so you can be easy tonight, like the one drink ho you are."

"Aten Ka, that shit is not going away," Katah groaned in his head.

"Make sure she picks something that makes her look beautiful."

"Actually, she wants to go shopping for me," Katah said.

"Ouch!" Scar laughed as he fixed his tie as the last piece of his business suit he put on. "No, I understand. She got to make sure her trophy boyfriend is looking sharp."

"Dude, you can eat a fat dick."

"You guys have fun tonight," Scar insisted with a laugh. "I can kill some time myself anyways. Benefit of having someone to share your light with, right?"

"You sure you don't want to come out with us?" Katah asked. "It'll be more fun for us if you came."

"Begone… thot!"

"Fuck you dude!" Katah laughed. "Later nerd!"

"Later," Scar said as he made some last minute adjustment, then headed out of his suite and towards the political science department of the campus. After he went inside the building and went to the faculty office to let them know he was there, he sat in a waiting chair, nervously twitching his leg, counting the time until he was called into the professors chambers.

"Sonlig?" Sneeze called out to him.

"Yeah, Sweat Pea?" Scar answered in his light.

"You're sure you don't want to go out with your friend?" Sneeze asked.

"No, I'll just be a third wheel on a bike," Scar insisted.

"I wanted you to go. I wanted to see you dance. I like seeing you dance."

"What, you wanted to rub one off while you watch me?"

"Shut up," Sneeze laughed. "You should go. You'll have fun."

"No," Scar said. "I think that Three Spheres' going to pop the question to Katah. She really loves him."

"Then you should be there," Sneeze said.

"Nah, that's okay. I'm happy for them, but it'll just make me think of you."

"Oh. I'm sorry."

"It's okay."

"You'll be able to graduate soon," Sneeze reminded Scar. "That's one step closer to us being together."

"Yeah," Scar agreed.

"Scar," a professor said as he poked his head out of the teachers chamber. "We're ready for you."

"Good luck," Sneeze said.

"Thanks, Sweet Pea," Scar said physically before he approached the teacher. "How's it going, Doctor Ah'cun?"

"Good Scar," Doctor Ah'cun said as he led him into an oval room with a wall covered with wooden bookshelves filled with books. In the center of the room was a circular table on a red rug that stood in the center of the wooden floor. Light flooded in the room from the windows, shining on the two other professors who stood by the table waiting for Scar.

"Hello, Doctor Isis, Doctor Maneki," Scar greeted the two.

"Hello, Scar," Doctor Isis said before they all sat down. "We are ready whenever you are."

"Alright," Scar said as he found a panel that was hidden on the wooden table and turned on the computer to access his files, creating a presentation for the teachers. "So, my thesis will largely go over the events that transpired during the Arkaim Secession War that happened over six hundred cycles ago. As we know, that civilization was part of the Moksha Empire, a third density culture that was on the cusp of the Fourth Density in the Solntse system. As most civilizations that are third density, they then used fiat currency as a social tool of cultural exchange.

"However, with the discovery of microwave technology, and the use of that technology to produce close to sound speed, the reaches of their solar system became more accessible. Because of this, the new resources found throughout the system, including quick travel to Erzya, a nearby un-inhabited garden world in there solar system, placed the current fiscal market under stress. Philosophical debate raged on the planet of Moksha at that time, about rather the current market should be scrapped and a new one made now that there was resources abound to ensure a good quality of life for all of Moksha's citizens.

"This coincided with the rise of the Arkaim monk culture, priests that were able to access the light. It was soon discovered that individuals on the world who went through the Ascension process like the monks were able to better navigate space by lowering their resistance to Aten Ka. As other entrepreneurs on the planet began to take on this new lifestyle, their success clashed with established oligarchy who refused to change their way of thinking."

"This lead to the creation of the Yamna culture, a new nation state comprised of these entrepreneurs that was entirely off-world and explored their system. This nation ended up being the default logistic service for the Moksha's Empire. Problems raised again when the Yamna nation contacted the Federation, and talks began for them to join the Federation and be a bridge for the rest of Moksha to join."

"Things didn't go well when Yamna introduced equivalent mass trade, and soon war was suggested on planet Moksha. It was then that the Yamna nation decided to colonize Erzya and make that planet their new home, creating the capital Arkaim and successfully joining the Federation. This did not sit well with Moksha, and a large invasion fleet was created in hopes of blockading the Federation from Erzya.

"Moksha fatal mistake was not understanding the Light and the capabilities of an individual who uses it. In the cycle of 25 AC on Erzya, when Moksha's fleet had just arrived into Erzya's orbit, Commander Ixchel of the 42nd Fleet flew into the Solntse system at faster than sound speed, and dove into the waters of reality above Erzya, creating a reality shockwave that decimated the Moksha fleet. Once the majority of the vessels were disabled, the 42nd and 103rd Fleets entered the system, safe guarding Erzya and ending the war.

"The problems that lead to the war may have been cultural in base, and in large part to the Yamna nation occupying Erzya without creating a proper agreement with the Moksha Empire. But there are other solutions that the Federation can use to help settle disputes such as these to help bring in systems that are on the cusp of the fourth density. One solution that can be utilized is to create an explorer colony near…Aten Ka she's right behind me isn't she?"

"Yes she is," Doctor Ah'cun said as the other teachers laughed in Ixchel's direction who was seated behind Scar on his side of the table.

"Ah…yes," Scar continued. "One solution that could be used would be to create a nearby explorer colony near the civilization, since cultures of the Moksha Empire had already established contact with the Federation. This was done in the Mangala system, when the society there had just contacted the Federation."

"But the colony was establish only after the population voted to join the Federation," Professor Maneki stated. "And with the popular vote of over seventy percent."

"Yes, but I propose that we should do so earlier," Scar suggested. "A colony should be set in a manner in which it should take an collective endeavor to reach the colony, to make sure that no one culture is disenfranchised from others."

"Or an opportunistic culture could go about and conquer their world and seize control of the planets resources to reach such colony," Doctor Isis said, scratching her Sirian light gray arm.

"Yes," Scar agreed.

"And what's more, what would differentiate such explorer colony from the conquering culture that it would soon exchange with?"

"Such colony would have to follow strict guidelines established by the Federation that no unethical misconduct will be practice with the civilization."

"Which will still be mute if we interact with the conquering culture," Doctor Ah'cun countered. "Also, this still would place such individuals who interact with the Federation in a significant social and economic advantage over everyone else in their cultures. If a problem was created before they contacted us, then there would be one after contact."

"What if we tried?" Scar offered. "What if I was to set up a colony to interact with a third…"

"Then I would disown you," Ixchel announced behind Scar, causing him to shudder from the coldness of her voice. Scar drew in a long breath, running his hand through his mohawk before settling his eyes on the table's surface.

"We know what you are trying to suggest," Doctor Ah'cun said. "That's why we suggest to all old light students to create two dissertations, knowing that the mass majority in this field would suggest what you have done. And it's not something that the Federation hasn't tried before. Rather it is the celestial or terrestrial colony, the interbreed culture or the divine messenger method, all of these methods failed because we tried to change cultures at the macro level.

"The only method that has ever found success for us at a higher percentage was the individual Ascension process. If those individuals were to create a following, a culture onto themselves, which would create similar problems that we discussed before, then so be it. But we are only interested in those particular individuals we work with. And if they fail, we would informed them of what they did wrong and offer them the chance to retry. We know that you want to help Earth, but you would do more harm than good if you did."

"Okay," Scar said after a sigh of deep reflection. "So I guess that I should present my second argument. So…um…recently the Chichen just joined the Federation, in House Xkit. It was a long process, due to the fact that they were an Andean culture that shun the use of Aten Ka for empirical principles. After decades of negotiations with the Federation they decide to join, but some of the breakthrough may have come about with the practice of the sport Jai Alai. The sport was very popular among the elite of the Chichen culture, and during heavily televised multinational games much progress was reached between the two cultures. I propose that we should develop different methods of using intracultural sport events to help bridge the gap of any civilization on the brink of joining the Federation…"

2

156 AA

"How long do you have until you go to boot camp?" Sneeze asked as she sat on Scar's bed looking out the window towards the city.

"Only a month," Scar said as he packed his clothes in his luggage case. "My mom doesn't want me to waste any time. The quicker I'm in, the quicker my ten cycles are done, we can get married and I'm sworn in as Speaker."

"You didn't want to be an officer?' Sneezed asked as she spotted a news outlet camera floating by outside the house.

"I thought about that, but my parents said no. I understand. Being an officer teaches you to separate yourself from your men. That would be a bad habit to build if I'm going to be Speaker. Plus, my way of thinking is NCO based. That'll be something other officers would hate."

"I don't know, it would have been nice to be married to an officer and a gentleman."

"Then you're engaged to the wrong dude," Scar laughed. "Plus, the best way to learn how to serve the people in House Xkit is to follow orders, not give them."

"Okay," Sneeze agreed, leaning back on the bed. "I still would have love to see you in an officer's uniform."

"The enlisted dress uniforms are nice," Scar said as he finished packing his clothes and walked over to Sneeze, cupping her breast through the Andean white shirt she wore.

"Your mom can see us," Sneeze reminded Scar.

"Uh huh," Scar said as he continued to fondle her.

"Scar, can I ask you something?" Sneeze asked as she bore into Scar's light, grabbing Scar's hand into hers.

"Shoot."

"Did you ever want to go see how Kathrine is doing?" Sneeze asked innocently, and Scar recoiled from the question, snatching his hand from Sneeze. His chest tighten a bit and a fear rose in his light, but Scar instinctively calmed himself like how Chac'chel taught him.

"I don't want to think about that," Scar said as he tried to compose himself.

"I'm sorry," Sneeze said as she studied Scar's light. "Do you miss her?"

"I don't want to think about that," Scar stated. "I love you. I'm here. I don't want to think about that."

"I'm sorry!" Sneeze said as she felt Scar's guilt in his light, grabbing his hand into hers. "I won't bring her up if you don't want to. I thought it would be a good idea if you saw her."

"It's fine," Scar said. "I'm good. I just want to think about you. Just what I have now."

"Sonlig, I'm sorry," Sneeze said as she stood up and squeezed Scar in her arms, her light mingling with his. She tried to comfort Scar with her light, with Scar feeling the sister, friend, and desperate lover in her washing over him.

"I'm sorry," Scar said as he held onto Sneeze. "I shouldn't have freaked out like that. Not to you. That was wrong."

"You haven't done that since you were on Earth," Sneeze said as she studied Scar's light again.

"I think it was a panic attack," Scar observed as he went over his emotions, the way his body shutdown, not wanting to take in anymore information to prevent overload. "Yeah, your right. I haven't done that since I left Earth."

"I'm sorry."

"Don't be," Scar insisted as he hugged Sneeze tightly, reaching down to grab an ass cheek in his hand. "Besides, I just graduated from this place. We need to go to town and have some fun."

"You didn't want to bring any of your friends along?" Sneeze asked as Scar lead her by hand to his luggage.

"No," Scar said as they walked downstairs. "I don't want to drag those guys back to Saltal. They're busy with their families."

"What about Katah and Three Spheres? They both just graduated too. Maybe they want to come back on campus."

"They're on a honeymoon right now," Scar explained as they walked out into the mid-day sun and over the his father's car in front of the house, ignoring the few cameras that took their pictures. "I think Three Spheres is more concern about making babies than hanging out with me right now. Beside, I want to spend some time with my girl before you have to leave."

"It would have been more fun with your friends along," Sneeze reminded Scar.

"You're right," Scar said as he open the front passenger seat for Sneeze, kissing her as he did. "But we all grow up and move on. We can't hold on to the past forever. Got to be an adult and do adult things."

"Hey Scar!" someone shouted from a group of students across the street. "You're leaving?"

"Yeah, man!" Scar shouted back. "I just finalized my doctorate."

"How does a prince of a major House drive around in a plain old sedan like that?!" another student asked.

"Which one of us is going to get some royal trim in the back of a sedan later!?" Scar asked, Sneeze squeezing his him in modesty.

"Oh, I bang princesses in the back of sedans!" another student yelled in a mocking voice. "It's not like I'm jealous or anything. Congrats, man!"

"Thanks!" Scar said after he closed the car door after Sneeze sat down.

"Who were those guys?" Sneeze asked.

"I don't know," Scar said as he sat in the driver's seat. "Once I played on the football team, random people just want to talk to you, like you're special or something."

"Like the cameras above us," Sneeze pointed out as she looked out the windows.

"Ya'ax Mont wanted to get pictures of me while I was still here before I left. It'll help with their recruitment."

"Life of a college jock," Sneeze joked as she reached out to Scar's lap.

"Heh, it is what it is," Scar said as he pushed his light into the vehicle and began driving off the campus. "Any other time back on Earth I would have bust the chops of anybody who was like me now. But I have to admit, graduating school, being a star football player, having a princess as a fiancé. This is the life."

"What are we going to do now?" Sneeze asked as she smiled at Scar.

"I want to go clothes shopping," Scar suggested. "I feel like doing a Three Spheres and have my fiancé looking hot before we go downtown to see the sights."

"You should buy some clothes too," Sneeze said, her light growing excited. "I want to see you in something that shows of that physique of yours."

"Yeah, that's okay," Scar said. "I'm not the fancy dress up guy."

"But you want to have me dress up like a piece of meat," Sneeze complained hotly to Scar.

"Okay, fine," Scar conceded. "Just one outfit though."

"Okay," Sneeze giggled as they drove off campus and into Teotihuacan's heavy traffic. The school was close to the central part of the city, so it didn't take long for them to get to the high end shopping district. After Scar managed to find parking in a hotel the family owned, he and Sneeze walked along the streets, looking inside the shops until they found one for clothes for Sneeze they both liked.

It was a retail branch for women as tall as Sneeze, with brands from across the multiverse, so there were more designs in that shop that Scar cared to think about, from elegant gowns to full body transparent suits. Scar wanted Sneeze to wear a short shorts and mini top ensemble to show off her perky assets.

"Do you think this is nice?" Sneeze asked as she stepped in front of a mirror, wearing a pair of thin white cloth shorts that were unbuttoned down so they could fit with a small white jacket that covered a black tube top blouse.

"Yes," Scar answered as he looked at her rear that peeked out of the shorts.

"I'll get these then."

"You want me to pay for them?"

"No, I'll do it," Sneeze said as she hurried over to the cash register to pay for the clothes. When she finished she put the Athena's clothes in the bag from the store and pulled Scar out of the shop, placing his hand on her rear as she looked for a shop for him. Sneeze stopped once she found a shop she liked, with a brand of clothing that made men's wear that was both athletic and stylish at the same time.

"Let's go in here," Sneeze said, not bothering to hear if Scar disagreed or not. She searched through much of the selection, while making sure Scar kept a grip on her. When she was satisfied with what she found she made Scar go put it on for her. It was a form fit black polo shirt paired off with a pair of gray and black striped flexible gym wear pants that was also snug to wear.

"I think these show off too much," Scar said as he looked in the mirror.

"Yes they do," Sneeze agreed before she pulled Scar to the register so she could pay for the clothing. Afterwards they walked out of the store, Scar's arms wrapped Sneeze's waist while her hand was now clamp to his rear. Scar could feel her hunger for him in her light, literally wanting to nibble on his lips as they walked through the streets, feeling good as people looked their way as they passed by.

"Are you hungry?" Sneeze asked, which she always was when she was feeling happy.

"Yeah," Scar said. "How about a movie afterwards too."

"That sounds fun," Sneeze said, and the two searched around until they found a small diner to grab a quick bite. They didn't bother with a fancy restaurant, not feeling that high about themselves. They did sit and talked for a while, and Sneeze felt even more pleased when someone came up to Scar wanting to talk about his college football career.

After their meal they drove to a movie theater where they decided to watch the latest summer blockbuster, which they didn't watch mostly. The movie had already been out for a while and no one was in a mid-day matinee showing, where they sat far in the back and made out. After that they decide to go to the Teotihuacan Zoo when Sneeze decided that she wanted to see the fire salamander enclosure. Afterwards was a walk in the city park, all the while doing what they can to keep their bodies and lights imbedded in each other.

When the day drew late and the sun began to set in the west, Scar drove Sneeze to the space port where Psssh's pyramid ship floated waiting. She had to leave and go home to keep her father from getting mad at her. They made their way through the passengers and towards the private VIP section of the port, tightly holding each other's hands, not wanting the day to end. They eventually made it onto a flight pad which the tech manning it flew upwards to dock with the ship, where at the entrance stood Spy and Tilt to escort Sneeze in.

"What time do you leave?" Sneeze asked as she stood in Scar's arms, holding onto his neck as she stared down the setting sun.

"My parents wanted to stay in their hotel overnight. I didn't want to bother them when they're alone. The get like rabbits when no one is in the house."

"Oh, I didn't want that image in my light," Sneezed giggled as she squeezed Scar's neck.

"What, this image?" Scar asked as he dove into Sneeze, enveloping her lips into his mouth. He was nursing his semi all day long, trying to keep it at bay, but his hunger was taking over now and he wasn't going to hold back. Scar slid one hand down her rear and between her legs, the other gripping her breast, enjoying her reaction when he did.

"They can see us," Sneeze informed Scar, but her light didn't want Scar to stop. She just let Scar do as he pleased, and he just felt too good to stop. He was a young, healthy happy teenager now, with the body of a god and the knowledge to please a woman taught by a preying cougar. He knew the right way to kiss, right where to touch and how hard to press, loving it when Sneeze grabbed his mohawk tightly when he did everything right. When he was feeling satisfied with his work, he stopped to stare into her eyes, studying the Fibonacci sequences that spread over the obsidian black almond surface.

"Don't look at me like that," Sneeze said as she stared back into Scar's light.

"Like what?" Scar asked.

"Don't look at me the way you're looking at me now. I have to go and I can't move when you look at me like that."

"I want to look into your eyes," Scar said angrily.

"Scar," Sneeze pleaded back.

"Fine," Scar snapped, closing his eyes.

"Don't close them," Sneeze laughed as she rubbed her face into his cheek.

"Dammit woman, make up your mind," Scar said as he picked her up from the ground, making Sneeze let out a small cry before Scar put her back down. She slowly walked towards her father's ship, with Scar reaching out until she was out of reached. She walk backwards to keep her gaze on Scar as she approached the entrance. She stopped at the open portal, her tall Kaggen maids standing patiently as they understood her unwillingness to go inside.

Sneeze waved every few seconds at Scar who wave back, until finally she reluctantly stepped inside with Tilt and Spy, the portal closing seamlessly behind them. The ship floated upwards in a constant rate, filling with Light as a window in the air opened before them that revealed the Space Between and their home universe. When the ship flew through the window and dove into their universe, the window snapped back into place to reveal red puffy clouds painted by the last light of the setting sun.

Scar stood there for a few moments, absorbing every emotion, feeling every urge that course through him. Other than that small tinge in his light from earlier he was so happy, cocky like any teenage boy on the cusp of adulthood would be. It may have been a good thing that he still has that small tinge, that guilt that refused to let go, otherwise he probably would have been like every other self-important god at Ya'ax Mont he bashed. If the tinge wasn't going to keep him humble, the next few months in Marine boot camp was certainly going to. With a huge grin, he stood by as the tech landed the lift pad and made his way back to his father's car and to his family's hotel.

CHAPTER 16

157 AA

1

Scar sat quietly on the bus that carried the group of recruits he would attend bootcamp with. It was an old clunker of a vehicle that still used liquid fuel so that the recruits can get used to the smell of carbon fumes they would find on most of the worlds they will eventually be stationed on. Everyone in the bus was excited for their stint on Camp Guerretal, the Marine training facility on Saltal.

As Scar looked at the enthusiasm of the passengers, his nostalgia brought him back to when he first went to Army bootcamp and how those guys on that bus was just as excited and naïve. The group he was with were all Nimans, Andeans and Pleiadeans from Scar's home world. All were dressed the same in rural Andean clothing, and most never being outside their home solar system. The innocence of the young men and women lights on the bus made Scar smile.

"Where do you think you're going to get station at first?" a Pleiadean brown hair woman asked the person next to her in front of Scar.

"I want to get station on a world that just entered the Federation," the Andean answered as he looked up at the woman. "I think that'll be fun just to interact with a culture that just got introduce to Aten Ka."

"Or maybe you just want to date some young exotic off-world girl that'll be enamored by your light," the woman joked.

"I don't think so," the Andean replied shyly.

"My names Boudicca," the woman declared. "What's yours?"

"Bolom."

"Nice to meet you Bolom," the woman said confidently as she gripped and shook Bolom writs. "So, you going to serve your full ten cycles to vote."

"Yeah," Bolom answered. "I'm also planning to go to University when I'm eligible. Hoping that I can get drafted into Congress too."

"It takes a while for it to happen," Boudicca stated as she pondered Bolom words. "You usually have all the older veterans whose numbers are ahead of you to finish until your number comes up."

"Yeah, I hear it may take a few centuries," Bolom added. "But I'm hoping that after I get a good job as a politician, I'll be able to create enough renown to declare myself a god of my own world, perhaps bring in business to start my own nation state."

"Oh, you already have plans to be a king," Boudicca joked. "That's why you want to go to a third density world, to find yourself an easy queen."

"Ha," Bolom laughed back sarcastically. "No, I'm just hoping that I can build some contacts on those world. Network while I serve. There's nothing wrong with having dreams. Besides, not everyone can be born a prince like his Highness behind us."

"Hey," Scar laughed at Bolom.

"I'm just poking fun at you," Boudicca said. "How long do you plan on serving? You can't get that much resources in the Marines."

"Just the ten cycles," Bolom explained. "Then I'm going to get a permit and start mining. After a few decades I'll get more permits and start the farming with livestock and crops. I'm hoping in a few centuries I'll have enough the make a city on a world so people would want to migrate there. Have everything ready to go once I become a Congressman."

"I like your dream," Boudicca said with a smile. "It's ambitious. I hope you succeed."

"Thanks. What about you, do you have any plans after you serve?"

"Me. No, I don't think that far ahead. I just want to serve me ten cycles so I can vote. Have some say in my life instead of others making all the decisions for me. Afterwards I was just planning on exploring the universe, meet some friends along the way."

"How about exploring it with me?" Bolom asked with a little tremble in his light. "I don't mind having a partner from Nima with me. Have someone from home I can relate with while I gather resources."

"I'll take you up on that, Bolom," Boudicca agreed while she looked out the bus and towards the base they were about to arrive at. "Holy shit, look at that place. It looks like some back-world village."

Scar looked out the bus himself at the barracks that comprised most of the buildings of Camp Guerretal, a normal looking base that stood on top of grassy hills in the midst of a secluded forest. There was no power that supplied the base, and it seemed to Scar's eyes that the barracks were open window, letting the elements inside. And since the base was father north away from the equator, that meant that during the summer the place was going to be humid and hot, and during the winter cold and miserable to all the fourth density recruits.

"Fuck yeah," Scar whispered to himself as he took note of the base.

"There isn't any power on base," Bolom said. "It's like were going to be camping out all the time."

"I think that's what bootcamp is Bolom," Boudicca giggled.

"I hope they have heated water," Bolom groaned in dread as the bus slowly made its way on base and towards the processing center where a few form fitted Marines stood by for the bus to stop.

"I think that's how they keep us vegan on base," Boudicca offered. "If you don't raise your density up you'll end up feeling the elements."

"Aten Ka," Bolom moaned as the bus came to a stop. Outside the three Marines stood, emblems of the Federation embroidered on their uniforms, three silver loops of the Light with the four heads of the prominent species on the outer loop, Pleiadean, Andean, Lyran, and Avian. A short green frog hominid with an elongated head walking smartly to the bus entrance, the passengers of the bus waiting with nervousness and joy as he stepped on the vehicle.

"GET THE FUCK OFF MY BUS!!" the Marine screamed into everyone's light, and the bubble of joy and nervousness popped as everyone scrambled off the bus as quickly as possible. All the while the Marine instructors screamed at the recruits, demanding them to get in lines of squad formation, yelling at some recruits to move positions, then yelling at them again to go back, anything to keep the recruits guessing. And no matter how hard the recruits got it, Scar seemed to get double the treatment.

"What the fuck are you doing in my training company, Bridge!" the green frog yelled at Scar as he stood at attention, facing forward at all times.

"I'M HERE AS ORDER, DRILL SERGEANT!" Scar answered.

"You think that just because your some hot shot prince able to bang any piece of pussy that walks your way that you can come train in my Corps, Bridge!"

"YES DRILL SERGEANT!" Scar said.

"Well shit, take a look at this cocky motherfucker!" the Marine laughed. "I'd almost be impress if you weren't IN THE WRONG FUCKING SPOT! MOVE TO THE END OF THE LINE, JAMARCUS!"

"YES DRILL SERGEANT!" Scar yelled as he ran down the line and fit in at the end, the other recruits moving over to readjust the formation.

"We are now going to proceed to the processing center!" the frog Marine stated. "There all of you will have your information inputted into the system, your hair shaved, your cloths removed, your new uniforms issued and your personal belongings stowed away until the end of training! Do you understand stand!"

"Yes Drill Sergeant!" the company answered.

"Bullshit, I can't hear you. Sound off like you have a pair of gonads!"

"YES DRILL SERGEANT!"

"Now at my command, you are all going to take thirty steps towards the entrance to the building! Only thirty! Do you understand!"

"YES DRILL SERGEANT!"

"You will start off with your left foot on the command of forward march!" the frog drill instructor continued. "You will all stop on the command of halt! Do you understand!"

"Yes Drill Sergeant!"

"I can't hear you, do you understand!"

"YES DRILL SERGEANT!"

"Forward…March!" the instructor commanded, and counted the steps until the reached there destination, commanding them to halt before the instructors guided the recruits into the center where they went from room to room, placing all their belongings in cotton like knitted bags in one room, stripping naked and putting on uniforms in another, all the while being screamed at by the instructors at any given moment, rather they made a mistake or not.

"What's the fucking problem Bridge!" the frog instructor yelled when the recruits lined up in front of phones to call home.

"I DON"T NEED TO CALL HOME DRILL SERGEANT!" Scar said to his drill instructor.

"Well shit, look at Mister Fancy Pants here! Jamarcus is so special that he doesn't need to give anyone a call, as if no one in his life is actually worth calling or is actually concern about him. Bridge, you better get someone on that phone right now! Don't fucking throw away a chance that some people in your company don't have!"

"YES DRILL SERGEANT!" Scar answered, and after a moment's thought, pick up the analog receiver and dialed a number.

"Hello?" Rhiannon answered.

"Ma'am, I am calling to inform you that Private Xkit has arrived on Camp Guerretal, and is doing well. Your brother is in good hands and his training will commence soon. This recruit loves you and is waiting to see you soon."

"Good luck, Scar," Rhiannon laughed from her end.

"Goodbye," Scar said before he hung up the phone and ran to his spot in his line.

"Source dammit, Bridge, you're in the wrong fucking spot again!" one of the drill instructors dug into Scar.

"YES DRILL SERGEANT!" Scar responded, trying with all of his might to keep from smiling from the harassment. All the other recruits were shaken from the treatment they were receiving, mainly from the tone that the instructors gave their commands. But Scar already served in a military force and has been through war. He knew that the instructors performed the way they did to get the recruits used to responding to situations that would be just as strenuous. And mostly the instructors were getting their own personal laughs with treating him like shit.

All day long the instructors drilled into the recruits, marching them to different locations, given instructions from different trainers they soon forgot due to the quick reaction sequences of their schedule. Everyone's light was spinning in confusion as they went stumbling throughout the day, until at last they arrived at their barracks at almost midnight, physically and mentally tired, some on the edge of tears. They were given orders to stand at the end of their twin bunks, doubled up and side by side, standing at attention as their head drill instructor began his introductory speech.

"My name is Gunnery Sergeant Anish," the frog instructor began. "This is Staff Sergeant Coatl, and Staff Sergeant Drona. We will be your drill instructors during your time here in Camp Guerretal. You will find that your training will be intense, where your body will break and your mind will splinter. That is our goal here.

"Make no mistake. There are pampered, silk clothed, self-righteous lights out in the multiverse that think that because they were born with high densities, that makes them gods. They are sadly mistaken. All gods are created here, in my beloved Marine Corps. By the end of your time in boot camp and the end of your first cycle of training, you will be sent out to remind this false gods on multiple occasions how inane their beliefs are, and you will enjoy it.

"Your training will be hard but fair, and your instructions given with strict discipline and with the intent to make you better each day. You will be driven, beaten down, exhausted, bled, broken, killed, resurrected, and put through the same process over and over again throughout the first cycle, to make sure that the last thing in the omniverse that will break is your light, because you can't break something that is already broken.

"Whomever you thought you were before today was insignificant. Whatever dreams you have of being in Congress are unreachable until you finish your training in my Corps. Because you may have believed that you were gods and goddesses, that you have achieved great accomplishments in life. You actually think that you were a somebody. I'm am here to tell you that you are less than nothing. You're are at this moment the lowest form of light in the omniverse. You are a recruit. But if you stick out this training, and receive all that we will try our best to give you, then you will gain the greatest title that any light in the omniverse can ever attain. You will earn the title of Marine."

"Hoorah," Scar whispered silently to himself.

"Pray," Gunnery Sergeant Anish ordered, and the recruits cited of their prayer.

I am Aten Ka

And Aten Ka is in me

My purpose is to increase how much Aten Ka shines in me

That can only be achieved through my actions

Therefore, when I act, I act with Love, Honor, and Commitment to all Light

However, I have sworn to defend my family in the Federation

Through hardship, pain and death

So let Aten Ka shine through my actions

For I am Aten Ka

"Good night recruits," Gunnery Sergeant Anish bid before the lights were turned off.

"GOOD NIGHT DRILL SRGEANT!"

2

Scar looked out over the beach from the sand fort he and Bernini made behind his home at the foot of Psssh's castle. As he leaned against the sand wall and accessed the enemy that stood before them, his light grew dim. It had been a long day of battle, a battle that even Scar was beginning to question rather it was worth it. It was he, Bernini, Horus, and the older teenagers of the beach, fighting off wave after wave of the younger siblings who were intent of taking their base, but they stood their ground with courage.

Scar turned from the beach and looked over his fellow soldiers as they summoned the strength from each other to fight on, or just slouched around because the fort gave them some really nice shade. It was a large circular wall of impenetrable sand to anyone not willing to climb like ten feet. The only entrance was a closed pathway that lead to the ocean, allowing a constant stream of water to gather in the pool Bernini and Scar made so Sneeze can relax in. It was guarded well by a naked Horus, who unfortunately was playing with the enemy just as Scar turned his gaze to him.

"Source dammit!" Scar hollered in fear. "Bernini, the walls have been breached!"

"No!" Bernini shouted as he rushed towards the entrance.

"Horus, stop betraying us to the enemy and repel them back!" Scar ordered as he blast the kids with sprays of ocean water.

"Okay!" Horus agreed, picking up the water at his feet and drenching the enemies that were his friends. The intruders fought back as much as they could, but when the other teenagers joined the fray, they could do nothing but retreat in anguish, cursing them as they swore to tell their mommies on them. Doubt was planted in Scar's light about his boy. He knew now that if the enemy made their final massive push, he couldn't rely on him, filling Scar with grief.

"Horus, are you hungry?" Sneezed called out in her sweet, beautiful voice to her child.

"Yeah!" Horus responded as he ran over to the precious cargo. In the other end of the pool was Sneeze, her ebony smooth skin lit from the red sun above, giving her the appearance of a Achaean goddess carved on Argive red clay. Horus rushed to her side, where the large blue and white top cooler stood, filled with ice chilled snacks and drinks. After Sneeze gave him sustenance, Horus hugged her pregnant belly before he sat down and ate his meal, Sneeze hugging him beneath her bulging bosoms.

"Scar, I don't think we can trust Horus in the next battle," Bernini advised. "Your wife spoils him too much. He doesn't have the heart for war."

"You know I can hear you, dumbass," Sneeze said as she gave her fiancé and soon to be brother-in-law a disturbed look.

"You're right," Scar agreed. "And our ranks and moral shrinks by the minute." Scar looked over the last of his loyal soldiers, who dutifully watched over the walls for any encroaching forces, except for two who were making out to pass the time. Many fighters were loss that day, rather by hunger, or boredom and wanting to go somewhere cooler, or Aten Ka forbid, being tattle tailed on by their younger siblings. The horror of embarrassed teenage Kaggen faces being drag home by their parents was something Scar believed he will never forget.

"King Scar!" one of his men called out, and Scar rushed over and laid next to the watchman, peering over the wall to see a number of children, green and red, black and blue, all rushing the fortress with balls of ocean hovering over their thin mantis frames.

"To battle!" Scar called out. "You two, stop sucking faces! Defend the precious cargo! A juice pack to the one who splashes the most kids!" A roar cry erupted from the soldiers as they rushed to the wall, standing their ground as line after line of children climbed the walls, driven by annoyance of their older siblings. Water was flung everywhere until the last of the young ones were driven back, mostly because one of them found something interesting in the small surf.

"Loyal Yawn," Scar proclaimed as he slapped a tall warrior on his back. "You have fought bravely. You have earned this reward. Your juice pack!"

"Thanks," Yawn said as he took his prize in his green hand and sucked it dry.

"Hey old man, we want some too," one of the soldiers protested in hot jealous fury. "I'm not staying in this dumb thing if we don't get something to eat."

"I have rewarded you all with rich bounty," Scar countered in divine rage.

"Dude, you made us share a few small packages," another soldiers explained in a disloyal tone.

"SILENCE!" Scar shouted, refusing to hear anymore disrespect from his subjects. "They are my divine riches. You should feel blessed that I partake them with you."

"Tis trouble times," Bernini lamented to his brother. "The people have revolted against their gods. This day was longed prophesized. What shall we do?"

"We stay strong," Scar said as he held Bernini's moping head against his chest. "We will win this day."

"Whatever," the young beautiful temptress of the group huffed, using her womanly ways to lure yet another soldier away. "Come on babe, let's go to the market."

"Wait up," the coward called after her as they both retreated in shame.

"Take heart soldiers," Scar spoke to his men in celestial vigor. "We shall win this day, and the spoils shall be yours to enjoy!"

"Yeah, like half a chip," one of the disillusion warriors replied in disbelief.

"Your Highness, this is it!" Yawn called out from his position. When Scar laid his body next to him, his heart drop when he saw countless (really like sixteen) enemy forces rushing the fortress, the sheer numbers of their feet shaking the sand beneath them.

"On the rear flank!" Bernini warned, and Scar turned in horror as more of the horde rush towards them from the opposite end of the beach.

"They changed their tactics," Scar said with a smile. "Rally, men, rally! Let us be true today. If we are to go down, let our loss be heard throughout history! To immortality… BWAAAH! Source dammit I just swallowed a gallon of water. Fuck it, I'm done." Scar retreated back to the pool, covering his head as the kids flung water at his face.

"Finally got bored with your game?" Sneeze asked as Scar reached in the cooler for something to drink."

"It was battle, my queen," Scar said before he squirted his juice down his throat. "Battle is never a game."

"Hmmm hmmm," Sneeze responded with a sarcastic smile.

"Do you guys have any pears in here?" Bernini asked as he searched through the cooler.

"I think so," Horus said as he helped his uncle look for some food.

"Man, I think I got more sand in my urethra than on my body from lying on that sand," Scar complained. "I don't know why I decided to go out naked today."

"Then you would whine about the kids making fun of you, Sonlig," Sneeze reminded Scar as she brushed sand off of him.

"Punk kids," Scar grumbled. "Well I'm bored."

"What do you want to do?" Sneeze asked as she and Horus looked up at Scar.

"WAKE UP TADPOLES!" Gunnery Sergeant Anish screamed into the barracks, turning on the lights and waking Scar up from his dream. He leapt out of bed, the vison of his pregnant wife and son still in his eyes as he jump from his bunk and stood at attention at its end.

"To all of you who thought that yesterday was the worst that you will experience, I have news for you!" Gunnery Sergeant Anish announced. "Things will start to get hard now!"

3

The first month were a blur for the company, with day after day of instructions crammed into their Lights. Scar was selected to be the company's recruit commander because of his military experience on Earth. His knowledge helped while they were being taught the basic that any light should know what to do, how to march in formation, to make your bed or clean your space. How to talk to your superiors or one another with respect and dignity. All with extreme discipline from the drill instructors, who hounded them at very minute to keep them on edge.

The next month was even harder. Once the regimen of everyday life got normal, the real training began. Light manipulation with intent to kill, exhausting nonstop physical training from before dawn till after dusk. All with nothing but raw vegetables to eat, and if you were lucky, a sweet piece of fruit was a reward for a job well done. It didn't matter what the elements were outside as the weather began to get colder. Rain or shine they trained, making it essential for the recruits to clear their energy nexuses to keep warm. If not the cold nights in bed were brutal.

No matter if it was actual combat training, flying through the universe, or searching through the silver sphered Matrix for strategic intelligence, the instructors kept at it with the company, until something clicked within them. Scar smiled when he saw it happen. All the yelling, the harshness, the frank criticism began to become normal to the company. After a while, smiles began to grow on the groups faces when they finally figured out not to listen to how the instructors was talking to them, but to listen to what they were saying. And what the instructors were saying were always full of wisdom and concern for the recruits, and sometimes flat out hilarious.

It was now the last month of boot camp, two weeks before they graduate and get assigned to their new forts in the multiverse. As the training began to sink in, the company began to get cocky, confident with their finely honed skills, which is what the Marines want with their new recruits. Warriors who can think for themselves and take on any challenge they may face without any fear, because fear was beaten out of them.

Today the company was at the proton accelerator range, where the recruits stood in the ever piling snow in front of mound shape cannons that fired bolts of solid accelerated matter at the recruits, who would grab the blast, redirect it at the cannons to destroy it, rewind time to put it back together, and repeat the process again for over a section.

"Aten Ka I hate this," Bolom moaned next to Scar as he grabbed a shot and flung it back at the cannon.

"You hate everything," Boudicca laughed at him as she did the same. "You're just cranky that you had watch last night."

"You didn't have to pull a watch last night," Bolom grumbled.

"That's because the drill instructors doesn't want us staying up at night by ourselves."

"Which wouldn't have been a problem if one of us had been silent about our status," Bolom said.

"Are you still mad about that," Boudicca snapped at Bolom.

"No," Bolom said.

"Source, you've been cranky lately. I think you need to get laid and released some of that frustration inside of you."

"It doesn't help if you're the one who's saying that," Bolom told Boudicca. "By the way, which stations did you choose."

"The ones you wanted," Boudicca answered as she destroyed her cannon and reassembled it. "I still say we should think about getting station in Ganesha space. There's some unexplored space regions that may deserve checking out.

"Do you want to change our selections?"

"It's just an idea. We may not end up in the same fort. If that's the case, then maybe we should increase our options, choose the stations with the most unexplored waters to maximize the most resources we might find."

"That's a good idea," Bolom said.

"I know," Boudicca concurred. "By the way, where do you want to go during our liberty after graduation?"

"Do you want to hang out around Teotihuacan?" Bolom asked.

"No way, let's go exploring," Boudicca suggested.

"How about Ganesha waters then. Your idea has me piqued. Let's go out there and see what we can find. Three days should be enough to explore a few galaxies."

"Shit!" a recruit cried out at the other end of the line. All eyes turned as a tanned Andean laid on the ground, his arm blasted off and wincing in pain.

"Are you alright?" the recruit next to him asked.

"Yeah," he grunted, his military training kicking in as he calmed himself before he restored his arm by rewinding space-time through his body, then stood up and triggered the cannon to fire another shot at him.

"What the fuck happened up here, Private Xibalba?!" Gunnery Sergeant Anish asked as he flew next to the recruit.

"I SCREWED UP DRILL SERGEANT!" Private Xibalba answered as he stopped his exercise cannon and stood at attention.

"Have you forgotten that you can get killed in this training, Private Xibalba?!"

"NO DRILL SERGEANT!"

"I think you did, which means I failed as an instructor!" Gunnery Sergeant Anish informed the recruit. "Are you implying that I failed as an instructor!?"

"NO DRILL SERGEANT!" Private Xibalba said.

"I think you are! Because your light simply can't be fading of somewhere else other than the training at hand. Perhaps your thinking about graduation?!"

"YES DRILL SERGEANT!"

"Well hot damn!" Anish laughed. "You must have something nice planned for liberty! I bet you have some nice hot dripping snatch waiting for you once you get off this base!"

"YES DRILL SERGEANT!" Private Xibalba answered, getting a chuckle from the other recruits."

"Then congratulations!" Anish shouted. "I hope she's a nice piece of ass. She better be worth it, because that next time your light gets distracted and you hurt yourself, you're going to need to repair your rectum! BECAUSE I WOULD HAVE SHOVED MY FOOT SO FAR UP YOUR ASS, YOU"LL HAVE FOOT FUNGUS AT THE BACK OF YOUR TEETH!! DO YOU UNDERSTAND PRIVATE XIBALBA?!"

"YES DRILL SERGEANT!"

"Carry on!" Gunnery Sergeant Anish ordered before he flew off, the other recruits barley keeping their laughter in check. They continued their exercise for another section, switching the patterns and speed of the cannons to keep the recruits on their toes, until the instructors told Scar to gather his company and have them form up off the range.

"Aten Ka, I can't wait to get back to the barracks and lie down," Bolom sais as they stood at attention."

"Damn, you're in a cranky mood," Boudicca silently laughed at him. "Did you wake up on the wrong side of the bed?"

"I didn't get any sleep last night, in case you forgot," Bolom grumbled.

"Oh, poor baby. Do you want me to tuck you in tonight before you go to bed?"

"I swear, you're asking for it," Bolom warned Boudicca.

"Or what?" Boudicca said as she slapped Bolom ass.

"Keep pushing," Bolom said with a smile.

"We must be having a party in the ranks!" Gunnery Sergeant announced as he dropped down in front of Boudicca. "This must be the club since you can't keep your hands off your fellow recruits, Private Boudicca!"

"NO DRILL SERGEANT!"

"Well are you going to slap me in the ass, private?!"

"NO DRILL SERGEANT!"

"Shit, Private Boudicca, are you racist?! You don't like Makans?!" Anish asked, the other recruits struggling to stay silent.

"NO DRILL SERGEANT!"

"I think so, because I think it's just plain rude that you're going to slap someone in the ass and not give me one! My feelings are hurt! Private Bridge, did you know that Private Boudicca is practicing some hanky panky in you ranks?!"

"YES DRILL SERGEANT, I ORDERED HER TO!"

"What the fuck, Jamarcus!" Anish yelled as he flew over to Scar, the company trembling as they waited for what was going to happen next.

"You're saying that you ordered Private Boudicca to slap someone in the ass?!"

"YES DRILL SERGEANT! PRIVATE BOLOM STATED THAT HIS ASS IS MORE SOLID THAN MINES, SO I HAD PRIVATE BOUDICCA CONFIRMED THAT IT WASN'T!" Burst of laughter erupted in a few of the recruits when Scar gave his answer, and Gunnery Sergeant Anish himself had a hard time keeping a straight face.

"I'm glad you think this is funny!" Anish said. "Because I'm going to bet that you think ten laps around the galaxy is funny too, don't you company?!"

"YES DRILL SERGEANT!" the company answered.

"Get going then!" Gunnery Sergeant Anish ordered, and the company filled themselves up with light and exploded up into the atmosphere. In a matter of dots they were out of the solar system, and in less than a minute they were at the outer edge of the galaxy branch Saltal was located in as they began their flight around the Andromeda galaxy. As they flew around, Scar watched as it seem in their flight that the inner section of the galactic branches seemed to flow like a river, faster than the outer edges of the galaxy. When they made their way to the other side, the flow of the river seemed to go in reverse. That sight always seemed to make Scar happy, giving him a child like glee.

"So what are you going to do after boot camp?" Bolom asked Scar as he flew next to him.

"Go home, show my fiancé my grandmother's castle, get her pregnant. You know, the usual."

"Holy shit man," Boudicca laughed as she overheard. "I guess divine rape is a thing."

"Something like that," Scar chuckled.

"A castle," Bolom said. "Maybe we should have a castle, Boudicca. It might look great for a city aesthetic."

"Already claiming me for a queen," Boudicca replied snidely. "This whole divine rape thing must be going around. Some kind of bug."

"Ha," Bolom responded.

"Hurry up recruits!" Anish ordered in the company's lights, and the recruits quicken their pace as they continued their flight around the galaxy.

Chapter 17

158 AA

1

Scar waited patiently in the driveway that was before the entrance to his grandmother's castle, a gorgeous marble and wood building that stood at the foot of a mountain south of New Scarborough. The white and gold pyramid like building was molded out of an immense slab of stone, with all of its fixtures shifted inside the rock and details exquisitely carved by amazing craftsmen. This day was the first day Scar saw the building. His siblings told him that their mother rarely went their because it just reminds her of Xkit and her decision to join Aten Ka. Yet it was Ixchel herself that suggested to Scar to have Kukulkan show Sneeze and her father around.

Scar bounced around on his toes, the gravel under him crunching as he kept himself busy until Kukulkan arrived with Sneeze and Psssh. It would be over a year since he last physically saw Sneeze, and he laughed inside as his body ached to be next to her again. The age old proverb of wishing to know what you knew now when you were young was playing itself in Scar. To know why his body was acting like a rampant horny teenage boy was more satisfying now than when he was on Earth. But then he never had a healthy relationship when he was a teenage Jamarcus.

Scar looked up at the mountains that stood above Xkit castle, its forest covered sides contrasting against the flat white construct that was carved form the marble vein of the mountain. Scar was told that there was a beach that was made from the weather marble, creating white sand that looks like it has gold flecks in it. Clouds formed at the top of the mountain shielding the morning sun that was creeping over the peaks.

Scar's light went back to his special forces training he went through from the previous cycle as he waited. Training he couldn't tell from either being brutal or fun. His station was Fort Dubnos, a military facility located by a Pleiadean colony. And like its name describes, it was a hellhole for new Marines entering the Vanguard training course. When he first got there, everyone called him by his Earth name instead of his new light name, thinking that it would knock his confidence down from is past trauma. All it really did was make him feel at home.

The first day on base was him going from building to building, either being ignored by the top brass that he had to report to, or told to go away and report to someone else and ignored all over again. It was due to the fact that he was promoted to Sergeant Major when he finished bootcamp, based on his previous experience from Earth and in no small part to nepotism. A lot of the senior NCO's were pissed that this young green recruit received a rank that took some of the soldiers over a century to achieve. Scar agreed too, but the rank came with painful responsibility that he had to fulfil to his House.

When he was finally registered on based after he arrived at the fifth office building he walked to, he was then given the run around on where he was going to stay. He wasn't allowed to stay with the other senior NCO's at their hotel like barracks. He couldn't stay with the lower ranked enlisted Marines. No way he was going to get in the open element barracks with the other Vanguard trainees, that was too nice for him.

He was sent to a storage depot, where he found a cot and bucket next to tanks and low density small arms. A place that served to remind him of what he really was. He shared the space with another Sergeant Major that had the same responsibilities as him. The two talk about their families and their previous old lives on third density worlds. The only real difference was that Scar's roommate chose to go enlisted to spite his father, who had a road cut out for him instead of creating his own.

The training was the things of nightmares. For countless sections they would operate in the emptiness of space, until it was more normal to swim in the waters above a planet than on it. There were gauntlet like combating sessions where they had to fight each other, many times to the death. Scar had reached the eleventh density due to his new vegan diet, even able to see the spiraling White Road of the Omniverse. But that didn't mean shit when about twelve or more sixth density Marines came at you, ready to do whatever it took to put you down. Many times they had to go out into the Space Between because the reality shockwaves from their battles were too dangerous for nearby galaxies.

When the easy stuff was done, things turned to the literal nightmarish. They were all sworn to uphold the ethics of light delving before they went to psionic warfare. The delving into each other's lights, searching for your target's deepest shameful secrets or fears and blocking your own. Manipulating your target to move and do things against their will, or sometimes without them knowing what was going on. It broke many of the trainees, with a good eighty percent quitting when they couldn't tell the difference from being awake and asleep.

Scar had no problem with this part of the course. He had to laugh at himself once when he woke up naked in the mass hall, not even realizing where he was until the last moment. Everyone there got a laugh too once he regain his light, especially the women. The nightmare tactics training was even more fun for Scar. He used to read a lot of horror books and watch horror movies on Earth, which was some of the best times he had with Kathrine. The other marines may have tried to used her memories to mess with him, but it just made him happy. Besides, if someone were going to use her against Scar, the tactic of making him scared wasn't going to work.

At the end of the course they put all of their new skills to use, going down to worlds mentally disguised in illusions to blend in with the species they walked among. There were days where Scar would just go to unknown worlds, arrive in cities as a local tourist and go exploring. He'd spend sections of the day noting important infrastructures, power lines, water and sewage plans, communication relays, VIP locations and schedules. All the while wondering if that wasn't already done on Earth when his light was there.

Scar's light snapped back to the present when he saw Psssh's pyramid ship pop up above the sea north of Xkit castle. Scar couldn't contain his glee, dancing on his toes as Kukulkan, Psssh and Sneeze, the Kaggen clothed in Federation fitted clothing, all flew down from the ship and landed in front of him. Scar and Sneeze ran into each other's arms, laughing at themselves as they spun each other around.

"Hi Sweet-pea," Scar said in between kisses.

"Oh, I want to eat you," Sneeze giggled as she bit softly on Scar's small lips.

"Hello, Kukulkan," Scar greet the old Andean, who was dressed in a smart Andean colorful suit and tie.

"Good mourning, your Highness," Kukulkan answered in a formal tone, still in business mood as Psssh's guide.

"Hi Psssh," Scar said as he reached up to his obsidian colored head

"Hello, Sonlig," Psssh clicked as he pressed his head against Scar's, his prideful joy shining into Scar's light.

"Welcome to Castle Xkit, my King," Kukulkan stated as he led the three up the marble steps and into the building, Psssh having to bend his fifteen foot tall frame so he could fit inside.

"Are you alright, King Psssh?" Kukulkan asked as he watched the large Kaggen. "We don't have to do this tour if you are uncomfortable."

"No no," Psssh chirped. "I'm quite fine. I want to see Ixchel's palace. It's different yet similar to my own."

"That's because the basic design was pyramid based to make it more stable," Kukulkan said as they walked the corridors. "But Queen Xkit and Lord Aapo wanted the interiors to be more contemporary like most other off-world structures, to make it more pleasing for visitors."

"I see," Psssh agreed.

"This castle was built over a millennia ago, when Lady Chac'chel was a little girl. I remember her and Lady Ixchel running through theses hallways, terrorizing the servants with their antics. Lady Athena spent some time here, but when it was clear that she wasn't happy, they moved to their Chateau on one of Ra's islands Xkit and Aapo gave him. Now it is used to entertain special guest of the House, like I mention partly earlier."

"This is all so beautiful," Psssh marveled. "Don't you agree, Sneeze."

"Oh, yes," Sneeze stuttered after she removed her lips from Scar. "Yes, it's all so beautiful."

"Indeed," Kukulkan spoke in an even tone, giving Scar a mindful eye. "The castle was designed from many artisans from many worlds. That's why you have a number of different cultural designs to the structure and interior decorating. Queen Xkit told everyone to build from their light, so you have what is before you. She loves the artwork that many wanted to create, the paintings and sculptures. The workers made the place so splendid that Lord Aapo had a hard time sleeping under this roof. He said it was like sleeping in a museum."

"By any chance can we see some of this artwork?" Psssh asked before Kukulkan gladly guided the group through the sunlit corridors of the castle. They walked on red soft carpets that cover all the halls and looked at many of the paintings that lined the walls, depicting important events of real or mythological origins on dozens of worlds. One showed a picture of a blacked furred Lyran dressed in ancient armor as she battled a giant snake that descended from the heavens, blotting out the sun with its size.

"I have to use the bathroom," Sneeze whispered to Scar as they stood in a room filled with statues of Andean political figures dressed in ancient Andean clothing.

"Kukulkan, I got to take Sneeze to the bathroom," Scar told his elder before dragging Sneeze from the room.

"Come back, Scar. This is your history too," Kukulkan reminded Scar before the couple walked their way through the hallways until the came to the interior of the castle, in an area where there was an square open space. The sun shined down on a garden with flowers similar to the ones Ixchel planted in front of the house on Suburbia.

"Here's the bathroom," Scar said as he opened the door for Sneeze. "Well, the only one I can find. This place is huge."

"It's nice," Sneeze said as she walked in the room. "It's like my father's palace, except much smaller."

"Do you like your tour so far?"

"Yes," Sneeze answered as she unzipped her uniform, her light buzzing with nervousness as she sat in front of Scar on the toilet.

"Where did you guys go?" Scar asked.

"Kukulkan took us to the Citadel to show my father around. That was fun, I love the food over there. That's why I have to pee so badly. Then we went through New Scarborough. I didn't like that too much. Everyone kept giving us the stink eye."

"I'm sorry, Sweet-pea," Scar apologized.

"That's alright," Sneeze said as she wiped herself and flushed the toilet, then rose to go to the sink to wash her hands.

"I'm having a good time though," Sneeze continued as she tried to zip herself up. "I like coming to visit…" was all she could say before Scar grabbed her from behind, yanking her uniform down to her feet. She stayed silent as Scar reached into her crotch, working his hand between her legs while he tried to loosen his pants. Sneeze help him along so that soon Scar stood ready to enter her, bending her over to do so. When he first penetrated, Sneeze face squinch in pain, trying to get use that new sensation.

"I'm sorry," Scar said, not wanting to hurt Sneeze, but Sneeze grabbed Scar's rear, thrusting her hips back to him, slipping him all the way in, her mouth opening in a constant Oh. Scar was shocked and thrilled by Sneeze action, and he was thrusting away before he knew it, his teenage hormones taking over his light. Sneeze stood there silently, her head bent over as she took Scar's motions, barely able to think. Scar himself was lost, not realizing until it was too late that he released inside of Sneeze.

"Did you go?" Sneeze asked quietly as Scar held her silently.

"Yes."

"You want me to get pregnant?

"Yes."

"Your mother is going to get mad at us," Sneeze warned Scar.

"I don't care," Scar spoke into her neck. "I need my family. I need you guys so badly."

"Are you done?" Kukulkan asked, shocking Scar and Sneeze up straight, quickly dressing themselves as the old man stared them down. Once finished they walked out shamefully as Psssh looked on from the side, a bit giddy from what he saw.

"I have no idea what is wrong with this family," Kukulkan stated as they walked out the square area. "You all want to get pregnant in that bathroom."

2

Scar stood barely awake in the early dark morning hours in black Marine uniform, waiting with the rest of his trembling platoon on a flight deck for a transport vessel to take them to their training destination. It was below freezing that morning, and due to the parameters of the mission, the group couldn't raise their light above the fourth density, and barely that. Scar looked about him as the platoon members huddle against each other, giving each other's body heat to fight off the cold, holding on to the back packs that carried their gear in for the mission.

"Do you know where you're going to get stationed?" Kane asked, his black tattooed cheeks shaking as he walked up to Scar.

"Most likely any station located in my families space of influence," Scar said as he shuffled up against his roommate. "From what the commanding officer told me, my grandpa already got plans for me when I leave base."

"Same here," Kane said as looked up into the night sky, pleading in his light for the transport ship to arrive. "My dad wants me serving in his star cluster. We've had a bad time dealing with pirates raiding our mining world. I've already talked to the base commander of the post close to where I live and my job of infiltrating the gang."

"Your dad already got you going?" Scar asked in knowing sympathy.

"Yeah. I would love to show you my home some time. You can meet my wife and menehune."

"That'll be cool. I'll have to take you up on that."

"What about you?" Kane asked, jumping up and down to keep warm. "Do you have any kids?"

"My fiancé is pregnant with our first one," Scar answered with a sad smile.

"You must miss her."

"Desperately," Scar muttered to himself as the platoon was flashed by blinding lights by an egg shaped solid craft appearing above them and silently came to a floating rest by the group. As a door appeared on the side of the craft, the platoon climbed in as quickly as possible, wanting the door shut to keep the cold wind out. They all sighed in relief as the ship closed up, leaving the cargo department they were in with a stable climate.

The pilots raised their lights to take the ship into the White, and soon they were speeding away above the universe to their planetary target. The platoon waited quietly as the ship flew, double checking their packs to make sure that all of their gear was in order. They were tasked to enter Lyran space, to a station that was part of the Federation. The station didn't know that they were coming, which makes their infiltration that more dangerous. They were to drop in air space thirty miles from a naval station on planet Agassou, swim to the fleet being repaired their and plant their dummy bombs on the bottom of the hulls. Once done they were to swim out of the port and rendezvous with a traveling firm where they are to catch a civilian flight off the planet.

"How does your fiancé's planet look like?" Kane asked to pass the time.

"Roi Son? It's gorgeous. It's hard to describe. The city that her father lives in is located at the foot of his pyramid castle. It's intwined with the jungle surrounding the area, but there are other cities all over the multiverse that are like that. It's the grass plains in the central part of their worlds supercontinent that is breathtaking. It's nothing but seas of steppes and grasslands. There are egalitarian cultures that live there, living in balance with their neighbors and the planet. There was this one time that Sneeze and I were walking with one of her friends near the friend's village. The red sun was raising above a small round mountain just as a herd of beetle buffalos were walking by. That was so beautiful."

"That sounds straight out of a wildlife documentary," Kane laughed.

"Dude, I had to pinch myself to make sure that what I was seeing was real," Scar said.

"Yeah. The Light Paradox. I get it. There's this mountain that's part of my father's island home. It's just the same as the one you're talking about, but it's tall enough to pierce the clouds. There are some nights when you go up there when the air is so clear, I swear that if you reach up you can touch the stars with your fingertips."

"That's amazing," Scar said as he perceived the image in Kane's light.

"Yeah. I guess that's one good thing about the Ascension process. If I hadn't went through it, I probably would have taken that mountain top for granted. Now I don't even want to walk on it, it's so precious to me."

"Entering drop zone in one minute!" their training officer yelled at the group, bring the platoon back into the present moment. They checked their gear for the last time, then gathered at the cargo area door ready to be released. No one was nervous, they were too busy to be nervous. They had done missions like this dozens of times a month, always something new, never getting into a regular rhythm. All to drive home the point that nothing stays the same, and change is permanent. The ship suddenly stopped, the cargo door opened to reveal a black ocean under the white covered universe screen below them.

"Go!" their officer order, and the group plunged out into the White, diving through the screen and into the night sky of planet Agassou. They fell in a control descent, flattening their bodies against the air to lessen the impact as they came close to the water surface, straightening out at the last moment to dive feet first into the dark ocean.

The platoon then began their long swim towards the naval station. Because they were higher density beings, there was no need to use any breathing apparatus. After long training days in the vacuums of space, Marines learned to breath using only the Light. It took the group just over two sections of mind numbing swimming, using only the stars that the team navigator was following for directions.

When they reached the edge of the repairing docks, the platoon separated into four groups, just as planned, and headed to different areas of the station where different types of sea and space vessels floated in the water. Scar's squad managed their way towards a group of frigates, where they once again split up separately as they each found their target ship and began their work.

Scar opened his back pack, pulling out one of the dummy charges, setting a timer of one hour before swimming towards the opposite end of the ship. It was then when he saw a patrol ship listing lazily in the water towards the frigate, the crew going about their rounds. Scar's light sparked up in reflex, then relaxed back down as he swam to the other side of the hull to hide from the ship. Luckily, no one of the patrol boat was searching with their light to see his reflex spark, and the boat gradually cruised away. Once the boat was gone, he set the timer on the second charge, then started both of them with a remote starter before swimming away from the port and towards the nearby city.

After a section of swimming Scar came on shore by a lone dark street, where he changed his form to a brown furred Lyran dressed in high end Agassou colorful fashion. After drying of his backpack, he slung it on his back and walked miles along the road until he reached the outskirts of the city, where he saw his squad all sitting under the lights of an open air restaurant, all disguised in local forms.

Once he arrived the group paid their check and walked back to the city, where they stopped by a tourist hotel. It was a half a section wait until a taxi vehicle drove up to them, who's driver took them to the city's spaceport. The squad piled out of the vehicle and paid their driver before heading to the Ku'uchil travel counter to receive their pre-ordered tickets for their flights.

"Hello sir," the gray fur attendant purred as Scar approached. "What can I do for you?"

"My name is Shango, and I have an eight AM flight to Saltal."

"Yes, here it is. You're here quite early. That's going to be a two section wait."

"Yes, I know," Scar concurred. "I don't mind the wait."

"Here you are sir. Is there anything else that you need?"

"No, thanks a lot," Scar said as he took his ticket and proceeded through the screening checkpoint. He made it to the waiting area for his flight where the rest of the platoon sat, either talking in pairs or separating from each other to give the impressions that they were all separate strangers.

"I'm so tired," Kane said as he slouched down in the seat next to Scar, playing with the orange stripped fur on his arm. "You get so amped up on these trips. And when it's done, all you mind wants to do is shut down for a day to reset."

"Yeah," Scar said. "We do enough physical training to make us ready when we have to go lower density. But when we actually perform, our bodies act like it's the first time. Every time. Maybe it's the stress."

"Probably. Want something to eat?"

"Did you eat at the restaurant?"

"No I was too nervous back then," Kane explained. "I just got something to drink. I'm starving now."

"I'm not hungry," Scar said.

"Watch my bag for me?" Kane asked before he went off to one of the space port restaurants for a quick bite. When he got back, Kane ate in silence as Scar and the rest of the group waited patiently for their vessel to arrive. Once the craft docked and the arriving passengers left and the departing boarded, Scar found his seat and slumped in, going into a meditative trance. Not going to sleep, but not fully awake as the vessel made its long flight to Teotihuacan.

As the platoon departed the ship, Scar and the rest of the group waited until they were alone to change back into their normal forms, raise their lights back and shifted to the military base in the central part of the city. It would be just under a section from the time the flight landed on Saltal until the whole platoon was waiting in a room in the Special Forces operation headquarters, where their instructing officers waited for their debriefing.

"Well done team," the officer said nonchalantly. "Infiltration of the repair docks went according as plan. All ordnances were planted on all target ships, and I can confirm that the commanding officer of the base was none too pleased on our success. Another morning done. Report back to Fort Dubnos for further instruction."

With that command, the platoon all raised their lights until they were in the White and zipped back to their barracks on their home base for some rest. Scar and Kane walked back to the weapons depot, their mind too tired to want to go anywhere else. The instructors had offered them months ago to move somewhere else for their resting quarters, but Scar and Kane liked it in the depot. The times they were in their were quieter than the barracks, and they were always busy training when it was being used. And it began to feel soothing to be in their cots after long days of training.

"I am going to past out for a few hours," Kane declared as they entered the depot, walking past the tanks towards their living area.

"I've never heard such a great plan," Scar yawned behind him, staring at Kane's feet.

"Hey, you have a package on your bunk," Kane said as he saw a brown package on Scar's pillow.

"I do?" Scar said as he waked over to his cot, picking up the item and reading that it was from Ra, Ixchel, and Sneeze. When he tore it open, he found that it was a pile of roleplaying campaign books, with a set of roleplaying dice. Scar's light brightened and solidified with the thought of his parents sending him something, then soften as he began to ache for Sneeze. Fighting back a tear, Scar open on of the books, his light brightening again on the prospect of creating another party.

"Have you ever played any role playing games?" Scar asked Kane as he sat down on his cot.

Chapter 18

161 AA

1

Scar stood silently with his arms crossed in the corner of the operation room in the Citadel. Ra, Admiral Aapo, Chac'chel and a few diplomats discussed a situation that was unfolding on a hologram screen. The Vanguard commander of Scar's newly assigned platoon stood patiently by Aapo, an elderly Andean with scruffy white hair and bony frame showing in his Navy uniform, waiting for orders to be given. Hostages were captured on a cruise ship floating in the night sky above an ocean on the planet Konotal, who was deciding to join the Federation, and specifically House Xkit. The perpetrators were part of an anti-aristocrat front that committed acts of terrorism throughout the multiverse, calling for the deconstruction of the Seven Houses.

Ra talked casually with diplomats that were in sync with representatives on that planet who were negotiating means that the Federation could help with the event. Ra was adamant with his decision that the Federation must remain neutral at this time, due to any actions they make being construed as colonialism. Scar and his commander were summoned to Nima for two purposes, in case the world government agreed upon a back door deal with the Federation, and to keep an eye or Scar during the crisis.

"If you are joining us now..." a news commentator said in an unique Andean accent from one of the screens. "...what you are seeing is the cruise ship Ochan's Path, where the passengers on this luxury liner were planning on taking a cruise through the solar system, but are now being held captive over the Yucatan Ocean against their will. The terrorist group O.O.L., a cell associated with the anti-aristocrat organization group, Liberation Front, has taken responsibility."

"We don't know what the purpose of the Ochan's capturing is. Only One Light hasn't released any statements besides the fact that they indeed hold the vessel, but the world waits for any demands they may give us. Joining me now is retired Lieutenant Colonel Uc'zip. He served in Konotal's Army for over twenty cycles, specializing in intelligence and counter-terrorism. Thank you for joining me, Colonel."

"I wish I could be talking to you on better terms, Cauac."

"So, O.O.L. hasn't released any statements yet on what demands they seek, but why do you think this hostage situation has occurred?"

"There could be many reasons," Colonel Uc'zip surmised. "Obviously, like you stated before Cauac, we all know that Only One Light is a subsidiary branch of Liberation Front, so it can be only for the delay and hopeful disavowing of House Xkit. Liberation Front isn't so much anti Federation, but anti Houses that supply much desired Light to many planetary nations that can't produce their own."

"Which makes since," Cauac interrupted. "It easy to see why any political group would want Konotal to join the Federation as an independent nation state. But the benefit of joining House Xkit, at least from the freedom of worrying about the resources required for energy consumption will eventually help us in the long run until we can develop our own Lights to do so. Polls say that over eighty percent of the population support the move."

"But that's the problem," Colonel Uc'zip pointed out. "Liberation Front is against any light supplying energy to a world. They have an extreme libertarian ideology that wishes that all lights live free in the multiverse from aristocratic or political rule. There against any individuals they deem 'false gods.' And to your question before Cauac, I think that O.O.L. is hoping that because they are associated with Liberation Front, the Federation will have to send in Sixth Density or higher personnel to deal with the crisis, which will be meet with the arrival of Liberation Front's forces. I can almost guarantee that O.O.L. is hoping that witnessing a battle like that would make Konotal rethink joining house Xkit."

"Jamarcus, come on up," his commanding officer said, and Scar pushed himself out of the corner and walked through the dark room to the paneled round table the military and political staff stood by.

"So we got word that Konotal has agreed to expedite the global vote for their nation to join the Federation, Major Yumcha," Admiral Aapo spoke to the officer. "That has given us a semi green light to conduct a black ops on the planet, hopefully without them noticing what is going on. This is by request of House Xkit. We want your platoon to board the cruise ship, using only small arms to not give away your light, and free the hostages."

"What is the situation on the vessel," Major Yumcha said as he ran his hand through his pale white crew cut hair.

"There are twenty known assailants on the vessel right now," Admiral Aapo stated as he made the televised broadcast vanished and brought up an image of the Ochan's path, a water and spacefaring cruise liner. "The mass majority of the passengers are being held in their rooms, the crew of the ship are being held in the helm and the engine department, and the terrorist patrol the ship constantly to ensure everyone stays put."

"I'm assuming that lethal measures are authorized?" Major Yumcha asked as he scrolled the interior of the ship, finding all the terrorist and watching them move about the vessels corridors.

"You are correct," Admiral Aapo said. "We need the terrorist taken out as quickly as possible to prevent them from notifying any help of the attack. Hopefully the initial confusion of death and travel through the Matrix will delay such communications, allowing us to evacuate the ship's passengers and crew before any reinforcement arrive. Liberation Front wants a conflict with the Federation televised. We can't give them that."

"Roger that," Major Yumcha acknowledge before he turned off the ship's image. "Do we know how many passengers are on the ship?"

"Right now, over twelve hundred," a diplomat suggested.

"Aten Ka," Scar muttered as he put his hand over his eyes.

"This needs to get done Sergeant Major," Chac'chel told Scar. "This is House Xkit responsibility, and we will see it done. You will see it done. Do you understand?"

"Yes, Lady Chac'chel," Scar responded.

"Let's get back to base," Major Yumcha ordered Scar.

"Sir yes sir," Scar said as he open a window into a room located in the Special Operations headquarters in Fort Ah'Pekku. In the room thirty two Vanguard members of Scar's platoon waited in chairs silently in black uniform for their operation that was going to commence.

"We got our orders ladies and gentlemen," Major Yumcha said to the group as he walked up to the white board at one end of the room. "Jamarcus, are you still entangled with the ship?"

"Yes sir," Scar answered as he made an image of the ship in the room, transperant so that the platoon could see all subjects in the cruise vessel.

"This is how it's going down. To prevent O.O.L. from knowing that we are there, we are to not use our lights once we slide on the ship, only small arms. There are twenty terrorists on the ship as far as we know, but there isn't any word on if the terrorists has someone embedded with the hostages. Alpha, Bravo, and Charlie go ahead and entangle with a target. When we slide on the ship, make sure your target is dead.

"Delta squad, you are to secure a window to Konotal's surface so the passengers can quickly leave by the ship's aft. Somewhere far enough from any populated areas to prevent tipping off news organizations. When we secure the hostages, make sure all electronics are turned off and no raising of lights. If some still insists to use electronics or the light to contact someone, stop them. Do you understand?"

"Yes sir," the platoon answered.

"Everyone grab their weapons and prepare to depart," Major Yumcha ordered, and the platoon calmly made their way to the armory room.

"Jamarcus, make sure to secure our exit," Major Yumcha ordered Scar as they left the room together.

"Will do Major," Scar replied as they joined the platoon in the weapons room, where each Vanguard member grabbed rifles off racks and large plastic container pods of ammo. The weapons they used had microwave coils in them that when activated created a strong displament field in the weapons rifling chamber. This allowed any object fired through the field to be shot at an accelerated speed. The weapons themselves were air pressurized, firing thirty two caliber pellets through the chamber that would get expelled from the weapon at ballistic rate speed.

After grabbing a rifle, pods of ammunition and three pressurized air containers, Scar and the rest of the platoon waited until Major received word for them to commence the raid. Scar fired of a few empty air shots to make sure his riffle was operating fine before attaching the cylindrical ammo pod to the side of the rifle, where the metal pellets poured out into the firing chamber. After a quarter section of waiting, Major Yumcha turned to his Vanguards, his face grim ahead of their task.

"Into the White," he ordered and the platoon filled their forms with light, slipping into the White and traveling to the Ochan' Path. Each group held on to their personal window, waiting for the major to give the order to infiltrate.

Scar's window showed the aft of the ship, which was a custom amphitheater that double as a movie and play theater. Two plain clothed terrorists walked side by side over the stage, walking quietly as they surveyed the air above the ocean.

"Want me to take one of them, Sergeant Major?" a Marine in Delta squad asked as she floated her small Andean frame next to Scar.

"Yeah," Scar said, firing off a few pellets shots that evaporated in the White and were cast out as subatomic dust across the universe. All the Vanguard did the same, relaxing their bodies the best they could before they began.

"On go," Major Yumcha announced, his eyes still on his target. "Three… two… one… go." Scar leapt through his window, lowering his light to stay fourth density, and lunging at his target who didn't have time to react as Scar plunged his hand through the target's back, blue blood spurting onto the deck as he fell. The Delta squad member leapt out the same time, shooting her target in the chest multiple times, and after the target collapsed placed two more into the terrorist skull.

"Are we clear?" Major Yumcha asked once the initial dust settle.

"Aft is clear," Scar responded, wiping the blood off his hand with his uniform while the other squads confirmed their status. The operation truly got under way as the Vanguard quickly searched for all passengers, instructing them to retreat calmly to the rear of the ship and punishing those who didn't listen to the no electronics or light part.

Scar searched out to the nearby continent, straining his light the best he could to create a window on the stage to a deserted road that lead to a nearby city. Having to stay in the fourth density limited how far he could reach out, which was only for a few miles if he wanted to make a window wide enough to allow all the passengers and crew to leave without constraint.

It didn't take long before a swarm of passengers, mostly Andean, Pleiadean, and Lyran, all headed towards the window. Scar immediately became concern as a large number of the passengers began to cheer their freedom.

"Shut the fuck up!" Scar screamed at the crowd, and from then on the rest stayed silent. The evacuation took just over twenty minutes, and Scar was just beginning to get paranoid that it was going too well when a Pleiadean passenger dressed in a white string top dress and beige sun hat pressed her wrist and a hologram screen appeared above it. She began speaking in Pleiadean into the screen, telling the device what was happening.

"Stop!" Scar yelled at the woman in her language, shooting the ground at her feet, causing the other passenger to scream in response. They woman ignored Scar, her face tensing as she continued to tell how the passengers were leaving the ship.

"Fuck," Scar grunted, shooting the woman in the chest three times before she fell dead on the deck, creating a panic as the passengers ran to the window to escape the violence.

"What's going on Jamarcus?" Major Yumcha asked in Scar's light.

"We're compromised," Scar stated as he made sure that the target was dead. "The terrorists had a sleeper imbedded with the passengers. I think she just told someone what we're doing."

"We're heading to you location, Jamarcus. Protect the passengers."

"Will do," Scar said as he and Delta squad picked out positions amongst the seats of the theater, waiting for the inevitable attack. It would be another few minutes until the other squads arrived with the last of the passengers, coinciding with windows opening up on the upper levels of the ships superstructures. As soon as Scar saw a figure appear above him, he let out a stream of pellets that punctured the hull of the ship in that direction. The rest of Delta squad began firing, laying down constant streams of pellet fire above them as the last of the passengers screamed as they left the ship.

Scar was reloading as the other squads secured the window when a shot hit him right in his throat, hard enough to pierce his flesh and sending him backwards in pain. Scar gathered himself as he rose back up, healing his wound and finishing his reload.

"Get out of there, Jamarcus!" Major Yumcha ordered, and Scar looked up to realize that the rest of Delta platoon was already heading towards the window. Scar bolted from his defensive position and towards the window, the other Vanguard giving cover fire inside of it as Scar was the last person to exit the window before he closed it.

2

Scar stood on the open exercise field in the early morning hours before dawn, waiting for the rest of his platoon to arrive. Other black uniformed Marines were gathering on the field that was placed in the center of a barracks complex, all beginning their morning physical training before jogging off to other training facilities. As the last members arrived from cars or air, Scar took in a deep breath of the cool tropical air before addressing his Marines.

"I see that Vanguards still struggle to get to where they're supposed to be like any other Marine," Scar joked as the last of his platoon arrived for morning exercise.

"Sorry, Sergeant Major. My kids school schedule changed, and I had to do some errands with the car before I left home," the Marine explained before he fell in at attention in his spot in formation.

"Oh, alright. So I guess it's okay that we arrive later than the other Marines on base for training," Scar said with an evil grin. "In that case, it's okay for us to leave after everyone is done on the field." The platoon groaned in response

"The first exercise of the day is the jumping jack!" Scar proclaimed.

"THE JUMPING JACK!" the platoon repeated.

"Starting position, move," Scar commanded, and the platoon quickly stood at attention.

"You'll count the cadence, I'll count the repetition," Scar informed the group. "Ready, begin! 1… 2… 3…!"

"ONE!" the platoon shouted, and increased the number of the candace until the performed two hundred. The platoon continued their exercises, moving on to pushups, sit ups, squats, lunges, scissor kicks, hops, and every forms of calisthenic movement that Scar could think of. They did this for sections, from the time the sun rose in the east to a section after the other Marines on the field left. Scar lost some weight due to the vegan diet he had to uphold in the Service, much to Sneeze displeasure. But the constant training kept him tone, much like his father. Scar laughed to himself when he thought Ra was huge.

Once Scar was satisfied that his platoon were the last one to leave the field, he reformed his Marines into marching positions, and the group ran over twenty miles to the beach where once again the platoon performed the same exercise, except this time in the crashing surf. In between Scar would add freestyle sprints and laps in the ocean to spice things up, making sure that the Vanguards were always wet, always miserable, and always moving.

"We're done for ocean exercises, now on to the waters above!" Scar announced, the platoon groaning again with the prospect of their clothing freezing as the flew out of the atmosphere.

"Sergeant Major Bridge!" a voice called out from the sky, and Scar looked up to see a Doggan marine flying down towards him, his yellow to blue scales sparkling in the mid-day sun.

"What's up Corporal?" Scar asked as the Marine landed in the sand next to him.

"I just got told by Operations Command that Lord Ra requests your presence at your home world. Your ordered to take two Vanguard with you before you go."

"Roger that," Scar said before he turned to his platoon. "Achtland, take over for me?"

"No problem Jamarcus," she said as she took his spot in front of the group.

"Thanks man. Hey, make sure you guys hit the firing range after your space training."

"I'll get it done," Achtland agreed.

"Enki, Anansi, come with me," Scar ordered as an green scaled Anunnaki and a gold and black spotted Lyran left the platoon and walked by his side. Scar increased his light and open a window to the Operation room in the Citadel, with the three Marines walking through as the rest of the platoon took off into space. After Scar closed the window, the three made their way silently through the room of military and political figureheads.

"It must be great to have your own personal Vanguard on call whenever a situation comes up," Anansi joked before Scar turned to him.

"Are we going to have a problem, Staff?" Scar asked him honestly.

"No, Jamarcus, I'm just kidding," Anansi said slapping Scar's arm. "I'm just digging into you."

"This is my life," Scar informed Anansi, his light growing hot. "If you want to go to another platoon, let me know. Just know this: you guys can leave the Marines anytime you want and leave this life. This is my duty for the next few thousand cycles."

"I'm sorry Jamarcus," Anansi pleaded, placing his hands together in front of himself to show his contrite light.

"It's alright Jamarcus," Enki insisted to calm to mood. "It's an honor to work with you. That's what Anansi was trying to say, right?"

"Yeah," Anansi agreed, with Scar giving him a calm look before he turned to lead them through the room. It wasn't long before Scar found Ra and Chac'chel talking with three humans by a panel table.

"Hello, Scar," Ra said before he shook Scar's wrist. "I want you to meet these fine gentlemen. This is Mayor Bruce Douglas, Commissioner Fanucci, and General Cartwright of their National Guard unit."

"Hello, Your Highness," Mayor Douglas said as he shook Scar hands.

"What up, Mayor."

"I just wanted to let you know, the book you wrote was really impactful for some people. It helped many of us through the scary parts of Ascension."

"Book?" Scar asked in confusion.

"You know, the book you wrote on Earth as Jamarcus Bridge. The one you barely finished before you died."

"Holy shit, someone found that!" Scar exclaimed before he quieted himself. "I completely forgot about that thing."

"It circled around some conspiracy theorist circles for a few decades, but everyone was shocked when Earth's representatives traveled here and found out you became Scar Amun as you wrote. It really solidified the Ascension and the Federation in many eyes around the planet."

"So it actually served a purpose," Scar wondered.

"The reason we called you here is because these men have a peculiar situation that can become very bad if not dealt with," Chac'chel said to bring the conversation back to the current issue. "These individuals here represent a colony of humans that left Earth to colonize a planet. New Terra, in one of the Makans' universes we supply light to. It was agreed upon with the Makan overarching governments that they could move to one of their worlds and begin trade with nearby nation planets after their vaccination process ends."

"Recently, we had a colony of Makans that landed on New Terra," General Cartwright said. "Close to our main city, Saint Jennifer. They believe that in the righteousness of their own religious doctrine that they are to lead us into the light, by teaching us, and, you know, popping out some kids with us."

"That sounds nice," Scar laughed. "But they moved on-world. Did they get medical clearance by the Federation to do so?"

"That's the problem, Lord Scar," Mayor Douglas pointed out. "They haven't gone through any vaccines regiments. They are a religious sect that doesn't practice medical science, relying only on the light. And they began missionary trips to the city multiple times, even when we requested them to keep their distance from us."

"How many humans migrated to New Terra?" Scar asked.

"There are seven million citizens in Saint Jennifer right now," Mayor Douglas said.

"Outstanding," Scar whispered.

"I don't have to tell you of the danger that this colony faces, Scar," Chac'chel stated to her nephew, staring into his light. "The Makans have to leave. Do you understand?"

"Yes Lady Chac'chel," Scar said before leaving the group, with Anansi and Enki following close behind.

"You guys are fifth densities, right?' Scar asked as he opened a window to the hanger of their family's air defense facility, where dozens of small long nosed, short winged blue scout planes stood before them.

"Yeah," Enki said as he and Anansi looked at awe at the planes.

"You guys grab a scout ship," Scar ordered. "I'm going to open a window to the universe and we are going to travel through the White as fast as we can to their planet."

"You can't open a window there?" Anansi asked as he walked towards one plane, climbing in the cockpit and filling it with his light.

"I've never observed their world. I'm going to follow my father's celestial lght to it."

"What, you don't want to ask your father for help?" Anansi asked.

"This is my responsibility," Scar answered solemnly, but recognized the wisdom of Anansi's poking fun. "You guys ready?"

"Almost," Enki said as he got set up in his scout plane, turning on dials and switches before he filled it with his light. When they were ready, Scar searched out into the Space Between, following his Father's energy until he saw the universe he was speaking about. Scar opened a window into the White of its universe, and when he, Enki and Anansi entered it, he closed the window behind him, speeding of in the White towards New Terra, just slow enough so the two Vanguard could keep pace with him.

It didn't take much time for the universe to scroll underneath them to find the planet, a green and white temperate world full of snow covered mountains in the northern and southern hemispheres, and hundreds of large, land locked massive lakes covering the planets continents. The perfect planet to start a interstellar civilization.

Scar scrolled down on the screen until the view of the planet surface was closer, where he swiped around until he found Saint Jennifer, and subsequentially the Makan colony across a river that separated them from the city. Scar once again open a window into the universe, which he and the two Vanguard flew through. Once in Scar flew towards the Makan colony, flying hastily over the surface of the river, the two Scout planes skimming the water surface but creating no spray as they slipped through reality.

"Aten Ka, they have sewage systems already emptying into the river," Enki noted as they arrived over the Makan town, where frog like beings gathered between bowl shaped houses as Scar, Enki and Anansi landed.

"Hello, Marines," a village elder in simple gray slacks and blue long sleeve shirt called out to them as Scar waited for the two Vanguard to leave their scout ships. "My name is Dene. I'm the so called leader of this village. Welcome."

"Good afternoon, Dene," Scar said as he waited for Enki to join him with Anansi. "How are you guys doing today."

"Fine up to this point," Dene answered with a nervous laugh. "Although I believe that this is going to change in a few moments."

"You can say that," Scar agreed. "These two are Staff Sergeant Enki and Staff Sergeant Anansi. My name is Sergeant Major Scar Amun of House Xkit."

"Your Highness," Dene proclaimed, his navy blue and lime green stripped cheeks expanding in excitement. "I've never met royalty before. I don't know what to say."

"We're not that special," Scar told Dene. "And I'm pretty sure you're going to find a bunch of words to say to me soon. I'm going to cut to the chase here, Dene. You and this village moved here in hopes of intermingling your light's and bodies with the humans across the river, correct?"

"Yes," Dene answered.

"I was briefed that your village did not go through the proper vaccination regimen before migrating here. Is that true?"

"We don't practice medical science in our culture," Dene explained. "We rely primarily with the Light to heal all our illnesses."

"Which is fine," Scar implored. "But the humans across the water don't do this. They are still third density beings. They require mechanical science to deal with sickness and injuries."

"That is why we want to mingle with them and teach them the way of the Light," Dene insisted. "To help them in their Ascension into the Light."

"Which will make their civilization completely reliant on you for medical purposes. So I'm going to ignore the fact that you may know the Federation policies on anti-colonial practices, something I actually went to school for. So no matter how you state it, you can't pull a blanket over my eyes."

"Whatever you may think you're trying to imply, your Highness," Dene said angrily. "…we have every righteous intentions to the people across the river."

"Scar, Dene," Scar requested. "And so that we are clear about how I stand on this issue, the righteousness of your beliefs doesn't excuse the fallacies of your actions. You have to realize that you are a walking plague to the beings over there. You're now spewing sickness out into the river. And to bring that plague to them, while simultaneously being the only ones to cure them of such plague is quite frankly Empty."

"Now I never insulted you Scar!" Dene shouted at him. "I ask that you don't insult our faith!"

"I'm not insulting you," Scar said as he took in a deep breath, releasing it in a slow sigh. "Look, Dene. I've been ordered to remove you from this planet. And I would like to add by any means necessary."

"Is that a threat?" Dene asked, his light trembling with concern.

"I'm just informing you of the parameters of my mission. These people across the water there are under my protection as a member of House Xkit. And I will. And if you all call yourselves members of the Federations, than you should know that what you're doing is wrong, and not of the Light according to the Federation's principles."

"Well, the Federation doesn't represent us then," Dene announced. "What kind of Federation can exist if it's going to trample on our beliefs."

"You know what, you remind me of a sect of people that lived on the planet back where these humans are from," Scar grumbled. "These guys used to go around with a flag that had a snake with the slogan 'Don't Tread On Me,' written on it. And that mentality is all well and good, but sometimes I think they believed it meant "I Can Tread On Other People…"

"Jamarcus, take it easy," Enki advised Scar, who took in another deep breath and released it slowly before speaking again.

"Your people have to leave, Dene," Scar demanded calmly. "I'm going to give you one month, and I'm going to wait here until you're gone."

"Do we have a choice in the matter?" Dene asked.

"Did any of you go through the process to become a member of Congress in the Federation?" Scar asked in earnest, waiting for a response. "Then no. And the Protection of Persons' Freedoms don't apply to this scenario."

"Well, I'm sorry that we couldn't convince you of the truth of our ways," Dene bemoaned.

"You and me both," Scar replied as he rubbed the space between his large eyes.

CHAPTER 19

164 AA

1

"So how much did we get?" Dewayne asked as Billy entered the safe house.

"We were able to buy about thirty seven kilos," Billy said as he closed the wooden door behind him and sat on a couch, placing a large duffle bag on a glass table.

"Let me see that shit," Dewayne said as he walked over the bag and opened it, pulling out a black plastic wrapped package. He pulled out a knife from his pocket and slit open a deep cut into it, revealing a clear crystal dust like substance. Dewayne's mind went blank, not seeing Billy in front of him as he scraped off some of the substance and put it on a steel plate place on top of a gas burner.

Dewayne turned from the table and walked about the disheveled stone brick house until he found his black needle kit, the only thing he had that was neat and organized. He returned back to the table, turning the burner on before opening up his kit. Dewayne breathed heavily, his gapped mouth open revealing crooked yellow teeth as he pulled out a rubber hose and tied it to his arm.

"You're going to burn the house down," Billy said as he moved the duffle bag from the table. "Watch what you're doing."

"I know what the fuck I'm doing," Dewayne said almost absent mindedly as he watched the crystals begin to melt into an brown substance. After messing with the semi-liquid substance with a metal stirrer he pulled out a needle and carefully drew the brown in, his teeth clinched as he stared down at the plate. Afterwards he wiggled back from the table, placing the needle in his mouth as he readjusted the hose on his pale, pimply arm, slapping it to find a good vein.

"Turn the fucking burner off," Dewayne heard Billy say, but his mind was focused on the needle that his poked in his skin, drawing blood into it and tapping the needle with precision, making sure that the mixture was right. He then plunged the drug into his vein, and after a few seconds of waiting, the world plunged forward and opened, as if his mind stepped back into the rear passenger seat of the car in his head. A numbing happiness spread through his body, as he gracefully laid back on the dirty floor, closing his eyes as he sunk further into his high, his brown bangs covering his face.

"Is it good?" Billy asked.

"What?"

"Is it good?" Billy said as he walked over to Dewayne, kicking him with his army boots. "Wake the fuck up."

"Yeah it's good," Dewayne said as he rolled over to his side, wanting to lie in that velvet hole he was in.

"Help me package this then," Billy said as he yanked Dewayne up with his dirty white and black sleeve t-shirt and pulled him to the table. He grabbed one of the packages and slit it open, grabbing a spoon to scoop much of the crystal out onto the table. Billy smacked Dewayne around enough to make him place much of the crystal into small plastic packages. After about an hour the two had enough packages to fill up a black garbage bag.

"I'm going to get the car," Billy said as he walked to the door, but Dewayne was ignoring him again, sitting quietly while staring at the wall. Billy walked over to their brown oval shape vehicle, looking out at the surrounding poor

Sirian neighborhood. There were kids playing in front of the other stone brick homes, or families hanging out on roof patios or the wooden stairs built into the outsides of the buildings.

Billy turned on the induction engine, then drove the vehicle over the mostly dirt grass yawn and right next to the front door. Billy went back into the house, putting on his black leather jacket and yanking up Dewayne, who stayed exactly where he was when he left.

"Get the fuck off me!" Dewayne muttered at Billy, his sunken eyes trembling in his sweaty face.

"Let's go sell this shit," Billy said as he swept back his unkempt black hair. "Grab the bag and put it in the car."

"Fuck, what the hell is wrong with you?" Dewayne said as he grabbed the bag and carried it outside, placing it in the trunk. Once inside, Billy drove the vehicle of the grass and onto the street, heading to their regular corner.

"We got to talk about Jeremy," Billy said as he looked at the gray skinned Sirians on the sidewalk.

"Jeremy? Why, what did he do?"

"I think he's a snitch."

"Fuck no," Dewayne said turning to him, his brown greasy hair barely keeping up with his whirling face. "He's human. Why would he snitch on us?"

"I don't think he's human," Billy said. "You know some of these aliens can shape shift, right?"

"Then how does he knows so much about Earth?"

"Maybe he's one of those old souls," Billy answered as he parked in front of an empty dirt lot, getting out and walking to the trunk.

"What'd he do to make you think that his a snitch," Dewayne asked as he walked with Billy, watching him grab a few packages and putting it in his pocket.

"He sought us out, trying to make some money," Billy said as they walked back to the hood of the car. "And he doesn't want to use any. That fucking gets under my skin. How many humans you know just walks up to a dealer and ask for a job but doesn't want to use?"

"Not many," Dewayne answered with a dejected look.

"The dumb ones," Billy said, looking straight at Dewayne's face. "But this motherfucker walks up to us, want's to get paid but doesn't want to use. I don't trust people that don't use this shit. So he either wants to go out on his own, or his a snitch."

"What do you want to do?" Dewayne asked as they watched a Sirian walking up to them.

"I don't know," Billy said as he gave the buyer a bag in exchange for a package filled with gold. For hours the two sold their product, exchanging it for a package of gold or two packages of silver. The one thing that has kept Earth from joining the Federation was the devaluing of precious metals. But open minded entrepreneurs like Billy realized that there were markets out in space for certain needs that they could supply if they brought it to worlds that thought that gold and silver was useless.

The day was going alright for the two until Billy noticed that Dewayne was coming of his high. He became more agitated with the customers, bossing some of them around when he didn't get what he wanted.

"What the fuck is this?" Dewayne said as one Sirian gave him a bag of some metallic substance.

"It's a metal, human," the Sirian said as he pulled on his dirty khaki colored open shirt. "What's the difference?"

"We want gold. You motherfuckers should know already. One bag of gold or two bags of silver. Nothing else."

"This is copper," the Sirian protested. "It does almost the same thing. The fuck's your problem?"

"Get the fuck out of here," Dewayne said as he turned from the man.

"Give me my shit," the Sirian demanded as he stepped up to Dewayne. "It's metal. What's your deal?"

"Calm the fuck down," Billy said, trying to break up the argument.

"Fuck it," Dewayne said, walking to the passenger side door. He reached into the car and pulled out a loaded forty five caliber pistol, pointing it at the Sirian. "How about lead, motherfucker You heard about lead?"

"Aten Ka!" the Sirian shouted, backing up from Dewayne with his hands up.

"Dewayne, stop!" Billy said as he grabbed Dewayne's arm.

"You heard about lead, right?" Dewayne asked again. "You know what it can do to you if I shoot you right now?"

"Hey, wait a dot, human. We are all lights here," the Sirian reasoned with Dewayne, backing away slowly from the two humans.

"DEWAYNE, STOP!!" Billy repeated at Dewayne, this time with Dewayne staring at him with his sick paranoid face.

"Lets go!" Billy ordered as he open the car door, yanking the pistol from Dewayne before shoving him into the car. Billy scrambled to the driver said and turned the engine on, peeling off with the Sirian male looking at them in confusion.

"Now we have to find another spot," Billy grumbled as he stared out the windshield, then grabbed the gun and pinned the muzzle against Dewayne's temple.

"DON"T YOU EVER TOUCH MY GUN AGAIN, BITCH!" Billy screamed. "YOU GOT THAT?!"

"Sorry," Dewayne said, his eyes clinched as he waited for Billy next move.

"Fuck!" Billy grunted as he put the gun under his seat, making a reminder to himself not to keep the gun out in the open. But Dewayne's outburst may have been fortuitous for Billy, as he drove through the neighborhood to a specific location.

"Where are we going?" Dewayne asked, his expression trembling with worry as he looked at Billy.

"You'll see," Billy said as he continued to drive until he parked across the street from a two story apartment building. Billy and Dewayne waited for almost an hour before they saw Jeremy, a skinny black guy with jeans and a multi colored t-shirt walk out of the apartment and into a blue sedan like vehicle. Billy turned his car after Jeremy as they drove off towards the downtown area of the local city. Billy eventually parked his vehicle down the street from where Jeremy stopped, right beside a restaurant. They waited in silence for a while before two more vehicles showed up, both with Naval Federation Emblems on them.

"No fucking way," Dewayne said as they watched Jeremy through the restaurant glass windows talking to the patrolmen. Billy looked at Dewayne, his drug fever spurring on his anger, until he knew the he was on to what he was going to suggest. After Jeremy left the shop, Billy turned the car away and drove back to their house.

"Call Jeremy," Billy told Dewayne.

"What do you want me to say?" Dewayne said as he pulled out his device and pressed a few icons.

"That I want to talk to him," Billy said in a calm voice as he drove, waiting patiently until Jeremy answered his phone.

"Hey Jeremy, it's Dewayne," he said into the phone. "Billy wants to talk to you…no, he didn't tell me why…you ask him."

"Hey Jeremy," Billy said as he grabbed the phone from Dewayne. "Dewayne fucked up earlier with one of our customers, didn't you Dewayne?"

"Yeah," Dewayne said shamefully.

"So we need to think up of place to set up shop again. Meet me at my house in a couple of hours."

"What the fuck happened?" Jeremy asked.

"Dewayne being Dewayne," Billy answered. "I'll let you know once you get there."

"You're not there now?"

"No, we're scoping out some places," Billy explained. "I'll talk to you then."

"Alright," Jeremy answered before Billy hung up the phone. He drove calmly back to the house, with both men heading inside where Billy grabbed the duffle bag and went back to the vehicle and placed it in the trunk, then grabbed his gun and slipped it in the back of his pants.

"Clean this place up," Billy ordered as he came back inside. "Put all the trash in garbage bags and put it in the car." For the next hour they cleaned up the house the best they could, then grabbed an gray oval sanitary droid they never used and had it cleanse the building even further, destroying all forensic evidence that they were in the building. Billy grabbed the plastic gear they once used to make drugs and made Dewayne and himself put on the gloves and boots. Then for half an hour they waited until they heard Jeremy arrived in front of the house, slamming his car door and walking up to the door, knocking on it.

"Hey, Jeremy," Billy said as he open the door after Jeremy knocked for the third time.

"Hey fellas," Jeremy said as he walked into the house. He smiled for a moment when he saw that the house was cleaned, then his expression turned to horror as he turned around, his eyes locked on Billy's gun that was pointing straight him.

"Wait!" Jeremy yelped before Billy fired five rounds into Jeremy's chest, the bullets plunging into the stone walls of the house. Jeremy dropped on the ground, a pool of blood spreading underneath him.

"I guess he was human," Billy said as he and Dewayne stepped out the door and towards the car, stopping when blinding lights flashed on in front of them

"This is Naval Drug Enforcement!" a voice screamed into their heads. "Get your hands in air and get on your knees, now!"

"Shit!" Billy shouted as he turned and ran back inside, but stopped when he saw Scar in his black Marine uniform standing in the spot where Jeremy laid. Before he could think, Scar leapt forward, grabbing Billy by the neck and yanking him into the air.

"Surprise motherfucker," Scar smiled with his too small mouth. Dewayne tried to run from the lawn, but was blasted off his feet by a concussive kinetic bolt that erupted in front of him, spraying dirt in every direction.

"This is entrapment!" Billy grunted in Scar's hand.

"You're the one who pulled the trigger," Scar said as he dropped Billy on the floor.

"You are being arrested for the charges of drug trafficking, resisting arrest, and committing homicide in the second degree," a voice called out again as Naval Patrolmen pinned the two on the ground. "You have rights as suspects. Do you need your rights spoken to you."

"Go fuck yourselves!" Billy said as the two were dragged out to the floating disk shaped vessels above the street. "I'll get out of this! This was a goddamn set up! This is bullshit!"

2

Achtland laid quietly in the back of a square transport vehicle, tied up and barely coherent as she stayed quiet next to two other women. A gray fur Lyran drove the broken down van like car on a deserted desert rode, with a gaunt Andean riding silently in the passenger seat next to him. Every once in a while the Andean would glance to the back of the van where their cargo was, the three women, all drugged and scantly cloth. One was a blue to green colored avian, another a gray to black Lyran, and Achtland, a red haired Pleiadean who was short for her species, but still taller than most other beings.

The Andean continued to sneak glances back at the women, one part his urges getting the better of him, the other part the uncertainty of the packages they bought. The transfer went off without a hitch. They traded with someone they dealt with for cycles. But this one night settle wrong in the Andean, not allowing him to be at ease, which was a normal paranoid state for him.

"Did they say that one of the girls was going to be a Pleiadean, Rui Shi?" the Andean asked as he shot another glance at Achtland's ass.

"What are you going on now?" Rui Shi asked.

"Did Pol'tats say that one of the girls was going to be a Pleiadean?"

"No, I don't think so. What's the deal?"

"We should have double check who we were picking up before we got there."

"What is your deal, Hunab?"

"Remember the last time we pick up a package that we didn't know about. It turned out to be some bitch that another guy bought. They sent guys after us, man. They were ready to kill us if Angus didn't broker a deal to clear shit up."

"I wasn't here when that went down," Rui Shi told Hunab.

"That scared the shit out of me," Hunab said as he looked out at the black desert wilderness surrounding them. There was no moon that night, and was abnormally overcast, with the clouds blocking most of the stars in the sky. Other than the light coming from the vehicle, they couldn't see that far out into the darkness.

"Anyway, when we get back to the city I'm going to get fucking hammered," Hunab said as he glance back at the women. "There's this bitch in this bar that I go to in Tunichtal, this fine ass Andean bitch. She's all over me when I go to that place. I'm thinking of turning her out."

"You think every woman is hot for your skinny tadpole ass," Rui Shi laughed.

"Shut the fuck up," Hunab spat at Rui Shi. "I can get any bitch I want. I bet these girls back here want some of this dick."

"They probably think your sprout is as short and skinny as you."

"Fuck you, you fur ball punk. Why don't you clean out the shit balls dangling from your ass."

"Ha!" Rui Shi snorted. "Why're you so angry?"

"Fuck you, asshole," Hunab said, his eyes still locked on Achtland. "I can still make the legs of these bitches numb from below the knees. The red hair girl wants some of this. I can tell from the way she's staring at me."

"What the fuck can you do to her?" Rui Shi asked, egging Hunab on as he stumbled to the back of the van, his gaze crawling over the three women. Anxiety sprang up in the other two women's light, which Achtland allowed to sink into hers, making her body shakes that more real when Hunab grabbed at one of her breasts.

"You like that don't you," Hunab asked Achtland, pinching down hard into her flesh, causing her to flinch in pain.

"Achtland, you okay?" Scar spoke into her light when he felt her distress.

"I'm good Jamarcus," Achtland reassured Scar mentally, but wretched when Hunab tried to kiss her on the mouth, receiving a punch in her eye for her response.

"Fucking cunt!" Hunab screamed at her, making the other two women groaned in misery, tears already flowing down their faces.

"Man, take it easy on them," Rui Shi said to Hunab to cool him down. "They haven't been broken in yet. Angus is going to be pissed off at you for breaking the merchandise before we get back."

"Fuck you," Hunab snapped at the Lyran before he took his seat next to the driver.

"Were you under distress, man?" Scar asked again in Achtland's light.

"Stop worrying, Jamarcus," Achtland insisted, letting the Empty into her like the women next to her were, crying with her fellow slaves. "Let me finish my mission."

"Dude, if you feel threaten, you are authorized to protect yourself," Scar reminded Achtland.

"I know," Achtland said laying in despair as they drove for sections until the square van drove off the road and onto a dirt path that would lead them to a rundown wooden shack out in the middle of nowhere. When Rui Shi parked the vehicle, he and Hunab climbed out of the van, heading to the rear and opening up the doors. They violently grabbed the women and yanked them out, forcing them to walk into the shack where a bloated Pleiadean man with a full grown black beard and tied up hair waited for them with the door open.

"Was she part of the deal?" Angus asked about Achtland as Rui Shi and Hunab dragged the women inside, throwing them all down in one corner of the shake.

"They said she was part of the package," Rui Shi insisted as he went to a table in the one room shack, grabbing a bottle of alcohol to take a long swig.

"Fucking hell," Angus sputtered as he closed the door. "Pol'tats better not have fucked up again this time. Didn't he say that it was supposed to be an Andean in the group."

"That's what I was trying to tell Rui Shi," Hunab said as he hovered over the girls. "Fuck if I'm going to have another Block trying to kill us over another mix up."

"I'll call Pol'tats tomorrow and give him a piece of my mind. Aten Ka, he pulls this shit again, I'll put a pellet in his head."

"No you won't," Hunab laughed at Angus as he walked over to the booze table and grabbed another bottle of alcohol. "You kiss that man's ass every time you see him."

"That's call networking," Angus argued as he walked over to the cargo, staring down the women who began the tremble yet again as they watched how his gaze crawled over them.

"Have you drugged these bitches," Angus asked as he bent down and grabbed the skirt of Achtland, raising it to get a glance of her under garments, his pot belly sticking out of his undersize shirt, ready to burst it open if he happen to eat one more morsel.

"When we left Pol'tats guys," Rui Shi said as he and Hunab stared at him with blank stares.

"I'm going to try this bitch out," Angus said as he pulled Achtland up and over to the room's bed. "I haven't had home pussy since I left Iau." Angus threw Achtland down on the filthy mattress, her mind filling with the other woman's terror as Angus began to pull his pants down before he laid on top of her.

"Aten Ka, Achtland! Are you in distress?!" Scar asked again in her light.

"I'm fine," Achtland mumbled verbally, the drugs in her keeping her from talking correctly, with Angus smiling from her statement.

"Yeah, you want this don't you?" Angus asked as he began to pull down her garments.

"Defend yourself!" Scar screamed in her head, waking her up enough so she could fill her body with enough light to lessen the effects of the drugs in her system.

"They haven't said where they're taking us yet," Achtland mumbled.

"What was that?" Angus asked as he laid on top of Achtland.

"That's and order Staff! Defend yourself!" Scar blasted in Achtland's light.

"Yes, Sergeant," Achtland said as she looked at Angus confused look above her.

"Wait…no!" Angus cried before Achtland broke free from her restraints, swiping at Angus face, her hand cleaving right through it and grabbing his small three looped Aten Ka in her hand. The women screamed in terror as Angus' blood sprayed all over the bed and Achtland. Rui Shi and Hunab stood slack mouth in disbelief at what they just saw.

"It's a raid!" Rui Shi exclaimed as he ran to the door and towards the van, only to be met with a blast of the White, knocking him prone on his back, the force of the attack and the pain in his body leaving him sucking air into his lungs. Hunab watch this unfold, his mind twitching at what to do. He lunged at the air pressure weapon in the room, turning the displacement field on before it and the wall next to him was yanked away into the black of night. Before Hunab could react a White blast hit him, flinging him against the opposite side of the room, hitting the wall and falling unconscious.

"You killed me," Angus' light said is it twirled around in Achtland hand as the room began to fill with Naval Patrolmen.

"You alright," Scar asked as he walked into the ripped wall to Achtland, who was still covered in Angus blood.

"Yeah?" Achtland answered, her mind still fuzzy with her injection.

"What a dot," Scar said as he reached out to her, rewinding her form back in time until the drugs were out of her system, Achtland's light and the blood covering her clearing up in the process.

"You killed me," Angus stated again in disbelief as he stared at Achtland.

"Yes I did," she stated as she handed his Aten Ka over to one of the Patrolmen before she walked over to free the other women.

"We can make a deal with you," Scar suggested to Angus before he was carried out of the house. "We can bring back your body if you tell us where these victims were going."

"You killed me," Angus repeated, his light still in shock.

"Get him out of here," Scar said as the Patrolmen left with Angus' Light. Scar walked over to Achtland who held the two women in her arms.

"Are you sure you alright?" Scar asked, keeping his distance from her.

"I'm good, Sergeant Major," Achtland answered with a small tremble in her voice.

"I'll be outside when you're ready," Scar said, leaving her to cope with what just happen.

CHAPTER 20

166 AA

1

"**W**ake up, Sonlig," Sneeze said as she kissed Scar on the cheek while he laid in bed.

"Hmmm," Scar groaned as he snapped awake, looking at Sneeze as she walked out of the bedroom.

"Can you go see if Horus and Hathor are awake while I make breakfast?" Sneeze asked before she left the room.

"Alright," Scar mumbled as he got out of bed, wearing nothing as he walked out of the bedroom door just in time to see Sneeze's naked figure descend the stairs. Scar slowly walked to Horus bedroom, who was still tangled up in his small sheets, his pale white hair tangled and draped over his face. His light grew and shrank with each breath he took as Scar approach his side.

"Wake up son," Scar said as he patted Horus arms until Horus rose with a giant yawn. Scar pick up Horus, who curled up in his arms and began sucking his thumb as Scar walked to the nursery. Scar made his way to the white lamp inside the crib, looking down at their one year old, her small hands crunched up against her white cheeks as she laid silently sleeping, her legs curl up under her swaddling garments.

Scar decided to let Hathor sleep so he could wash Horus in the shower. He walked back into his bedroom and into the bathroom where he prepared the shower's temperature before stepping in. He placed Horus in the stream of the shower, who covered his eyes as he got soaked. Scar handed him a bar of soap, and as he washed himself, watched Horus closely to see if he did the same. When he saw that Horus was missing some areas, he tried to help him, but Horus just pushed his hands away, wanting to wash himself like a big boy.

Scar laughed at his son, seeing that Horus was in a lot of ways a big boy. He was seven cycles old, even though his body still looked like a toddler. He wanted to do things boys his age usually did, but was still too young or too small to do, like play sports or rough house with the older kids in the neighborhood. Which made it more satisfying when Scar had to treat him like a baby, such as when he picked up Horus after they finished showering, trying to dry him off when Horus refused to, grabbing a towel himself to do it.

When they were both dry enough, they climbed down the stairs and walked into the kitchen where Sneeze had just finished putting a freshly cooked hot cake onto a plate and placed it onto a table. After placing pieces of blue and black seeded fruit on it, she gave Horus a fork who began to consume his meal.

"Here, Sonlig," Sneeze said as he handed Scar a bowl of the same chopped up fruit.

"Thank you, Sweet Pea," Scar said as he wrapped his arm behind her, cupping one of her perky breasts in his hand.

"You know you can't stop once you start," Sneeze scolded Scar as she turned back to kiss him.

"Sorry," Scar said as he sat down next to Horus, the two eating happily next to each other. The peace was broken when Hathor began to cry from her nursery, waking from her slumber.

"Horus!" she shouted in her light as her form began to cry in successive bursts. Horus jumped off his chair without finishing his breakfast, dashing off to the nursery.

"You should have woken her," Sneeze sighed in grief as she listen to Hathor from the sink while washing dishes.

"I'm sorry," Scar said as he swallowed the last pieces of fruit in his bowl. "She looked so peaceful lying there. I didn't want to disturb her."

"I better go get her," Sneeze said as Scar handed her his bowl. "She's probably hungry."

"I'll go get her," Scar said as he walked to the stairs, not wanting to bother Sneeze any more than he should. He walked into the nursery to find Horus jumping up and down with his finger in Hathor's hand as she continued to cry.

"I think she needs her diaper changed," Horus informed Scar as he walked to Hathor, reaching down and sniffing her garments, wincing his nose as he found the source of Hathor discomfort.

"I think you're right," Scar said as he picked up Hathor and took her over to the changing table. "Do you want to help me change her?"

"No," Horus answered, his face squinting as Scar removed Hathor's garments and placed them into a bin close by. Scar grabbed some wipes and quickly cleaned Hathor bottom, thin pick her up again as he took her downstairs to the kitchen.

"Sweet Pea, where's the baby bathtub?" Scar asked once he returned.

"Under the sink," Sneeze said as she reached down into the cupboard and pulled out a pink colored tub with soft rubber lining. Sneeze filled the tub with lukewarm water as Scar grabbed a bottle of baby soap, squirting some in to create some lather bubbles. Scar slowly put Hathor in the tub and began to washed her body with the soapy water.

"Horus!" Hathor cried again, wanting her brother to wash him. Horus grabbed a chair and pulled it next to the sink, where he began to bug his sister with picking up water with his hand and pouring it on her head. Hathor would grumble, pushing away his hand when he did so then cry for him to do it again, her body trembling every time he did.

"I swear, you two love to fight, don't you," Sneeze giggled as she rubbed Hathor's pale white skin, staring into her eyes that were as obsidian as hers. Once Scar was done he picked up Hathor and took some more lukewarm water in a cup and poured it out over Hathor to rinse her off. When he dried her off he handed her carefully over to Horus who bounced impatiently next to Scar, wanting to hold his little sister. Horus held her tightly, trying to mingle his light into hers.

"Horus, you have to watch your lessons," Sneeze said as she picked up Hathor from his arms.

"Okay," Horus said as he ran into the living room, touching a wooden shelf against one of the living room walls so a large hologram screen popped up. Scar and Sneeze sat next to each other, Sneeze adjusting Hathor so she could breast feed while Horus flicked through programs until he reached a visual recording where an elderly Lyran woman waved into the living room.

"Hello," the woman greeted in her language.

"Hello," Horus responded in the same tongue. He continued to have a conversation with the woman, the recording repeating a phrase whenever Horus made a mistake. Lesson after lesson Horus continued, absorbing the information that the screen placed into his light, even after Hathor had finished feeding and went back to sleep in Sneeze's arm. It would be another couple of sections that Horus parents watched him learn until the house phone began to ring.

"I'll get it," Scar said as he absent mindedly walked over to the hologram screen to answer it.

"Sonlig, you're still naked," Sneeze told Scar, who stopped dead in his tracks, raising his light to create a black uniform over his body while she retreated to the upstairs bedroom.

"Horus, put some clothes on," Scar said to his son, waiting after he ran upstairs to his bedroom before answering the call.

"Hello, this is Scar," he said as he pressed the red glowing icon on the television shelf. The screen turned blue for a moment, then flashed into an operation's room located in Fort Ah'Pekku.

"Jamarcus, are you busy," Major Yumcha asked as he stood before Scar in a set of khaki military uniform with shorts.

"Not right now," Scar said as he shot a quick glance up the stairs.

"Thing's have escalated over in Ganesha territory, and the Federation's brass are wanting all assets available to deal with the situation. We've been ordered to mobilize to assist the fleets."

"Which means that they are forcing you to go with me," Scar grumbled.

"It's the job, Jamarcus," Major Yumcha responded. "I have no problems with it."

"Any word on what my sister is up to?" Scar asked.

"For now nothing," Major Yumcha sighed. "Liberation Front has a fleet blockade in the Darshana system. They tried to form one in the Mangala system, but your sister has destroyed every ship that entered Mangala space. But the Federation doesn't want her to over reach into Darshana."

"How did they get their hands on enough vessels to form a fleet?" Scar asked himself.

"That's something we're probably have to deal with later," Major Yumcha said.

"I'm guessing they want us mobilized yesterday?" Scar asked with a sad smile.

"I'll see you in a hour," Major Yumcha said before he hung up on his end.

"Sweet Pea, did you hear that?" Scar asked as he walked up the stairs to their bedroom.

"Yes," Sneeze said as she stood at the foot of the bed, clothed in one of her favorite set of clothes of Athena's with a worried face. "Do you want us to leave?"

"Momma doesn't want you or the kids in this universe if there are any conflicts," Scar said as he linked his light with Psssh's to let him known what the situation was.

"We could just stay on Nima," Sneeze said as she walked out of the bedroom to gather Horus up who was playing on his video game console.

"Yeah, no," Scar laughed. "I don't want to get in it again between her and Psssh. They bicker all the time about what their grandkids should be doing."

"Come on Horus, we're going back home to Grandpa," Sneeze said as she turned off the game.

"Dad, do you have to go fight?" Horus asked as he walked over to Scar.

"Yep," Scar said as he pick him up in his arms, following Sneeze and Hathor downstairs and out the front door.

"Are you going to come visit us?" Horus asked as he held on to Scar's neck.

"Not anytime soon, but I hope in a few weeks," Scar said as he kissed Hathor on her chin a few times. A flash of light burst above them in the night sky and a hole to Sneeze's universe appeared with one of Psssh's ships hovering next to it. A smaller diamond shape craft dropped down out of the sky towards the house.

"Is the ship cleared to be above Teotihuacan space right now?" Sneeze asked.

"I'll deal with it when I get to base," Scar said as he held his family in his arms, lingering from not wanting to let them go.

"Honey, we have to leave," Sneeze said as she kissed Scar's neck. Scar loosened his grip on them, just enough so he can look up into Sneeze's eyes.

"Don't look at me like that," she said placing a hand over his eyes. "You get that hungry look and I can't think."

"I'm sorry," Scar said. "It's just that I had a dream similar to this. I just wanted to be sure that you guys are real."

"Light paradox, Sonlig," Sneeze said as she kissed Scar firmly on his lips. "It should be more important that you're happy."

"Yeah," Scar agreed before he kissed Horus on his cheek, making him squirm in his arms before he put him down to walk with his mother to the waiting ship.

"Let me know when you're ready to deploy," Sneeze requested as she waved to Scar.

"Love you guys," Scar said before they shifted into the diamond craft and flew up to dock with the large pyramid in the sky

2

"Are all fleets accounted for," Admiral Unicob asked as the flagship carrier drop out of the White and into empty space.

"Not yet, Admiral," an officer answered as he walked next to Unicob. Unicob waited patiently while he looked out of his ship's helm and into dark space as more ships began to drop out of the White and into attack formations. Miles long black elongated pyramid shape carriers, the aft of the ships longer than the bow, dotted the area in front of Unicob, their hulls sprinkled with lights. Dozens of frigates and fighters were either dock to or flying by the carriers, all going about their final preparation for the assault.

"Admiral Unicob, Admiral Aapo is calling you," an communication Patrolman called out from his station.

"Bring him up, shipmate," Unicob ordered as he walked next the Patrolman. An hologram of Admiral Aapo appeared above the two, the old man staring at them with concern eyes.

"Admiral Unicob," Aapo greeted him. "How are we this fine Navy day?"

"Outstanding," Unicob laughed. "Any day we can help out House Xkit is a fine Navy day."

"I thank you for your assistance," Aapo laughed with a sarcastic smile. "Has all the fleets assembled yet."

"From what I could gather, eight attack fleets have arrived. The 228th and 374th fleet hasn't assembled yet."

"Do you want to link lights for intel, Admiral?" Aapo asked.

"One moment," Unicob said as he placed his hand on a slick black panel, allowing Aapo's light to sink into his, ordering the Patrolman to turn the link off. "What do have for me, Aapo."

"Not much," Aapo began, worry trembling his light. "We know that Liberation Front has a fleet. What size, we're not sure. They have also recruited the help of one of the secular nations on Darshana, a few hundred thousand. They have been cautious with assembling all there ships in the system, but what has been confirmed is seven Rukma class frigates, several hundred Sundara class fighters, and one confirm sighting of a Tripura class carrier."

"If we don't have an exact number, we can't make a solid strategy," Unicob grumbled in his light. "Will your granddaughter be joining the fight?"

"I hope not," Aapo answered. "Knowing her, she would have dove right in over Darshana to take out as much of the blockade as she could. She has been ordered to stay on Mangala to secure that space. Not to worry Unicob, we have a battalion of Marines standing by, including a platoon of Vanguards."

"Your grandson," Unicob surmised. "He won't be able to act how I like unless we deem it necessary for strategic deployment. We will have to lure out Njord if he is there."

"Which means we must use a bait tactic to bring any ships they have to Darshana," Aapo said. "That's why we asked for so many ships to assemble. We should be thankful that Darshana asked the Federation for aid. Otherwise we would have lost more lights from our fold."

"We'll have the Seventh fleet arrive first, to drop off as much Patrolmen onto Darshan surface as we can. Then we'll have to wait and see how Liberation Front responds."

"Hopefully they won't send in their higher density fighters," Aapo suggested to Unicob.

"I hope they do," Unicob physically spoke to himself. "We can end this today if they choose to fight."

"Admiral Unicob, the 228th and 374th has arrived," an officer reported to Unicob.

"Here we go," Unicob said as he took in a released a deep breath. "May Aten Ka shine its Light on our path. Captain Bitol, you may commence with the attack."

"Yes Admiral," the captain responded, a tall, darkly tanned Andean with blazing blue eyes, and after a few moments ten battle frigates rose into the White and speed over and back out into the waters of reality above planet Darshana, a major metropolitan city planet. The ships waited in orbit above the planet for over a minute, the crew on the ships watching anxiously for anything to appear out in empty space.

"They're not taking the bait, Captain Bitol," Unicob said. "We have to force their hand. Send in your carrier and deploy Patrolmen onto the planet's surface."

"Aye aye, Admiral," Bitol answered, and ordered his carrier to move above Darshana. As soon as his massive ship drop out of the White, hundreds of metallic sphere deployment pods were ejected out of the carrier and down to the planet. Suddenly seven golden coned Rukma tower ships, the base section of the towers wider than each ascending level, appeared and began to blast the pods out of the ionosphere.

"All frigates attack," Captain Bitol ordered, and the ten Federation battle frigates lunged forward towards the Rukma class frigates. Bolt after bolt of the White was sent at the Rukmas, which shrugged off most of the blasts with their shields, forcing them from targeting the pods and focusing on the approaching frigates. As the Federation frigates got within miles of the Rukmas, a colossal size golden city appeared above all of the ships, literally casting a shadow over all of them. The Tripura class carrier released nearly a thousand butterfly like Sundara fighters towards the Federation frigates, and soon their blasts began to overwhelm the Federation frigates with holes being punched in their black hulls.

"2nd, 29th, and 101st fleet, take care of that carrier," Unicob commanded, and three flotillas appeared above the Tripura city carrier. As the new influx of Federation frigates targeted the city, trading bolts of White with it, the new carriers released thousands of long nose fighters to attack the Sundara dragonflies. The sky above Darshana crisscross with countless blasts and explosions, and soon the Liberation Front fleet was beaten closer to a breaking point as one of the Rukma golden towers exploded and split in half, falling to the planet surface.

"Fucking Empty," Unicob muttered as he saw the ship falling in his light.

"This was to be expected," Aapo reassured Unicob.

"Still…" Unicob said, not wanting his true emotion to leak out into his Light.

"Admiral Unicob, one of the frigates from the 29th flotilla has reported a breach," a technician reported out.

"About time," Unicob grunted as he searched out with his light and saw the black diamond ship begin to explode from the inside. Soon a large rupture of energy burst from its hull as a Anunnaki clothed in tatty clothing exploded out of the ship and towards another frigate. Hundreds of rag-tagged flying beings from different species join the first infiltrator, who began to shift into the Federation ships and wreak havoc.

"2nd Battalion, Third and Fourth Marines, engage," Admiral Unicob ordered, and soon close to a thousand Marines in black fitted uniforms shifted above Darshana, commencing in close combat with the flying Liberation front insurgents. The tide of battle began to turn in favor of the Federation due to attrition, and Unicob once again grew anxious, waiting for the inevitable final battle.

"He's going to show up," Aapo guessed. "You can't commit your most powerful fighters and not go in yourself."

"I hope you're right," Unicob mumbled, and as if on cue, he felt a large sensation of force as a seventh density light appeared. Scrying for it, he discovered a massive shaved head Pleiadean, clothed in dark slacks and a leather jacket, his sky blue eyes inspecting the Marine he was gripping in his hand. With one punch the Pleiadean sent the Marine unconsciously hurtling out into space.

"It's Njord," Unicob told Aapo as he watched the Pleiadean rampage through the Marine forces like a lion upon lambs. The Federation fighters mustered together to take on the new threat, but they stood no better chance than taking down a mountain with a shovel.

"Major Yumcha, send in your platoon," Unicob ordered calmly.

"Aye aye, Admiral," Major responded before he and his platoon shifted to and attack Njord. He was taken by surprise by this new group, as the Vanguards' techniques and experience showed as they were able to go almost blow for blow with Njord. All it did though was make Njord fight less sloppy, and one by one he was able to dispatched each member of the Vanguard platoon, either by disintegrating one or breaking another. Eventually only Yumcha was left, his thin Andean frame pale in comparison to the over eight foot tall frame of his foe.

Without hesitation, Njord came in for a final blow against Yumcha when he was suddenly blasted from the side as Rhiannon shifted in. As her light shined through her old Marine uniform, her teeth cliched as she pummeled Njord with punches and kicks, her long black hair flowing behind her as she commence her assault.

"Source dammit," Aapo muttered in Unicob light as they watched Njord, Rhiannon and Yumcha go at each other with lethal relentlessness. When the strikes from the terrorist became too much for Rhiannon, she ceased he attack, floating by and waiting as Yumcha was in the midst of an exchange before she plunged into Njord, sending them both crashing onto the surface of the Tripura city carrier.

Infuriated, Njord picked up Rhiannon and threw her plowing through the superstructure of the ship. Njord filled himself up with light, planning on vaporizing Rhiannon before Yumcha kicked Njord in the back, breaking his concentration as he shifted his attention back on the officer. Yumcha managed to dodge most of his strikes before Rhiannon joined back in, and as they shifted their fighting strategy of keeping their distance and blasting Njord, they began to hold their own against him.

Seeing this, Njord upped the ante by creating a sword capable of holding his light in it. He was able to lunge forward at Yumcha, and with the added reach, slashed at his chest, cutting him open as he curled in a ball, holding his chest together in his hands. Rhiannon shifted over Njord, grabbing his arm and trying to wrestle the sword out of his hand. Njord tried to grab Rhiannon, but she stood up on her hands on Njord arm, twirling around to dodge his grab.

Thinking quick for a strategy to end his fight, Njord yanked down a huge water reality well under Rhiannon, slowing all of her movements. Rhiannon tried to fly away, but Njord was too fast, grabbing her arm with one hand and plunging his sword completely through her with the other. Soundlessly she screamed as Njord pulled the sword from her torso and flung her towards the planet's surface.

"Request permission for the release of strategic assets," Unicob asked.

"Stand by Admiral," Aapo said as he spoke to a waiting council of politicians and military personnel.

"You have a green light," Aapo spoke out.

"Send in Sergeant Major Scar," Unicob told Major Yumcha.

"You're up, Jamarcus" Major Yumcha grunted from somewhere above Darshana, working to heal himself.

"Roger that," Scar said, as he floated above the White Road of the Omniverse, a spiraling beam of white light that had multiverses springing forth from it like lotus blossoms from a vine. Upon looking into the window that he used to observe the battle, he filled himself up to his fullest density, with eleven loops springing from his head. Scar froze time in the universe so that the only thing that appeared to be moving was Njord.

After searching in the White Road, he found Njord's celestial energy and yanked it almost completely from him, leaving Njord at the fourth density. Scar then shifted right next to Njord, and the insurgent leader hardly had enough time to glance at Scar before Scar punched him right on the chin, knocking him unconscious and falling down as a fire ball. He slammed against Darshana atmosphere in an explosion before descending to its surface.

"Is the target eliminated," Unicob asked Scar in his light.

"Negative Admiral," Scar answered as he waited for Njord to land in a large flash of white concussive force in an isolated dessert. Scar shifted next to the crater, the sun blazing above him as he walked slowly in as Njord gradually gained his wits.

"Do you need any help?" Rhiannon asked in a raspy voice, shifting next to Scar while still holding her wounded stomach with her hand.

"I think I'm good," Scar said as Njord slowly crawled at him, his deep anguish boiling up in the light Scar allowed him to have.

"You false god," Njord muttered, his battered frame shaking as he spoke. "You think you can rule over all lights. You have no right to own beings. You have no right to take freedom from them."

"I offer energy and protection," Scar told Njord as he stood above him. "I do nothing more."

"You're a tool," Njord spat at Scar, barely able to look up at him. "You've been brainwash from birth. Mentally tortured and conditioned. You think you have free will, but it's a lie. You think these people are a slave to you. But you'll be nothing but a slave to the Federation." As Njord looked into Scar's light, a cruel smile spread across face.

"But you think you are a slave master. You all but changed your skin to one."

"You know what?" Scar began as he bent down to Njord. "You're right. Everything you said is right. And even if I think I had some agency in my choice, it doesn't change a thing. But I've come to copes with what I am. And more importantly, with what I am not. And my 'I am not' is only defined by my actions. When you come back, don't even bother doing all this terrorist bullshit. You come see me. And I will do what I was created to do." Scar then opened up the White and blasted Njord into subatomic particles, creating a massive fireball mushroom cloud that could be seen for miles.

"Target eliminated," Scar informed Admiral Unicob.

"Send in the rest of the attack force," Admiral Unicob ordered from his ship before the rest of the fleet traveled to Darshana to end the battle.

CHAPTER 21

168 AA

1

"I'm back home," Scar told Sneeze as he got off the public bus, throwing his green military duffle bag over his shoulder.

"Wait…hold on…Horus is acting up…are you back?"

"Yeah," Scar said as he walked along the road that lead to his father's house on Suburbia. "I just got off the bus. I literally came here right from the spaceport. I didn't even wait to change out of my uniform."

"Wait, let me see…I like your ass in that thing."

"What ass," Scar said as he look at his rear in his slim black Vanguard uniform. "I had a better ass when I was Jamarcus. This body's flat."

"It's muscular." Sneeze laughed in his light. "How was your flight?"

"Long and boring," Scar answered as he looked at the houses in his old neighborhood, seeing how beautiful some of them are in the late spring day. The trees were in bloom and the blossoms were falling into the wind whenever a strong breeze swept through them, filling the air with a rainbow of colors.

"Did you get any sleep?"

"A little bit. I shouldn't complain though. It was a normal domestic flight. I can't expect every navigator to be as fast as I am in the White."

"I've gotten the same way," Sneeze admitted as she chased Horus around her chambers in Psssh's castle. "I love my maids and the workers for my father, but I get so annoyed if one of them is navigating instead of having your light taking us where we want to go."

"Aten Ka, we sound like a bunch of spoiled rich people," Scar grumbled.

"We are," Sneeze said as she finally grabbed Horus up. "Say hello to your father, Horus."

"Hi Daddy," he said as he pressed his forehead against Sneeze's. "When are we going to come over to your place for the wedding?"

"When are you guys going to leave?" Scar asked as he wave to one of his parents' neighbors.

"We were supposed to leave as soon as you got home," Sneeze said as she put Horus down. "So I guess it was fortuitous that you called out to me."

"Are you guys all set to leave?"

"No, not yet," Sneeze said. "I have to make sure that Proclaim, Whisper and Nibble are ready to go."

"The royal bridesmaid gang," Scar laughed as he approached his neighbor's gray wooden fence as he walked out to greet him.

"Good morning, Scar," he said, taking off his sun hat and wiping the sweat from his brow from working in his garden. "Did you just get home from the military?"

"Good morning, Mr. Ahmak," Scar answered as he reached down from the fence and shook Ahmak's wrist. "Yeah, I just got off the bus just now."

"Has it been ten cycles already?"

"Eleven," Scar laughed. "But who's counting?"

"So what's the first thing that you're going to do when you get home?"

"Oh, I'm raiding our fridge and fixing me a cheeseburger, maybe with mushrooms and Nimian onions."

"Ready to get off the vegan diet," Ahmak chuckled at Scar. "I don't blame you. Will that get in the way of your light once you become Speaker."

"I should come back down to a resting tenth density," Scar assessed idly. "I shouldn't have a problem sharing my light at that point."

"You're in the eleventh density now," Ahmak whispered in awe. "I don't think I'll ever see something like that again in this lifetime."

"It is what it is," Scar said shamefully.

"Are you ready?" Ahmak asked.

"No," Scar answered.

"Well, I hope you get ready pretty soon," Ahmak said as he waved Scar away. "You go home now and get some rest. Tell your mother I said hi and I hope her Arrow Head roses wilt."

"Wow," Scar laughed as he walked towards his house. "Bye Mr. Ahmak. Sneeze, you still there?"

"Hmmm," Sneeze answered in his head.

"Are you busy?"

"Oh no, I'm just helping Hathor put on her shoes she wants to wear for the wedding."

"Daddy?" Hathor called out as Sneeze place their heads together.

"Yes, baby?"

"…Daddy?"

"Yes, I'm here."

"Do you…do you know where my other shoes are?"

"Which ones?"

"Don't encourage her," Sneeze said as she put Hathor down. "She's been obsessed with shoes lately. She's been that way ever since we visited Athena and Rhiannon on Firmament."

"Has she been?" Scar asked with a smile.

"She was so happy when she found out she had feet like them. All the kids on Roi Son make fun of her because of them. Now she wants to wear shoes like Rhiannon all the time."

"She just has a role model that she wants to be like," Scar said as he walked into the front yard of his home, the pathway wreath in Ixchel's flowers that she grew around the white wooden archway. "I forgotten how beautiful Momma's garden is during the spring."

"By the way, where did your mother tell we're staying at when you told here you were back?"

"Oh shit, I didn't tell my parents I was back," Scar said as he stopped in front of the door.

"Source, Sonlig! She wanted you to tell her when you were home so she could get everything ready for the wedding!"

"I'm sorry," Scar said as he winced from Sneeze's anger.

"You have to tell her now," Sneeze instructed Scar.

"Crap," Scar said as he searched out for Ixchel's light. "Momma?"

"Scar?" Ixchel asked in surprise. "Oh, you are home. Welcome back son. Ra! Scar is home!"

"Hello son," Ra greeted Scar.

"Did you just get on world?" Ixchel asked, Scar feeling the excitement in her light. "We can come pick you up from the spaceport."

"I'm actually at the front of the house on Suburbia," Scar responded ruefully.

"You what?!" Ixchel yelled into Scar's light, her son wincing from her anger. "Scar, I told you to tell me when you arrived home. I was to call Sweet Pea to come over as soon as you got here."

"I told Sneeze already," Scar said as he walked into the house, standing still for a moment as nostalgia rushed back into him, imagining Bernini chasing him through the house when he was a baby.

"She is in your light right now?" Ixchel asked.

"Hello Ixchel," Sneeze answered hesitantly.

"Sneeze, you and I are going to talk separately for a while. Scar, you stay in the house and do not go anywhere. Wait until Kukulkan contacts you. Do you understand?"

"Yes ma'am," Scar said as he walked over to the refrigerator.

"Do as your mother tells you, Scar," Ra said to emphasize that Ixchel was serious.

"Yes sir," Scar sighed, first getting annoyed, then laughing that he got annoyed. It didn't take long before Scar found all the ingredients he need to fix himself a cheeseburger, and after cooking it placing himself on the floor before the family hologram to watch television. Bored and alone, Scar instinctively reached out to Popol to see what she was doing.

"Hello... Sonlig... Sonlig, is that you?"

"What up girl," Scar said as he watched sports new. "How's my waifu doing?"

"I'm good Sonlig. Aten Ka, it's been a while since we've talked. How have you been? Did you get out of the Marines yet?"

"Just did," Scar said as he took a bite out of his sandwich. "Hey, are you home? My mom wants me to stay for a while at their house before I do anything, and I'm bored."

"Sonlig, I haven't been on Nima since we graduated from Coba."

"Oh shit, I totally forgot about that," Scar said as he sat straight up. "I'm sorry. I got back home and just thought I was like a hundred cycles old. Fuck dude, are you busy? Where are you right now?"

"I'm at…oh shit…man…I'm on my island right now."

"Wait, what!" Scar laughed, having to put his burger down before he crushed it. "Didn't I call that?! I so called that!"

"Aten Ka," Popol moaned in Scar's light.

"Man, I nailed it. Aten Ka, I'm fucking psychic. What are you doing on your island now anyway?"

"Sonlig, don't even start with me, you're the last person to talk. I'm actually with my husband right now. We're having our donor mother over so the kids can play with her."

"Oh shit dude," Scar mumbled in between bites. "You got married. Congrats, girl. Why didn't you invite me to the wedding?"

"Because you're the Speaker," Popol answered. "I didn't want Backlum to meet you. I felt nervous about that. Especially about what happen."

"Oh yeah, I totally forgot we made out that time," Scar laughed after he finished his burger.

"Sonlig, I swear," Popol growled.

"So I have to ask you something. How's it going to be like if Backlum has to share you with me?"

"Fuck you Sonlig."

"Oh man, I missed having you pissed off at me," Scar laughed, then went silent for a while. "I missed having someone treating me normal, actually."

"Sonlig, you okay?"

"Yeah," Scar answered as he put his plate in the sink to wash. "I'll leave you alone with your family. Oh, by the way, Sneeze and I are going to get married soon. Do you want to come to our wedding?"

"Congratulation yourself," Popol said. "Yeah, when is it?"

"I'll let you know as soon as my parents tell me. See you later homegirl."

"Bye, Sonlig," Popol said before her light left his. After Scar finished the dishes he went up to Bernini's bedroom and laid down on his small bed. He looked up at the ceiling, thinking about how in about a week he was going to be the Speaker of his own House. A god. It didn't feel right, like something that you read in a book and sounded nice at the time. But when you are about to have it as an adult, it becomes nothing more than a fancy you might of had as a child. The last eleven years wore a somber wake up call for that young boy he once was.

The more Scar thought about it, the more his light was troubled. He rolled over to his side, thinking about the happiness he had with Sneeze and his kids. If he could spend the rest of eternity with them, watching all of his offspring fill his existence, he would have been more than happy. It would have been a life without responsibility, only to his wife and children. But responsibility was all he had been taught for almost two hundred cycles. He was afraid that he would become a slave to that.

"Scar?" Kukulkan called out into Scar's light. "Are you free?"

"Yes sir," Scar answered.

"Where are you now?"

"In the house on the hill of Suburbia."

"Look out your window to the Citadel," Kukulkan ordered.

"Why, what's going on?" Scar asked as he walked over to Rhiannon's old room, which was kept the same by their parents. When he looked towards the Metropolis, his jaw slacked open as he saw a massive oval shape craft hovering over the city, it's shadow blanketing the southern part close to the ocean river.

"Holy shit," Scar whispered to himself.

"Come take a look at your yacht," Kukulkan told Scar. "Your parents had it made for you for to use as Speaker."

"My yacht," Scar repeated, not sure what he was saying. He remember the Tripura class carrier above Darshana, how massive it was and its purpose for war. He didn't realized that individuals used such crafts for leisure.

"Come here, Your Highness," Kukulkan demanded, and Scar shifted to where his light was. He floated a mile above the city looking up at a bronze like metal craft that was twelve miles long and one and a half miles wide, with ten miles long oval rails below and on the side of the main hull, connect with three rail arms each.

"Ra and Ixchel suggested that you may need a forward base of operation," Kukulkan explained. "Since you seemed to prefer to handle situation hands on, you can now always have your capital city with you."

"This is amazing," Scar said as he watched other crafts flying by it, those vessels dwarfed by the enormity of the bronze colossus.

"What will you name it?" Kukulkan asked as he floated over to Scar.

"I…hmmm…yeah…I know. The Fetu Auala."

"I see Earth is still in your heart," Kukulkan noted with a smile.

"Yeah," Scar said, not taking his eyes off of the ship.

"Do you want to test drive it?"

"Like a car?" Scar asked, then chastised himself for acting so amazed by what he was seeing. He was going to be Speaker soon, he told himself, so he need to act like one. He followed Kukulkan as they shifted into the helm of the ship, which seemed more like a luxury suite than a piloting chamber. After filling the Fetu Auala with Scar's light Kukulkan order the pilots to take the ship out of Nima's atmosphere and out through the solar system.

2

Scar stood in front of his parent's mirror in the Chateau bedroom, readjusting the straight brown tie that matched his father's rural dress suit. Scar adjusted the red blazer and brown slacks the best he could, trying to make it feel like it fits, but they never seemed to. They fit physically, but in his light they didn't.

Scar looked out into the night from his parents window to watched all the visitors that filled the acres surrounding the Chateau. Lights floated above the grounds, shining upon representatives from different nations in House Xkit or the Federation. All were excited to be there at this occasion, as any person should. Who would turn down an invitation to see the new god of a pantheon. It's just that Scar didn't know who that god is going to be. It isn't him, no matter how much he would tried to be.

"Are you doing alright?" Chac'chel asked as she walked into the bedroom. Scar turned to see her small round frame dressed in a sparkling blue dress that accented the small amount of blue left in her pale white skin tone.

"I don't think that this suit is the right thing to where," Scar said as he continued to fidget with it.

"Did you want to wear your father's clothes for the party?" Chac'chel asked as she walked next to Scar.

"This outfit, yes. I believed that I wanted to wear it. Now I'm not sure what I want to wear."

"You don't think you can fill your father's role," Chac'chel surmised.

"Yeah," Scar said blankly.

"Well, if you truly were telling the truth, then it would be the both of us taking that role," Chac'chel stated as she looked at her dress.

"Yeah…yeah, your right. The both of us," Scar said as he grew more confident with that fact.

"Or maybe you're still not comfortable in your form?" Chac'chel asked as she stared at Scar's face in the mirror.

"Oh, that thing," Scar laughed. "I don't care about that. At first I had a hard time looking at it. But the Marines knocked that right out of me. That thing has been blasted and shredded so much I don't see myself as it any more. I'm Aten Ka, nothing more. I am not."

"That's good to hear," Chac'chel said as she patted Scar's thigh. "But I do believe that you should were something better than what your father wears. He always looks like he just left a small village on some back water world."

"There's nothing wrong with looking like some country bumpkin," Scar laughed.

"Not when you're meeting some of the most important individuals in the multiverse," Chac'chel chastised Scar.

"Okay Auntie. But what should I choose?"

"Something that's in your light, that is you," Chac'chel advised. Scar thought for a moment, then went with his first instinct, changing his father's clothing into bright light before it changed into a black t-shirt, a brown leather jacket and blue jeans.

"You can't switch out one rural outfit for another," Chac'chel growled.

"Ouch," Scar chuckled. After a few more dots, Scar stared at himself, then he glanced down at Chac'chel. After a spark of inspiration, his clothes glowed again and turned into a fancy black evening suit and tie, although his bare feet still reveal themselves on tip toes in the mirror.

"That looks very nice," Chac'chel commented. "I think your mother may like this choice."

"Where is she?" Scar said as they walked out of his parents' bedroom.

"She's with Sneeze and King Psssh, fighting with her father about the wedding plans."

"Hah, I would give resources to see them fight over that."

"You must have a death wish," Chac'chel snidely remarked.

"No, it just feels good to have to worry about that," Scar explained as they climbed down the stairs that lead to the Chateau's entrance. "Them bickering makes this ordeal feel normal."

"It's an ordeal then, becoming the Speaker?" Chac'chel asked sarcastically.

"Yes it was," Scar snapped back in an even tone. "The reward is great, yeah. I mean, all of us wants to be surrounded by people who worships them. Just a little bit. But you guys made sure to beat that out of me. So I'm stepping into a role that deep down inside I don't want."

"That's a lie," Chac'chel guessed. "And you know it is."

"Maybe," Scar said as they stopped before the entrance. "I want the responsibility. I was created for it. I don't think I can walk away from that path.

I would probably go insane if I didn't serve as the Speaker. I just don't want all the material things that goes with it, the prestige."

"Which means you are ready for the role," Chac'chel said.

"No I'm not," Scar said as he grabbed the door handle. "But the only way to swim is to get wet." Scar opened the door and walked out into the waiting crowd with his aunt, lights flashing as they stepped out from the covered entrance and amongst the people. Chac'chel introduced Scar to hundreds of beings from many species for close to two sections, their names becoming a blur in his light. He stopped trying to remember all of them, knowing he could always recall them in the Matrix.

Many of them congratulated him with his service in the Marines. Others with graduating from Ya'ax Mont with a doctorate, even mentioning his college football career. Scar really became engage with the visitors when they talked to him about services that House Xkit could provide for their planets or interstellar nations. Scar knew that he was probably getting suckered into promising actions he didn't know much about, and luckily Aunt Chac'chel was there to rush him along to the next dignitary.

Scar heart jumped when he saw his siblings all standing in a group, talking amongst the guest. Thor and Athena both wore black Bla'nik type dress suits and gowns, with Athena's dress being tightly fit and a white head scarf covering most of her black hair. Rhiannon wore an Earth inspired revealing thigh long flowery dress, with matching sparkling heels. Bernini was the only one wearing a normal Federation style fit uniform, its blue color inspired from his service.

"Hi guys," Scar said as he stepped towards them, lights from cameras flashing as he approached his family.

"Jamarcus!" Thor yelled as he grabbed Scar into his large thick arms. "Aten Ka, you lost weight. You looked bigger in college."

"It's the diet," Scar said as he reached down to hug Bernini. "I lost a lot of weight when I got out of boot camp."

"You look like Daddy," Bernini said as he peered up at Scar with a weird look.

"I know, it's crazy. Except for the freckles. Hi Rhiannon."

"Oh, did Scar tell you guys about how he almost vaporized me on planet Darshana?" Rhiannon asked as she reached up to hug Scar.

"Momma told me about that," Thor laughed. "Grandpa was so mad at you when you showed up."

"I didn't try to vaporize you," Scar said shamefully.

"He didn't even give me any time to react. He just rambled off some cool speech like from a movie and blasted Njord right into Aten Ka. I barely shifted off the planet."

"I'm sorry," Scar emphasized at Rhiannon, wary of what the news may say of that knowledge.

"It's alright Scar," Athena said as she wrapped Scar in her motherly embrace. "You did what you were supposed to. Rhiannon is the one who screwed up."

"Me?" Rhiannon yipped at her sister. "That's my star cluster that I have to protect. We all have that responsibility."

"No, you were supposed to protect Mangala," Thor informed Rhiannon. "Jamarcus was to be used for Darshana."

"But the insurgency is over for now," Athena noted to break up the argument. "Thor, don't you have something to give Jamarcus?"

"Oh, right," Thor said as went over to a nearby table to grab a football.

"Here," Thor said as he clumsily threw the ball to Scar, who caught it in one hand and naturally tucked it one of his arms.

"Cool," Scar said. "I thought I never would hold one of these things again."

"I can't throw it like your quarterback," Thor said as he walked up to Scar. "Teach me how to do that."

"Oh yeah, you see the seams?" Scar asked as he put the ball in Thor's hand. "Hold it with your ring and pinky fingers on top of the seams."

"Which fingers?"

"The two farthest from your thumb," Scar chuckled. "Then when you throw it, swing your hips and shoulder forward before you throw with your arm."

"I think I got that," Thor said with a excited look on his face. "Run out for a throw?"

"Children," Chac'chel called out in a forewarning tone.

"I'll block that," Bernini said as he tried to keep up with Scar, who ran past the tables and out into the open grass knolls. Scar adjusted his direction when he saw Thor's throw go awry, and he separated from Bernini with an agile quickness, grabbing the ball from the air and receiving a cheer from the guest.

"That is not very diplomatic," Chac'chel grumble to herself as Scar threw the ball back to Thor.

"Didn't Jamarcus get his doctorate on the use of sports to help with diplomatic cultural exchange?" Thor asked as he gave his aunt a sneaky look.

"Look at your grandchildren, Mother," Chac'chel muttered in her light as Thor came over to hug her. Bernini and Thor continued to pester Chac'chel as Athena and Rhiannon walked out to Scar on the knoll he stood on, looking out to the night sky in the direction Earth was in this universe.

"I'm so proud of you," Athena said as she hugged Scar from behind. "You accomplish so much."

"I haven't done shit," Scar confessed. "Anyone could have done what I did."

"We haven't," Athena said. "You should be pleased."

"Yeah, well, enough about me," Scar said as he sat down on the grass. "How are you guys doing. How's your boyfriends, Rhiannon?"

"Oh, those two," Rhiannon spoke as she and Athena sat next to him. "I dumped them a while ago. Sura wanted to get more serious in our relationship, and it got weird between him and Deva. And I don't want to stop the single life just yet. I'm having too much fun being free."

"That's good," Scar said truthfully. "I wouldn't know what I would do if I wasn't going to be Speaker or marry Sneeze. Freedom can be scary."

"Well, I'm not that free," Rhiannon added while giving Athena a mean look.

"What about you and Twin Pillars?" Scar asked Athena. "Did you make any progress in your relationship."

"No," Athena said. "He hasn't asked me to marry him. I know he's intimidated with my density, but I don't know what I have to do to get him to overcome that. Maybe I should break it off."

"No, you're still thinking like you're back in the Bla'nik culture. You got to let go of the concept that the guy has to ask the woman's hand in marriage. You're the goddess, so seize the moment. Ask him to marry you. Sweep down from your divine mount and bring him back to you hallow halls. Make him your cup bearer…wait…I should phrase that better."

"Aten Ka!" Rhiannon laughed as she fell on her back.

"Where did that come from?" Athena asked with a smile.

"Yeah, divine rape never sounds good no matter how you phrase it," Scar agreed, smiling as he looked up at the night sky.

CHAPTER 22

1

Scar sat down on Bernini's bed in the Suburbia household, trying to keep Hathor still so she could put on the bride's maid gown that she needed to wear. It was a much more modest style that was similar to what Rhiannon was going to wear that morning, a silver and white gown with reflective speckles insinuating a woman's curvature. Scar didn't want her to wear it at first, but Rhiannon and Sneeze convinced him to let it slide. They just thought she looked so cute in it because of how she just wanted to be like her aunt.

Scar decide that today he was going to wear his father's red and brown outfit like it was, in its Andean rural style to match Sneeze wearing Athena's clothing she loved so much. Why she did Scar didn't know. Maybe it was the sense of having a sister to look up to perhaps. Or it was the fact that Ixchel told her to wear it when they were younger like a mother making sure her child didn't do something foolish. It's funny how the light choses certain items or moments that makes it happy deep within.

"Daddy, are we going to live with Grandpa," Hathor asked as she put on her white short heeled shoes, her eyes fixed on them like a pirate looking at her golden treasure.

"Which Grandpa?" Scar joked as he picked her up.

"Grandpa on Roi Son," Hathor answered smartly. "Are we going to live in Groen Stad in your house there?"

"I haven't built it yet," Scar said. "But it should be done very soon. Why?"

"Aren't we going to live in Grandma's castle?"

"Do you want to live there?" Scar asked as he put her down once she began to wiggle to get out of his grasp.

"We're going to have a lot of brothers and sisters right?" Hathor asked in a matter of fact tone, walking around in a circle like she was wearing a wedding gown herself. "We're going to have a big family in the castle."

"We are now," Scar ponder as he sat down on the floor by Hathor. "What makes you say that?"

"I know," Hathor said as she looked at her father, absently sweeping back her pale white hair from her obsidian eyes, her light shining through her pale white skin. She and Scar then turned at the same time when Ixchel walked into the room, herself wearing a fancy Andean outfit, with a yellow vest covering a silk shirt and dark gray cotton pants.

"Hi grandma!" Hathor shouted as she ran to hug Ixchel, rubbing her face against her belly.

"Are you ready for your father to get married?" Ixchel asked as she rubbed Hathor's hair.

"Yeah," she said as she kept rubbing Ixchel belly. "I can't wait till I get married. I'm going to have a bunch of kids."

"Yeah, you're a little too young to be thinking about that, kid," Scar groaned as he walked over to them.

"You already see your kids?" Ixchel asked as she bent over to look Hathor in the eyes.

"Hmmm hmmm," Hathor answered with a big nod. "I'm goin to marry a dragon man, and his tail is going to be this long," she said while stretching her arms as wide as she could.

"Really?" Ixchel chuckled.

"Yeah. We're going to live in your castle with all of my brothers and sisters. And we're going to have parties on the beach."

"Wow, she has all of that planned out," Scar laughed. "Just wait until you're about two hundred and fifty cycles to start."

"So Scar, we are almost ready," Ixchel informed him. "We are going down stairs and we are going to wait in the living room until Kukulkan announces us. King Psssh, Horus and Sneeze are going to come down with your father when her family is announced. After your announcements, he is going to explain your responsibilities as royal progenitors of a new species, and he will then swear you to those oaths. Are there any questions?"

"No ma'am," Scar said as he bent down to hug his mother.

"Are you ready?" Ixchel asked Scar.

"You have no idea how long I've been waiting for this day," Scar said as he picked up Ixchel from the floor, slightly irritating her.

"Are you going to put me down any time soon?" Ixchel asked into Scar neck.

"Momma? Remember when I told you that I hope there would be a day when I could thank you for all that you and Papa did for me?"

"Yes."

"Thank you," Scar said, trying to smother her in his light.

"Alright Scar, you can put me down," Ixchel ordered as she patted Scar on his shoulder.

"Sorry," Scar said as he put her down.

"Why do you boys always want to pick me up?" Ixchel bemoaned as she lead Scar and Hathor down the stairs and to the living room. Outside in the backyard were all the family guests his parents told Scar and Sneeze to invite to the wedding. Nibble, Whisper and Proclaim all stood together, all garbed in Kaggen necklaces and covered in colorful body paint, almost as tall as the tree that Kukulkan stood next too. On the other side was Scar brothers and sisters, all dressed in their home world's formal attire.

Seated before the tree were most of the people Scar grew up with. Popol and her Sirian husband sat with their children. Their mother donor was a third density being and still had a hard time meeting other species, so she stayed on her home world. Oki decided not to come, his light already moved on from his childhood friends, his wonder lust still not satisfied as he traveled about his universe.

The party all managed to show up, which pleasantly surprised Scar. Katah, Three Spheres and their kids sat by Popol's family, their children running amuck through the aisles. Uncir, Chamahez, and Utu brought their wives, but decide to not bring their kids. Scar didn't understand why, but they kept having this notion that they were going to a god king's wedding, and didn't want their kids ruining it. Which almost hurt Scar, figuring that if they knew him then they would know what type of wedding he would have.

Enki and Anansi showed up, but none of the rest of his Vanguard platoon did, too busy with their duties to the Corps or their personal lives. Major Yumcha did come however, dressed in his khaki uniform, sitting up front next to Twin Pillars so he could talk to Rhiannon. As strong willed and independent as she was, it was surprising that she struck up a friendship with his commanding officer. Or maybe it shouldn't have been a surprise.

"Welcome guest of the Royal House," the old family servant began to start the wedding. "My name is Kukulkan and I'm am the Royal Butler to Her Majesty Xkit and to her bloodline. I welcome you all here today for this wonderous day, where the new Speaker of House Xkit shall take on the duty with her Royal Highness Sneeze of Roi Son to fill House Xkit with their offspring, so that this multiverse shall be blessed with their Light.

"Does he have to make it sound like this is important?" Scar grumbled under his breath.

"Shush," Ixchel silenced Scar, waiting with discipline until Kukulkan called them.

"It is with great pleasure now that I shall call for our Speaker. He has graduated with great distinction from Coba Private Academy and Ya'ax Mont University. He also served for ten cycles in the Federation Service with the unique Third Vanguard Battalion. At all times he was a service to House Xkit and to the Federation. May I introduce His Royal Highness, Scar Amun of House Xkit."

"Come along Scar," Ixchel said as she lead Scar and Hathor out the house and through the seated guests, all the while Scar waving hi to his friends. They stopped in front of Kukulkan and the tree, with Ixchel joining her children as Scar and Hathor waited together for the rest of their family.

"Now I shall introduce King Psssh, ruler of Roi Son and one of the Twelve Rulers of the Web Universe. His empire spreads through out a galaxy and services other species throughout his universe, helping many of those species in the Ascension process. He is accompanied with the fiancé of Scar Amun, a graduate of Groen Stad Academy and University. May I introduce to you, Her Royal Highness, Princess Sneeze."

Scar and Hathor turned around to see Ra, wearing a fancy Andean green, red and gray suit, leading Sneeze, Psssh and Horus out the house. It was surreal how Psssh managed to fit his large frame inside their house, but he was able to crawl out of the open back glass wall and stand with Sneeze's friends. Horus was dressed just like his father, his hair combed back nicely for once as he lead his mother hand in hand.

"Horus!" Hathor called out as soon as she saw her brother.

"Be quiet!" Horus hissed at Hathor, giving everyone a giggle as Ra guided him and his mother next to Scar and Hathor before joining the rest of House Xkit.

"I shall address Scar and Sneeze, two beings who now and for the for seeable future shall be task with a divine duty. It is primarily through the Speakers of the Seven Houses that the thousands of worlds in this multiverse are filled with the Light. It is through them we are able to reap the providence of Aten Ka, and with their Light have peace and abundance.

"This is a harsh task, to know that for the rest of your known existence that your sole purpose is to the service of your subjects. And that the purpose of your children shall be to spread Aten Ka to other worlds or universes. That is why it is needed for the Speaker to be forged through the Ascension, so that the Speaker no longer identifies as form, but only as Aten Ka, so that every action the Speaker commits shine with its divine Light.

"So now I ask you, Your Royal Highness Scar Amun, and Your Royal Highness Princess Sneeze, do you swear by the Light of your lives, to forever serve House Xkit, to provide us with the Light of Aten Ka, and to provide House Xkit with security, abundance and with love?"

"Yes," Hathor answered gleefully, causing the audience to laugh in response.

"Yes," Scar and Sneeze answered together.

"So be it. Let the multiverse be blessed, for we have a new god king and queen. Welcome Your Majesties, King Scar Amun and Queen Sneeze." As the congregation began to cheer, Scar reached over to kiss Sneeze, he happiness swelling up his light. He was finally in the place he wanted to be. Scar felt almost bad, thinking that now Sneeze was stuck with him, and it would be a hassle for her to leave, but perhaps that was Jamarcus still inside of him.

He picked up his two children, grabbing them and their mother in his arms, squeezing them tightly until his light began to shine like the mid-day sun, his ten loops swirling about him like a buzz saw. He looked into his wife's light, her feminine eyes looking right into Scar's. Her light no longer had the long hair that used to show when she was younger. She used to have it because she wanted to look like her human mother, but she changed it when she noticed Scar loved her bald head. She loved when Scar would stare into her, and that love ricocheted back and forth.

"Where is Lady Chac'chel?" Sneeze asked as she kissed Scar's ear.

"She didn't want to come to the wedding," Scar explained. "I understand. She's sees into the future like Hathor. And when what you want in the future isn't with you, it hurts when people or events reminds you of that Emptiness."

"I see," Sneeze said, a bit worried for her. "Are you happy, Sonlig?"

"Me? Fuck yeah. I'm the guy in the dream now. I'm finally the person that I want to be."

2

Scar sat in a waiting chamber with Sneeze inside the Citadel, both dressed in Federation uniforms, waiting patiently for the House assembly to summon them to the council chambers. Scar held Sneeze's hand in his while she ran her fingers through his crew cut hair, trying to calm his trembling nervous light. Scar looked around the teal colored room, staring at the pictures of the important figures who were part of the assembly. Some of the pictures were of people in the assembly room right now, a couple of beings long past reincarnated or has joined Aten Ka.

Scar glanced over to Chac'chel, as she stood before the door to the room, her round frame dressed in another exquisite black formal gown that matched her hairstyle. Her light was solid and focused, already calculating what Scar's next steps will be once he is voted in as Speaker of the House. Scar watched as she held her hands together in front of her, her finger tips tapping each other from pinky to index with her thumbs pressed together. Scar had to remember that telltale sign when he spoke with his aunt.

"What are you thinking about?" Scar asked Chac'chel to pass the time, feeling uncomfortable while no one was speaking, something he used to have no problem with when he was Jamarcus.

"President Ixazal had spoken with Ra a few months back about her planet wanting to leave the House," Chac'chel informed Scar. "They were able to establish a few high density lights to supply their star cluster. If they are to leave then we should begin talks with other nations that has been contacting the Federation."

"Did you already have a few nations in mind?"

"Just a few. There is actually a nation of systems that presides in the same galaxy branch that Earth and Roi Son does. They are spread out over hundreds of sound cycles, and their trade empire is stable. But their logistic capabilities are far behind what they need to be."

"Not that many high densities in that universe," Scar said. "I'm surprised that they were able to establish such a network. It must have taken hundreds of cycles. What is the name of the empire?"

"The Dingir," Chac'chel answered. "They are a Draconian species. Intelligence say that they call their ethnic nation the Anunnaki. Very empirical. That's why they have been reluctant to join the Federation, due to their skepticism towards the Light. Scar, we should take advantage of this before the rest of the Federation does."

"You and Hathor have been thinking about this for a while haven't you," Scar noted with a smile.

"Don't mock me Scar," Chac'chel snapped, giving her nephew a sharp glance. "We could spread our influence in that galaxy before the rest of the Federation start to take an interest."

"You mean before they want to bang them," Scar joked. "What do you suggested?"

"Establish a trade route for them, providing must faster travel services in exchange for a portion of the resource profits."

"Are we going to supply them with ships or have our people navigate theirs?"

"That's what I wanted to ask you about," Chac'chel said.

"We aren't going to just give them our ships. In exchange for resources, yes, but if they still need either navigators or Light to travel through the waters, then we should demand that we set up colonies on their worlds. Primarily for logistic stations for our ships, but also for genetic and culture exchange. It's easier to join a House if you're related to the people in it."

"I'll have our negotiators contact Dingir to give them our terms. We won't claim all of them. They're stubborn like most lights in that universe."

"What about my father's services," Sneeze asked. "We could help establish contact. We made contact with the Dingir before. My father did before they decided to be more independent."

"We should ask your father if we can use his castle for a meeting site," Scar suggested. "And we should talk to him anyway. It would be kind of bad if we tried to set up a competing shop in his back yard."

"My father's business is in other galaxies," Sneeze explained. "We just live there because it's a back water galaxy. Our own private island in the ocean of reality."

"Scar, it's time," Chac'chel said as the door opened and Kukulkan appeared with two classically dressed Andean guards.

"Hello Kukulkan," Scar and Chac'chel greeted the old man in unison.

"Hello, children. The Assembly is ready to receive you now. Guards, will you kindly escort Queen Sneeze to her seat."

"Queen…fancy," Scar laughed as Sneeze left with the guards.

"I like the name," Sneeze said. "I like being your queen. Don't hate me for it."

"I'm sorry," Scar apologized as Sneeze left the room, walking next to Chac'chel and composing his light to be more calm. Once they heard the crowd's applause in the chambers quiet after Sneeze took her seat, Kukulkan lead Scar and Chac'chel out into the semi-circular assembly chamber were the nations in house Xkit's representatives stood. Before them were polished brown wooden counters in rows that stood before the pulpit at the flat wall part of the chamber. Scar and Chac'chel went to their seats at the rear of the chamber near where they entered and stood as the two hundred and fifty eight members applauded them.

Two thirds of the Assembly were Andeans, with Lyrans, Sirians, and Pleiadean members composing most of the remaining third. They stood and clapped as Kukulkan marched to his position behind the pulpit, and then the cheering grew louder as he joined the thrall, all wanting to give authentic praise to Scar and his accomplishment. Scar was pleasantly surprised when he saw a human in the chamber, giving the assemblyman a teenage like wave when he saw him.

"Welcome distinguished guest," Kukulkan stated to bring the meeting to order. "To Lord Ra and Lady Ixchel, we in this Assembly room thank you for blessing all of us with your Light. To Queen Sneeze, may we be blessed with the Light of your children. Representatives, Kings, Queens, Presidents, Prime Ministers, welcome to the voting ceremony for King Scar of House Xkit. As customary, we shall now hear from any member of this Chamber who wish to bring up their argument against the voting of King Scar as Speaker of the House. Do we have an argument."

"I shall like to bring up my argument," a bright light Sirian announced by his counter, wrapped in white cloth with royal blue linings.

"The House recognizes President Diogenes of planet Thetis," Kukulkan said before sitting down behind his pulpit.

'Distinguish members of the Assembly," Diogenes began as he stood. "Lord Ra and Lady Ixchel, who I wish was here today, but understandably didn't want to take away from their son's moment. To Queen Sneeze and her father King Psssh. To King Scar and Lady Chac'chel, I thank you for the service that you have provided for Thetis and our cluster. Without such service, we would not know the peace that we have right now, nor would I be able to enjoy the status that I have.

"But if we are to talk about status, then lets us examine the status that we are now voting to give to King Scar of House Xkit. Speaker of the House of Xkit. What does that mean? If we were to go to the literal meaning of the term when House Xkit was created, then it is the right of the person who hold such title to give any command and have such command be followed. What ever that being says, must happen. To put it plainly, to be a god.

"But what is a god? And more importantly, is a god needed to serve as the Speaker of House Xkit. Not to take away from the service that King Scar shall provide for us, but shall we also give him our eternal servitude. I'm in the minority that a god is someone who's social status and material wealth is used to separate themselves from the people that serve such a being.

"The purpose of the Federation is to insure the persons, citizens, vice-voices, and voices in the Federation the ability to live without need, in balance with the multiverse and the lights in it. That is the purpose of the tenants of the

Federation. Discipline, Education and the Light. So that if any light were to establish each of those tenants, they could live a life without worry.

"So is not the voting of placing a god in rulership of us in violation of the purpose of such tenants? Is it not contradicting to say that we are all Aten Ka, but create a culture that raises a Light above all others for whatever reasons. Can we truly say that we live by the purpose of the Federation if we live in our personal lives in defiance of it.

"This is still house Xkit, and King Scar has every right to be ruler of such House. He has done more than enough to earn such a title. But shall we also give him a title of Speaker? Of a god? Let us then hold true to the tenants of the Federation, and chose instead to separate the powers of House Xkit, and give such powers to the people who assembles in this chamber, to better insure our freedoms and liberties. Only then can we say that instead of being in House Xkit, then we are a family in House Xkit. Thank you Lord Kukulkan."

"Those were some valid points," Scar whispered to Chac'chel.

"We can discuss them after you are sworn in," Chac'chel advised. "We are still running a business before being a family."

"Understood."

"Would any other Assembly Person like to present an argument or counter argument?" Kukulkan asked as he stepped back to the pulpit.

"I would like to present an counter argument," a blue skinned Mangalan proposed as she stepped to her counter.

"The House recognizes Lady Saraswati of planet Jain."

"Thank you Lord Kukulkan, for your service here and to your service to the House," Saraswati spoke. "To Lord Ra and Lady Ixchel, may you enjoy your retirement, because you certainly earned it. To King Psssh and Queen Sneeze, welcome to the family of House Xkit, and let this be a doorway so that more of the Kaggen be introduced into the Federation. To Lady Chac'chel, thank you also for your service and guidance. And to King Scar Amun. Congratulations for all that you have worked for and the sacrifices that you have made.

"Now, we have heard our argument from President Diogenes about the ethics, or perhaps to say the unethical merits to name a Speaker to the house of Xkit. To have a person be voted to be our god and divine ruler. Yes, Assemblyman Diogenes made legitimate arguments against being ruled by a god. But there are major flaws in his argument, both in his own character and in the process that Scar was trained to become Speaker of House Xkit.

"Let's first tackle the definition of what a god is. Yes, one could use such an argument that if any individual who uses social status and material wealth to separate and elevate themselves from the rest of society, then yes, such a being is a god. But if we were to go by such criteria and apply them to ourselves in this room, then wouldn't all of us here in this assembly hall be considered gods. You yourself President Diogenes have the title of god on your world.

"And as per material wealth, House Xkit provides a service of Light and protection for all lights in the House, as well as those of the Federation. In essence, they are the energy provider and military establishment that is the basis of all of our economies. In the business stand point, Scar most likely would have primary ownership or stake in all businesses in our nations. So does not the major stock holder of such businesses have every right to make final say over how such operations are handled.

"Lastly, Scar has put in his service to the Federation during time of war, and is eligible to vote and serve in Federal Congress, which some of us in this chamber are not able to claim. So for someone who has not actually applied the tenants of the Federation to their own lives to criticize someone who did, let alone went through the Ascension process is hypocritical.

"Let us not forget that Scar was trained from birth to become Speaker of the House, something he choose to do and accomplished, something I know that I probably never could. He was closely monitored and groomed, being put through the harshest of circumstances to ensure that he is capable of rulership.

And he still must be voted into position by the members of this Assembly. I wouldn't know how to feel if I were to go through what King Scar has done and still be uncertain that I would be voted Speaker.

"We ask House Xkit to provide Light, security, and above all else, love to every individual of our civilizations. Lord Ra and Lady Ixchel would not have provided their Light if they didn't love us, and I believe King Scar will also. So I ask you, by these merits, how else would you want to define a god? Because I have no problem being ruled by such an individual. Thank you Lord Kukulkan for hearing my argument."

"Thank you Lady Saraswati," Kukulkan said as he stepped back to his podium. "Are their any others who would like to present their argument for or against Scar becoming Speaker of House Xkit?" Kukulkan asked before being answered with silence.

"Then we shall begin the vote. When your names are called out please give your vote of yea or nay to the record secretary." When the secretary called out to each Assembly person, each one giving their answer to be imputed into the Citadel records. Almost all of the Assembly voted in favor of Scar, with only a handful voting against.

"I guess the libertarian ideology of Liberation Front has taken root," Chac'chel mused.

"Any argument based on logic must be listened too," Scar said. "I'm kind of an in-the-closet libertarian myself."

"Yet you're literally about to become a god who will rule over an intra-universal empire," Chac'chel chastised.

"Which means I'm perfect for the job, right?" Scar laughed. "But in-the-closet only. There's too much Jim Crow in that philosophy."

"Jim Crow?" Chac'chel asked in confusion.

"Never mind," Scar laughed as the assembly finished their tally.

"Now that we have the final count, we have two hundred and fifty three votes for Scar being Speaker of House Xkit, with only five against. Then let it be recognized that King Scar Amun has been voted as Speaker."

"Okay," Scar whispered as he rose from his seat, with Chac'chel and the rest of the beings in the chambers erupting in applause. Scar calmly walked forward, shaking the hands of the dignitaries he walked by, who all gave light felt praise of his new position. When he stood behind the podium, he shot a cheery glance up at Sneeze, as she and her father sat on the upper visitor level with the news media and special guests from the Federation. Sneeze waved gleefully as Psssh held her, his prideful light shining bright.

"Thank you Kukulkan, for all that you have do for our family," Scar said as the cheering ended. "For my Aunt Chac'chel, I will lean hard upon your experience as we work together on this endeavor, which I'm sure you will regret. To the King, Queens, dignitaries, and other representatives in this Chamber, I thank you for voting for me to serve you as Speaker.

"My sole purpose, the thing that I have been forged for over two hundred cycles to do is to bring Light to all of you. But right there is the ultimate question that every sentient being has probably asked throughout the existence of the omniverse. What is Aten Ka? Many have spent extensive sections of the day trying to know what it is. On Earth this was due to the Uncertainty Principle, that you can't make a measurement of the location and velocity of the Light at the same time, meaning that you can never really tell what you're are observing with the Light.

"So if we can't tell exactly what the Light is with science, then let us use philosophy to come up with an answer. If you go by certain religious principles, such as Judeo-Christian-Islamic teachings back on my old light planet, then Aten Ka is an omnipotent, omniscient, omni-benevolent entity that created the universe for the sole purpose of the beings and culture of such beings who observe it. We can find fault with this theory, because if one can find Aten Ka in other beings outside of your culture and species, then how could have Aten Ka created the universe and all things in it for you?

"There are others that emphasize that Aten Ka is a dream state, a higher level of consciousness that allows all who are able to Ascend their Light to attain this elevated plane of existence. And in this dream state, we can intermingle our light with other beings and objects in the dream, to change ourselves and the environment to fit our needs. But we can literally observe Aten Ka outside of our forms. And if that's the case, are we dreaming of Aten Ka, or is Aten Ka dreaming about us?

"We may try to find and study Aten Ka in all objects in the omniverse and never find the answer. So I have decide that to find the answer, I must look inside myself. I can tell you who I was. I was a naïve little boy that actually thought the Ascension process was important yet fun, and couldn't care less about being Speaker of a House. And even now, the title and status is of no concern to me.

"When I was on Earth, I was an awkward and scared little boy who couldn't find acceptance in the culture and family I grew up in. When I was an adult I served in the military because on that world there was no other option for a child like myself for a stable life. In that service I fought in a futile war that lined the pockets of the politicians and oligarchs who sent us there instead of the soldiers who fought in it.

"I also met a woman and her friends who I loved more than anything, and a culture that I grew to appreciate. I loved that woman and her friends because they were the first people that I could call family. But the people of that culture rejected me because of the color of my skin, and the woman that I loved was taken from me, in my own selfish point of view.

"But then I met my true Family, and in the process I met you. When I was young on Earth I loved learning about science, about quantum mechanics and cosmology. When I got into college, I develop a love for anthropology and philosophy. And when I met all of you, my light exploded with anticipation that I was able to practice all the things that I love while I encountered you the second time. Something I still enjoy.

"Now, I'm a person who stays in the realm of means when describing something. If you desire to achieve a certain goal, and the means in which you chose to do it is the same as someone else, no matter how you may disagree with and are appalled by the ends, you are the same. Some here may say that I'm a omni-benevolent being who is willing to share his Light with all to ensure your security and prosperity for all time. There are others who say that I'm a malevolent, jealous god who demands tribute and worship from those I ensnare in my aura. If through philosophical debate one can find sufficient evidence for either claims, then make no mistake, I am both.

"Therefore, I will swear an oath to you and to the Federation that all my actions will be in service of you, through pain and death. I'm a single minded individual, and because of that I can be confused with and rightfully so called arrogant. Yet I can still say that I need your help, for what is the point of having people in a House if they can't speak for me. And hopefully with you speaking for me, my actions will shine with Aten Ka. Thank you, and may the Light shine on the path of House Xkit and the Federation."

The chamber erupted in cheers and applause as Scar stepped from the podium and Kukulkan lead him through the Assembly, who all once again greeted him as he walked by. Chac'chel hurried to his side, eager to go with him as Kukulkan eventually guided them from the chamber and through the Citadel into the Entanglement Chamber, an enormous black walled, floored and ceiling room that also seem brightly lit. In the middle of the large room was a black monolith that stood from floor to ceiling where Ra and Ixchel stood next to, their light fluxing in and out of the monolith.

"Congratulations, Scar," Ra said as he hugged his son.

"Thanks Papa," Scar said into his ear.

"Are you ready, Sweetie?" Ixchel asked as Scar approached the monolith.

"No, but let's get this over with," Scar chuckled. As Scar placed his hands on the monolith, an immense surge of energy filled his entire form, filling him to the bream. His skin felt tight on his body, and it was as if the energy tried to suffocate him like a waterfall being poured into his mouth. He felt his parents light in the monolith, and slowly they pulled themselves out leaving Scar entangle with thousands of locations across hundreds of world, over galaxies and universes.

Thousands of windows appeared around Scar like being in an egg, and he felt the environments and the lights in those windows. When he was about to become overwhelmed, he remembered what Chac'chel instructed him to do when he would confuse his light with countless others. To know that I am not. And he remembered how she asked him how to describe his I am not.

"Through my actions," Scar said as he swept all the windows to the back of his light, turning to Chac'chel as she waited beside him.

"So what's up on the docket?" Scar asked, ready to get to work.

<h1 style="text-align:center">3</h1>

"What movie are we going to watch today?" Ra asked as he cycled through the video selections on the hologram screen.

"Don't pick anything boring," Thor said as he laid on the living room floor, Horus climbing over his massive frame.

"What constitutes boring?" Ra mumbled to himself.

"Anything you pick," Rhiannon said as she sat next to Ixchel and Sneeze on the couch, with Hathor sitting quietly on her lap.

"That's just plain rude," Ra said as he finally settle on a documentary he liked. "Do you guys want to watch a nature film about the sea life on Nima?"

"No," the whole family answered, making Horus and Hathor giggle uncontrollably.

"Fine, someone else pick a show to watch," Ra spat detested as he sat down next to Ixchel, placing his arm around her shoulder.

"How about we watch a horror film from Earth?" Scar asked, sitting in front of Sneeze, her legs dangled over his shoulders. He remembered how happy he used to be when he would watch those movies with Kathrine and her friends, wanting to share that emotion with his parents.

"Oh yeah, that's a good idea," Bernini agreed as he sat straight up next to Athena, both of whom sat crossed legged in the middle of the room. "Earth has some frightening movies."

"I do not want the children watching any movies that will keep them awake all night long," Ixchel warned with a concern tone.

"Oh no," Scar said as he reached out to the floating screen and flipped through the selections. "I'm not going to pick an actually scary one. I going to choose one of the bad ones. Those are the best movies ever."

"I remembered watching movies like that with you and Bernini when you were on Earth," Sneeze remarked.

"You do?" Hathor asked as she climbed from Rhiannon's lap and into her mother's.

"Yeah," Bernini laughed. "I couldn't get why you found them so hilarious, Scar. Sneeze and I wouldn't be impress when we watched, and he would just laugh at us. Now I get it. Oh, we should watch an alien abduction movie!"

"I do not want to watch one of those," Ixchel complained as she leaned against Ra. "Those are horrible, xenophobic films."

"That's what makes them so good," Scar said as he choose one. "I love this one. It's call Invasion: New York. It's the typical alien invasion scenario, but it's actually about the U.S. invasion into Iraq and the Battle of Fallujah. I loved this film. It was like vets were the only ones who understood what the movie was about."

"I don't know," Ra said as he felt Ixchel's anxiety. "You think it's going to be good."

"Just meld into my light, you'll understand" Scar suggested as he started the movie. As they all settled in, feeling the love in each other's light, the movie began and after half a section, Scar began to feel the emotions he wished for as the family watched the movie. From the directing, cinematography, acting and action scenes, one thing was apparent. This movie was awful, and Scar laughed in the misery his family was in.

It was based on Earth during the early twenty first century. Aliens had come to the planet saying that they have arrived to protect them from the horrors of an empire pillaging countless worlds, but Earth soon realized that the aliens were stealing their resources. The invaders paid well, but to the wrong people, and soon wars broke out across the planet over the new currency, with the aliens trying but failing to control the conflicts.

There were pockets of resistance in different sects of the world's population, specifically New York City. The citizens their never accepted alien ruled and openly told the world that any foreign forces who chose to enter the city would enter at their own risk. And of course the invading species did, where spectacle after spectacle occurred in the ever losing battle the humans fought against their overseers.

"Why do the actors have to give these way too specific lines of dialogue when they perform a stunt?" Ixchel asked as she watch confused while a U.S. rebel shot a grenade that created a too large explosion, while also asking his enemies if they saw that shot coming.

"Momma, that's par course of all action movies in the United States," Scar explained as the family cringed at a horrible line an alien commander spoke about cooking the humans. "You have to have at least five witty one liners in movies like these."

"Which was the first one?" Thor asked as Horus slept in his arms. Scar could only smile as they watched in discomfort until the movies sad but hopeful ending.

"That was terrible," Athena said as she rose from the floor, stretching her body out.

"That was great," Bernini laughed.

"I use to hate that one," Sneeze said as she rubbed Scar head. "The first time I saw it I was mad that there was a movie about insectoids hurting humans. Now I watch it in Scar's eyes, and it's so obvious. Do you think the director knows about Kaggen people."

"Could be," Scar said as he stood up, stroking Hathor's cheeks as she slept in Sneezes arms. "Maybe he was using his alien encounters to show the fallacy of the war."

"We should put the children to bed," Ixchel said as she walked over to pick up Horus, his head slump back in her arms as she walked up the stairs, followed closely behind by Sneeze.

"We should leave too," Athena said. "I can't afford to stay too long away from Firmament, and Thor's got to get back to supervising the construction of New Nippur."

"Alright," Thor said as he lazily rose and walked over to Scar, hugging him in his big arms. "Love you, Jamarcus. You deserve everything you work so hard for."

"Thanks," Scar said. "I still think you did more. You created your own trade nation."

"Not yet, but it's getting there."

"You're recognized by the Firmament. That counts, I don't care."

"Come on Bernini," Thor said as he and Athena walked to the front door.

"Bye Scar," Bernini said as he hugged his chest. "Tell Sneeze I love her."

"Yeah man," Scar said. "How's it like working for Thor?"

"Like I'm back in the Navy," Bernini said. "Except I'm almost the boss. But the stress is still there."

"You'll get used to it," Scar suggested as Bernini made his way to the front door, with Rhiannon waving bye next to him.

"I hope so too," Bernini wished. "Later Scar."

"So you guys are going back to the Chateau," Scar asked when he and Ra stood alone in the living room.

"Yes. We we're thinking that we wanted to renovate this house to accommodate all the grandkids that we're going to have. But we figured that the Chateau would be better suited for that. That's why we wanted to know if you wanted to live here when Sneeze wants to be on Nima."

"That's a good idea," Scar agreed. "But the kids love Roi Son. They can't stop playing by the beach during the day, and looking out at Earth's sun at night. Horus seems to already know that he will be going there for their Ascension."

"Do they talk about it already?" Ra asked.

"Yeah," Scar said as he watched Sneeze and Ixchel descend down the stairs. "Hathor already sees her husband. Which I don't like."

"That's just Jamarcus in you, Sonlig," Sneeze explained.

"No, that's just being a father," Scar complained under his breath. "Still, I love this house. It makes me happy when I'm in it. I loved when Bernini used to pick on me when I was kid in this place. That's why I'm going to build a house like this in Groen Stad. I already have the utilities lines from Psssh's castle already set up. We just have to start building."

"Why do you not just take this one?" Ixchel asked. "We probably will not use it. Since you and Sneeze love it so much, why not take it. Our wedding gift to you. Just stay in the Chateau when you come and visit."

"That's a plan," Sneeze said with her best impersonation of her husband, which tickled Scar to no end as he hugged her with a laugh.

"Then it is settle," Ixchel said as she and Ra walked to the front door. "Remember Scar, your aunt is expecting you early in the mourning for your talks with the Dingir Empire."

"Yes ma'am," Scar said before his parents left.

"Are you going to shift the house over now?" Sneeze asked.

"Yeah, wait a dot," Scar said as he raised his light, creating a window to the open field at the foot of Psssh's pyramid castle. With one mental motion, Scar made the house and all its underground fixtures intangible, then molded them into the ground on Roi Son, rearranging the pipes and powerlines so they disconnected from their sources on Nima and connect to the ones from the castle on Roi Son. When he was done he molded the grounds in the field until he released the house in its new location, closing the window to Nima.

"I thought you would have a harder time doing that," Sneeze joked as she followed Scar through the invisible wall and out into the back yard.

"I did learn something from construction class in Coba," Scar said as he looked up into the night sky, finding the small yellow star that Earth orbited, surrounded by five of the many bright planets orbiting Roi Son. Scar wrapped Sneeze in his arms before him, grabbing her breasts in his hands.

"What are you planning on doing?" Sneeze asked as she placed her hands on Scar's crotch. "You know you have to work early in the mourning."

"You know I can't stop once I get going," Scar said as he kissed her brown skin. She turned to face him, kissing him, wanting to nibble on his lips while he gave her that hungry look he always gave her.

"I can never do anything when you look at me like that," Sneeze jested as she stared into Scar's eyes. "You look like you're about to do something terrible."

"Good…good," Scar muttered menacingly at Sneeze as she giggled in his arms.

"Aten Ka, what are you going to do with me?"

"I'll show you," Scar said as he led her to the nearby beach.

Foundation Issac Asimov Gnome Press

Pagani Automobili S.p.A

Tom Sawyer Rush Atlantic

The Road Not Taken Robert Frosting

Coruscant Star Wars Lucasfilm

Bahamut Kelemvor Sword Coast D&D Dungeon Master Guide Wizard of the Coast LLC

Standard Oil Co. Inc

ExxonMobil

Chevron Corporation

BP plc

InfoWars

Reptile Mortal Kombat Midway Games

BET ViacomCBS

Fox News Fox Corporation

Shrek DreamWorks Animation

Crom Conan The Barbarian Universal 20th Century Fox

Prince Charming The Walt Disney Company